About the author

I'm a widow, blessed with four beautiful children (two boys, two girls), grandchildren and great-grandchildren — my family are my life!

I have lived near Newbury for the past fifty years.

I suppose I would call myself an artistic 'Jack of all trades, but master of none'. I have spent my life making and creating. I appreciate and love all genres of artistry in any form, to me it colours and enriches the world we live in.

In the past, amongst numerous other things, I have written many stories for my children (unpublished).

I began writing *Fill My Empty Heart* a few years ago, shelving it, to become a carer, first for my aging parents, then my dear husband. Then along came the virus and lockdown. What do I do in isolation?

The characters and story have lived in my head for so long, it was a golden opportunity for me to finally complete my book, at last.

Live life… Love life… Enjoy life!

FILL MY EMPTY HEART

Moni Jay

FILL MY EMPTY HEART

Vanguard Press

VANGUARD PAPERBACK

© Copyright 2021
Moni Jay

A CIP catalogue record for this title is
available from the British Library.

ISBN 978-1-80016-083-5

Vanguard Press is an imprint of
Pegasus Elliot MacKenzie Publishers Ltd.
www.pegasuspublishers.com

First Published in 2021

Vanguard Press
Sheraton House Castle Park
Cambridge England

Printed & Bound in Great Britain

Dedication

I dedicate this book to my beloved sister, Chrissy, who died, far too young, due to pancreatic cancer, earlier this year, so cruel, so heart breaking. I miss you so much, my beautiful sis'.

DISCLAIMER

Acknowledgements

My very grateful thanks go to the following people:

To my children who have given me their unwavering support and love.

To dear Charlie, (you know who you are), you are a shining star! I thank you for your never-ending patience!

To Piotr, a true friend, my grateful thanks.

To my dearest friend, Bridget, in the USA.

Finally, to all at Pegasus, I'm sure without your great support this book would not have been published

CHAPTER 1

Magnified by the soft glow of an oil lamp, animated shadows in the bedroom window, along with the accompaniment of a fierce, bellowing voice, signifies that all is far from well within the dilapidated farmstead at Penfold Grove.

'Git yer clothes orf and git on me bed, now, yer good fer nuffin' useless bitch!' The all too familiar, vociferating demands of the head of the household, one Albert Sebastian Soames, yells at his timid, long suffering young wife, Katerina.

Albert, both woefully uneducated and totally ignorant as to any of the niceties of life, shows not one iota of forethought regarding the effect that his perverted demands might have on his innocent six-year-old daughter's ears, in the adjoining bedroom.

Consequently, in the adjacent room, his young daughter, Lilibeth suffers yet another chilling shudder of dread running through her body, as the voice of her father's string of violent, sadistic threats and obscenities grow louder and ever more forceful.

Unrelenting, the slurred raging voice of her highly intoxicated father continues, echoing around the small child's bedroom, reverberating a chillingly cold fear, penetrating every crevice. 'I ain't askin' yer! Git 'em orf, yer good fer nothin' frigid mare!' For a few seconds there is an eerie silence. Lilibeth gasps when suddenly a heavy crashing noise startles the child, her eyes widening with trepidation. She can just make out the weak, and barely audible voice of her longsuffering mother, crying out pitifully, 'Oh please, no, no! I'm begging you Albert, I can't, you know I'm not well.'

Her pleadings ignored, there follows the sound of another heavy sickening thud and Katerina cries out, 'No, no don't! Please. Oh, please, you're hurting me, no! Her mother's feeble voice fades.

Completely oblivious of anyone's feelings, other than his own, he heartlessly persists. 'Shut yer snivelling trap woman. Now I ain't askin',

I's telling yer… git on me bed, or else!' he threatens, without a shred of mercy in his crass voice.

Crouched in the cupboard in the adjacent room, his daughter, her knees tucked firmly under her chin, rocks back and forth, wincing, as the sound of slapping noises intermingle with her mother's pitiful whimpering cries for mercy, filling the child with terror.

A nauseating cold fear engulfs the small child, her entire body trembles with fear, as her cruel father's foul demands on her mother continue relentlessly. 'Yer a useless fuckin' whore! Git in me bed. Now!' rebounds his rasping filthy demands. 'Right, yer been askin' fer it, yer stupid bitch, I'll bloody learn yer!'

Holding her breath cringing, she hears her mother's high-pitched scream. the terrified child presses her plump little hands over her ears, in a futile attempt to block out the unyielding demands of her formidable father.

His demanding tirade continues relentlessly. There's a combination of furniture crashing and heavy-handed slapping noises, accompanied by bloodcurdling screams from her poor mother echo around her room, chilling the air further, 'Argh! please, no, I'm begging you, For pity's sake. Help me someone. Dear God. Help me…!'

Her mother's desperate pleas are the last straw. Quivering with fright, Lilibeth can tolerate it no longer. Forgetting her own terror, she flees the safety of the wardrobe, running barefoot to her parents' bedroom.

Pushing the door open she gasps in horror. Amidst the array of broken furniture, she sees her mother, petrified, her nightdress ripped and torn, her bruised and battered body, cowering in a corner.

Her father is stood above her, his trousers pooled around his ankles, his fat hairy legs and buttocks in view, his hand held high, ominously clasping his dreaded buckled leather belt, about to strike her terrified mother.

Clenching her tiny fists, Lilibeth's body goes rigid, she screams with all her might, 'No…! Stop papa! Stop!'

With a sharp intake of breath, Katie's eyes dart towards her daughter, 'No, hush Lilibeth! Go back to your room baby, now!' she implores, desperate fear in her eyes.

Bravely standing her ground, defiantly facing her father she says, 'No won't! Don't hurt Mamma. Stop! Nasty Papa!'

Narrowing his bloodshot eyes, he stares down at his offspring, his fiery weather-worn face gleaming with sweat, glowing a vivid crimson, doing his best to focus his beady eyes on his contemptible child.

Inwardly, Lilibeth shrinks with fear, but stubbornly she meets and holds her father's evil gaze, as his thick bushy eyebrows frown intimidatingly, his cold, grey, eyes narrowing.

He scowls at his whippersnapper of a daughter, a tiny wisp of a girl that has the sheer audacity to stand there, daring to intervene and answer him back. 'Why yer little brat, yer just like yer fuckin' useless mother. Shut yer gob, yer insolent little runt. I'm gonna tan yer wivin an inch of yer bloody life!' he snarls.

A glance at her helpless mother strengthens her resolve. Despite visibly trembling, she courageously stands steadfast, defiantly rooted firmly to the spot.

Nostrils flaring, Albert's burning stare towards his insolent daughter, holds uncontrolled hatred and implications of murder, in his evil blood-shot eyes. Irrationally, and without reason, he throws back his head, laughing through the few filthy rotten teeth left in his mouth. Slimy spittle bubbles from his mean, contorted lips. 'Why yer... yer good fer nuffin' little dollop of shit!' he splutters. 'I'll bleedin' learn yer!'

His arm swings high, cutting a vitriolic figure, incandescent with pure hatred towards his much despised, unwanted child, his vengeful eyes glowering at his helpless daughter. 'I'm gonna thrash yer wivin an inch of yer bleeding life, yer brat!'

With her blood running cold, Katie, awash with fear for her precious daughter's life, cries out, imploring, 'Dear God, no Albert! I'm begging you, don't touch her, please, she doesn't understand, she's only a baby!'

Albert, his attention momentarily distracted, shoots a venomous glance in the direction of his wife, taking perverted pleasure in seeing his pathetic wife, reduced to begging him for mercy. He grunts, there's a sick sadistic smirk of pleasure written on his face, 'Shut yer whingin' gob misses! I'll learn that ruddy brat of yourn, make no mistake!' he bellows. Returning his gaze down on Lilibeth, he spits, 'I'm gonna tan yer bleeding hide red raw kid, yer useless little bit of nuffink!'

13

Aware that if she continues to protest, she will only exacerbate his foul temper still further, Katerina lunges forward and grabs at the waistband of his pants, preventing him reaching her beloved daughter, 'No Albert... oh please, I'm begging you, not my baby!' she pleads, 'I'm so sorry, I'll do as you say Albert, I will, I promise, just let Lilibeth go back to her room,' she offers feebly.

Albert, completely oblivious to the pleadings of his wife, makes another concerted effort, dragging his trouser entangled legs, enabling him to make another unsteady shuffling step towards the helpless child.

Gripped by terror, Katerina lunges forward, clinging frantically to his pants, she cries out to her daughter, 'Run baby, run to your room, for pity's sake, go to your room child. Now!'

The effect of his elongated, heavy alcoholic binge serves to make his bloated, rotund body even more unstable, roaring thunderously, like a wounded lion, he attempts to make yet another step towards his terrified daughter, his broad leather belt snaking menacingly in his white-knuckled fist. But his balance is impaired by Katerina's firm grasp of his trousers. He lurches forward, loses his balance, stumbles awkwardly and topples sideways.

There's a sickening crack as first his shoulder and then his skull strike against the marble-topped washstand, his grotesque, whale-like body slams heavily to the floor. There follows a deathly silence.

Gasping for breath, Katerina struggles to her feet, sweeping her long, tussled, hair from her tear-stained face, she notices blood on the back of her hand, but she is numb and feels nothing, she stands motionless, her mind vacant.

The pitiful sound of her daughter sobbing brings Katerina to her senses. Lilibeth is stood frozen in the doorway, her eyes transfixed on her father's alarmingly still, prostrate body, shaking uncontrollably from head to toe.

'Oh God.' Katerina gasps, shifting herself bodily sideways, to block the conspicuously lifeless form of Albert, from her distraught child's vision.

'Look, M-Mammy, look... blood, Papa deaded,' Lilibeth stutters through her deep sobs, pointing down at the ever-growing pool of blood emerging beneath her father's head.

Gritting her teeth, Katerina inhales deeply, she must reassure her daughter and get a grip on the situation, 'No, no, don't worry, darling, Papa fell and banged his head a little bit, that's all. Don't cry. Hush baby, please.'

Kneeling before her daughter and lightly grasping her arms, she whispers, 'Hush, listen to me very carefully. I know this might sound silly, but I want you to go back to your room, straight away. Get dressed, put your clothes on, all of them. Your petticoat, frock, cardigan, stockings, shoes, hat and coat, everything! Now can you do that for me, Lilibeth?' she asks, her voice, although very soft, denotes a strong tone of urgency.

Lilibeth sniffs and nods, wiping her runny nose on the sleeve of her nightdress. Obediently she does as she's asked, returning to her own room, casting a worried glance over her shoulder as she goes.

'Hurry, Lilibeth, do as I ask!' Katerina urges as she fights to hold back her impending tears.

With her daughter safely out of the way, Katerina turns and stares wide-eyed down at the lifeless form of her husband and the blood, emerging from beneath his head, is he...?

Unable to tell if he is breathing and fearing the worse, her heart is gripped with fear, there's only one way to find out.

Grimacing, she holds her breath, and gingerly, with her heart pounding so heavily that it physically hurts her chest, she kneels apprehensively beside him. His ample chest is heaving, albeit very slowly and laboriously. Katerina is filled with a surge of relief. 'Thank God,' she mutters, 'he's alive.' Simultaneously, as her anxiety subsides, the relief that she feels turns to sheer trepidation, as she realises the dire consequences that she would have to face when he wakes, she trembles violently. She has suffered so much at the hands of her husband, but she knows that this latest episode, when he had actually raised his hand towards her precious daughter is the last straw, their lives were now in mortal danger, they simply had to get away from Penfold Grove, and fast.

Holding her breath, desperate not to disturb him, she cautiously rises to her feet, she gulps, nervous fear parching her throat as a chilling sense of foreboding grips and envelops her. Panic sets in and takes over her. Grabbing a frock from the chest of drawers she pulls it over her torn nightgown then, impulsively, rushes around the room, throwing the few clothes that she possesses onto the bed. Snatching a cake of soap, a flannel, her hairbrush and a towel. Quickly scanning the room, her eyes fall on the large metal trunk, her trunk, containing the beautiful gown and shoes her beloved mother had made and given to her, on the very same day that her dear mother had passed away. It would break her heart to leave it behind, but it was obvious that she couldn't even contemplate taking it with her. Without daring to glance down at her husband, she gathers up the two top blankets from the bed, holding her breath she tip-toes uneasily over Albert's body and carries the contents along the landing to Lilibeth's room.

Stood beside her bed, fully clothed with Daisy, her rag doll, clasped firmly to her chest, the small child watches in silence, her sweet cherub-like face full of bewilderment, as her mother dashes around her room in a frenzy, flinging her clothes in an untidy heap on the blankets that now cover the floor. All the while, Katerina remains acutely alert, her ears straining for the slightest indication that her husband might be stirring. 'You've gone too far this time, Albert Soames,' she mutters under her breath, 'I can't take any more, we're leaving... and we won't be back... ever!' She vows.

With the contents of the drawers emptied, Katerina kneels before her tearful, confused daughter and gently clasps her shoulders. She can barely speak but she does her very best to sound calm and composed. Lowering her voice to a breathless whisper, she looks into her daughter's eyes, 'Listen to me Lilibeth, we're going downstairs now, I want you to be really quiet, we don't want to disturb your papa, do you understand?'

Lilibeth nods.

Together, they creep cautiously down the narrow unlit stairs. Lilibeth, hugging her precious rag doll goes first, Katerina follows behind, dragging the soft awkward bundle, wincing and cursing under her breath as it makes a deafening thud, thud, as it dropped down each step.

Safely down to the scullery, Katerina's hands shake as she struggles to light the lamp with a taper. As light floods the room, two small wicker hampers are hastily filled with an assortment of food grabbed from the larder, along with a pan, a few utensils, and finally a chipped enamelled jug with a hinged lid, which she hastily fills with water. Pausing very briefly at the foot of the stairs, Katerina strains to hear any sign of movement upstairs, to her relief all she can hear is the heavy pounding of her heart and her own shallow, gasping breath. Despite the warmth of the spring night, Katerina pulls on her heavy winter coat, a wide brimmed hat and her sturdy leather boots, slipping her soft leather house shoes into her pockets. Under her daughters puzzled gaze, and gripped by fear, she is finding it difficult to work with any degree of concentration, she is simply acting on impulse.

Clearly agitated she searches the scullery. 'Something to tie the bundle,' she keeps repeating, over and over. 'Something to…' Her eyes settle on one of Albert's dreaded leather belts draped over the arm of his chair, it will have to do. Drawing the corners of the blankets together, Katie fastens them securely, then exhausted, leans against the table, looking forlornly at the cumbersome bale and the two heavily packed baskets, she shakes her head, wondering how on earth, she can possibly manage to take it all with them? The horse and cart seem the obvious mode of transport but harnessing them would be both noisy and nigh on impossible in the dark, besides, it would take up precious time, something she simply didn't have. 'Think woman, think!' she chides herself.

Looking despairingly down at her young daughter she sighs mournfully, unless she can come up with an idea and quick, it would be too late. Albert will wake, and when he does…? She shivers as she thinks of the potential consequences if he were to catch them now. Her eyes settle on Lilibeth, 'Oh my poor baby, what can I do?' she mutters.

Like a bolt out of the blue it suddenly comes to her. 'That's it, baby!' Of course, her daughter's old perambulator, stored in the outhouse, 'I'm sure I can manage with that,' she mumbles to herself.

Dropping to her knees, Katerina speaks softly to her daughter. 'Now I want you to be a good girl and follow me outside, no noise, darling, be as quiet as a mouse,' she urges, putting her finger to her quivering lips. 'Remember, not a sound,' she adds, then heaving the heavy bundle towards the back door, she literally holds her breath as she tentatively slides the bolt and lifts the latch. Breathless with fear, she cautiously opens the door, to her dismay it creaks predictably. 'Please God, don't let it wake him,' she murmurs under her breath.

With their belongings now out in the yard Katerina listens. To her relief the house is as ominously as silent as the grave, so she ushers her daughter outside and gently closes the door behind them, sucking in a huge lungful of air to steady her nerves, then exhales a sigh of relief at managing to jump the first hurdle. Next step is the perambulator. Retrieving it from the outhouse proves to be relatively easy, though loading everything onto it is a much more difficult task. How she manages she doesn't know, it takes every ounce of strength she can muster, but after a determined struggle, manage she does. The problem is, by the time she's finished, it's piled so high that she can barely see over the top, so she's obliged to wedge the two wicker baskets beneath the pram on the chassis. Finally, with everything loaded haphazardly and precariously and the minutes ticking rapidly by, Katerina knows only too well that there is no time to lose, she's aware that when Albert wakes, they will undoubtedly be at his mercy. She'd pushed him too far this time, indeed, they would be fortunate to survive his ferocious vile temper. Without a moment to lose, they had to make a move, and now! Inside, Katerina feels sick to the stomach, and takes another steadying lungful of air, to steady herself. Feigning a relaxed, confident smile, she kneels before her daughter, looking into her eyes, telling her, 'There's no time to lose, we must leave now, baby, we must find somewhere safe.' she explains gently, 'Remember, we have to be very quiet, we don't want to wake your papa. Hold Daisy really tight, we don't want to lose her,' she adds in a broken whisper.

'Oh, I won't lose my Daisy coz she's my special friend, isn't she, Mamma?' says Lilibeth, squeezing her beloved doll even closer, her sad, tear-stained face breaking into a sweet, trusting smile.

Filled with trepidation, Katerina takes her first determined steps towards freedom and the unknown. Before the farm disappears from her view, Katerina ventures to pause for a few precious seconds, to steal a last, very nervous glance back towards the farmhouse. To her immense relief, all appears to be quiet and still, so with yet another fortifying breath to further her courage, she puts her daughter's hand on the handle of the pram, declaring, 'Hold tight darling, it's time for us to go.'

Go, but go where? She wonders despairingly. Penfold Grove might have been her home for more than seven years, but thanks to Albert's possessive dominance, she was never allowed out on her own. Her knowledge of the surrounding area limited. Left would take her to the tiny little hamlet of Fennydown and one mile beyond, to the market town of Holdean. She has friends living in Fennydown. Two close, trustworthy friends. Her first instinct is to flee to them, but she reasons Albert would automatically expect her to turn to them, wouldn't he? Yes, it would surely be the first place he'd look, and she couldn't possibly risk him turning up at their cottage, causing riotous mayhem for Margo, Stan and their dear son Freddie, so Katerina dismisses the idea out of hand. No, it is out of the question, they are kind, gentle countryfolk in their early fifties, no she couldn't go there, she just couldn't. Besides, what would be the point? Once he'd found them, he would surely drag them back home again.

So, on reaching the end of the lane she turns right. In her heart she knows what ever fate befalls them, surely nothing could be worse than living seven long terrorising, painful years with Albert Soames. It had been hell on earth, and she owed it to her daughter to flee before it was too late. With no thought as to where they might be heading, at that very moment, her only aim is to put as much distance between themselves and her volatile, lecherous husband as is physically possible. To ensure escaping his clutches, she would just have to take a chance, hoping the good Lord would guide them.

Beginning their journey into the unknown, they walk in silence, but Katerina's mind is working overtime, where exactly could they go? She gnaws her quivering lip as she takes a last lingering look across the field towards the Penfold homestead and a tear falls, surely there is nowhere more desolate and foreboding on God's earth than Penfold Grove, she decides. To her daughter, outwardly she is looking straight-faced and calm, yet inwardly feeling desperate. Gritting her teeth, they walk on and after eighty yards or so, her eyes fall onto the row of three derelict and roofless farm workers' cottages, their craggy outlines silhouetted eerily against the silvery light of the moon. She slows her pace, just a little, to observe the cottages that until just a few years ago, housed the unfortunate, hard grafting, yet always pathetically grateful farm workers and their families. Previously good homes that now sat deserted, ravaged by the elements of time and sheer wanton neglect. Such a fitting testament to their worthless owner, Albert Soames, thinks Katerina dryly. She shakes her head, such a waste. Three, lovely, tied cottages, that the downtrodden farmworkers had been driven to abandon and flee, as their tyrannical employer descended further and further into the depths of uncontrollable state of foul drunkenness.

The inhabitants, in turn, fearing that they were in mortal danger from their employer's completely unreasonable demands and ferocious temper if they stayed a moment longer, reaching the end of their tether, each family, in turn, decided that they could take no more, that it would be a more desirable option for them to up sticks with their families, taking their chances elsewhere, rendering themselves both jobless and homeless, to go in search of difficult to come by work wherever they might find it. Destitution and the workhouse being a more palatable option to them all, in preference to being beholden to their evil slave driving, drunken employer, Albert Soames.

Ivy Cottage, the first and by far the largest of the properties, boasted three small bedrooms, previously occupied by Ernest Brooker, along with his brother Zachariah, sister-in-law Maude and their three young children. Sadly, they had left just eight weeks after she herself had arrived at Penfold Grove, so she didn't get to know them that well. After their departure, word spread of the terrible way Soames treated all his workers, consequentially the Brookers were never replaced, so their pretty cottage quickly fell into disrepair. Ivy cottage is now a pathetically forlorn sight. In its hey-day, it had been a serviceable family home crowned with a thick thatched roof, sadly now a roofless shell with most of the tiny rotten windows, missing several panes of fragile glass, dangling limply from their hinges and swaying in the wind. The accommodation, now only suitable for wildlife, appropriately, completely smothered in a thick blanket of rampant, life suffocating ivy.

The second cottage, Fourwinds Cottage, the tiny one-up- one-down home, which previously had housed Herbert and Millie Long and their new-born infant, Eva-May. That was until the sudden untimely death of poor Herbert, at the tender age of just twenty-nine. Tragically he died from a massive heart attack, almost certainly induced by the persistent bullying from Soames, into doing not only his own work, but the work left undone by the last deserters, Ernie and Zacharia Brooker and family. Despite not being a particularly strong man, Herbert had been a real grafter who had ended up working all the hours that God sent, out in all weathers, yet barely living hand to mouth. He had died very suddenly, leaving poor Millie a widow, alone with a ten-week-old infant to support. Katerina had liked Millie from the moment she'd met her, Millie had made her first few lonely months at Penfold more bearable with her kindness and witty humour, but sadly theirs was doomed to be a very short friendship. The premature death of her beloved Herbert, meant that, at Albert's insistence, Millie was forced to leave the tied cottage with immediate effect.

With revulsion burning in her heart, Katerina recalled the sadistic enthusiasm that Albert had shown as he heartlessly threw them out, leaving them not only homeless but penniless. Oh poor, sweet Millie. It might have been a brief friendship, for Herbert had died just five months after the departure of the Brooker family, but she would never forget dear Millie and her beautiful tiny infant. Katerina grimaces, she wonders how Millie and her baby had fared after they were forcibly evicted from their cottage with only the clothes she stood up in, a carpet bag and the princely sum of seven shillings, and sixpence three farthings, a sum of money that Katerina herself had secretly pressed into her hand when Albert wasn't looking. Katerina gnaws on her lip, now she too was in the same position as Millie, except her own pockets were completely empty.

Minus further subsequent occupants, the third and final abode, Rose Cottage, home to the Murphy family, had long ago crumbled into nothing more than a heap of rubble, save two of the four stubborn corners and a sturdy stone chimney stack left standing ominously against the skyline, like an arthritic finger pointing objectionably heavenward in protest of the dwellings sad demise. The property that was once surrounded by Esme's lovingly tended gardens, the rear planted with much needed vegetables and fruit trees, the front with an abundance of tenderly cared for flowers which during the warm summer months had filled the air with their fragrant heady scent. Now, six years after their predictably hasty departure, the choking weeds and brambles had taken over in abundance, even the tough old fruit trees had been strangled mercilessly by the life strangling ivy and had given up hope of surviving, they had withered and died, leaving the naked and fruitless gnarled branches forlornly stretching outwards in despair.

As Katerina leaves Rose Cottage behind her, she recalls the very last of the tenants to flee Penfold Grove. Poor old Fred Murphy had flitted under the cover of darkness with his wife Esme and two young teenage sons, some nine months after her own arrival. She could still remember clearly, Fred sneaking round to seek her out in her scullery, to give her notice of his intentions to take his family and leave later that night, and to voice his ominous warning to her. 'I's just letting yer know that we'll be orf ternight gel. I's sorry, but we gotta go lovey, or else I can't be responsible fer me actions. By gawd I could cheerfully swing fer that man of yourn! I'm sorry gel, but I got all me kith and kin to fink of. Now if yer got any sense yer should come wiv us, yer more than welcome gel. Get yerself away from him now, Katie, come wiv us while yer got a chance to save yerself, coz I's warning yer gel, yer should get away from this God-forsaken hole and that drunken bastard afore it's too late!' he had warned her with genuine fear in his eyes. Katerina exhales. Dear Fred, if only she'd listened, if only she'd known then what she knew now.

Life had been hard enough when there were farmhands around, but the minute the third cottage was vacated, she had learned to her cost just how cruel, vile and degrading her life with Albert Soames would become.

As they amble onwards, Katerina, caught up in painful memories, loses her concentration, not noticing the blanket slither from the pram, entangling her feet. Lurching forward she stumbles, tipping up the pram, depositing all their worldly possessions on the ground, yelping in agony as her knees meet with the rough and stony ground.

'Mammy!' Lilibeth cries out. 'Are you hurt?'

Ignoring the sharp pains shooting up and down her legs, Katie shrugs her shoulders and smiles down at her daughter, 'I'm fine darling, just fine,' she lies, brushing herself down and picking their meagre possessions, slinging everything back on the pram. Doggedly she limps onward.

Trying to think positively, Katie thinks they are more than fortunate, for the first week in June, it is comfortably warm and dry, their heavy coats and hats are soon discarded, and slung carelessly over the handle of the pram.

In the dead of night, Katerina trudges on aimlessly, her head filled with a mixture of emotions. Fear of Albert catching up with them, relief to be leaving Penfold and optimism for their future, yet on the other hand, worried stiff as to what exactly that future might hold.

Pushing the pram is proving to be a harrowing ordeal, causing her untold misery, at only five feet three and of very slender build, Katerina is really struggling to cope with not only the unbalanced weight on the pram, but the precarious way in which it had been hastily loaded and repeatedly re-loaded. It was giving her no end of problems, problems that she could well do without. Every so often, to her frustration, the moon would suddenly disappear behind a wayward cloud, plunging everywhere into an inky darkness, she had lost count of the number of times that the pram had fallen foul of ruts and potholes, forcing her to stop and reload all their worldly possessions. Not only having to contend with the rough terrain, she now finds herself walking through a dense wood, the enveloping velvety darkness holding an eerie, spooky sort of atmosphere which is giving her the jitters. Hedgehogs snuffle and grunt, as they go scurrying about their business, as does a pair of very handsome, lumbering old badgers. Then there's the heart-stopping episode with the owl. She'd almost had a heart attack when, without warning, like a haunting shadow of a ghost, a large pale owl, flies silently across their path, heading for an open field, shrouded in a swirling mist, it is all so unnerving. She takes to singing nursery rhymes to try to distract her daughter from the spooky surroundings, she also makes up funny little stories, anything that can keep her young daughter's mind occupied, and hers too, for that matter.

For what seems like an eternity, they both trudge wearily on. Snap! Katerina freezes as sounds of rustling dead leaves and a nerve shattering series of sharp cracking twigs seems to come from the bushes, no more than twenty or maybe thirty feet in front of them. Caught unawares, they both stand stock still, their clasped hands gripped tightly together. Beads of perspiration bathe Katerina's brow and her weary body stiffens, she swallows, mumbling the semblance of a prayer. For one heart-stopping moment she is convinced that Albert had tracked them down and is about to step out in front of them. A large fox emerges from the thick tangled bushes, she exhales a long gasp of relief when it pauses for a brief second, just long enough to cast a furtive, lightening glance directly at them, then just as quickly it slinks from sight, back into the safety of the shadows of the night. That unexpected encounter serves as is a reminder that she should stay focussed. She knows that Albert will surely be out there somewhere, tracking them down, of that fact she can be certain.

'Ow, stop, no more,' says Lilibeth tugging at her mother's skirt. 'My feet is hurting, I'm tired,' she declares, stubbornly plonking herself down on a grassy knoll. Although reluctant to stop, Katerina has to admit she's in desperate need of rest herself Having to contend with the heavily loaded and unbalanced pram in the dead of night is bad enough, but she's still weak, after suffering a miscarriage some four months earlier, yet another contribution towards her dire state of fatigue. Dispirited, Katie sits down, reluctantly, yet thankfully, beside her daughter. 'I know, darling, Mammy's tired too. Come, sit on my lap, we've walked such a long way. Let Mammy rub your feet, it'll make them feel better.' Lilibeth duly obliges and snuggles down gratefully on her mother's lap. Katerina kicks off her own boots then carefully removes her daughter's shoes, 'Wiggle your toes sweetheart,' she tells her, massaging the life back into her daughter's red and swollen feet.

Katerina wraps her shawl around them both, though it is more for comfort than warmth. With doleful eyes Lilibeth looks up at her mother, 'Is we nearly there? Coz I'm sleepy, and so is Daisy?'

'Um… no, not yet, sweetheart, we have a little bit further to go, but don't worry, I'm sure we will find somewhere really nice, very soon,' she replies reassuringly.

'Nasty Papa won't come with us, will he?' asks Lilibeth frowning.

Katerina shudders at the very thought and shakes her head. 'No, darling, just you, me, and Daisy, of course?'

Lilibeth looks relieved.

'Yes sweetheart, you, me and your Daisy makes three! Hey, that's clever, it rhymes, doesn't it?' says Katie forcing a smile.

Lilibeth nods, trying unsuccessfully to stave off a yawn.

Clearly the small child is completely exhausted because within minutes of settling down, her eyelids flutter, and she drifts into a welcome sleep.

Holding her close, Katerina kisses her daughter's forehead, gently rocking her back and forth, 'Sleep tight, my precious baby,' she whispers, sighing a long woeful sigh.

With her eyes now adjusted to the darkness she looks about her. She feels vulnerable, lost and very alone, with only her thoughts to keep her company, the enormity of their desperate situation truly dawns on her.

Undoubtedly, she had foolishly acted on impulse, she decides, after trudging around aimlessly for several hours in the dark, she now had no idea where they were and even worse, not the faintest idea where they could possibly go! They had no-one, they were completely lost, alone and penniless! She struggles with her conscience, trying to convince herself that she had done the right thing in running away.

Life with Albert Soames had been intolerable. For seven long, agonising years it had been a living nightmare, she sighs as a tear rolls down her cheek. Hadn't she spent her every waking moment working tirelessly and uncomplainingly, all the hours that God sent for that ungrateful tyrant? Hadn't she silently suffered his terrifying, drunken mood swings and the pain of his sickeningly enforced, sexual depravities demanded of her? So many of which, invariably ending up with a series of tragic and very painful early miscarriages? Sadly, for the sake of her daughter and a roof over their heads, she had stupidly endured his wickedly perverted ways without question.

But tonight! Albert had done the unthinkable, for the first time ever, he had vented his foul temper on her precious daughter, he had raised his filthy hand to her, threatening her with physical violence, and for that act alone she knew that she would never forgive him, it makes her determined to resolve that it can never happen again!

Miserably she sits cradling her daughter, the only thing she knows for certain, is that there was no going back, for no matter what lay before them, surely nowhere on God's earth could possibly be worse than living under the same roof as Albert Soames at Penfold. Confidently she vows there and then, that they would never set foot in that house again!

The cool misty light heralds the start of a new day, which in turn encourages the start of a noisy dawn chorus.

Katie opens her eyes to see the sun flickering through the canopy of the trees above her, her body aches from head to toe.

Lilibeth is still sleeping soundly in her arms as they lay huddled together.

Dismayed, as the terrible events of the previous night comes flooding back to haunt her, she lifts her head, surveying the spot where they had been obliged to bed down for the night. Closing her eyes and opening them again in disbelief, she lets out a long sigh of frustration. What a nightmare, no shelter, merely a grassy, dew-covered bank on which they had gratefully slept off their fatigue.

Now they were, stuck in the middle of…? God only knows where, their situation apparently hopeless, and to cap it all, now her feet are throbbing furiously, she struggles to search for solution to their dire predicament.

Katie has no family to turn to, not a single penny in her pocket, and the huge responsibility of providing for her young daughter, to clothe, feed and most important of all, the obvious need to put a roof over their heads, and what has she got, absolutely nothing!

Filled with sorrow, tears well up in her eyes, what had she done? For just a fleeting moment, Katerina foolishly considers that maybe they should return to Penfold, but with the horrific memories of the previous night revolving around in her head, she instantly dismisses the idea as utter madness, she can't go back, she won't! Anyway, isn't this the second time in her life that she'd been forced to fend for herself? Katie frowns, but this time it is so very different, this time she is not alone, this time she has the added responsibility of her six-year-old offspring to consider. Looking down at her daughter peacefully sleeping in her arms, so blissfully unaware of their shocking state of homelessness, a cloud of depression envelops her, she wonders how far they had walked and if Albert was far behind them.

She expels a long sorrowful sigh, the first of the day.

It is obvious that they have to move on, but it is as plain as the nose on her face that she can't expect her little daughter to walk any further, she had to face the facts and be practical.

After much soul searching, she decides to sort out the badly loaded pram before they can move on, they won't get far with everything constantly falling to the ground. Her thoughts are interrupted as Lilibeth wriggles and stirs. 'Where is we, Mamma?' she asks, rubbing the sleep from her eyes and looking about her.

'I'm not sure, darling, but don't worry, we're going to find somewhere really nice, very soon,' she tells her, trying hard to make her reply sound convincingly positive, though deep down she is not only worried, but scared stiff. Worried, because her impulsive actions had not only reduced them to living as nothing more than common vagrants but scared witless that they would be tracked down by her husband at any moment and forced, against their will, to return to Penfold Grove, the very thought makes her skin crawl.

In the cold light of day, she is now wishing with all her heart that she had gone to Margo and Stan's house, after all, their son Freddie would surely have protected them, he was a strapping nineteen-year-old and probably well able to deal with the likes of an obese, fifty-nine-year-old abusive alcoholic.

Why-oh-why hadn't she stopped to think before she went blindly marching off into the night? But it's too late to turn back now, she sighs. Wandering around aimlessly in the dark she has completely lost her bearings, now she wouldn't know how to find Margo and Stan's house in Fennydown, even if she wanted too.

Filled with despair, Katerina scolds herself. Snap out of it, stop the self-pity woman, think positive, think!

Lilibeth gazes up at her mother, her pretty pale blue eyes filled with trust, 'Me and Daisy's hungry, can we have breakfast now?' she asks, busy picking the pieces of moss from her crumpled frock.

Forcing a cheerful smile, Katerina shrugs. 'Well then, I'd better find something for us to eat,' she says, struggling to release one of the wicker baskets, wedged firmly beneath the pram.

After a scrummage through the second basket she finds what she is looking for and busies herself cutting rough chunks of bread, spreading it with some of her homemade butter and strawberry jam.

'Can I have some milk, please, Mamma?' Lilibeth asks politely.

Katie sighs, 'I'm sorry, darling, there's no milk, but we've got water.'

Lilibeth shrugs with indifference and carries on happily tucking into her rather bulky, ill-prepared sandwich with red jam plastered around her mouth.

With breakfast over, Katerina uses just a few precious drops of water from the jug and a flannel to freshen themselves up.

Lilibeth's deep auburn hair is naturally curly, as is her mother's, it needs constant daily grooming, already it is tangled and matted, so she ransacks the pram to find the hairbrush. 'My goodness, just look at this lot piled up on the pram, what a mess, I think perhaps we should re-pack it all, darling, will you help me to fold everything nice and neat?' asks Katie, lovingly brushing her daughter's tangled hair. More than seven long years spent with Albert has taught her that if she occupies her time, she can bury her problems to the back of her mind.

Lilibeth nods, as always, only too happy to help, especially if it means her mother would stop pulling and brushing her hair, she will agree to anything.

Setting to, enthusiastically helping her mother, the entire contents of the pram are spread out on the ground. With meticulous folding and clever packing, she finds all their clothes can be stored in the deep well of the pram beneath the mattress.

The morning holds a clear blue sky now, the strong sun has already dispensed with the early morning mist, so their two coats are neatly folded, to serve as a pillow. One blanket is placed on top the mattress, the other will provide a warm top cover, if needed later.

Satisfied with a job well done, Katerina now feels a sense of urgency, time is getting on, the sun is fast rising in the sky and warming the earth. Strangely she feels more vulnerable in the cold light of day, she shudders, anxious to make a move. 'We must move on, darling. Would you like to sit in the pram, now it's tidy?' she asks.

'Yes, please, Mammy, Daisy says she wants to ride in the pram with me,' replies Lilibeth enthusiastically, offering her arms to be lifted.

Katerina cringes in agony as she forces her swollen, blistered feet into her damp leather brogues. She toys with the idea of wearing her lightweight leather house shoes, they would be far more comfortable, but she knows they won't stand up to country walking over rough terrain, she'd wear them out in no time. No, it would have to be her boots.

'What about my shoes, Mammy?'

Katerina, smiles thinly, 'You won't really need them if you're sat in the pram, will you, darling?'

Clearly enjoying her new elevated mode of transport, Lilibeth is all smiles, the pram giving her a good view of the countryside, but Katerina is concerned. For all she knows, they could be walking straight back to Penfold Grove and into the hands of her evil husband, so she ponders as to how they can manage to walk in any one direction and keep in a relatively straight line. She would be the first to admit that she isn't very worldly wise, but she does know that the sun rises in the east and sets in the west so, after a great deal of thought and some careful calculations, she comes to what she thinks is a practical decision. They will walk with the morning sun on her right side and her shadow to her left, then, when her shadow shortens, around midday, they will walk with the sun on her left and her shadow on her right in the afternoon. Her logic tells her that they should keep heading in a reasonably straight line, and hopefully northwards. 'At least if I'm right, we won't keep going around in circles, or even more disastrously, end up back at Penfold Grove,' she tells herself.

As they prepare to continue their journey, Katie glances at the sun then her shadow to get her bearings. It is time to make a move.

Straightening her shoulders, she can't help but notice there are large, steely grey clouds looming on the far horizon, her heart sinks, 'Oh please, don't let it rain.' The very thought of walking the countryside in heavy rain fills Katerina with dread, she knows they will have to find shelter, sooner rather than later.

Determined she shrugs her shoulders and gives her daughter a confident carefree smile, 'Are you ready, darling?'

Lilibeth nods.

'Then let's be on our way!' she declares cheerily.

With Lilibeth sat high in the pram and the weight more evenly distributed, Katerina finds the going is nowhere near as problematic as walking in the dark, and despite her boots making her feet throb, causing her untold agony, she now feels more confident. At least in the daylight, she can see all the holes and ruts and take avoiding action, and besides, she can also keep her eyes peeled for her husband.

The sun warms them like a comforting blanket. The entire countryside is wide awake, but the difference now is it can all be seen and understood.

They chatter constantly. 'Look, sweetheart, lots of rabbits in the field over there,' Katerina points out, pausing momentarily to show Lilibeth at least a dozen or more, happily running around the field carefree and bobbing their tails, disappearing then emerging once again from the numerous warrens that are scattered all over the field.

Every so often she spots other interesting things to see and would point them out. Like the couple of squirrels scampering adeptly up a tree and along the branches.

They stop briefly and only when necessary to go to the toilet or maybe snatch a bite to eat and quench their thirst, then they would move quickly on again.

Considering it was the first week of June, the unusually long warm spring had encouraged many of the flowers to bloom early, the hedgerows are filled with a profusion of wildflowers. Katerina points them out to her daughter, trying as she does, to remember all their names. Large white trumpet shaped flowered bindweed stubbornly weaves its way through the thick green hedgerows, tussling with wild, sweet-smelling honeysuckle. Little periwinkle flowers and deep yellow buttercups happily sway in the gentle breeze, nodding neighbourly together. A few brightly coloured butterflies flit daintily from flower to flower, compete with the buzzing bees, whilst the fluffy old man's beard tangles with a sturdy hawthorn hedge, and all the while the air is filled with a myriad of beautiful bird song.

Tall flat heads of white yarrow stand proud above the lusciously thick carpet of green grass that frames a whole meadow full of even more wildflowers, a pleasing, colourful picture that if it was under any other circumstance, decides Katie, she would have thoroughly enjoyed the glorious beauty of the Wiltshire countryside.

As the day wears on, the temperature begins to drop, the air holding a vague hint of a chill. Katie shivers. The sun is lower in the sky now, and her shadow, when it isn't disappearing behind the increasingly darkening clouds, stretches out long and thin to her right, indicating that it must be well past teatime.

Heavy foreboding clouds gather menacingly overhead, heaping further misery on her, the light darkens ominously, a strong wind whips up from nowhere, agitating the flora and fauna. Katerina grabs her hat and coat then pulls up the pram hood and quickly attaches the storm cover, just as the heavens open and the rain falls to earth with a vengeance.

Katerina quickens her pace, though for the life of her she doesn't know why, after all, where exactly, were they hurrying too? Despite feeling utterly exhausted and her feet now totally numb, she bows her head, gripping the handle of the pram even more tightly, trudging wearily on.

The sad, drenched little trio of Katerina, Lilibeth and the large cumbersome pram, cross cautiously over a rickety, ancient wooden bridge, through the gaps beneath her feet she can see the rushing water, swirling furiously, racing over the large boulders.

She grimaces, her sodden boots squelching with every painful footstep. Gritting her teeth, she uses the last of her energy to push the heavy pram up an unfriendly, steep hill that has rivers of water gushing down and swamping her feet.

Rounding the bend at the top, Katerina stops dead in her tracks. Behind an unruly copper beech hedge, nestles a very tempting, homely looking large cottage, mauve clematis ambling decoratively against its crude flint wall.

Slowly she pushes the pram past the gate, her eyes enviously taking in the welcoming abode, she's sorely tempted to knock at the door. The rain is now falling relentlessly and showing no sign of letting up, and to make matters worse the light is beginning to fade.

On the verge of approaching the cottage door, a large barn in the adjacent field catches her eye. Looking at Lilibeth she gnaws her lip; she has reservations about approaching a stranger's home. We'll probably be safer if we take refuge in the barn, she reasons, after all, she has no idea who lives in the cottage and the last thing she wants to do is draw attention to themselves, so she resists the temptation of the lovely homestead, trusting her instincts, she opts for the barn instead.

Wheeling the pram to the wooden gate, she lifts the latch and swings the gate open, just enough to squeeze the pram through the gap.

Tears well in her eyes as she stands looking down at the ground despondently, it's a muddy quagmire. Her heart sinks, for no matter how hard she tries, everything seems stacked against them. Cows obviously graze in the field, the wet sodden ground is uneven, with deep, water-filled hoof prints that would make it nigh on impossible to push the narrow wheels of the weighty pram over the flooded ground.

Sighing wearily, Katerina looks at her daughter in despair, trying to force a smile.

Lilibeth responds with trusting smile back.

Spurred on by her daughter's unquestionable faith in her, she resolves not to be deterred. Fuelled by tenacity to reach the barn, no matter what effort it takes, she clenches her teeth, there's only one thing for it, 'I'm sorry sweetheart, you're going to have to walk,' she says, lifting her gently to the ground, 'It's very muddy darling,' she warns, 'so lift your skirt and tread very carefully, I don't want you falling in the mud.'

Turning the pram around so that she can drag it backwards over the rough pitted ground, Katie fastens the gate securely behind them. Dragging the pram, slipping and sliding, they both somehow managed to reach to the barn door unscathed.

Once safely inside, Katerina breathes a long sigh of relief. Giving their dripping wet hats and coats a sharp flick she hangs them on some wooden pegs to dry.

Lilibeth is puzzled, 'Why is we in here?' she asks, 'I don't like it, Mammy, it's dark,' she says, looking warily around the huge barn.

'We need somewhere to shelter from the rain. It's nice and dry in here, sweetheart, we can stay here until morning. Tomorrow, when the rain has stopped, we can move on,' she explains brightly.

Lilibeth shivers. She's wet, cold, hungry, and extremely tired.

'Let's get out of these wet clothes, or we will catch our deaths,' Katie explains, searching through the bottom of the pram to find a change of clothing. Within no time they are both stood in clean dry clothes.

'There, that's better, isn't it?' Katerina says brightly, rubbing her daughter, perhaps a touch too zealously, to warm her.

Lilibeth objects to her mother's vigorous enthusiasm, 'Ouch, no more, Mamma, I'm lovely and warm,' she protests, her cold red nose, now a very healthy pink.

Katerina, looks forlornly at the pile of filthy, bedraggled, sodden clothes laying in a heap on the earthen floor, 'Hum, I think we should try to dry our clothes, darling, I suppose we could hang them on the straw bales to dry out, what do you think, sweetheart?'

Despite feeling completely exhausted, Lilibeth perks up, 'I'll help, and we can hang my Daisy up, coz she's wet too,' she volunteers.

Hearing voices approaching, Katie stiffens, grabbing her daughter's hand, 'Quick, someone's coming!' she whispers, pulling her behind a stack of straw bales, 'Quiet, darling, not a sound.'

Stooping behind the bales, they listen, as male voices grow louder, 'Hush darling, hush,' she whispers, holding her breath until finally the voices fade away. That was a close thing, it was fate that she had chosen the barn, at least they were safe for now.

'Why is we whispering, Mamma?'

Kneeling beside her daughter she explains that they desperately need shelter from the rain. Yes, the barn is nice and dry, but the problem is, they don't have the farmer's permission to be there.

Looking worried, Lilibeth asks, 'Will the man be very cross and shout at us, Mammy?'

'I don't think so, sweetheart. Perhaps we should have asked him when we first arrived, but not now darling. You see it's getting late so it's not worth disturbing him at this time of the night,' she explains, 'Anyway, I'm sure he won't mind, you see we will only be here tonight, we'll leave tomorrow, bright and early, so he won't even know that we've been here.'

Lilibeth yawns and rubs her eyes, 'I'm tired and my poor Daisy says she's sleepy too.'

The light is fading fast, and the lack of windows makes it even darker inside the barn. Lilibeth is perched on a bale, barely able to keep herself awake, Katerina realises that if she doesn't organise somewhere to sleep and soon, it will be too dark to see anything. As quickly as she can, she uses the two blankets to make up a bed of sorts in the hay, stacked in the furthest corner, away from the wooden doors

'Here darling, bring Daisy, lay with me, try this lovely warm bed I've made for us,' she suggests, patting the blanket, inviting her daughter to join her.

Though Lilibeth looks unimpressed with the makeshift bed, she is dead beat, she lays beside her mother, still clutching her doll in her arms.

Appreciative of having somewhere warm and soft to lay, Lilibeth cuddles down, 'It's lovely and warm, Mammy,' she concedes.

Katerina softly hums a lullaby and within minutes, her daughter, now cosy, and comfortable, flutters her eyelids and drifts gratefully to sleep.

Looking down at her sleeping child Katerina frowns and whispers, 'Oh my poor little lamb, what have I done? Here we are, stuck in the middle of…? I honestly don't know where and reduced to sleeping rough in a big old barn. God help us.' Not for the first time, she lets out yet another long, drawn-out sigh and whispers, 'I swear I will do whatever it takes to work things out for us.' she says, kissing her slumbering child tenderly on her pouting rosebud lips.

With Lilibeth now in a deep sleep, Katerina creeps over to open the barn door and peers outside. Everything appears quiet and still, even the rain has eased up, now it's little more than a fine drizzle.

To her right in the distance, she can just make out the silhouette of the cottage, a ground floor window, lit with a softly glowing light tells her that someone is home.

The lack of moonlight restricts her vision, so she opens the door warily, just a little more, looking cautiously around.

Enticingly, to her left, about forty or fifty feet away, a small herd of cows are huddled together beneath the boughs of a large tree, the very sight of which, stirs her into considering a crazy notion. Biting her lip, she pauses to think, all she has to do is keep her head and be extra vigilant, after all, right now the moon is hidden by the heavy cloud cover, so it would be perfect to reach the cows unseen.

Weighing up the possibility. She knows there's very little water left, and they would have to drink something, was it worth taking the risk? 'Oh dear, I suppose necessity dictates, what choice do I have?' she asks herself.

Her mind made up, she searches in the second basket and pulls out an enamelled bowl and after yet another cautionary check through the gap in the door to ensure the coast is clear, she makes a swift, light-footed dash for the nearest cow.

'Easy girl, nice and steady there,' she whispers, gently patting the cow's hindquarters, setting the bowl down beneath its udder. Stooping on her haunches she begins milking, whilst talking softly, reassuring the animal, though all the while her nerves are on a knife's edge. Whilst milking she remains vigilant and alert to everything about her. Inevitably a few precious drops of rich creamy milk are spilled but it can't be helped, she simply can't afford to get caught. Milking cows or even goats, comes as second nature to her, but in the darkness, without a stool and shaking with fear, it was proving to be very difficult.

Minutes tick by, 'That will have to do, for now,' she decides, and with a quick nervous glance around, she lifts her long skirt from her ankles and makes a dash to the barn door.

Safely back inside the sanctuary of the barn, she congratulates herself for the bravery she'd shown in venturing outside for the milk, even if her excursion had scared her half to death.

Exhausted but a little happier than the previous night, she cuddles up to Lilibeth for much needed sleep.

CHAPTER 2

Shards of light pour through gaps in the walls. The sound of footsteps on the gravel, approaching the barn, wakes Katerina with a start, sitting bolt upright, her nerve ends tingle all over her body. She looks down at Lilibeth, thankfully she is still sleep. Her brow creases, oh please, don't wake up, not now!

As she listens, terrified of being discovered, for a few worrying moments she thinks they are coming into the barn, but to her relief the sound of their footsteps passes on by and out of earshot.

Rain is still pummelling relentlessly on the rusty corrugated tin roof making a deafening racket, there's no need for Katerina to look outside at the weather. It seems an obvious decision to make, they would have to stay where they are for now. After all, it is warm and dry and they have plenty to eat, and now, thanks to last night's hairy escapade, they even have a convenient source of fresh milk too.

Fuelled by an unshakeable determination to find a better life and freedom from her obnoxious husband, she knows in her heart, that staying put in the barn is almost certainly their best option, for now at least.

Hearing someone outside the barn, has made Katerina realise their vulnerability, surveying every nook and cranny of the barn, she decides that it might be advisable to move out of sight, up in the loft, a possibility that she would explore later.

Stirring, Lilibeth frowns, 'What's that noise, Mammy?' she asks, looking up at the roof.

'What noise? Oh that, it's just the rain sweetheart, it's nothing to worry about, we're nice and dry in here.'

'My tummy's hungry, can we have something to eat?' adding, 'Daisy's hungry too.'

Doing her best to prepare a slice of bread, Katerina smears it with butter and honey, 'There you go Pet, oh, and look what we've got, fresh milk,' she says, handing her daughter the recently acquired precious milk.

'Umm, nice,' exclaims Lilibeth and drinks the entire contents without stopping to draw breath, 'lovely, just like the milk at home.' she says, wiping her mouth with the back of her hand, in an unladylike fashion.

The innocent comment strikes a nerve, Katerina feels sick to the stomach. Home, where exactly is home?

Whilst they eat, Katerina gives further consideration to the idea of moving up into the loft, it seems to be a sensible precaution, though she had yet to persuade her daughter, 'I've been thinking, it's a bit draughty down here, perhaps we could put everything up there, in the loft, we'd be much warmer, what do you think darling?' she asks, waiting for her reaction.

Mystified Lilibeth looks up, 'But how do we get up there, Mammy?'

'There's a tall wooden ladder, over there in the corner, see?' she points out, relieved that her daughter appears to be readily accepting of her somewhat strange proposal without question.

The idea certainly appeals to the adventurous, tomboy side of Lilibeth, 'I'll take Daisy up the ladder,' she says making a dash towards the ladder.

'No wait. It's very high!' warns Katerina, grabbing her arm, 'we must be very careful, let me stand at the bottom of the ladder and hold it steady for you.'

Before she'll allow her young daughter to scale the ladder, she takes charge of her doll, 'Best I carry Daisy up for you, you'll need two hands to climb up there, we wouldn't want you to drop her, would we?'

Reluctantly she hands her precious doll into her mother's safe keeping.

Standing at the bottom, she holds the ladder firmly, watching with her heart in her mouth, as her excited daughter climbs to the loft, without showing the slightest sign of fear.

'Come on, Mammy, you come up now!' Lilibeth cries out gleefully, peering over the edge.

'Get away from the edge darling, you'll fall!' she warns.

As usual, her offspring does as she is told, thankfully unquestioning obedience has always been one of her daughter's virtues.

Struggling, desperate to keep her balance, Katerina hoists her skirts, and somehow manages to carry the baskets, one at a time, up the ladder and set them down, well away from the edge. 'Just the blankets then that's everything,' she tells Lilibeth.

'What about my pram, are you going to bring it up the ladder?'

'Hah, I couldn't possibly bring it up here darling, it's far too big and cumbersome,' she says managing a chuckle.

Mind you, her daughter had raised an important point. Thinking for a minute she realises there isn't any point going to the trouble of literally hiding up in the loft, then leaving the perambulator out to be discovered. Looking around the barn, she can just make out, at the far end, a small, stable like partition strewn with tackle and a few bales of straw, she smiles gratefully, it's the perfect hiding place.

With the pram now safely hidden from view, she rummages around the barn, she finds a large, galvanised pail, deciding it would be ideal to use as a toilet, she can empty it when it's dark. She also finds several decent sacks that can be filled with the straw to provide them with a soft bed.

Gathering up their clothes they'd had hung up to dry the previous night, she throws them over her shoulders along with the sacks. Grabbing the bucket, she gathers her skirt and carefully climbs the ladder once again.

Frustratingly, fatigue overcomes Katerina and she's obliged to sit and rest a while to recover. Whilst she does, it occurs to her that the edge of the loft could be a potential danger to Lilibeth, they are at least twelve feet off the ground. Searching around the loft, she finds several sturdy wooden boxes, so as a measure of safety, she places a row of them as a barrier, at the leading edge of the loft. Three more boxes, one large and two smaller ones, are upturned to provide somewhere to sit and eat, a further two boxes are placed side by side, on which she stands the baskets containing their provisions.

The next job on the agenda is to sort out the sleeping arrangements.

'If we stuff some straw into these sacks and use our blankets, we can make a comfortable bed, right here in the corner,' she suggests, 'what do you think sweetheart?'

Home making, even if it is in a barn, appeals to Lilibeth, 'I'll help,' she offers, and the pair set about stuffing straw into sacks to make up a satisfactory mattress.

'There, so what do you think of our handiwork then?' asks Katerina.

'It's all right,' says Lilibeth, shrugging her shoulders, she had settled down, and was playing happily with her doll Daisy.

Katerina smiles to herself, hum, that should do for now, surveying their new, albeit temporary makeshift home. 'Time for something to eat, cheese sandwich, a jam tart for afters and a mug of milk all right?'

Lilibeth nods her approval.

Katerina decides the pots of jam and honey should be put by, they would last so much longer in the warm weather than the cheese and butter etc.

They sit on the boxes eating their lunch.

Lilibeth is especially thirsty and manages to finish off what was left of the milk in the bowl. I'll have to get some later, Katerina decides.

Twenty minutes later it falls silent, Lilibeth is taking her afternoon nap.

Resting beside her daughter, she stares up at the corrugated roof, deep in thought. After her highly successful escapade the previous night and with her daughter now sleeping soundly, she's thinking that she could perhaps seize the opportunity to replenish their depleted milk supply whilst she can, it wouldn't take long. Minutes later, putting her hat and coat on, armed with the bowl, she pulls the door open a little, glancing nervously around, she's in luck, she can see and hear no one.

Stepping tentatively outside the door she pauses, straining her ears and searching for any sign of movement, but she is having second thoughts. Perhaps I should wait until it's dark? she considers, but on the other hand, the cows are even closer than they were the previous night, and it would only take a few minutes... her mind is made up.

One quick look to double check that there's no-one around and she lifts her skirts and runs towards the herd.

'Steady up there, take it easy,' she whispers nervously, 'easy now, good girl.' Fortunately, the cow that she has chosen appears at ease, so she sets the bowl down. 'Here we go, good girl, steady up, nice and easy girl,' she says soothingly as she stoops on her haunches and begins milking.

'Hey, you! What the fucking hell d'you think you're doing?'

The blood drains from Katerina's face. She freezes in horror.

Beneath her wide brimmed hat, she tentatively glances over her shoulder, a man is stood outside the cottage with his legs astride his fists on his hips.

Her instinct is to turn tail and flee as fast as her legs will carry her, but it's out of the question, there is Lilibeth to consider.

'What the fuck do you think you're doing? Stay where you are!' he demands, striding purposely down the yard towards her.

Still crouching, Katerina bows her head, her face hidden below the brim of her hat, and although her back is turned away from him she can hear his footsteps getting ever closer.

'What the fuck's your game? Speak up man!' he demands forcefully.

Katerina feels him right behind her, her heart sinks, she swallows, I'm done for, she stands up and slowly turns to face the music.

The tall man is stood intimidatingly, just three feet in front of her.

Beneath her brim she can see his long legs and rolled up shirt sleeves, his clenched fists resting on his narrow hips, she doesn't dare to raise her head and face him, trembling with fear she gulps.

Fast losing patience with the audacious vagrant, the farmer draws a lung full of air through his nostrils, 'Answer me, damn you!' he demands, his deep voice gradually rising through his apparent frustration. 'This is private property, you've no right to be on my land, let alone stealing my fucking milk!'

Katerina glances nervously towards the barn, to her horror, Lilibeth is stood in the open doorway.

Attempting to distract him she spins round, but he's ready for her, grabbing her wrist before she can run, 'Oh no you don't, I've gotcha, you ruddy thief!' he growls, his hand restraining her firmly.

Struggling like a wild thing, she is desperate to break free of his grasp.

Horrified, Lilibeth sees everything and panics, screaming wildly she leaves the sanctuary of the barn and runs towards them yelling, waving her arms frantically in the air. 'No! Don't hurt my mammy!' she yells as she batters and kicks as hard as she can at the farmer's legs, 'Noooo! Nasty man! Stop it, stop it!' she screams.

Katerina scoops her daughter up in her arms and as she does so, her hat falls to the ground, her long auburn hair to tumbles about her shoulders.

Stunned, the farmer's jaw drops open, he gasps and stumbles backwards raising his hands skyward, noticeably shaken, 'Dear God, you're a... a woman!' he exclaims, 'Hey. I'm sorry Miss. I'm so sorry, I didn't mean to... I didn't realise...' he stutters. Shocked, he backs off.

Katerina hugs her daughter closer, whispering. 'Hush darling, hush, Mammy's all right, sweetheart,' but Lilibeth is distraught, refusing to be consoled, she wails even louder.

Astonished, the farmer backs off even further, his look is one of genuine shock, he shakes his head in disbelief, 'Miss... I'm so sorry, I didn't mean to frighten you.'

Katerina rocks Lilibeth from side to side, doing her best to comfort her, 'Hush now Baby, it's all right, I'm fine, please don't cry.'

'Miss,' he says, looking suitably humble, 'I um, I'm really sorry, I didn't realise you were a wo...' he pauses, amazed. He was about to say woman, but the thieving rogue of a villain had not only turned out to be a woman, but an extraordinarily striking young woman too, he's shocked.

Frowning deeply, he shakes his head, the poor girl stood trembling before him, is looking more akin to a hunted fox, trapped by baying hounds, waiting to be torn limb from limb, 'Is um... is the little one all right?' he inquires, looking bemused.

Katerina bites her lip and fights back the tears.

Alarmed, he can see that the young woman is about to shed as many tears as the little girl, 'Look here, you're both soaking wet, would you um, would you like to bring her up to my cottage, out of the rain? Perhaps I could make a pot of tea or something?' he offers, by way of an apology. Seeing this young woman so distressed his anger immediately dissipates and his heart softens. Well, what else can I do? The pair of them look like filthy drowned rats, and scared witless.

Distrustful and wary, Katerina frowns, what choice has she got? She chews on her bottom lip, they had, after all, been caught red-handed, stealing on his property. Warily she nods, whispering, 'Um, thank you very much Sir, that's awfully kind of you Sir. '

The farmer picks up her hat, handing it to her then strides towards the cottage, glancing back, he beckons them to follow.

Katerina hobbles meekly behind him, carrying Lilibeth in her arms, cursing herself for being stupid enough to risk getting the milk in broad daylight.

Lifting the latch, he swings the door open, 'Please, do go in Miss,' he said politely, he stands back, his outstretched arm inviting them inside.

Lilibeth, her arms wrapped around Katerina's neck, clings even tighter as her mother, steps cagily inside.

'Here, let me take your coat.' he says and helps her to remove it. 'Um, do take a seat, I'll just put the kettle on and make a pot of tea.' he offers, hanging her wet coat on the door peg, he disappears into the scullery, but before she'd even had chance to cast a glance around the room, he pops his head around the door, making her jump. 'Oh, I'm so sorry Miss, I didn't mean to startle you. I'm just wondering, would the little one, rather have warm milk perhaps?'

Uncomfortable, Katerina squirms in her seat, it's very generous of him, considering he has just caught her red-handed stealing his milk. 'We um, we don't want to be a nuisance Sir,' she says meekly, but the offer of a cup of tea is irresistible, she would be a fool to refuse. 'That's very kind of you Sir, if it's not too much bother, yes please Sir,' she replies timidly, her pale face blushing a deep pink with shame.

'It's no trouble at all Miss,' he said smiling warmly.

'Ahem, are you hungry? I'm sorry, there's not much in the larder?' he tells her as he places a tray with three mugs on the table. 'If you are, I've some porridge already made. I could warm it up, I might even have an egg or two,' he offers.

'Oh, please Sir, there's really no need. We've just eaten, thank you Sir,' she lies, praying that her daughter will keep silent.

Fortunately, Lilibeth remains mute, her head still tucked firmly beneath her mother's chin, she's scowling at the farmer.

They both sit in silence drinking their tea, as they drink, both sneak the occasional discreet eye over the rim of their cups, using the opportunity to weigh each other up, there is an understandable air of awkwardness between them.

Katerina is surprised to realise that he is a very young man for a farmer, possibly in his mid-twenties, a second glance and her eyes meet his, they are a striking deep cornflower blue, and from the odd fleeting glance she decides he is very handsome.

Joseph's brow is furrowed, not because he's angry, but because he is genuinely concerned for their welfare. The small child, he notes, is curled up tight, on what he assumes to be her mother's lap, keeping her head bowed low enough to avoid his gaze, she is obviously scared stiff of him.

Emptying her cup, Katerina takes a fleeting glance around the room, it looks cosy, very comfortable and tidy. Stood in front of the fire is a basket of tastefully arranged dried flowers, above the mantle, a large wooden framed, somewhat grimy old mirror, mottled with age. Sat on the deep windowsill are two oil lamps, gracing a small, silver framed photograph of an attractive woman, his wife perhaps?

At least the child has stopped crying, the farmer thinks to himself.

Curious about his guests, he lifts the cup to his lips, studying the woman a little more closely. The woman is undoubtedly very young, probably in her very early twenties and despite the fact she's filthy and dishevelled, it does nothing to hide her strikingly good looks. He can't fail to notice her large, soulful, pale blue eyes, they are the colour of a summer sky, enhanced with thick dark lashes. Her exquisite face is framed by her long, curly, deep auburn hair. He gulps, she's simply stunning. Who is she? Where the hell, have they come from? What on God's earth are they doing here at Sweet Briars in such a terrible state? So many questions.

Then there's the little girl, the grubby little infant who is still clinging fretfully to her mother as if her life depends on it, poor little soul. At a wild guess, he estimates the young child is no more than about four at most, not that he is an expert on children, of course. What on earth were they doing here at Sweet Briars? Out in this terrible weather, so obviously ill-prepared, and desperate enough to be stealing his milk! He shakes his head, it's beyond his comprehension, it beggars belief!

Aware he's been caught staring, he shifts and clears his throat, placing his empty cup on the tray, he smiles kindly, and lifts the teapot, 'Perhaps you'd like another, there's plenty left in the pot?'

'That's very kind of you, um… if there's one to spare that would be most welcome Sir, thank you,' she answers politely, though she feels riddled with guilt at accepting his generous hospitality, but she has to admit the tea is more than appreciated.

He pours two more fresh cups.

The poor woman's terrified, he observes, he can see it in her eyes, also he couldn't help but notice she's still trembling. He resolves there and then to get some answers, perhaps the tea would encourage her to talk. He hands Katerina a fresh cup of tea, 'What about your little girl, perhaps she would like some more warm milk?' he offers.

Looking down at Lilibeth she's embarrassed to find she'd sobbed herself to sleep. 'Oh no, I'm so sorry Sir, she's fallen asleep Sir, she says, sounding alarmed.

'Aw bless her, poor little mite, she's sound, I'll fetch a blanket, we can make up a bed on the sofa,' he offers, rising to his feet.

'Oh no thank you Sir, she's fine here with me,' she insists, clutching her daughter even tighter.

'Stuff and nonsense, even a fool can see that the child is completely exhausted, surely she'd sleep easier if we make her up a bed?' he reasons, then without even waiting for a reply, he leaves the room. She hears him climb the stairs, returning almost immediately, carrying two blankets and a pillow. He promptly proceeds to make up a bed on the sofa with the blankets and a soft plump pillow. 'I would take her shoes off, if I were you, they're very muddy,' he suggests, 'Can I give you a hand to settle her?' he offers considerately.

Wishing the ground would open up and swallow her Katerina frowns, 'Thank you, sir, but I can manage,' she replies curtly, struggling doggedly to her sore, tender feet.

He smiles to himself, hum, not only extraordinarily attractive, but she apparently has a stubborn, independent streak too, he observes.

Lilibeth doesn't stir as she's tucked beneath the blanket, so Katerina perches herself precariously on the end of the sofa at her daughter's feet.

'There you are, she looks a lot more comfortable now,' he says, sitting down and picking up his pipe.

She nods in agreement, 'Yes, thank you, sir. I am so sorry about this. We really don't want to put you out, sir,' she says apologetically, cringing at his kindness.

Uneasy with constantly being addressed as, sir he leans forward, 'Look, let me introduce myself. I'm Joseph, Joseph Markson,' he says offering his hand, 'My friends call me Joe, and I can assure you, you are not putting me out at all, my dear.'

'I um, I'm Katerina,' she volunteers quietly, 'my friends call me Kate or Katie, and this is my daughter, Lilibeth, or Lily for short,' she says, nodding in the direction of her daughter, warily she stands and shakes his outstretched hand. 'How do you do, Sir?'

Joe's eyebrows lift; she had set him thinking. She said friends, if she had friends then what the hell is she doing out here in the sticks in the middle of nowhere with such a small child, and in such foul weather too? He liked the name Katerina, a very unusual, pretty name, he thought it suited her. He smiles a kindly smile that shows his pearly white teeth, 'Well it's very nice to meet you, Katie, even if it is under such strange circumstances. Perhaps you would like another cup of tea?' he offers.

'Thank you, sir, but I'd better not,' she tells him fidgeting, 'I, um, I need to go to… the um,' her face a rosy red.

He looks at her quizzically, 'The um…? Oh right, the lavatory,' he says, as it dawns on him what she is getting at, 'Ah yes, it's straight through the scullery, out the back door and immediately on the left,' he explains, 'help yourself.' quickly adding as an afterthought, 'Don't turn right, or you'll end up down the well.'

Katerina's torn, doubtful of leaving Lilibeth but she is desperate, 'I um, I won't be long,' she tells him, glancing a worried look at her sleeping daughter.

'Don't worry, I'll keep my eye on her,' he assures her, and proceeds to pack tobacco in his pipe.

Minutes later she comes rushing back through the scullery to check on her daughter.

Joe is sat quietly in his chair, drawing on his pipe, 'Hey, she's fine, she hasn't moved at all,' he says reassuringly. 'Sit yourself down, you look all in yourself.'

As she sits down, he stands, 'I won't be a minute,' he says and disappears into the scullery with the tray of empty cups, he puts some milk in a pan on the stove and rinses the cups.

He is only gone a few minutes but when he returns with the hot milk, he finds the young woman has fallen asleep in the fireside chair, he shakes his head, the poor loves, the pair of them are all in.

Fetching another blanket, he carefully drapes it over Katie, she doesn't stir so he sits back in his chair, draws on his pipe and takes the opportunity to study the sleeping young woman in more detail.

Her long, dishevelled auburn hair tumbles around her extremely attractive, well-defined features, her long dark eye lashes resting on her pale cheeks. His heart races, she's the most beautiful woman he's ever seen. Noticing an ugly bruise on her cheek and a nasty looking cut just above her left eye, he frowns, how the hell did that happen? Her beautiful face is grubby, as is the small child's. What on earth are they doing out here in the sticks and in such dreadful weather? He notices the bottom of their skirts are wet and muddy too. Who are they? It's obvious that they're in trouble of some sort, but what?

He has so many questions running around in his head, but they would have to wait, tomorrow will come soon enough, right now they are obviously in need of a good night's sleep, any questions he has can wait until morning. After stoking the fire, he turns the oil lamps down low, then retires upstairs to his bedroom.

He doesn't sleep at all, most of the night is spent tossing and turning, as a consequence he's up and dressed well before first light.

Creeping gingerly down the stairs he's half expecting them to be gone, but he finds Katie, cuddled up on the sofa with her daughter cradled in her arms, both are sleeping soundly. He shakes his head and smiles to himself.

With guests to feed and very little in the larder, except a couple of eggs and some porridge oats, he decides to replenish his depleted food stocks.

Quietly he closes the back door behind him.

The cows are relieved of their milk and a small churn filled. The goat is milked too. The chickens are fed corn and their eggs collected, plus one unfortunate chicken meets his maker, in the name of a decent dinner for his unexpected guests.

A small sack is filled with freshly dug potatoes and a spring cabbage cut from his vegetable garden, everything is loaded onto a small wooden handcart. That'll do for now, he decides and makes his way back to the cottage.

The wooden cart rattles as it strains under its heavy load, the metal rimmed wheels scrunch noisily on the gravel as he approaches the back door, Joe curses the racket it's making. If they weren't awake now then they soon would be.

Pushing the kitchen door open with the blade of his heavily muscled shoulder he carries the box of his early morning's work into the scullery.

The house is totally silent, his heart sinks, for one awful moment he fears they might be gone, disappeared just as mysteriously as they had appeared the previous day. Popping his head around the parlour door he sighs with relief, they are still there, the child now wrapped in her mother's arms, they are both fast asleep on the sofa, he shakes his head, they make such a sad little picture.

As Joe flicks the sizzling hot fat over the eggs, he hears someone stirring. It's Katie. 'Good morning my dear,' he greets her genially, as she enters the scullery.

Looking sheepish, she stands fidgeting, looking ill at ease in the doorway, her face highly flushed with embarrassment, she clears her throat, 'Ahem, I'm so very sorry about yesterday, sir, I owe you an apology.'

He interrupts her, 'Did the smell of breakfast wake you up?' he asks cheerily, 'I hope you're hungry. Here, take a seat,' he offers, pulling a chair from beneath the large wooden table. 'There's plenty of fresh tea in the pot and a jug of fresh milk, help yourself,' he adds.

Katie grimaces, wondering if his offer to help herself to the milk is meant to be a sarcastic comment, referring to her audacity of helping herself to his milk yesterday, though he seems relaxed and friendly, 'Please sir, allow me to cook the eggs,' she says, taking the egg slice from his

CHAPTER 3

'I wouldn't hear of it,' he retorts, promptly taking it back again. His eyes have a boyish mischievous glint in them, he looks highly amused.

'Oh, please, sir, I'd like to cook. You've been so kind allowing us to stay the night,' she protests, anxious to make amends for all the trouble that they've caused him.

Ignoring her offer he stands firm, grinning at her, 'Oh no you don't, Katie, you're my guest and I'm more than capable of cooking the breakfast. Please, take a seat, drink your tea before it's goes cold.'

Katie looks surprised, 'You have more tea?'

'Aye, um, let's just say I've got a friend in the know,' he says smiling broadly, 'Please, drink your tea.'

'I still think I should cook the eggs for you,' she stubbornly offers again.

Amused he chuckles, 'I can manage thanks, I'm not a bad cook, even if I do say so myself.'

'My mammy is the bestest cook in the whole world, so she is!' A little voice of protest interrupts their conversation.

They both spin round, Lilibeth is stood in the doorway.

Joe raises his eyebrows.

Katerina bites her lip and frowns.

Stood looking determined, with her hands on her hips, Lilibeth pouts. 'She is too, mister. Everybody says so!'

Appalled, Katie snaps, 'Lilibeth please, don't be so rude. remember your manners child. Come, sit at the table. Now!' she says in a forthright manner that tells her daughter that it is actually an order, not a request. 'Mr Markson has been kind enough to cook us a breakfast, come and sit at the table!'

Eyeing Joe suspiciously, Lilibeth looks back to her mother for reassurance.

'It's all right, sit here,' says Katerina, patting the chair next to hers to encourage her.

'All right,' she answers with a scowl that's directed at Joe, a look that doesn't become her at all, 'Can you pick me up please Mamma?'

Katerina obliges, then sits timidly beside her daughter.

Joe is about to serve the eggs when, suddenly and without warning, Lilibeth bursts into tears, wailing uncontrollably. 'What's wrong darling, have you hurt yourself? She asks, trying unsuccessfully to pacify her.

'Daisy, she's gone! I want my Daisy; I want my Daisy!' she sobs.

Alarmed, Joe spins round, 'Daisy. Who the hell's Daisy?'

'Don't worry, sir, Daisy's her doll, they're inseparable,' Katie explains, 'and she isn't lost, she's um… in the barn. In the loft to be precise,' she admits, looking red faced and lowering her eyes, embarrassed. She turns to her daughter, 'Hush darling, hush, Mammy will fetch her for you,' she offers trying to console her distraught daughter.

Clinging to her mother like a limpet, she wails louder 'No! Don't leave me, Mammy!' Clearly there's no way the anguished child will let her mother out of her sight for a second.

Deeply concerned to see the little one so upset, Joe shakes his head, 'It's all right, you stay with her, I'll go find her doll. It's in the barn you say?' he offers, putting the eggs to one side.

'Yes, sir, it's in the loft actually, if you wouldn't mind, thank you, sir I'm afraid she's simply lost without her.'

He smiles kindly at Katerina and rests his hand on her arm, 'Joe, please.'

She smiles back, 'Um… thank you, Joe.'

'That's better and if you have no objections, I shall call you Katie?'

She shrugs her shoulders and nods.

'Right then, Katie it is, now where's my jacket?' he says smiling.

He strides down to the barn, but after climbing the ladder to the loft, he stands stock still, completely dumbfounded. There's a bed of sorts, a makeshift table and chairs, two baskets and some clothes. Good Lord, just how long have they been in here? Visibly shocked, he shakes his head in disbelief. A quick survey tells him that they had made themselves a proper little home from home. After a brief search he finds the missing doll wedged firmly between the two wicker baskets. He decides everything else will get damp, so he takes it all back to the cottage.

The door swings open, and Joe enters carrying the two baskets, the blankets slung over his shoulder and a rag doll beneath his arm. 'Um, yours, I believe Lily.' He says, returning the doll to the little girl, who stops crying instantly, delighted to be reunited with her precious doll.

Unceremoniously putting the baskets down on the floor, he drops the straw covered blankets beside them. Frowning he waits for an explanation. 'Hum. Can I take it all this is yours?' he asks, his voice sounding a little more sarcastic than he intends.

Katie does more than blush, her face turns bright scarlet, she feels sick to the stomach with unadulterated humiliation. 'Oh no, I'm... I'm so sorry, I don't know what to say,' she blurts out.

'Well, I'm hoping you've got an explanation for this lot,' he retorts, his voice now low, but firm.

Joe's apparent change in attitude frightens Lily, she clings to her mother's skirt and her tears flow once more.

'Mr Markson, sir. I'm so sorry, we didn't mean any harm, we didn't do any damage, I promise you. I um, we...' Katie clears her throat and tries hard to explain, 'naturally we shall be leaving, of course,' she says nervously, 'But before we go sir, I'd like to do some baking and cleaning, by way of recompense for all the trouble we've caused you, and for the generosity that you have shown us by allowing us to stay here last night. You've been so kind, we're very grateful sir.' Katie sighs, she knows she is rambling on, making no sense at all, even worse, she can feel the tears welling up in her eyes. To make matters worse, Lilibeth begins wailing even louder so Katie sweeps her up in her arms, to comfort her.

Realising he sounds unnecessarily harsh, his voice softens, 'Have you quite finished, my dear?' he asks softly, 'Look Katie, I'm not cross with you, I'm just worried about you both. And can you blame me? Here I am, living miles from anywhere or anyone, when out of the blue yonder I find a young woman and a very small child are apparently living rough in my barn. I'm not annoyed my dear, I'm just very concerned for you both.'

This time it's Joe's turn to sigh, 'look, you say you'll go,' he shakes his head, 'where exactly, may I ask, are you going too? If you don't mind my saying, you look ill-prepared to be travelling far in this awful weather with such a young child.' He pauses and steps forward, placing his hand over hers, 'Can't you tell me what's wrong? Tell me what circumstances have brought you both here? You never know, I might even be able to help you.'

Katie is getting flustered, her head is beginning to spin, Lilibeth just won't stop crying and he's firing so many questions at her she feels giddy, she just can't think. Reeling she slumps down on the chair.

Joe studies them, both clinging to each other, as if their lives depend on it. 'Katie please. Come, sit in the chair beside the fire, my dear, you'll be more comfortable.' he suggests and helps her, along with Lilibeth, from the table to the fireside chair, he sits in the chair opposite. 'Look, it's obvious to me that you've got a serious problem, but I've no doubt it can be sorted, though it would help if I knew what was going on,' he says gently.

Gratefully she leans back against the soft cushions but remains tight lipped.

Continuing to cry, Lilibeth nuzzles her head beneath her mother's chin.

He notes the little one seems to be eyeing him with trepidation, it's heart-breaking to see such a young child so distressed. 'Um, I'm thinking, perhaps it might be better if we talked about this um… business later, you know… out of earshot,' he says nodding at Lilibeth. 'What do you say Katie?'

Katie shrugs her shoulders and nods, 'If you think it's for the best, sir.' She answers timidly in barely a whisper.

Frustrated he frowns, 'Look Katie, you both look completely exhausted, you're welcome to stay for a few days, if you want. You're both more than welcome, you can use the front bedroom if it suits you,' he offers.

Katie looks bemused, wary of his motives, 'Oh I don't know…'

'Come, let me take you up and show you the room,' he suggests, 'it's a very comfortable little room,' he adds persuasively.

Apprehension fills her, but there was no denying his unexpected kind offer would give her some breathing space, time to think and make proper plans, perhaps she shouldn't be quite so hasty, she concludes.

Looking down at Lilibeth she decides for the sake of her daughter maybe she should, at the very least, consider his generous offer, after all, they could hardly stay in the barn, not now they'd been discovered. 'Really, are you're quite sure Mr Markson? Perhaps for a couple of days then, and I promise we won't be any trouble, sir,' she assures him.

Breathing a sigh of relief, he smiles at her persistent formality, 'Like I said before, it's Joe. Let's not be so formal Katie,' he says as he rises from his seat. 'Good, well that's settled, follow me upstairs and I'll show you the room.'

At the top of the stairs, he opens the door to reveal a reasonably sized, very pretty room, Katie peeps inside, 'Oh my, it's a lovely room Joseph,' she tells him, 'Are you quite sure about this?'

He nods. 'Of course, and at least you'll be warm and comfortable,' he smiles kindly, 'so, would you like to stay for a while?'

Katie nods gratefully, 'Oh yes please, that's very generous of you, thank you, sir.'

He nods, 'Good, well then, make yourselves at home,' he invites her.

'That's very kind of you Mr Markson, thank you very much, sir.'

Shaking his head, he sighs, 'No problem Katie, and for the umpteenth time, it's Joe,' he reminds her yet again. 'Hum, well that's the first of your problems solved,' he says, somewhat relieved, 'and maybe we can talk about your apparent housing problem, when a certain little someone goes to bed tonight, what do you think?'

With a flick of her hand, Katie brushes away a tear, it's as if a heavy load has been lifted from her shoulders, for now at least. 'Thank you, Mr Markson, you're so kind.'

He claps his hands together, 'Right, now that's sorted, I reckon there's a small matter of breakfast that needs attending to, are you hungry Lily?'

Lilibeth is still wary of Joe, he had grumbled at her mammy about being in the barn. Still, she considers, he did find her darling Daisy and the bedroom did look lovely, a lot nicer than the dark old barn, 'Yes, please mister,' she agrees through her plump, pouting lips.

Back in the scullery they are greeted by cold congealed eggs. 'Oh dear, I'll cook some more,' he says, throwing the eggs in the bin.

'Mr Markson, perhaps you would allow me to cook the breakfast,' she offers humbly. 'I could make some scrambled eggs if you'd prefer.'

He chortles, 'Hum, Mr Markson yet again? Oh dear, what's up, don't you like the name, Joe?'

Shrugging her shoulders, she blushes deeply, 'Joe, or rather Joseph does seem a bit personal Mr Markson, after all, we hardly know each other.'

'Look my dear, there's no airs or graces in this house, Joe's fine, honestly Katie,' he tells her.

'Well, if you insist, Joe,' she smiles shyly, 'so, can I cook the breakfast?'

His grin grows even wider, 'Aw go on then if you insist.'

Sensing that her mother is no longer upset, Lilibeth pipes up, 'My mammy's eggs is lovely.'

Joe's smile is warm, 'Really Lily? Well, who knows, with a bit of luck, they might be as good as mine,' he quips, highly amused.

Not convinced that he believes her, Lilibeth, who, despite of her very young age, has never been one to be defeated, sticks her chin out and chips in again, 'My mammy really is the best cooker in the whole world mister,' she declares scowling.

He smiles down at her mockingly, 'I'm sure you're right little Lily.'

The small child feels he's still not taking her seriously; she's determined that he should know what a wonderful cook her mother really is. 'She is the bestest cooker. See!' she says, swiftly removing the cloths that cover the two wicker baskets, 'Look!' she declares, puffing up her chest with pride, 'My mammy did make all this! '

Astonished, Joe's mouth drops open in amazement, 'Well I'm blessed,' he says, feasting his eyes on the contents of the baskets.

Katie recoils in embarrassment, 'Oh no, Lilibeth, put the covers back, immediately!'

But Lilibeth is adamant that Joe should see that her clever mummy can cook anything. 'See mister, my mammy did make all this…! Lovely crusty bread, and plum jam, and a big bit of cheese, and butter and pickled eggs and…'

Irritated, Katie quickly replaces the cloths over the baskets, 'That's enough Lilibeth, please! I'm quite sure Mr Markson… sorry, I mean Joe,

I'm sure he is not in the least bit interested.' she says sternly. Annoyed with her daughter's unashamed boasting, Katie's pink complexion now an even deeper pink.

'You've got to be joking Katie,' says Joe grinning, 'I've never seen such fine food,' he turns to Lilibeth, he's smiling, 'and I'm not at all surprised that you're so proud of your mammy's cooking, it looks delicious.'

Lilibeth beams, 'I said so, didn't I?'

'You certainly did Lily,' he nods in agreement, 'All this wonderful food is making me hungry. Now, how about breakfast? It's getting so late it must be almost dinner time and I'm absolutely famished.'

At Katie's insistence, she scrambles half a dozen eggs, slices some of her ham and cuts her bread, spreading it liberally with her home-made butter.

In the meantime, Joe lays the table with the willing assistance of Lilibeth, who has now decided that she quite likes Joe, just a little bit after all.

As they eat, Lilibeth studies Joe's every mouthful, 'Does you like my mammy's cooking then, mister?'

'Mmm, delicious, just perfect Lily,' he replies, as he wipes his plate clean with the last piece of bread, 'all thanks to your mother's excellent homemade bread and butter,' he tells her, 'So, what did you think of my chickens' eggs, little Lily?'

'The eggs are lovely, and my name is Lilibeth,' she admonishes him with a very straight face.

Raising his eyebrows, he struggles to supress his mirth, 'Is that so, little Lily.'

Looking determined she glares at Joseph, 'You called me little Lily, again!' she corrects him.

Shaking his head, he chuckles, 'Hum. really, little miss clever clogs.'

'Oh, Mammy, he says I'm clever, didn't you mister? '

He smiles at the cute, likeable child, 'So I did Lily, you're very clever indeed,' he says, giving her playful wink, 'and there's no need for the mister, plain old Joe will do, young lady.' he says, giving her another wink.

Lilibeth giggles, 'I think Joe's got something in his eye Mamma, coz he keeps shutting it. '

Katie looks up, smiling lovingly at her daughter, she even manages a small chuckle, it's heart-warming to see her daughter so at ease and dare she say… happy?

Though it's an everyday pleasure for most children, thanks to her evil father, up until now happiness had sadly been lacking in her daughter's short lifetime. She smiles lovingly, 'I think Joe is winking darling.'

Joe himself, is beginning to feel a lot more comfortable, a little humour has worked wonders to break the ice with his guests, but never-the-less, he had work to do. 'Hum, I guess it's no good me hanging around here all day,' he says, picking up the dishes, 'I'll get this lot washed up, then I'll get off to work.'

'Please, allow me, it's the very least I can do, you've been so kind,' she offers, springing to her feet.

Smiling back at her, his eyes shine mischievously, 'What's that, you mean you want to go to work?' he scoffs, blatantly teasing her.

Katie grabs a couple of dishes as the colour rises in her pale cheeks. 'I um, I actually meant I'd be more than happy to do the washing up, Joseph,' she corrects him, shyly lowering her lashes.

'There's really no need Katie, it won't take me long,' he chortles.

'Perhaps we might do it together, it will take half the time?' she suggests diplomatically.

Shrugging his broad shoulders Joe laughs, 'Right then, have it your own way, sounds like a good deal to me.'

Katie hands him a tea towel.

'I was thinking,' he says stacking the dry dishes and eyeing the two baskets crammed with delicious, fresh, but highly perishable food, 'I reckon it'll be a real scorcher today, perhaps it would be wise to empty your baskets, put everything in the larder on the marble slabs, just to keep it all fresh. I'd hate to see all that lovely food go to waste.' Now, Joe's being the diplomat.

'Hum, yes, I suppose you're right,' she agrees.

Bending to put on his boots, Joe frowns, 'Look Katie, the fact is, I have work to do, will you be all right here, whilst I'm gone?'

The prospect of being left alone fills Katie with a rush of anxiety, a knot of fear tightening in the pit of her stomach. Right now, she's feeling safe and secure from the outside world in Joe's company. But on the other hand, she has no right to expect him to neglect his work, just for their benefit. 'Honestly, Joseph, I told you, we don't want to be an inconvenience to you, so you get off to work, we'll be absolutely fine.' she assures him, perhaps a little too keenly for Joe's liking.

Feeling somewhat doubtful he takes his jacket from the peg behind the door, he hesitates, 'Hum, well if you're quite sure? You'll find fresh milk and plenty of food in the larder and there's some clean sheets and all you need in that cupboard, over there,' he tells her, nodding his chin towards the cupboard under the stairs.

Looking a tad uneasy, Katie frowns, it doesn't feel right somehow, going through somebody else's cupboards. 'Are you quite sure it'll be all right, Joe?'

Grinning broadly, flashing his pearly white teeth he nods, 'Sure I'm sure, just help yourself to whatever you need.'

Despite his assurance, Katie still feels awkward about rooting around in a someone else's cupboards, helping herself to their linen. For all she knows, there might well be a lady of the house, 'You're quite certain you don't mind?' she repeats, her voice sounding full of doubt.

He smiles, 'Good heavens no, of course not,' he insists, then he frowns, Katie is suddenly looking uncomfortable. Does she intend to leave the minute his back is turned? Or perhaps she's genuinely worried about being left alone? She definitely looks anxious, a fact which perturbs him, perhaps he should stay home after all, he wonders? 'Look Katie, I'll stay if you really want.'

'Oh no, Joseph, I told you, we'll be fine.' she assures him cheerfully, 'You get off to work, please don't worry about us.'

Perhaps she sounds a little too enthusiastic about packing him off out of the house, hoping she isn't considering doing a runner the minute his back is turned, 'Well, if you're quite sure? I really do have work to do.' With his finger on the latch, he hesitates and turns back. 'Look Katie, I could be gone four or five hours, you, um... will you still be here, when I get back?' he enquires tentatively.

Taking a deep breath and putting on what she thinks is a nonchalant expression Katie smiles, 'Why yes, of course we will.'

There's still a nagging doubt in the back of his mind, now he's feeling reluctant to leave them both, but at the end of the day his mate had said he was in desperate need of an extra supply of wood, and he had less than three weeks before the order was due to be collected. 'Right, well, in that case, I suppose I'd better be off,' he declares, adding, 'Feel free to make yourselves at home.'

Katie dries her hands on her pinafore, 'Thank you, Joe, you're so kind and we'll make sure we'll have a dinner ready for you when you return.'

The fact that she had promised to have a cooked meal for him, reassures him that she does indeed intend to stay put, he smiles, 'Lovely, I'll look forward to that, thank you. Anyway, time marches on, the sooner I go, the sooner I'll be back. Now make sure you both have a proper rest today, put your feet up, relax,' he said wagging his finger, 'Anyway, I'll be off. I'll um… I'll see you both later?'

It sounded more like a question than a statement to Katie, 'We'll be here,' she promises.

Running to the open door, Lilibeth stands watching Joe striding off down the yard towards the woods pulling a handcart, 'Bye, Joe, don't be long!' she calls after him as she waves furiously.

With a grin on his face, Joe turns and waves, 'Bye Lily, see you later!' he calls back.

Lilibeth waits until he's out of sight then goes back to join her mother in the scullery.

After all the trials and tribulations that she'd had heaped upon herself in the past few days, Katie, now feels somewhat reassured and relieved as she sits at the table finishing the last of her tea. She decides they had been fortunate indeed to have met such a kind and generous man.

'Why's Joe gone, Mamma?' asked Lilibeth, joining her mother at the table.

'He's a very busy man. He has a lot of work to do darling, and so, for that matter, do we,' she tells her, standing to brush the crumbs from her skirt.

Catching a glance of herself in the grubby mirror Katie is shocked. 'Goodness gracious! Would you look at the pair of us, we look like a couple of rag-o-muffins.' She tuts, 'Good heavens, what on earth must Joe think of us? Right, young lady, first things first, we'd better see if we can find the bath, it should be outside somewhere. I can heat the water up in the copper,' she shakes her head, 'We desperately need a bath.'

'I don't want a bath, coz my clothes will make me all dirty again. Look Mamma,' says Lilibeth, pointing out her filthy clothes.

'Tusk, well that's easily remedied young lady, whilst the water is heating up in the copper, we'll go to the barn and fetch some clean clothes from the pram.' Cleanliness had always been her priority, she is also desperate to change her heavy leather shoes, she has red raw blisters on her sore, dirty feet, and she can't wait to slip into her soft leather house shoes.

Anxious to take advantage of the opportunity to bathe and change in a civilised manner, Katie stokes the fire beneath the boiler, then takes untold trips back and forth to the well with the heavy bucket before there's sufficient water to provide a decent bath.

When finally, the tin bath is filled she ushers her daughter outside into the yard, 'Race you to the barn, last one there gets in the bath first!'

Before bathing, Katie goes to great lengths to ensure that they can't possibly be disturbed in the scullery. Both back and front doors are securely bolted, and after a great deal of effort she manages to drag a cumbersome oak cupboard in front of the back door as an added measure of security, finally the grubby curtains are carefully drawn at the window before they both strip and bathe in the luxury of the glorious warm tub.

Despite her initial protests, once she was in the bath, Lilibeth's happy enough, though she knows it also means her mother brushing out the tangles in her hair afterwards. 'Ouch, you're hurting me, stop Mamma, please. Ouch!' she winces as her mother does battle with the stiff hairbrush and the mass of tight unruly curls.

Normally Katie would take great pride in grooming her young daughter's wonderful mane of dark auburn curly hair, but the effect of living rough had turned it into an ordeal for both mother and daughter. 'I'm sorry darling, I'm doing my best,' she tells her, struggling to tease out the tangles as gently as she can.

With their ablutions satisfactorily taken care of and dressed in clean clothes, Katie finds a long pinafore hanging in the pantry, rolling up her sleeves she slips gratefully into her light weight, house shoes, then knuckles down to make a start on the housework, she's determined to work hard to repay Joe for allowing them stay in his lovely home.

With more logs wedged beneath the boiler, bucket by bucket, Katie transfers the bath water back to the copper tub. With the aid of some old wooden boiling tongs, she submerges their filthy clothes plus two of Joe's discarded grubby shirts for good measure, finally adding a few precious flakes of soap and a handful of soda, she'd found under the sink.

As she plunges and agitates the clothes in the steaming water she feels her energy ebbing, her head beginning to swim. She's overwhelmed with a feeling of dire fatigue, an infuriating inconvenience that, like it or not, she's obliged to accept from mother nature. She curses her wretched husband, even now, when she was finally free of him, she is still to suffer from her husband's filthy legacy. At her cost, she knows it's a waste of her time trying to fight it, like it or not she just has to stop, rest a while and gather her strength again or she would find herself sprawled on the floor. Once all the washing is rinsed and hung out on the line, Katie mops her brow and sighs, reluctantly giving in to her tiredness, taking Lilibeth out in the garden with a plate of hastily made sandwiches and some refreshingly cool water from the well. Rest, refreshments and a brief spell in the fresh air will do them both good.

Delighted to be outside in the garden, Lilibeth is happily occupied, dashing eagerly around the garden, in the hopes of catching a colourful butterfly as it flits from flower to flower.

Completely drained and weak, Katie relaxes gratefully in the shade of a tree. Her thoughts wander back in time, recalling the cautionary words of advice, given to her by her dear friend, Margo, who had done her level best to persuade, or was it warn her, about her husband Albert? Now you listen ter me, Katie love, that bleedin' Soames will be the death of yer at this rate. She would tell her. Mark my words gel, that filthy, man of yourn will finish yer orf, if you're daft enough ter let him. Margo had warned her oh so many times. Yer getting old afore yer time gel. She would say. Stand up ter him, tell him ter keep his filthy ways ter himself and leave yer alone, else your poor body's never gonna recover from losing them babies. Yer do know yer can always come and live wiv me and Stan, ducky, she would offer.

A lump comes to Katie's throat as a vision of her dear friend Margo settles before her eyes. Tall and willowy, with unusually large breasts and bright red hair. Sweet caring Margo, she meant well, bless her heart, always nagging her, trying to persuade her to stand up for herself.

Sat deep in thought, Katie had a faraway look in her tear-filled eyes. My dear, dear Margo, if only it had been that simple. Hadn't she begged and pleaded with him? But the truth was she simply had no choice. Albert was so much stronger than her, so when he wanted to take her, then he did just that, any way that satisfied him. Of course, to begin with, she had tried to refuse, oh so many times, but after many heavy-handed beatings with his belt he always had his way with her, regardless of her protestations. Always roughly, always violently and even worse, always against her will. Katie sighs heavily, it was like he always told her, 'You're me bloody wife, damn and blast yer, it's yer duty ter satisfy all me aching needs when I ruddy well wants yer!'

A chilling shudder runs through her body, she feels nauseous as she recalls his filthy, heavy body and his permanent, stinking, putrid odour. No matter how long and hard she had spent scrubbing herself, it made not a scrap of difference, his vile smell always lingered, his lewd sexual demands always left his permanent rancid smell on her.

For more than seven years, she had suffered an incredible eight, or was it nine, painful, regrettable miscarriages. To her dismay she realises sadly she had lost count, but each one had drained her young body further.

Shuddering she exhales another long, sorrowful sigh, it had been nothing short of a living hell. Never again Albert Soames, she vows silently. Never... never again!

Lilibeth's endless chattering returns her thoughts back to the present, she nods a satisfactory approval at the sight of their clothes, freshly laundered and flapping wildly in the wind. Having regained her strength she calls her daughter, returning to the hot, steam filled scullery.

The brief rest had certainly done her a power of good, now it's time to tackle the housework.

Feeling invigorated she takes an enthusiastic, fresh look around the scullery. It had obviously been someone's pride and joy at some point, but somehow, with layer of dust on every ledge and Lord knows how many spiders that had taken to spinning their webs just where they pleased, it all looked a little sad and neglected.

Katie decides all that is needed is a thorough scrub, some dusting and a good polish. Wasn't it the very least that she could do, to repay Joe for his generosity?

First job is to fling the windows and doors open wide allowing the warm breeze to sweep throughout the cottage, then, with the willing assistance of Lilibeth, the entire ground floor is methodically swept, scrubbed and polished with beeswax.

As she works with enthusiasm, she hums and smiles to herself, the softly spoken Joseph Markson had treated them both with such kindness and respect, he had unselfishly allowed them to share his home for a few days, especially when you took into consideration the exceedingly embarrassing fact that she, a complete stranger, had not only taken the bare faced liberty of secretly moving themselves into his barn, but also stealing his milk. Katie knows they are deeply indebted to him and no matter how hard she works, she can never repay his life saving, generous kindness. Surveying their handiwork, she looks about her, at least they had made a good start.

Not wishing to waste the hot soapy water, the shabby excuse for tea towels, curtains and dusters are the last items to be unceremoniously submerged in the bubbling water of the boiler.

Finally, the rag rugs are savagely beaten until they are completely dust free and draped over a small wooden fence to air.

If truth be known, thinks Katie, as she reviews their morning's work with pride, spring cleaning the cottage hadn't been a particularly difficult task at all, for the dust and spider webs were merely superficial.

Not until the curtains and the dusters join their clothes on the line does Katie allow herself the luxury of stopping for a well-deserved, but necessary rest.

Sat at the table with her daughter, she looks around the room and smiles, feeling a strong sense of satisfaction with a job well done, but never-the-less, lurking at the back of her mind she can't help but wonder if she's treading on someone's toes with all her cleaning, she sincerely hopes she hasn't.

The larder yields sufficient supplies to make some bread. Using some of her butter she makes a tray of scones and a few biscuits. By early afternoon, two large, very crusty cottage loaves and a selection of her baking, sits on the freshly scrubbed and polished dresser.

By late afternoon, their bedroom has been thoroughly cleaned and the bed made up with crisp clean linen, plus a beautiful, quilted overlay that she'd found in the tall boy, was carefully spread, crease free, to dress the bed, she's hoping the weather will be just as good tomorrow, so that she can wash the used bedding. The day is passing rapidly by it is time to prepare dinner. A working man needed a hearty meal when he'd done a hard day's work, so whilst the newly plucked chicken is roasting, Katie prepares an assortment of fresh vegetables and the new potatoes Joe had left in the larder.

Unlike Katie, Joseph Markson on the other hand, has had a totally useless and completely non-productive day, busily getting nowhere.

He had sat idly on a tree stump in the spinney, staring blankly into space, with the axe, a saw and the wood splitter laying idly at his feet. The huge pile of wood that in the past six hours, should have been chopped into a cart load of logs, was still scattered completely untouched around him.

How could he possibly concentrate on anything other than his two, newly acquired, extremely charming and fascinating guests? It was all so... intriguing, he can concentrate on nothing else.

There's no doubt about it, the whole episode had certainly shaken him to the core when he'd happened upon them, indeed he still couldn't quite take it all in. Yet here they were, large as life, staying in his home. Now the stunning young woman and her cute little offspring seems to occupy his every moment. What in hell's name, he wonders, could have happened to bring them all the way out here in the sticks, miles from anywhere and in such a terrible state too?

He's remembering the very moment he'd first clapped eyes on them both.

He could still picture them vividly in his mind's eye, as they stood huddled fearfully together in his yard. Both were trembling with terror at being discovered. Poor Katie, standing frozen to the spot looking wide-eyed and terrified, and the wailing child, ferociously kicking and punching at his legs to protect her mother, then clinging desperately to her mother's skirt, clearly frightened to death of him.

Oh yes, the whole experience had undoubtedly been a dramatic shock and given him plenty to think about.

Deep in thought, the astonishing young woman seems to stand permanently before him. He closes his eyes… she's there, he opens them again, she's still there, this beautiful young woman, with a sad haunting look of desperation in those alluring, very beautiful, pale blue eyes.

Replaying the exact moment, he had discovered them, he recalls his shocked astonishment, when he'd discovered that his no-good thieving rogue of a filthy vagabond was in fact a desperate young woman. Despite the mask of fear that was written all over her grubby, bruised and battered face, he recalls being truly pole-axed to discover she was in fact no tramp at all, but a delightfully attractive young woman! From the very moment he'd clapped eyes on her he was immediately entranced by her large haunting sky-blue eyes and fine facial features, all framed by the most striking shock of dark auburn, unruly curls. He had also discovered that she was very well spoken with good manners. To add to the mystery still further, he'd also noted the little child accompanying her, was equally polite and well spoken, too.

He shakes his head, and his lips break into a smile, such a fascinating young woman, without a shadow of doubt. True her clothes are filthy and of poor quality, but they take nothing away from her small, but perfect hourglass figure, he swallows, his heartbeat quickening.

The woman had introduced herself as Katerina, but Katerina who? He smiles to himself, Humm, Katerina, such a pretty, unusual name, it suits her perfectly, but there again, so does Kate or even Katie.

Then there's the young child with another unusual name, Lilibeth. Apart from the chubby cheeks and impish looks, she is her mother's mirrored image in miniature. A broad smile breaks over his face, they are simply delightful, the pair of them.

However, his smile fades to a deep frown. Who are they, where on earth, have they sprung from? What terrible course of events has reduced them to living rough in a barn, his barn…? Even worse, what were their future intentions, did they even have anywhere to go at all?

Questions, questions, he knows he won't rest until he gets answers and hopefully, this evening she might enlighten him.

Like a bolt out of the blue, a terrible thought strikes him, for all he knows, they might already be gone! Gone out of his life just as quickly as they had entered it, and that possibility worries him most of all.

It's no good, he decides, there's nothing to be solved by wasting his time hanging around the spinney, loafing about doing nothing, his interest in work had long vanished so his tools are left where they lay on the ground. Joe strides purposely homeward, feeling apprehensive and tense, wondering, with every footstep if he will be greeted by an empty cottage when he opens the door.

As he marches up the yard, telling wisps of curling smoke is rising from the sturdy chimney, lifting his spirits and putting the smile back on his face, they are still here. He's filled with a sense of relief, though he is ill prepared for what is to greet him.

Opening the front door to the parlour, he stands stock still on the threshold, the carefree smile on his face vanishing instantly, he's flabbergasted. His jaw drops open and his eyes widen in amazement, it is as if someone had quite literally turned the clock back in time.

The room is exactly as his dear mother had always kept it, looking spick and span, even the dusty furniture has been polished until it gleams.

As if that wasn't enough, something else gives him highly pleasurable feelings of nostalgia from the past. His nostrils flare as he inhales the unmistakable, enticing aroma of baking. 'Hello, I'm back, anybody here?' he calls, stepping into the parlour and removing his jacket.

A giggle from Lilibeth draws his attention towards the scullery, as both mother and daughter emerge.

Joe gasps a sharp intake of breath; his eyes widen in amazement at the sight that greets him. The nerves in his body tingle, his heart misses several beats, for the sight of Katie quite literally takes his breath away.

She stands before him in a long, elegant but simple pale blue frock, the colour of which imitates her captivating eyes perfectly, Katie looks simply amazing. He gasps. Her previously unkempt, straw entwined, tousled hair, now gleaming a fiery deep burnished auburn that cascades down in soft curls, caressing her delicate shoulders and curling around her breasts. For the first time in his life, he is rendered totally and utterly speechless by a woman.

Eventually he manages to tear his eyes away from her, they fall on little Lily. Her transformation is nothing short of a miracle, the grubby little waif of a girl has disappeared completely, the improvement is simply astounding! Just like her mother, her tangled hair is now a mass of shining bouncing curls, though Lilibeth's hair is tied back from her face with two blue ribbons that matches her frock. Over the dress is a crisp white pinafore. Her little face, now scrubbed clean, reveals the cutest semblance of her mother's fine features. 'Oh, my dear Lord, I can't believe it, what a picture!' he exclaims breathlessly.

Relaxing, he smiles broadly, his eyebrows still raised in pleasant surprise, 'Well I'll be blowed! Phew! This home coming has fair taken my breath away. Why you both look... look...'' he struggles to find the words and his heart misses another couple of beats, 'Oh my dear God, the pair of you... look absolutely stunning, so beautiful,' he blurts out.

Modestly, Katie lowers her head to conceal her blushes, whilst young Lilibeth stands with a grin so wide that it wrinkles her cute little button nose.

'Phew!' he exclaims as he hangs his coat behind the door and pulls off his boots. His eyes meander around the room, 'Katie, you've fair created miracles, you've turned my parlour into a little palace. I can tell you, it's a quite a while since it looked as good as this, if ever!'

Shrugging her shoulders dismissively, Katie returns to the scullery, 'Oh it's nothing Joseph, we wanted to repay you for the kindness you've shown us,' she tells him, tying the strings of her clean pinafore around her very trim waist.

Lilibeth grasps hold of Joe's hand as they follow her through to the scullery. 'We been busy, all day, Joe, come and see what we did for you.'

Still reeling from the dramatic transformation of the girls and his home, yet another huge shock is in store for him, the scullery is a real sight to behold. He stands, totally flummoxed. Absolutely everywhere had been scrubbed to within an inch of its life, now everything and everywhere is meticulously clean and tidy.

Taken aback yet again, he is temporarily rendered speechless, he can't help but notice the shelves of the dresser are filled with newly baked bread, scones and even a plate of biscuits.

A large oven pan filled with assorted roasted vegetables is sat appetisingly in the centre of the kitchen table. The plump chicken, cooked to golden perfection, is resting on a plate on the draining board, waiting to be carved, it all smells utterly delicious. He purses his lips, blowing a long, drawn-out whistle, 'Good God! All this... surely, it's not just possible, you've never done all this in the few hours I've been gone. Katie?'

Shocked and visibly shaken, he slumps back into his chair beside the range looking somewhat bemused. Good grief! Katie is full of surprises and all of them, it would seem, extremely pleasant ones too. 'I um... I just can't take it all in, you've done all this...! Katie...?' he stutters, shaking his head in utter disbelief. 'It's just not possible!' he looks at Katie and shakes his head again, 'Good Lord girl, I'm stunned. Come, sit here, please,' he says, nodding to the adjacent chair.

Katie bites her lip, she'd obviously overstepped the mark, she had taken liberties in his home and displeased him, now it seems she had to face the consequences. Reluctantly she does as she is asked, perching nervously on the edge of the chair, looking sheepish.

He leans forward, 'You've obviously worked extremely hard Katie, and God alone knows how you've managed it all in the few short hours that I've been gone. I'm completely stunned, I truly am,' he glances at Lilibeth who is stood close to her mother's side.

Aware that the small child would easily take umbrage, if he dares to question her mother, he deliberately lowers his voice to almost a whisper. 'Look Katie, I want you to know that I really appreciate all that you've done today, thank you,' he says, 'but really, there was no need to do all this, all I did was offer you a roof over your heads for a few days, not the job of a skivvy, for heaven's sake!'

'But I don't mind, we wanted to repay you for the trouble and inconvenience we've caused you,' she insists. 'Anyway, we, enjoyed every minute of it. I'm so sorry we've upset you, Joe, we really didn't mean to offend you,' she adds apologetically, wringing her fingers.

'Yes, we do like cleaning things, doesn't we, Mammy?' pipes up Lilibeth, scowling defiantly at Joe, as always, ready to back her mother up to the hilt, no matter what.

'I can assure you, I'm not in the least bit upset Katie. On the contrary, the truth is, all this has been an enormous shock, that's all.'

Sidling up to her mother, Lilibeth holds Katie's hand and speaks up, 'Me and Mammy just wanted to make your house beautiful, Joe.'

He smiles at Lily who, without a hint of insolence towards him, in fact quite the opposite, had squared her shoulders and spoken up loyally, for her dear mother. He thinks Lily's gesture is highly commendable and brave for one so young. For such a tiny child she shows more pluck than any grown woman he'd ever known, he can't help but admire the child's unwavering loyalty to her mother.

Lifting her up he hoists her onto his knee, 'Well I think you have both done a wonderful job, thank you Lily, thank you Katie.' He gives Lily a squeeze, 'Do you know what Lily? You're a joy to have around the house.'

'Ooo, am I, really?' she asks, eyes wide.

'You most certainly are Lily,' he tells her, giving her nose a playful tweak.

'What about my mammy then?' she asks.

Joe looks directly at Katie, his deep blue eyes twinkling, his lips curl with a hint of hidden pleasure, 'Oh believe me, your mammy is a real joy to have around too,' he replies, giving Katie a playful wink.

Katie squirms at his all to freely given compliment, she's just not used to them, and for the sake of her dignity, quickly changes the subject, declaring, 'Ahem, it seems to me that everyone has forgotten that the dinner is getting cold. Would you mind carving the chicken, please, Joseph?'

The urgent, nagging questions that had been chasing around in his head, demanding answers, now fade into insignificance, he decides that they maybe they can return to the subject sometime later that evening, perhaps when little Lily's ears are tucked up in bed and safely out of earshot.

About to carve the chicken, he can't help but steal an appreciative glance in Katie's direction. She really is stunning, who couldn't help but admire such a woman? He swallows hard, 'Katie, I um…' his mouth dry as parchment, his words failing him. Looking down at his hands he tuts, he'd been so caught up in all the dramatic and pleasurable changes that had occurred in his short absence, he'd completely forgotten to wash. Embarrassed he looks at Katie, 'Oh dear, look at me, I'm filthy, I'm sorry about this, I'd better freshen up first. I won't be long.' he says, taking the bowl and towel and hastily disappearing outside in the back yard.

A short while later he returns, bare from the waist up, droplets of water dripping from the tips of his long wavy hair running down over his lean, muscle defined torso.

Shocked and acutely embarrassed at the sight of his naked torso, Katie averts her eyes and dashes outside to the washing line, returning with a freshly laundered towel, handing it to him, along with one of his newly laundered shirts. 'Here Joseph,' she says, modestly lowering her eyes, 'I washed them today, actually I took the liberty of doing quite a bit of laundering, I um, I do hope that was all right?' She asks breathlessly, her eyes fixed firmly on the floor.

Picking up on her obvious awkwardness at the state of his undress, he pulls on the clean shirt a bit sharpish, 'My dear Katie, of course it's all right. Good heavens, you're unbelievable, you really are.' He says, in awe of her, joining them at the table, aware that Lily is staring at him. Her obvious admiration is written all over her face, he grins at her and picks up the carving knife, 'Mmm, lovely, you know what Lily, if this tastes as good as it looks then I reckon we're in for a real feast, young lady,' he says, taking a long, exaggerated sniff.

Lilibeth puts her hands to her mouth, attempting unsuccessfully to stifle a giggle.

Sharpening the knife and distributing the slices of the succulent chicken, falls to Joseph, whilst Katie serves up the new potatoes and roasted vegetables.

From the corner of his eye, he spies the large plate of delicious scones and a jar of dark red jam sat temptingly, waiting to complete the feast, his mouth waters, but even more pleasing, Katie is sat opposite him, she is looking simply stunning. He can't help himself; he can't take his eyes off her.

Looking up, Katie realises he is watching her, she blushes.

Self-conscious, he tears his eyes away, trying to concentrate on his dinner.

'Well, you were certainly right about your mother's cooking, Lily,' he declares, stretching his torso and patting his well-satisfied stomach, 'that was, delicious!'

A comment that draws a smug look of I told you so, from Lilibeth.

'Thank you, Katie, that was smashing,' he tells her as he rises from the table, trying to disguise his acute pleasure at not only the tasty meal he'd just devoured, but her very presence at his table. 'Now you just take yourselves into the parlour, you both deserve to put your feet up. I'll wash up and then I'll heat us all a mug of hot milk,' he says, trying to dismissively shush them from the room.

'Oh no, I wouldn't hear of it,' says Katie, picking up some dishes herself.

Shrugging his shoulders, his eyes dance with pleasure as she joins him at the sink, 'Humm, well as I'm not a one to argue, it looks like we'll have to share the washing up, soonest done soonest rest, as my dear mam used to say.'

Katie smiles and nods in agreeance, tying her apron strings she plunges the dishes into the hot water.

Clearly tired but content, Lilibeth sits beside the range, deeply engrossed in conversation with her doll Daisy, whilst the chore of washing the dishes is amiably shared by Joe and her mother, she yawns, rubs her sleepy eyes, unable to supress another yawn.

'Hello, I think someone's ready for her bed,' says Joe, placing the last of the dishes on the shelf.

'Yes, you're right, Joe. The trouble is she's used to a set routine, normally she would have been in bed ages ago. I expect the last few days have taken their toll on her,' explains Katie, looking suitably awkward.

'Nothing a good night's sleep in a nice soft bed won't cure, I'm sure. Tell you what Katie, I'll go up and turn back the covers whilst you get her ready for bed,' he suggests, then disappears upstairs, leaving them to it.

Setting to, Katie washes and changes her daughter in the scullery, 'Shall we sleep in that lovely room upstairs tonight, darling?'

Rubbing her tired eyes, Lilibeth nods wearily, 'Yes Mamma, you and me and my Daisy, coz we like the pretty room and it's got a nice, big soft bed to sleep in,' she replies, sounding tired but relaxed.

Katie smiles lovingly, 'It certainly is a lovely room. Up we go, I think Joe is waiting to say goodnight,' she tells her daughter, scooping her up in her arms.

Despite being tucked up alone in a strange bed in an unfamiliar room, Lilibeth seems quite happy to snuggle down beneath the covers with her beloved doll.

'Good night little Lily, sleep well,' whispers Joe, gently stroking her rosy cheek with his finger. Leaving them alone to say their goodnights, he pauses briefly on the stairs when he hears Lily call out to him, 'Nighty night, Joe!'

He smiles to himself, 'Good night Lily, I'll see you in the morning, Dear,' he calls back.

'Ooo, did you hear what Joe said Mamma?' says Lilibeth, scrunching up her shoulders with pleasure, 'he called me dear.'

'It took a little while for her to fall asleep,' explains Katie, when she eventually returns to the parlour, 'unfamiliar house and a strange bed, I expect.'

Although it's on the tip of his tongue he resists the temptation to quip, not as strange as my barn, as he doesn't wish to appear either sarcastic or sound judgemental. 'All perfectly understandable I suppose, she's certainly a bundle of energy bless her, besides, she's only little. By the way, how old is she?'

Trying to look a little more assertive in her conversation, Katie pulls back her shoulders and looks him in the eye, 'Lilibeth is just six. Actually, it was her birthday three weeks ago. May the twenty eighth to be precise.'

An element of surprise is written on Joe's face, to him, Lily looks small for a six-year-old, yet on the other hand, she appears to be extremely bright and knowing, for one so young. He tuts noisily, and frowns.

His reaction makes Katie feel uncomfortable.

He is shocked, 'Six, really?' he exclaims, 'Good grief, a bit young to be living in a big old barn full of drafts in foul weather, wouldn't you say?' he blurts out before his mouth has engaged his brain.

She recoils, visibly flinching, trying to bravely fight back her impending tears. Knowing she's obliged to proffer answers to his barrage of inevitable questions, she's feeling seriously cornered.

Instantly he regrets his crass comment the minute it leaves his lips, he sighs, 'Oh hell, I'm so sorry Katie, I didn't mean to sound so caustic or opinionated. Who am I to criticize?' He shakes his head, 'I really am sorry Katie. Oh hell, what am I saying? It's just… I can't help it, I've been worrying about you, both of you, all day. I mean, where have you come from, and how come you ended up living in my barn, of all places?'

Katie sits tight lipped, looking away, unable to face him.

He leans back in his chair and shakes his head, 'Sorry, I guess I shouldn't pry my dear, but surely you can't blame me for being curious?'

Biting her lip, Katie struggles to hold back the impending tears that are about to spring to the surface.

He leans forward, 'Look I'm sorry Katie, I can't help but worry about you both.' He sighs heavily. 'I guess it's really none of my business, so please, just forget I asked,' he says remorsefully, trying to placate the situation.

In her heart Katie feels he is not really prepared to let the matter drop. His persistent curiosity makes her feel obliged to proffer some sort of explanation. It is, after all his home, he'd been generous enough to take them in when he didn't know them from Adam. Besides, she is all too aware that they wouldn't have lasted long, lost and alone in the countryside. What would have become of them? She shudders to think. I guess I owe him an honest explanation, she decides, albeit reluctantly.

CHAPTER 4

Trying to re-assert her dignity, she straightens her back and clears her throat, 'Actually it was just the one night in the barn,' she confesses, looking shamefaced, 'and I can assure you, it was only intended to be an over-night stay,' she adds defensively, sighing. 'Regrettably, it was a necessary and temporary measure. We simply had no choice. It was the torrential rain, you see.'

He shakes his head at her illogical explanation. 'But that doesn't make sense Katie, if that's the case, why on earth would you choose an uncomfortable old barn, for goodness sake, when my cosy cottage is right next door?'

Feeling her resolve weakening from his intensive gaze, Katie fights to hold back the tears that are bubbling like a cauldron beneath the surface, 'I'm afraid it's a… a very long story,' she whispers.

He leans closer, his eyes looking into hers, his expression one of compassion. Gently patting her hand, he says in a soft, sympathetic tone, 'Why don't you tell me all about it, my dear, surely it can't be that bad. You never know, I might even be able to help you,' he offers.

Oh, how Katie wants to confide in him, dish out the whole sad sorry story, but it isn't that simple. On the surface he appears genuine enough, but inwardly she's still wary of him, how did she know that she could trust this man, after all, they were virtually complete strangers?

Stubbornly she sits tight-lipped as she weighs up the pros and cons. Maybe he is a stranger, but hadn't he been kind enough to offer two complete strangers the hospitality of his home without question?

Interrupting her thoughts Joe leans forward, 'Look Katie,' he says gently, 'you're obviously in some kind of trouble, what, I don't know, but until I know what the problem is, what it is that has led you to end up in this sorry state in the first place, how can I help you?'

Nervously she toys with the ribbon on her frock, she wants to tell him, she really does, but… the minutes tick by.

Quietly he waits patiently, but with Katie remaining stubbornly silent, he eventually decides that if she is to be forthcoming it would be necessary to press her again. 'Surely it can't be so bad that you can't tell me?' he asks, as he lifts her chin so that he can look directly into her eyes, 'Try Dear, try.'

Katie gulps, 'I'm sorry Joseph, but if I'm honest I really don't know where to start,' she tells him truthfully.

'Why not start at the beginning,' he suggests, 'It's as good a place as any, just take your time. You talk, and I'll sit and listen,' he suggests gently.

Feeling she is in an inescapable position, Katie mulls over what he'd said. Yes of course he deserves an explanation, and the more he presses her the more she feels obliged to enlighten him.

The knot in her stomach tightens, she feels nauseous, it's crunch time, like it or not she feels she has no choice, though she would have to be very careful not to mention Albert Soames, or Penfold Grove.

Resigning herself to his incessant pressure she relents, inhaling a deep breath she focuses her eyes squarely on the floor. 'Yes, all right Joseph. But first, I must thank you. We are indebted to you for your kindness and generosity, and of course, I owe you an explanation, I will tell you, but I warn you, it's a very long story.'

He nods, sits back and lights his pipe, 'I have all the time in the world my dear, take your time.'

Knowing it won't be easy, Katie takes a deep fortifying breath and licks her lips nervously. 'I um… I was born and brought up just outside Selchester, on the Sheybourne Estate,' she begins, 'We, that is my parents and I, lived in a cottage that was not too dissimilar to this one, though a great deal smaller, of course. My father was head of maintenance on the estate. My mother was the seamstress.' Katie stops and inhales another deep breath. 'Anyway, I suppose my life changed when I lost my father. He was repairing a roof when the ladder collapsed, he was killed instantly.' Katie's brow creases, she sighs. 'Our greatest fear was that we'd be thrown out of our home, but Sir Edwin Barton-Smythe, the Master of the house, told us that as the accident had happened on the estate, he would bear the cost for a simple funeral. He told my mother he was prepared to stretch my mother's hours a little, she would receive a small increase in her salary which in turn, meant that we could stay on in the cottage. I remember, at the time, we were relieved and grateful for his generosity.'

Clearly finding it difficult to talk, Katie pauses briefly, avoiding his inquisitive gaze, searches her pockets for her hanky, knowing she will be needing it soon.

Joe exhales a puff of smoke. Although his own father had died when he was a baby and he had no recollection of him at all, in a way he could relate how the difference in circumstances of losing her father could make to a young girl's life. Her father's death had obviously had a devastating effect on her childhood. No wonder there was such sadness in her voice. 'I see, so you lived in a tied cottage on the estate,' He mutters quietly.

Katie nods, 'Yes, though with hindsight I realised there was another good reason for his so-called nobleness. The Barton-Smythe's desperately wanted to retain the services of my dear mother, she was a remarkably fine needlewoman. the Lady of the house knew it all too well. Do you know Joseph, my mother could make absolutely anything, from huge heavy lined curtains to embroidering sheets and pillowcases? She made many of their fine clothes too, they were beautiful. Fine lace petticoats, day frocks and delicately exquisite evening gowns.'

Reliving her past Katerina barely pauses to draw breath. Joe sits listening quietly, not wishing to intervene, it is obvious that Katie has a stubborn streak, he could also see why little Lily was so vehemently loyal to her mother, it would seem it was a strong family trait.

'Everyone said so,' says Katie interrupting his thoughts. 'However, it wasn't long before we found out that his so-called generosity meant that my poor mother had to work from dawn till dusk, six days a week, and what for, I ask you? A measly one and four pence halfpenny a month extra. 'She pauses briefly and sighs, 'Huh, a shilling of that was taken from us because he increased our rent!' she adds, her brow creasing again.

Stopping, her eyes cloud with deep rooted sadness, she's wringing the handkerchief in her hands continuously.

Joe can't help but admire her steely determination, recalling her past to him, but the more she speaks the more her sadness becomes interlocked with strong undertones of bitterness in her voice, he shakes his head, it doesn't suit her at all, though perfectly understandable.

He shifts uneasily in his chair, after all, he had instigated her out-pouring in the first place. It was painfully clear to him that recalling her life's history was upsetting her deeply, he feels guilty. Clearing his throat, he interrupts her, 'Ahem, Katie, I can see this is all proving to be difficult for you, so I think perhaps we should take a short break. I'll heat some milk, it might help,' he suggests caringly.

Resting his pipe on the grate, he stands and disappears into the scullery.

The very moment he leaves the room, Katie seizes the opportunity to dash up the stairs and check on her daughter, though she has no need to worry, she is snuggled down beneath the covers and sleeping soundly. Katie creeps meekly back down to the parlour, only to find Joe stood in the middle of the room holding a couple of mugs, looking perplexed. 'There you are,' he says, handing her the mug of frothy steaming milk.

'Sorry, I was just checking on Lilibeth,' she says sheepishly, knowing she appears to be needlessly over-protective of her offspring, but she can't help herself.

'And... how is she?' he asks kindly.

Taking her drink and thanking him she sits down. 'She's sound asleep, thank you very much.' Then without being cajoled into continuing where she'd left off, she quickly drinks her milk, places the empty mug on the hearth and clears her throat. 'With my poor mother having to work much longer hours, I took over all the household duties at home. Cleaning, washing and cooking, anything that would make my dear mother's life a little easier. I really enjoyed it too.'

Completely transfixed, listening to Katie's soft voice recalling her past, he draws fruitlessly on his pipe that, unbeknown him had long ago expired, he simply can't take his eyes off her. He takes the opportunity to study her as she talks. He had never met a woman like her before, she is simply fascinating, or was it breath-taking? Hum, most definitely both, he decides.

Conscious of his eyes resting on her, Katie glances at him and fidgets nervously.

Realising he's staring and distracting her, he rests back in his chair, concentrating on re-lighting his pipe, settling down, listening intently as she doggedly carries on recalling her story.

'Fortunately, Percy Dobbins, the gardener, supplied us with fruit and vegetables. I used to help him out in the vegetable garden. That's when I discovered how much I loved gardening.' she says. 'We never went short of meat either. The gamekeeper, Tommy Palmer, supplied us with a supply of fresh meat, even the occasional fish.' A faint smile crosses her lips as momentarily she recalls happier times. 'I really liked Tommy. After my father died, he did what he could to help us out, like chopping our firewood etc.' She sighs yet again, weaving her handkerchief around her fingers so tightly her fingers turn white. 'Most of my time was spent alone, though it wasn't always a solitary life. When the Barton-Smythes were away and the weather was fine I often spent time with Miss Elsbeth and Master Edward, they were the two children that lived in the big house,' she explains, 'Miss Elsbeth was three years my senior, and Master Edward, my dear friend Edward, was nine months older than I. He was always making us laugh with his practical jokes, he was tall and very handsome.'

Deep in thought, Joe frowns, he can't help but notice Katie's wistful smile when she speaks of this Edward fellow. Then there was Percy Dobbins and Tommy Palmer, somewhere deep in the back of his mind, the two names seem to ring a bell, but for the life of him he can't recall where, he had never been to Selchester and never even heard of Sheybourne, so that couldn't be it. Katie is still talking, so he dismisses his own distracting thoughts and listens intently, hanging on to her every word.

'When the weather was fine, we, Miss Elsbeth, Master Edward and I, would play in the vast grounds. Hide and seek, paddling or fishing in the stream, and... on the swings,' she continues, 'that was great fun, they were strung from the boughs of the Great Oak. Sometimes, when the Master and Mistress were away and it was raining, Freda Loveday, their nanny, would allow us all to play in the nursery. We used to dress up in old clothes from the trunks. Oh, Joe, it was all such fun.'

Joe notes the strong tone of melancholy creeping into her voice and a sad, faraway look in her eyes, it's on the tip of his tongue to interrupt and maybe ask a question or two, but he resists the temptation, merely sitting silently, so that she can carry on, undisturbed.

Clearing her throat Katie carries on where she'd left off. 'It was Elsbeth and Edward that taught me to read and write,' she says looking wistful, 'they were such happy times. I can honestly say my mother and I might have been poor, but we were more than content with our lives.'

Katie interrupts herself momentarily, sighing long and hard, as if she was mourning those happy carefree days way back in her childhood. She sniffs and shrugs, dismissing the blissful bygone memories, then proceeds to continue where she'd left off.

'On reflection, Joe, I suppose when we're young we don't stop to think about what lies ahead in the future,' she says philosophically, causing Joe to raise his eyebrows in surprise. 'But as time passes by, things change, and sadly, so do our lives.'

With that profound statement Katie clams up, a tear trickles down her cheek.

Joe looks on feeling helpless. From what he'd heard so far, Katie had enjoyed a very happy childhood, albeit without a father, her upbringing obviously accounting for the very nice way that she speaks and her good manners too, but he's becoming increasingly concerned by her obvious distress. He wants to take her in his arms and comfort her, but he holds back. Also, there's the issue of Lily, he's curious, where did she fit into all this? Had Katie suffered at the hands of this vile, Sir what's his bloody name, or even the snobby Edward fellow? After all it is common knowledge that the toffee-nosed gentry think they have the God given right to take liberties with their staff. Poor Katie wouldn't be the first young girl in service to be taken advantage of, he was in no doubt that she wouldn't be the last either, he reasons. So, is this where young Lily, comes into the picture, he speculates? With an unexplainable anger building inside him, he surmises that that was almost certainly the case. Flaming gentry, born with a silver spoon in their ruddy mouths and not an ounce of decent morals between any of them, they needed taking down a peg or to and taught a hard lesson.

He watches helplessly as she sits unconsciously twisting her hanky, she's agitated and clearly distressed, which in turn makes him feel responsible. Her obvious misery is tugging at his heart strings, tempting him to call a halt to her ordeal, so without saying a word, he rises to his feet. The light is beginning to fade, casting gloomy dark shadows across the room so he lights both oil lamps, draws the curtains to make the room feel more cosy and secure. Although the past few days had been exceptionally warm and comfortable, as daylight falls, the darkening clouds are gathering and the temperature has dropped significantly, the air now feels chilly. Kneeling at the grate, he prepares and lights the fire, then taking the cups, disappears into the scullery, returning with two more welcome mugs of hot milk. It gives Katie the time to compose herself a little.

'Here,' he says, handing her the milk and returning to the chair opposite her, 'I think you're finding this too difficult,' he says gently. 'I hate to see you so upset, so if you want to call it a night, perhaps continue tomorrow evening, when little Lily is in bed?' he suggests considerately.

Nervously she swallows, he is a good listener and so very easy to talk to, but she had started and now feels compelled to get it over and done with. 'Yes, it's true, Joe, this is difficult, but if it's all right with you I'd rather carry on. I've got this far.' Gratefully she takes her time drinking her milk.

'If that's what really you want Katie, take your time, you're doing so well,' he encourages her, then rests back in his chair.

Katie glances up at him momentarily, 'I guess over time, things change Joe, and sadly we can do nothing about it. I vividly remember the day when Elsbeth and Edward called to see me, they were clearly excited about something. Lilibeth, guess what, I'm orf to finishing school. Oh, golly gosh, can you believe it? I'm going to Switzerland! Isn't it just the most wonderful news? Miss Elsbeth was gushing, barely able to contain her glee. Well, I can tell you Joe, I was shocked. What do you mean, you're going to Switzerland, that's abroad isn't it? I asked her, why on earth do you want to go to a foreign country? I couldn't believe that she could even consider leaving Sheybourne! I remember the puzzled, patronising look on her face. Why my dear Katerina, you funny little girl, don't you just yearn to see the big wide world? Before I can answer she delivered the next big bombshell to me. Go on Teddy old thing, she prompted her brother, tell Katerina your good news too. Well, I looked at Edward expectantly but before he could open his mouth, Miss Elsbeth took the greatest pleasure in blurting out, Teddy's orf to Oxford, isn't it so exciting?'

Though Katie's story is serious and compelling, Joe struggles to supress his amusement, as Katie expertly takes off the voice of this hoity-toity Elsbeth girl who obviously spoke with a plum in her mouth, but with Katie upset he manages to control himself and keep his amusement to himself.

'I can tell you, Joe,' says Katie interrupting his thoughts, 'I was absolutely mortified, I tried desperately to hide my disappointment, truly I did, Joe, but they were both leaving Sheybourne! I mean 'Oxford', I'd never even heard of Oxford! I had lived my entire life within the boundaries of the estate, but somehow it seemed beyond them to understand how hurt and upset I felt that they would even contemplate leaving, walking out of my life forever!'

Katie sniffs, sighing yet again, 'I suppose Master Edward must have noticed my disappointment. Hey, we'll be back old thing, he assured me, for the holidays you know. Well, I can tell you Joseph, I wasn't impressed. Some consolation, I thought, they're deserting me, it was as if my feelings… well as if I didn't matter to them at all! They were going to walk out of my life forever, how could they? How dare they?'

Katie stops, dabs her swollen eyes and blows her nose.

For the past two hours or more, Joe had sat quietly drawing on his pipe, listening to her every word, but as time passed, he'd grown more and more concerned for her welfare, Katie is becoming increasingly distraught, 'Katie, this is getting to much for you,' he interrupts her quietly.

Sitting with a vacant expression and not even aware that she had stopped talking, Katie's mind is rooted firmly back in time at the Sheybourne Estate.

He clears his throat loudly, disturbing her concentration, breaking her train of thought. 'Ahem, please Katie, I've heard enough.'

Blinking, she stares at him, 'Oh, I'm sorry Joseph,' she apologises, 'I was miles away. I suppose you might consider my reaction was one of pure selfishness?'

Shaking his head slowly, his kind face is full of understanding, 'No my dear, not at all. I've no doubt I would have felt much the same as you, in those circumstances. It must have been quite a shock, losing both your lifelong friends in one foul swoop,' he agrees, feeling a pang of guilt, poor Katie looks exhausted.

The room falls silent and for a few moments, not a word is spoken.

After a brief spell of awkward silence, it's Katie that speaks. 'I remember, after they'd gone,' she says, carrying on where she had left off, 'my life seemed dull and boring, Joseph. I was so lonely and missed their company. My days seemed full of nothing, except miserable solitude. But as time passed, I decided that I needed to occupy my time, so unbeknown to the Barton-Smythes, I started going up to the kitchens at the big house, helping wherever I could. Maizey Brown, the head cook, taught me how to make bread, preserve vegetables and fruit. I learned to make jams, cheese, butter and all sorts, at least our larder at home was always well stocked with food,' she quips, 'Edward often came home for the holidays. We used to stroll around the grounds, and he'd tell me about all the things he'd seen and done.'

Noting the definite tone of affection in her voice when she speaks of this young chap Edward, Joe notices the very mention of his name seems to bring out a hint of a reminiscing smile of days gone by to her lips, the look in her eyes seemed to hold a denotation of her first love perhaps? Joe bites on his pipe and frowns, it's totally absurd, but for some ridiculously stupid and unaccountable reason, he feels a pang of jealousy towards this Edward fellow. 'I see, it all sounds very idyllic,' he comments, hoping he doesn't sound sarcastic.

She appears to ignore his comment, licking her dry lips, she makes a concerted effort to carry on. Her faint smile disappears. 'Yes, I suppose it was for a while. Then...' she stops abruptly, her face pales, contorted with pain. 'Oh God, it... it happened on Edward's visit home, a special visit to celebrate his seventeenth b...birthday.'

No longer able to contain herself, Katie gives in to tears.

Alarmed, Joe sits bolt upright as she sobs uncontrollably, wishing with all his heart and soul he hadn't pressured her into all this business in the first place. Leaning forward in his chair, he bows his head, lifts her chin, looking into her eyes, 'Katie, please, that's enough, don't upset yourself. I think you should stop, now.'

Stubbornly she ignores his compassionate offer, she had come this far, gulping a lung full of air she continues as best she can. 'Edward's parents had arranged this huge party to celebrate his seventeenth birthday, even the staff would have our own party, held below stairs, of course,' she says, sniffing for the umpteenth time. Patting her puffy eyes, she sighs mournfully, then valiantly struggles on as best she can. Her head lowers as does her voice, 'Little did I know then that my course of destiny in life would be so cruelly and abruptly altered forever!' Again, Katie pauses briefly, unceremoniously blowing her nose, then stubbornly carries on.

'The evening before Edward was due back, my dear mother came home from work a lot later than usual, bless her, she looked all in.' Katie draws in a long deep breath, 'I suppose I was too engrossed with my own thoughts of Edward's homecoming to notice that my mamma was ailing for something.' She mops the tears from her eyes, as distressing, morose memories fill her mind and hold her captive. In her mind's eye it was as if it had all happened only yesterday.

Joe can bear her distress no longer. 'Please Katie, stop.' Leaning forward he grasps her hands, running his thumbs gently over her knuckles, he'd heard enough. Compelled to intervene and end her suffering, he says more forcefully. 'That's enough Katie.'

Again, she ignores him, trying to withdraw her hands, but Joe holds them tight.

Obstinately she steels herself and opens her mouth to continue.

'Katie, please, I said that's enough!' Frustrated he interrupts her again, but his words go unheard.

'I um… I couldn't wait to see Edward, to spend time with someone of my own age for a change,' she admits frowning, 'Anyway, that night, Mamma and I sat eating dinner, I listened, as my mother told me how hectic it had all been up at the big house preparing for Master Edward's party. It's been bedlam all day, she told me. We didn't know whether we were coming or going. Mamma told me that the Mistress had them all running around like scalded cats. Do this, do that, I want this, I want that. You mark my words Katerina, tomorrow will ten times worse. Oh, my dear Lord, I'm so weary, perhaps I'll get off to bed, I've got a very early start tomorrow. So, I packed Mammy off to bed with a cup of hot milk, Joe.'

Katie stops, squeezes Joe's hands, dreading what she was about to impart, she steels herself in order that she can carry on. 'The next morning, we were up at first light, I remember thinking that Mamma looked a little better, though she refused her breakfast. Anyway, Mammy was about to leave for work when she remembered something at the last minute. Oh, before I go Katerina, there's a large box under my bed, be a love and fetch it for me? Full of curiosity I ran to fetch it, returning with the huge fancy box. Mammy explained that she'd made me a gown for the birthday party. Oh Joseph, what do you think? I lifted the lid and buried beneath a mound of soft black tissue was the most exquisite gown that I had ever seen. It was the palest cream satin, trimmed with handmade lace and tiny pearl buttons. There was also a lace trimmed petticoat. She also handed me an old paper bag. Inside were a pair of cream satin court shoes. Apparently, they were my darling mother's wedding shoes. Oh, Joe, I cried, Mammy cried, we were so happy.'

The moment of joyfully reliving those few precious moments suddenly dies, her face darkens, her expression full of pain. 'Then Mammy kissed my cheek, I… I love you darling, she said as she left for work. Smiling at me and calling back, I… I'll see you later.' Katie's croaking voice trails away, words deserting her, she starts sobbing so deeply that further conversation is now impossible.

Joe feels worse than dreadful, because of his stupid curiosity he knows he is wholly responsible for instigating Katie's misery, he can bear it no longer. He kneels before her, prising her handkerchief from her trembling fingers and gently he pats the tears from her eyes. Despite his efforts to console her, and his insistence that he'd heard enough, Katie's head slumps forward onto his shoulder. 'I need to tell you, please,' she whispers hoarsely

Grimacing, he shakes his head, 'Katie, please,' he says quietly but firmly. 'No more, you're making yourself ill.'

Whether she hears him or chooses to ignore him, he doesn't know, she sits there in a daze, her head still resting on his shoulder.

Determined, she'd got this far she insists stubbornly, 'Please, I'm all right, Joe,' she says, taking several deep steadying breaths.

He puts his arm around her shoulder, 'Christ Katie, for God's sake, enough is enough!' He takes her hand and leads her to the sofa, pulling her onto his lap, he wraps his arm around her, to comfort her.

Grasping his hands, she whispers softly, 'Please, Joe, I'm nearly finished.' Ignoring him, she carries on. 'Someone was banging at the door, it was Maizey. She grabbed me, telling me my mammy had taken poorly. I ran as fast as I could Joe, but when I reached the house, the master was stood at the door. I'm sorry Miss Seymour, you're too late, your mother has passed away, he told me in his cold impassive voice.'

Katie's body seems to collapse, her pretty face contorts, wracked with pain.

Gently he tightens his arm around her. 'Oh Katie, I'm so very sorry.' he whispers. Her deep throated sobs consume her as she buries her head in her hands, her body shaking as she cries pitifully. 'Hey, let it all out, sweetheart.' He says soothingly, rocking her gently, holding her close to pacify her. He too had lost his dear mother Violet, only a few short months ago. Katie's story had touched a raw nerve, he knew exactly how she feels, he feels her pain too. 'Oh, Katie, you poor sweet girl, you cry, let it all out,' he whispers, drawing her closer, rocking her back and forth.

Silently they sat together in the dimly lit room, Joe holding her firmly, gently offering what he hoped would be soothing words of comfort.

'I...I'm, I'm s... so sorry Joseph,' she sobs, looking up at him with her doleful, tear-swollen eyes.

'Sorry? Hush, there's nothing for you to be sorry about, sweetheart. I know exactly how you feel, believe me. You see, I lost my own dear mother just three months ago.' he explains. 'Katie, sit here, take it easy, I want to get you something, I won't be a minute.' Reluctantly, he releases her, stands and disappears into the scullery.

Katie is left alone with her misery for only minutes.

Whilst the pan of milk is heating, Joe takes a bottle of brandy from the shelf, adding a good measure into her cup.

Sitting beside her again, he slips his arm around her shoulders pulling her close, offering her the milk, 'Here Katie, drink this. It'll help.'

Katie sips it and coughs, 'Yuk, what is it?' she asks, pulling a face.

'Warm milk with a drop of brandy, my mother had it when she was poorly, it should help,' he explains, 'Come, be a good girl, drink it all down, it'll do you a power of good, I promise.'

Feeling so low and miserable, she has neither the inclination nor energy to argue, so she does as she is asked, handing him the empty mug sighing woefully, she rests her weary head back on his shoulder, sighing for the umpteenth time.

Sorely tempted to have a drink himself, Joe had decided against it, he needed a clear head to think. Sat listening, whilst Katie had struggled to relate the events of her young life, he'd found the experience extremely harrowing, remembering the death of his own mother, just three months previously. He feels her pain and anguish.

Lifting her gently, he sits her on his lap again, enfolding her in his arms once more and they sit in silence. Exhausted, she falls into a fitful sleep, her head resting on his chest, sobbing intermittently.

Deep in thought he mulls over her story. Although he had found out a great deal about her, it hardly explained her present sorry predicament, being reduced to living rough in his barn with a very young child.

What she'd told him about losing her mother, merely confirmed his suspicions that with her mother dead and Katie being left alone and vulnerable, either that bastard Edward or his high-and-mighty father had taken the liberty of 'taking care of her'. The consequence of which had obviously resulted in the birth of little Lily, Katie's sweet, innocent young daughter, he deduced.

Full of remorse he's genuinely regretting persuading her to talk at all. Unwittingly he'd opened an ugly can of worms and now poor Katie is paying the price. It pains him to see her suffering.

Determined to wipe the misery from her mind, he vows there and then, to start tomorrow with a clean slate.

Whilst he cradles her in his arms, his thoughts turn to dear little Lily, born out of wedlock and ruthlessly shunned by her so-called, high-society father. Feeling her sorrow, he sighs, he has an uneasy feeling that there was a lot worse to come, but the poor girl had been through enough misery. At least she's talking, though he decides if she wants to divulge any more, it will have to be her choice and certainly not his. He'd heard more than enough.

Holding her close he feels her body shudder with heavy spasmodic dry sobs.

Knowing she'd cried herself to sleep, he hugs her even closer, whispering, 'Hush, sleep Katie love, I'm here for you now, everything's going to be all right.' He tightens his arm around her, burying his face in her hair.

The arrival of Katie had been earth shattering. She had undoubtedly turned his life well and truly upside down and inside out, even now he was still struggling to take it all in.

After more than two years spent looking after his arthritic mother, then her subsequent passing, he had become a virtual recluse, accustomed to living a quiet life, alone, content with his own company and happy with his lot in life. What with the daily running of the farm, tending the animals, working in the reed beds and the woods, there was no time for socialising and courting, though it was true to say that in the past, he'd had his moments.

Regular fortnightly visits to the market, had meant he'd had several very enjoyable, albeit short lived intimate relationships with many a pretty young girl.

Of all the young lads at market, Joe always stood out from the crowd. The girls adored his good looks, not to mention his tanned, lean, muscular body and easy-going nature, they all enjoyed his quick witted and often wickedly saucy sense of humour too.

So, more through circumstance rather than choice, Joe, with his mother now recently departed, had found himself living alone, supposedly happily resigned to living the life of a bachelor at his beloved Sweet Briars, for the rest of his days.

But now? With the unexpected invasion of Katie and Lily into his life, for some inexplicable reason, he now feels an over-whelming compulsion to take care of this beautiful, vulnerable girl and her young daughter, he had taken them both under his wing, determined to do whatever he could to protect them, come what may. They had entered his life out of the blue yonder, and now they both occupy his every waking moment.

He groans, it's madness, days ago he didn't even know they existed.

Poor Katie has really been through the mill tonight, and her state of anguish has really affected him more deeply than he ever thought possible. Now, here she was, snuggled down safely in his arms, seemingly calm and sleeping.

How long they remained there, he couldn't be sure, he'd held her so close whilst she slept. Whatever their past, he decides, come what may, he resolves to support and protect them from... whatever, whom-so-ever?

A few hours pass, the fire is now glowing embers, reminding him that soon it would be daybreak and he would have to milk the cows and goat. Sadly, he would have to wake her. Shifting a little, he puts his finger and thumb to her chin, raising her face to look in her eyes, 'Hey Katie, it's been a long, tough night for you. It's very late and you're completely exhausted. Why don't you get yourself off upstairs, join young Lily, try and get some proper sleep?' he suggests gently.

If the truth were known, Katie feels comfortable and safe where she is, but he's right, it's very late, and she desperately craves sleep. 'Yes, you're right, Joe,' she agrees, albeit reluctantly.

As she stands on the bottom stair, she turns and whispers, 'Thank you for listening Joseph, you're so very patient, I'm sorry I got so upset, I hope I didn't embarrass you.'

'Not at all.' He replies, shaking his head. The tears from her swollen eyes glisten in the light of the oil lamp, He's very tempted to call her back, but... he smiles kindly, 'There's absolutely no need to apologise, my dear. You did so well tonight, but you look all in. Now off you go to bed. Sleep well, I'll see you in the morning.'

Katie lays in bed staring at the ceiling, reliving the feel of him as he'd held her so close, comforting her, wishing with all her heart and soul he could hold her like that forever. She feels so confused, her emotions are at odds with all that she'd ever known before.

Joe returns to his chair and lights his pipe, shaking his head and pondering the events of the evening. It seems so cruel that Katie had suffered so much pain and misery for such a young woman, if only there was something, he could do to put things right. Deciding there is at least half an hour before it's time to start the milking, he settles himself in the chair, frowning as he mulls over all that Katie had told him. He tries to grab forty winks but with so much going on in his head, sleep is impossible, so he decides he'd be more productive milking the cows and the goat. Unenthusiastically he drags on his jacket and boots, and closes the door quietly behind him, with thoughts of Katie still revolving round and round in his head.

Lilibeth is the first to wake in the morning.

Katie, who had lain restlessly, for the best part of what was left of the night, had only just given in, to much-needed sleep.

Noises coming from the scullery downstairs catches Lily's attention, she slides silently down from the bed and with Daisy held firmly in one hand, she pads barefoot downstairs.

Joe is stood at the range stirring a pan of porridge, 'Good morning little Lily. Is your mammy not awake yet?' he asks brightly.

'Mammy's sleeping,' she answers.

'Oh well, your mammy must be extra tired, so how about some porridge, with a nice blob of your mother's red jam for breakfast?' he suggests.

'Yes please, Joe. Is you having some too?'

He smiles down at the sweet little girl that is so polite and full of innocence. 'Why of course young lady, best breakfast there is you know, porridge served with fresh creamy milk and your mother's tasty red jam,' he says as he dishes up two good sized portions, each with a generously large dollop of jam in the middle.

'Mmm, lovely, I like it with my mamma's jam,' says Lily, stirring in the jam and tucking in, 'my Daisy likes it too.'

Her last comment raises his eyebrows and causes him to chuckle, he can't pretend to understand the world of make believe that this sweet little child seems to be living in, he finds her highly amusing. 'Why don't you go up and get dressed while I wash up,' he suggests. 'If your mammy's still sleeping, perhaps we can go and collect the chickens' eggs before she wakes.'

Lilibeth is all in favour of any excursion and the collection of eggs sounds exciting, 'Yes please. Can we take Daisy with us?'

'I don't see why not,' he says shrugging his shoulders, he is happy to play along with this charming child. 'Right Lily, get yourself upstairs sharpish, get dressed and I'll wash up the dishes, do we have a deal?'

Lilibeth screwed up her face with curiosity, 'What does deal mean?' she asks politely.

He struggles to find an answer that was simple enough that a six-year-old can understand, 'Umm, let me see… it means um, I will do something for you, if you'll do something for me, it's a sort of an agreed exchange, a deal, do you understand Lily?'

She shrugs her shoulders, 'Don't know,' she replies, 'I'll get dressed now, then we can get the eggs, deal, Joe?'

He grins, 'Right, little one, it's a deal. Off you go, and Lily, try not to wake your mammy, she's obviously very tired?'

Lily nods.

Returning minutes later, fully dressed, she smiles sweetly, 'Mamma's fast asleep,' she tells Joe. 'So, is we going to get the eggs now?'

Concerned for safety of the eggs he suggests that Lily carries the basket there and he will carry it back, 'Is that a deal Lily?'

Excited, Lilibeth nods enthusiastically. 'Deal.'

'Good, then let's shake on it,' he says grinning.

Much to Lilibeth's delight, Joe takes her hand and shakes it, 'Deal agreed Lily.'

'Deal agreed,' she replies beaming.

Half an hour later, after helping to collect the eggs and feeding the chickens, at Joe's suggestion, Lily picks a bunch of flowers for her mother, in the hope of cheering Katie up.

It is time to return to the cottage. Lily proudly carrying her flowers and Joe pulling the cart, loaded with eggs, a churn of milk and more vegetables.

Just as they reach the door it flies open and Katie dashes out, ashen faced and highly agitated. She scoops Lilibeth up in her arms, 'Oh thank God, Lilibeth! Are you all right darling? Where have you been? You scared to death when I woke up and realised that you were gone!'

This time the shoe is on the other foot. It's Joe's turn to feel embarrassed, as if Katie hadn't enough worries, on her lovely shoulders. 'Christ Katie, I'm so sorry, I just didn't think.' He apologises profusely. 'We shouldn't have gone off without letting you know. It was a stupid thing to do, I swear I didn't mean to worry you.'

Katie shakes her head and sniffs, 'No harm done I suppose, it's just that, when I woke up and she was gone, I was absolutely terrified... I thought... I thought...' She clams up, hugging Lilibeth even closer. With her daughter held safely in her arms again, relief is written all over her face.

Lilibeth on the other hand is more than happy with her early morning jaunt. 'Look what I got you Mamma, pretty flowers. Joe said they would cheer you up and make you smile, coz he says you got a beautiful smile,' she says as she thrusts them under her mother's nose.

Katie's face turns bright red. Whether it's relief at finding Lilibeth, his compliment, or the bunch of flowers that were unceremoniously pushed into her face, Joe can't be sure, but Katie's laughing and crying at the same time. 'I reckon I should cook us all a decent breakfast, by way of an apology. I'm really sorry Katie,' he says, anxious to make amends for causing her even more unnecessary strife.

'Thank you, but there's really no need,' she shrugs.

But Joe is adamant. 'I said, I'm cooking.'

Unsurprisingly, last night seems to have knocked the stuffing out of Katie. Halfway through breakfast, he realises she isn't eating, 'No appetite this morning, Katie?' he inquires, looking concerned.

But she's deep in thought, her mind very obviously elsewhere, the strained look on her face tells him that she is still extremely upset.

Joe shakes his head, despite last night's revelations, dozens of questions were yet to be answered, he is still none the wiser as to why they had turned up at Sweet Briars apparently homeless and living rough in his barn and in such a terrible state. Everything about Katie is one huge mystery, but he isn't about to start pushing her for answers, most definitely not, after last night.

Normally he would have been hard at work in the spinney at this time of the day, yet here he is, mid-morning, hanging around the scullery deep in thought. Katie and Lilibeth's welfare troubling him deeply, they deserve some happiness. If only there was something constructive, he could do? It was true that he didn't yet know the reason why they were seemingly homeless, but the more he thought about it, the more it made sense to him that they should stay on here, at Sweet Briars. A young woman and her child should have a decent roof over their heads, so why not here? Until he heard differently, the solution seems obvious to him, they appear in need of a home, and he was willing to offer his, without questions and obligations of course. It would give them some space, time to sort themselves out.

As he sits watching Katie prepare the vegetables for their midday meal, he wonders what she might think of his suggestion. Maybe he should broach the subject now? On the other hand, perhaps he would be better off making less of an issue of his offer, take them out for a long stroll in the fresh air after they'd eaten, then drop his proposal into the conversation, sort of matter-of-factly.

If he's totally honest, he could well afford to put off his work for a bit, the weather has been kind to him, spring had been unusually warm and pleasant, enabling him to build up his stocks quite considerably, so why not, he reasons? After all, it would be quite a while before Stan will turn up to collect his wood and deliver his next lot of supplies.

An idea forms in his head. Yes, that's it, he decides, I'll take them both out for the afternoon, after the trauma of last night we could all do with some fresh air and happy relaxation, plus it would be an ideal time to chat with Katie about my offer, but first things first, I'll get cleaned up and then I'll sit Katie down and suggest my plans for a nice trip out together this afternoon. His decision is made.

Behind the out-house, well out of sight of his female guests, Joe had a thorough strip wash, including washing his hair, then draping the towel around his neck, props an old, mottled mirror on the toilet window ledge, built up a lather on his brush, after vigorously sharpening his cutthroat on the strap, he begins shaving, trying hard to concentrate on the job in hand. But the eyes that look back at him in the mirror are not his own eyes at all, they are the sad, alluring pale blue eyes that are glistening with tears, Katie's tears. His mind drifts back to the moment his supposedly blissfully, peaceful and uncomplicated life was well and truly highjacked. The ensuing outcome had undoubtedly had an incredulous effect on him. It felt like he'd been struck by a lightning bolt, when out the blue yonder, and without any hint of foresight, these two desperate strangers had literally walked into his life, and from that moment on, everything he has ever known and been seemingly content within his life, has changed entirely, quite literally overnight. The unexpected arrival of the pair had simply turned his world upside down and even more astonishing, he now found himself, most surprisingly, relishing the sort of family orientated domesticity that had been foisted upon him, just like that! It was ridiculously surreal. As he rubs the moisture from his freshly washed hair, those beautiful bright eyes, misted with fear and misery, are looking back at him, it wounds his heart.

Thinking about it, if he was totally honest with himself, he'd have to admit he had not taken this young woman and child into his home solely as an act of gentlemanly chivalry, for surely any decent human being would have done the same in that situation. Oh no, there was far more to it than that, because the moment he'd first laid eyes on Katie, this extremely attractive enigma of a beautiful young woman had captivated his lonely being in an instant, he'd felt inexplicably drawn to her, leaving him awash with a strong compulsion to protect both Katie and her delightful young daughter, no matter what!

Which was why, on this bright sunny day, he was determined to try and eliminate her misery with an enjoyable, relaxing afternoon out, for all of them. Smiling to himself he hums cheerfully as he swishes the razor clean in the bowl, pats his smooth jaw dry, then puts on a clean shirt.

Uplifted, Joe enters the scullery full of good intentions, only to find Katie, looking somewhat subdued, stood at the sink with her hands submerged in the soapsuds, absentmindedly toying with the dishes.

'Ahem, um Katie, I hope you don't mind me asking, but have you made any plans for the rest of the day?'

The crockery shatters into little pieces as it crashes to the flagstone floor, Katie whirls round to face him. 'You w...want us to leave... today?' she stutters. Strangely, his look is one of mortification, even Lily drops her doll open mouthed, staring up at her mother, looking highly vexed.

Joe's sudden, forthright blunt question has caught Katie by complete surprise, her heart sinks, it certainly hadn't occurred to her that he was expecting them to leave today. Frowning she bites her lower lip, wishing with all her heart that she hadn't been so foolish last night, to talk so openly, telling him so much about herself. Now she was going to have to pay for her stupidity. 'Plans, today...? Oh yes, I see what you mean, I um... well no, not yet exactly.' she whispers meekly, 'but of course, I do understand why Joseph. Please believe me when I say we are both so very grateful to you for the hospitality you've shown us, you've been so generous and kindness itself,' she tells him, her voice quivering, 'Joseph, I feel I must apologise to you, I'm so sorry I burdened you with my problems last night. I shouldn't have said anything. I realise it's not your concern,' she takes a deep breath, 'and yes, of course, I'm aware that we cannot impose ourselves on your hospitality any longer, so indeed, we will be leaving later today.'

Both stunned and horrified at her reply, Joe's eyebrows shoot up in disbelief, his jaw drops open, this is not the response he was expecting!

Slowly it dawns on him that Katie has completely misconstrued his good intentions with his ill-phrased inquiry. Glancing at Lily he lowers his voice and grabs Katie's arm, 'Leaving…! What do you mean, you're leaving, Katie? Hey, just hold on a minute, that's not why I asked about your plans for today. Good grief! I most certainly wasn't suggesting you leave at all!'

Lily is glaring at him intensely, full of mistrust, he lowers his voice further, 'Listen to me Katie, please. The reason I asked was, I was hoping we could talk, um privately. I was merely going to suggest that we all had a nice afternoon out together.' But Lily is eyeing him suspiciously, so he moves closer to Katie, lowering his voice to barely a whisper, he says, 'I was merely going to suggest we could go out, the three of us, get some fresh air, enjoy the weather, relax and maybe take a picnic with us. I also want to talk to you about your housing predicament. You see I've been giving the matter a great deal of thought and I hope I may have found a positive, viable solution that will benefit all of us,' he explains.

Looking confused Katie breathes a small sigh of relief. 'I um… I don't understand, Joseph.'

Noticing Lily is giving him a definite look of mistrust, he decides it might be better to discuss the pros and cons of his offer out of the earshot of young Lily. 'Katie, maybe it might be better if we discuss the situation in the garden, preferably alone.' he suggested quietly.

With no objection from Katie, he gently takes her arm to lead her outdoors, but Lily, who likens to her mother's forever present shadow, sticking close by her at all times, overhears the conversation and springs to her feet, 'Where are you going with my mammy?'

Thwarted by the youngster, Joe has to think quick on his feet, 'Where are we going? Ah yes, I thought we might go to the vegetable garden, the weather's been so good, I thought we might even find a few ripe strawberries,' he tells her. 'Do you like strawberries, Lily?'

Lily's eyes light up, 'Mmm, yes, lovely.'

'Good,' he says searching for the assortment of baskets that are normally stacked on top of the log basket and had now, apparently vanished, 'Do you know where the baskets are, Katie?'

Although Katie appears to give off a casual air of matter-of-factness, inside her stomach is churning so badly she feels she might be sick, she's wondering what exactly he wants to talk to her about, did he want them to leave or not?

'Katie?' he says lightly touching her arm. 'The baskets, can you give me a clue where you've put them?'

'The baskets? Oh yes, sorry, Joe, they're in the larder, bottom shelf, right at the back.'

He disappears into the larder and comes out grinning, 'There we go Lily, the small one is for you and the bigger one is for me and your mammy.'

Beaming broadly Lilibeth places her doll in her basket and slips her little hand into Joe's, 'Come on, Mammy, let's get some strawberries with Joe.'

Together they set off. Lily skipping merrily beside Joe, excited at the prospect of another adventure.

Joe is hoping that Katie will hear him out, see sense and accept his offer. But she's dragging her heels a few steps behind them, filled with foreboding, dreading what Joe is going to say.

'I hope the birds haven't eaten the strawberries,' says Joe as they walk.

Lilibeth, who was now leading the way, impatiently tugging Joe along behind her, stops suddenly, 'I hope there's lots and lots, coz my mammy makes the loveliest fruit pies and very tasty jam puddings and pots of jam and jam tarts and...'

'Hey up child, take a breath Lily.' He shakes his head, 'I don't know, you're a right little chatterbox and besides, all this talk of food is making me hungry,' he says turning back to Katie. 'I reckon your Lily could talk the hind legs off a donkey. The only difference is your Lily doesn't have a tail, and big pointy ears,' he throws back his head laughing.

For a fleeting moment Katie forgets her troubles and giggles.

The talk of a donkeys' ears puts a predictably quizzical look on Lilibeth's face. She opens her mouth, but before he can utter word, he grabs her from behind and lifts her up, sitting her on his shoulders. 'There you go little half-pint; you'll see a lot more up there.'

Beside herself with joy, Lily is delighted, 'Look at me, Mammy, I'm up in the sky, flying like the birdies!' she says, flapping her arms as if flying.

In a panic, Katie runs up behind them, 'Hold on tight sweetheart, please, you might fall!'

'Hey, lighten up Katie, she's fine, I've got her, she's perfectly safe,' says Joe, 'If flying like a bird makes her happy then let her enjoy it, she deserves some fun bless her.'

Joe's last quip miraculously lifts the tension that Katie feels, she relaxes a little.

Setting Lily gently to the ground, Joe waves his arms, 'Shoo, go on, clear off!' he claps his hands, 'Go on, shoo!' Dozens of assorted birds squawk their protests, flapping their wings and flying up into the many trees, surrounding the vegetable garden.

Surveying the damage, Joe shakes his head, 'Would you believe it, the greedy little devils have been at my fruit again! Oh dear, I suppose it's my fault, I need a new scarecrow, I should have replaced it when the old one fell to bits last year.' Then inspiration strikes him, 'Hey Lily, are you any good at making scarecrows?'

'Don't know,' she says shrugging her shoulders and pouting.

'Well, if it's all right with your mammy then perhaps you can help me make new one?' he suggests, looking at Katie for her approval.

Before Katie can speak, Lilibeth is jumping up and down with excited anticipation, 'Can I, Mammy, oh please, can I?' she pleads.

Looking uncomfortable, Katie is only too aware that the subject of their accommodation is far from resolved, for all she knows they could be trudging aimlessly through the countryside later that day, so now is not the time to make rash promises. 'I don't know darling, I'm going to have to think about it, I'm sorry.'

Lilibeth pouts her lips disappointed, looking dejectedly to Joe, hoping he'd say something to sway her mother.

Changing the subject, Joe spots some ripened strawberries, 'Hey, you're in luck, see, some red strawberries,' he points out. 'Take your basket and pick some, but only the red ones, or you'll get tummy ache.'

Unsmiling he looks at Katie and nods his head the direction of an old dilapidated wooden bench, strolling over he sits, patting the place invitingly beside him, saying, 'Please Katie, come join me.'

Dubiously Katie does as she's asked. They sit side by side, watching as Lilibeth crouches with her basket, happily searching for the ripened strawberries.

Turning to Katie, Joe takes her hand in his, his eyes looking directly into hers. Clearing his throat, he begins, 'We need to talk seriously, Katie. Look, I realise I don't know the whole story as to why you both ended up here, roughing it in my barn of all places, but don't worry my dear, I certainly won't be asking you to enlighten me again, I promise you.'

Preparing to hear the worst, her pretty face is now wearing a worried frown. Withdrawing her trembling hand, she's about to intervene when Joe holds up his palms, saying firmly, 'Now just hold on a minute Katie. Please, hear me out.' He dithers a bit, he hadn't yet worked out the best way to put forward his suggestion. Deciding the best way is to take the bull by the horns he clears his throat and takes a deep breath, 'Look Katie, what is clear to me is that you are both in need of a decent roof over your heads and I think I have a sensible offer to put to you. But before any more is said on the subject, I do I realise that we are all but strangers, so I want to tell you a few things about myself first, I think it's necessary, so if you'll bear with me?' he pauses, taking hold of her hands again looking straight into her eyes.

Lowering is voice he continues. 'I have spent my entire life here at Sweet Briars, twenty-six years man and boy. I have my own highly successful wood business. In the past I ran the business with the assistance of Will, a family friend and hired help. He worked with me in the spinney and with the animals. Sadly, he died three years ago. Then it was just me and my dear mother.' Joe sighs, 'A little while ago my mother fell ill and within a couple of weeks, she died.' Joe sighs heavily again and shakes his head. 'That was just over three months ago, God rest her sweet soul.' He squeezes her hand, 'You see Katie, like you, I do know how hard to is to lose someone close to you. Anyway, since then I have lived here alone.' he explains, 'Not that it bothered me, I didn't particularly crave company, or so I thought. That was until now. Ahem.' he clears his throat again. 'So, believe me Katie, you and Lily turning up like you did, well you've both been like breath of fresh air blowing through the cottage,' he continues, 'It's as though you have opened my eyes and shown me what I'd been missing all these years. Katie, I love having you both here, I really enjoy your company, yours and little Lily's. So, the point I'm trying to make is, here I am, all alone, rattling around in that big old house of mine.' Gently he squeezes her hand again, 'Katie, it's blatantly obvious to me that you both need a proper home, a roof over your heads, and my house is plenty big enough, so I'm wondering if you would consider staying on here, you are both very welcome, but on a more permanent basis. That's if you'd be happy to stay of course?' He looks at Katie intensely, waiting for her to say something, willing her to agree to his proposal.

The response from Katie is silence whilst she mulls over what he'd said. Apart from his surprisingly wonderful, unexpected offer, she had to consider Joseph. Would he really be prepared to accept her young daughter running around his house, under his feet all day, every day, she's such a chatterbox? Though it is true they seemed to get on extremely well together.

Then there was Lilibeth to consider. No longer under the dictatorship of her vile father, in the short space of time that they'd been here, she had seen her daughter blossom. She had to admit that for the first time in her short life she appears to be genuinely happy and carefree. Then there's Joseph, there's no doubt his thoughtful and compassionate, understanding ways had come as a culture shock to her, he's so different to her husband, indeed, they were worlds apart. Joseph is always calm, never raising his voice or losing his temper, he also treats her with respect, and she loved the fact that he was more than happy to make lengthy conversations with both herself and her daughter, a revelation that she simply wasn't used to, she'd been shocked to learn that any man on God's earth could be so kind, considerate and caring as Joseph.

'Katie?' he breaks into her thoughts, 'Have you any thoughts on my offer? Would you like more time to think about it? Because if you do then that's fine by me,' he tells her.

Naturally, her instinct is to jump at his offer immediately, but being realistic she knows it isn't as simple as that. The first problem is the highly embarrassing matter of the necessary rent, she's completely penniless. Deep in thought, Katie bites her lip, when she considers the alternative to accepting his offer, she knows she has to be practical. Just how long did she think they could possibly last, walking the highways and byways and living rough off the land, she asked herself? Realistically, she was thinking ahead to the long freezing months of winter to come.

At the end of the day, Joe's offer is too tempting, 'I don't know what to say Joseph, do you really mean it?'

He smiled kindly, 'Indeed I do. So, what do you think?' he asks, his voice full of enthusiasm.

'I think… I think…' Katie grimaces.

He frowns, 'Oh dear, do I feel a 'but' coming on?'

Shrugging her shoulders, she looks at Joe, 'No, not exactly, though I'm afraid that accepting your wonderful offer isn't as straight forward as it seems Joseph. You see, if I'm honest, the truth is we are totally penniless, we simply can't afford to pay you rent.'

Taken aback, Joe looks shocked, 'Good grief Katie, I don't expect you to pay rent!' he shakes his head, 'My home will be your home, it's as simple as that.'

Blinking back a tear she gnaws her lip, 'I'm sorry Joseph, but I insist, we must pay our way.' She thinks for a moment, 'Perhaps, you would consider my doing all the housework, washing and cooking for you would be sufficient recompense, then maybe…? Like a housekeeper.'

Joe frowns, he knows she is stubborn and has her pride, 'Oh well, if you insist Katie, that's fine by me,' he agrees. 'Now, is that it?'

Taking a deep breath Katie leans closer and whispers, 'Thank you for your generous offer Joseph, we love it here, we really do, but I think, if we are to live here, then we need to talk Joseph. You see there are things about me that you should know before you decide if you really want us to stay.'

'Hum sounds ominous, Katie,' he mutters rubbing his chin. He looks at Lily, who having picked as many ripe strawberries that she can find, has obviously got bored and eaten the lot, Lily is now watching them both curiously, clearly interested in their conversation. 'I um, I think perhaps we should wait until a little someone goes to bed tonight before we talk any more, don't you?' he suggests.

'Yes, I suppose you're right, we'll talk later Joseph.'

The rest of the afternoon is spent digging, weeding, pulling and cutting vegetables and collecting logs, so by the evening, after they had eaten dinner, Lilibeth was so tired out she happily went to bed without protest.

Whilst Joe is in the garden having a strip wash, Katie sits anxiously waiting in the parlour, she'd promised to tell Joe everything tonight, though she wasn't looking forward to it, she still wasn't sure she could trust him. On the other hand, earlier today he had entrusted her with his frank innermost feelings, on the passing of his life-long friend Will and the oh so recent, sad death of his dear mother. He had also told her about his life's history at Sweet Briars. She couldn't help but feel a strong empathy with him. Joseph Markson, she decides, is indeed a one off, a rare breed of the male gender. He is clearly an honest, sensitive soul who speaks from his heart. She sighs. Now it's her turn to bring Joseph up to date concerning her past. She knows she must be brutally honest, then he can decide for himself if it's worth taking the risk and be prepared to allow them to stay at Sweet Briars, or not. It had to be Joe's choice.

Entering the room, Joe smiles at Katie, 'I've made up a tray with a pot of tea and some of your lovely biscuits,' he tells her, 'If you pour the tea, I'll light the fire, it's getting chilly.'

With the fire burning brightly, Joe lights the oil lamps and pulls the curtains, to make the room feel cosier, then they settle down to drink their tea.

Joe is the first to break the ice, 'Have you given any more thought to my offer, Katie?'

'Indeed, I have Joe, but like I said earlier, there are things about me that you need to know before we go any further on the subject,' she tells him nervously.

Lighting his pipe, he sits back, 'You know this really isn't necessary Katie,' he says, shaking his head, remembering how upset Katie had been, the previous night, 'and if it's going to upset you as much as it did last night then I would rather you didn't bother, there's no need for you to explain anything to me at all,' he says gently.

'I only wish that was true Joseph,' says Katie sighing, 'but what I'm about to tell you could um… could possibly change your mind about allowing us to stay here, so I feel obliged to put you in the picture, then it's up to you to decide,' she tells him bluntly.

'Hum, well if you insist, but I'm warning you now, if you get upset then that's it, finished, end of conversation!' he says firmly.

Nodding her head, Katie reluctantly agrees, she takes a deep breath to bolster herself and begins. 'You remember I told you about my mother's sudden passing, Joe?' Katie sighs deeply, 'Well I assume that Edward's party went ahead. I guess I was in shock so, at my own behest, I spent the entire evening alone in our cottage grieving and worrying how I could possibly pay for the rent and my Mamma's funeral etc. Anyway, fortunately for me, as with my father, the Barton-Smythe's paid for a simple funeral for my mother. Two days later, myself, and all the staff, attended the service and my mother was laid to rest with my beloved father in Saint Peter's Church cemetery, at Malvarney. Sadly, my parents would have no headstone, but at least they are reunited now,' she adds with a sad wistful look in her eyes. Shifting uneasily, she continues, 'After the funeral I returned to our cottage alone. An hour later, there was a knock at my door, naturally I took it for granted that Edward had come to comfort me, but no, I was so disappointed. In walked Sir Barton-Smythe looking stern. "Good afternoon, Miss Seymour," he greeted me, "I trust the funeral met with your satisfaction?" he asked me formally. I nodded my grateful approval. "Yes, sir, thank you, sir. I um, I thought, for a moment, you were Edward coming to see me, sir," I told him. "Ah yes, Edward, he has already returned to Oxford," he told me curtly. "Now, Miss Seymour, about the cottage, you must realise that this cottage goes with the job, so now, with your mother deceased you must vacate the cottage, forthwith," he declared impassively. As you can imagine, Joe, I was completely dumbstruck. "Leave here, sir! But where can I go sir? I have no family, no-one!" I protested, but the grim look on his face told me he meant every word. "Now, now, Miss Seymour," he continued, I have taken considerable time and trouble to make extensive inquiries on your behalf, and I have found you a position as a housekeeper. The poor chap lost his wife and child in childbirth, hence his need to fill the position. It's most fortunate indeed that you can start immediately, so I will send Jenkins along with packing cases shortly. Then at nine sharp tomorrow morning, Jenkins will bring the carriage to deliver you to your new employers' residence."

Listening intently, Joe could see Katie is becoming distressed again. Although her head is bowed low and he can't see her face, she is constantly wringing her hands and breathing heavily, her voice was getting quieter too. He leans forward and gently places his hand on her arm. 'Katie,' he says softly, 'you are doing really well my dear, but I think you should stop, just for a while. I'm going to make us a drink. You deserve a break.' He tells her.

In the scullery, whilst he heats a pan of milk, he mulls over what she'd told him. It seems obvious to him that this, sir bloody what's-his-name had realised that she was with child and heartlessly wanted to be rid of her as soon as possible. The bastard obviously had no principals, he concludes. He shakes his head, he worked out that Katie must have been just over sixteen when all this had happened.

Pouring the milk into the mugs he adds some brandy to both cups, he had a feeling they would both be needing fortification, very soon.

'Here Kate, I've made a hot drink, I um, I took the liberty of adding a drop of brandy, I hope that's all right,' he says handing her the mug and settling back in his armchair. 'Katie, listen to me, you know I am not really interested in your past, what's in the past stays in the past as far as I'm concerned, it's the future that really matters, so perhaps we should call it a day and leave it there,' he suggests kindly.

Looking serious she shakes her head and looks up at him, 'I only wish that was true Joseph, but as I explained earlier, if we are to accept your offer, then believe me, it's essential that I warn you of the possible implications of what you might be letting yourself in for, if we stay here,' she explains, placing her empty mug on the fire grate.

Intrigued by her profound statement he frowns and raises his palms, 'Fair enough Katie, have it your own way, I'm listening,' he tells her, shaking his head, exasperated.

'Thank you, Joseph, I really do feel it's necessary,' she says, licking her dry lips nervously, she swallows then carries on, 'With absolutely no choice and a heavy heart, I spent the night packing the few things that I possessed,' she carries on, 'I also wrote a lengthy letter to Edward. When morning came, the staff and of course, the Barton-Smythes were there to see me off. Just before we left, I approached the Master of the house and gave him Edward's letter, I asked him to see that Edward received it, he nodded and put it in his pocket. As we drove down the drive, all the staff waved and called out their good wishes to me, but I couldn't look back, Joe, I was leaving the only home that I had ever known.' Kate pauses to wipe her nose and dab her eyes then obstinately carries on, 'After a very lengthy journey we reached our destination, Jenkins pulled up in the farmyard. It took just minutes for him to unload my few possessions, then with a tip of his hat and a nod of his head he leaned down and whispered, "best of luck ducky, I reckon you're gonna to need it," and with that he was gone!'

Joe tries his best to stop her, but Katie's having none of it. 'Please, Joe, I've nearly finished,' she straightens her back and squares her shoulders. 'The next shock followed almost immediately when the door opened and this enormous, revolting, filthy man came out to meet me. He looked me bodily up and down and growled, "I take it yer the new housekeeper. Bring yer stuff in and I'll show you, yer room." I was petrified of him, Joseph. His voice was slurred, I could tell he was extremely drunk, he could barely stand up.' Katie lets out a long, drawn-out sigh, 'I would have given anything to turn tail and run-away Joseph, but it was hopeless, where could I go?' Suddenly Katie stands up she needs some air, 'I'm sorry, you'll have to excuse me for a minute, please, I need to go outside, I won't be long.'

He jumps to his feet, 'Hold on, I'll get you a candle.'

Taking advantage of the break, Joe rinses the cups and makes a pot of tea, adding more sustaining brandy to each cup. Whilst he prepares the tray, he is thinking hard, something in the back of his mind is troubling him, though he can't quite put his finger on it, he needs time to think.

As she returns, he hands her the cup of tea, 'You're looking tired Katie and it's very late. You're obviously finding it too much, I think we should call it a day?' he offers kindly, but she looks at him mulishly and straighten her shoulders. Being strong-willed, Katie decides that if she doesn't get it over with here and now, she can't face waiting for tomorrow, though she would have to be very careful not to mention her husband Albert by name, or even Penfold Grove, after all, Joe might well know of her husband and even worse, he could possibly be a friend or maybe a neighbour of his.

Determined, it's now or never, Katie braces herself, 'I'm sorry, I do realise it's getting late, Joe, but if you don't mind, I need to get it over and done with. So, if it's all right with you, I'll cut my story short. When I tell you why we are here, then I hope you'll understand the reasons why I'm so wary of accepting your generous offer.' She pauses, chewing her lip. 'Believe me, you really need to know, Joseph, then it's up to you to decide if you're prepared to allow us stay.'

Eyes rolling, Joe shakes his head, 'If you feel you really need to, it's entirely up to you, but I won't have you getting upset again.'

'I'm going to be completely honest with you,' she begins, her voice wavering, 'it's about when you found us, we were both homeless and desperate. The truth is we were running away from... from someone. You see the man in question is an extremely violent drunkard, and if, God forbid, he was to find us living here, with you, I dread to think what he'd do to you,' Katie bites her lower lip, 'and as for Lilibeth and I? To be perfectly frank, I'm certain that if he found us here, he wouldn't hesitate, he'd kill us both!' Katie shudders and clams up, the flood gates open, she weeps copiously.

Leaping to his feet, Joseph kneels before her and lifts her chin with his finger, 'Oh Katie, please don't cry.' Gently he pulls her to her feet, wrapping his comforting arms around her, holding her close, whispering, 'Hush Katie, this has all been too much for you,' he leads her to the sofa, 'Here, come, sit with me.'

Timidly she does as she's asked.

'In view of what you've told me. I think I can allay your fears, my dear. Please listen to me, I need to tell you about my property Katie, I hope it will set your mind at rest with regard to you both living here. I can assure you that the unsavoury man looking for you, will never find you both here,' he says softly.

Frowning Katie looks at Joe, 'How can you possibly know that Joseph? I'm telling you now, he won't stop looking until he finds us, and when he does...!' she says, her body shudders violently in his arms.

Lifting her chin, he looks into her eyes, his own eyes filled with warmth and compassion, 'You have no worries on that score Katie. You see I own almost eight hundred acres of land, including Sweet Briars. We're quite literally in the middle of nowhere. Besides, there's only one access to Briars, a mile long, narrow dirt track that leads here and nowhere else, so I never see passers-by, and I never have visitors, indeed my nearest neighbours are many miles away. Don't you see Katie? You will both be absolutely safe here with me, I give you my word.' he reassures her.

Then after a hasty afterthought quickly adds, 'Oh, I tell a lie. I do get one visitor, a chap normally comes roughly once a month or so, he brings my supplies and collects his wood order from me,' he admits, 'He's a really great, trustworthy bloke, I've known him all my life.'

Katie sighs, 'I knew you weren't telling me the truth Joseph,' she says despondently, 'that evening, when we were in your barn, I distinctly heard you talking to someone, so I know you get visitors,' she says shaking her head.

'Just hold on a minute Katie, listen to me please, I wasn't trying to miss-lead you, I honestly forgot.'

Sceptical Katie shrugs her shoulders.

'So why do I get a visitor, you may ask? Well after Will died, my mother was unable to travel to market, her joints were painful and swollen, and I couldn't possibly leave her here alone, so I did a deal with a pal, he would come here to collect his order of wood and bring my supplies at the same time, it's as simple as that.' he explains. 'Look Katie, if you are concerned that he might find out you're living here then I'll simply change my arrangement with him. You see there's really no need for him to come up here into the yard at all. In future, I will tell him to go straight to the spinney and meet me there, your paths never need to cross, I promise you.'

It all sounds so convincing to Katie, but nevertheless, there are other issues to consider. She had to admit that the whole dynamics of his home would change dramatically for him if they were to live there permanently. The one question remained; would Joseph be prepared to accept her daughter? Lilibeth could be hard work, what with her constant inquisitiveness and running around under his feet all day, could he cope with her?

'But Joe, what about Lilibeth, she can be so tiresome at times.'

Raising his hands, he interrupts her. 'Your daughter is a credit to you Katie, I think she's bright and amusing, I like her company as much as I appreciate yours. So, what do you think, will you say yes to my offer?'

Patiently he waits, the silence is deafening so he decides to intervene, 'The truth is, your turning up on my doorstep, has woken me up to the fact that I'm lonely Katie. I love having you both here, and if you agree to stay then I can wake up each day with a new purpose in life. Good company to share my days and evenings with, someone and something worthwhile to work for. Don't you see? If you say yes, then we all gain.' Adding seriously, 'You will always be safe with me Katie.' He gives her hand a light squeeze, encouraging her to accept his proposal.

There's no denying his sincerity, and at the end of the day she had to be practical for the sake of her daughter, what other choice did she have anyway?

Finally reassured and convinced he will keep his word, to protect them and keep them safe, she decides to put her trust in him. Her lips break into a beautiful smile, 'If you are quite sure, then yes, we'd love to stay Joseph, thank you.' Adding ominously, 'I only hope that you don't live to regret it.'

A wave of elation sweeps over him, 'That's wonderful Katie, my home is now your home too,' he pauses, looking serious, 'Just one more thing Katie. I want to make it absolutely clear to you, that if you ever want to leave Sweet Briars, for whatever reason, you are perfectly free to go, you are under no obligation to me to stay. Do you understand what I'm saying?'

'Yes, I do Joseph, oh I'm so very grateful, I think you're a lovely, big-hearted and very generous man,' she says, and without thinking, leans forward and impulsively pecks him on the cheek.

Blushing, Joe's cheeks pink, 'Katie.' He beams, 'Yes well, tomorrow is a new start for all of us!' He yawns and stretches, he's glowing, he feels ten feet tall, 'You know it's getting late Katie, you don't need your beauty sleep, but I certainly do, I have to be up at first light. I'll see to the fire and wash up the couple of cups, you get yourself off to bed,' He suggests.

Katie smiles, 'If you're quite sure? I am tired, I'll say goodnight then Joseph, and once again, thank you.'

'I'll see you in the morning,' he replies, 'Goodnight Katie, sleep well.'

After damping down the fire he sits, going over all that Katie had told him. She'd said she was running away from a violent drunkard, which accounts for those terrible cuts and bruises when he'd found her, but if he was honest, she'd told him little else. He clenches his fists, if he could get his hands on that bloody Barton-Smythe bloke, his cowardly son, or the drunken bastard that she'd spoken of, whichever one it was, given the opportunity he would make sure they'd never take advantage or abuse a young girl, ever again. However, something is still nagging him, at the back of his mind, but try as he may, he can't figure it out. There seems to be a huge gap between being forced from her home when her mother died, then being dumped on a complete strangers' doorstep, he figures it was her last employer that was almost certainly responsible for her turning up here in such a terrible state. It was a mystery that was to remain unanswered for a while.

With his early morning chores completed, Joe returns to the cottage to find the table laid and Katie cooking breakfast. 'Good morning girls, I'll just get cleaned up, then after we've eaten, I'm going to make a start on building that new scarecrow in the barn.' he declares. 'Can Lily give me a hand Katie?' he asks tentatively.

Wide eyed, Lilibeth, stares imploring her mother to say yes.

After a moment or two Katie agrees, with the proviso that there are a couple of rules that her daughter will have to adhere to. 'Only if you promise you will stay with Joseph at all times, and you don't run off, then yes, you can.'

Squealing with delight, Lilibeth jumps up and down with joy, 'I will, Mammy, me build a scary crow, whoopie!'

'I have lots of baking to do this morning so I'm trusting you to look after her, Joseph,' she says to Joe, looking stern.

'I won't let her out of my sight for a second,' he promises.

'All right, Joe, thank you. She turns to her daughter, 'Lilibeth, make sure you do exactly as Joe tells you, and when I've finished baking, I'll bring you something to eat.'

As he works, Joe encourages Lily to help him make and stuff the scarecrow and by lunchtime they sit, proudly admiring their handiwork.

The scullery has been hot and stuffy, as Katie strolls to the barn she inhales the fresh country air, appreciating the breeze as it cools her body. Approaching the barn door, she stops, hearing the sound of Lilibeth giggling and Joe laughing raucously as they chatter away, it warms her heart.

'Mammy, Mammy, look what we made!' says Lilibeth, dragging her mother over to inspect their morning's work.

'Oh my, what a handsome scarecrow, I must say you've both done a wonderful job.' Katie is genuinely impressed.

'And Joe said we could put him in the vegetable garden when you get here, didn't you?' she says looking up at Joe.

He nods, 'If it's all right with your mammy, then why not?'

'But I've brought your lunch,' she says. Lilibeth looks disappointed so Katie relents, 'Oh well, I suppose we could take it with us and have a picnic in the vegetable garden.'

To the joy of Lilibeth, the scarecrow is proudly erected in the centre of the vegetable patch, 'So what is we going to call him?' Lily asks Joe.

He looked puzzled, 'Call him? I don't know that scarecrows have names sweetheart.'

Lilibeth's face is a picture, 'Course he's got a name, everybody's got a name,' she insists.

After a moment or two, Joe has a brainwave, 'How about we call him Windy Will?'

Looking inquisitive Lilibeth grins, 'That's a funny name, why call him Windy Will then?'

A smile creeps over Joe's face and he chuckles, quite frankly he was wondering where on earth he had suddenly acquired such patience to deal with this perpetually curious pip squeak of a child. 'Simple, I used to know someone called Will, he was a very good friend of mine. See, the scarecrow is wearing Will's old clothes and hat. And Windy? That's because hopefully, the wind will blow all the strings around his hat and rattle all the bits of tin, scaring the birds away.

Unable to come up with anything better, Lily claps her hands, 'I like Windy Will, I think it's a lovely name,' she says approvingly.

After enjoying their leisurely lunch, it's decided they will all help with the weeding in the vegetable garden and replenish the larder with more vegetables.

Deep down, Joe couldn't be more delighted that the girls were staying on a more permanent basis, when he considers that until recently, he had become a virtual recluse. Now, with their arrival, he found that he was rapidly becoming pleasantly adjusted to the joys of family life and all it entails. The only fly in the ointment is the cause of them turning up in such a dreadful state in the first place. To some degree she had inadvertently let the cat out of the bag already, intentionally or otherwise, he now knew that out there somewhere, was the cowardly lowlife that thought he had the God given right to abuse an innocent young girl and rule her with his heavy fist! Joe decides to say nothing, but to bide his time, then perhaps one day?

After several hours, the handcart is groaning with the weight of the produce, Joe is about to call it a day when a startled cry from Lily draws his attention towards Katie, she's clinging desperately to the cart for support, swaying as if she's about to collapse.

Flinging the spade aside he dashes over, sliding his arm around her waist, supporting her as she sinks to the ground in a heap, he carries her over to a bench so that they can sit.

'Katie! What happened. Are you hurt?' he asks, grave concern written all over his face.

Dazed, Katie clings to his arm trying to steady herself.

'Are you ill Katie?' he repeats, 'What happened, did you hurt yourself? Lily, be a sweetheart, come and sit with you mother while I'll go and get some cold water,' he says calmly.

Looking deathly pale, Katie sweeps her hair from her face, trying to pull herself together, 'No, please, Joe, don't make a fuss, it's nothing. I'm perfectly fine thank you.'

'My poor mammy is always falling on the floor,' proffers Lilibeth.

Alarm spreads over his face, 'Always falling... Katie?' he looks at her, searching for answers. When she'd collapsed, he'd automatically surmised that she had hurt herself, but Lily had inferred that it was a regular occurrence. 'Katie, tell me, is there something I should know?' he asks anxiously.

Feeling embarrassed, she averts her eyes from his concerned gaze, how could she possible tell him of her torrid past and of the very personal women's problems that she must suffer, as a consequence of her vile husband's filthy demands?

Tidying her skirt, Katie shakes her head, forcing a smile to dismiss his worrying, 'I'm fine, Joe, really I am. It was hot in the scullery and this afternoon... the sun is so hot, I suppose I've been over doing it,' she says, by way of an explanation.

Not entirely convinced by her justification, he decides not to press her, not here, not now, and most definitely not in front of young Lily. Then a shocking thought occurs to him, that she might well be pregnant!

Colour gradually returns to Katie's face, the enforced rest and cool water has fortified her, she appears to be fine again. 'Oh my, would you look at that lot on the cart, I'll be baking and bottling for a week or more, with a good summer there will be more than enough fruit and vegetables to see us through a long hard winter.'

Secretly pleased that Katie is implying that she is intending to stay long term by declaring her intention to preserve enough food to see them through the winter, Joe's spirits rise. He stands, 'If you feel up to it, I think we should call it a day, we can all go back to the cottage together,' he declares.

Walking homeward, Lilibeth latches onto Joe, doing her best to help push the cart, with Joe doing his best to let her think she's helping.

Katie, somewhat amused, tags alongside them, listening with interest as the unlikely pair laugh and chatter nine to the dozen. Lilibeth has so obviously taken a shine to Joe, and he appears more than happy to play along with her. It's as if they had forged a comfortable, natural bond between them. She can't help but wonder about Joseph. There can be no denying that he is an extremely handsome young man, he is lean and very muscular and speaks with an enchanting, easy to listen to, deep husky voice. He is both affable and considerate, with a really generous heart. It seemed inconceivable to her that some lucky lady had not yet caught his eye, settled him into marriage in his lovely cottage and produced many children, his children. He appears to be a natural family man, who clearly gets on so well with children.

Now her curiosity is aroused. It raises many questions about Joseph. Had there been someone in his past? Was there someone even now? Whilst spring cleaning she had discovered a room next to the parlour, a pretty bedroom with a bed a chest of drawers, pretty pink and green floral curtains, with a bedspread to match, it was a lovely feminine room, but as he'd made no mention of this particular room, she had decided to leave well alone, after all, it was not for her to pry into his affairs. Nevertheless, she couldn't help but wonder about its occupant.

Katie smiles to herself, with the exception of her best friend's son, nineteen-year-old Freddie and dear Edward of course, all the men she'd ever known were in their sixties and seventies, all with bent workworn bodies, little or no hair and rugged weather worn faces. But Joseph? He's so very different, he is young, he has a fine head of thick long wavy hair with unruly curls that flop over his forehead, his beautiful deep blue eyes are pleasurably enticing, somehow, they seemed to be able to talk to her intimately, his chest is sculptured and golden from hours spent in the sun. Katie feels her colour rising, as unfamiliar feelings engulf her. Closing her eyes, she inhales the fresh country air, after more years than she cares to remember, she feels content, happy, safe and at peace, she knows they were more than fortunate to have come across Joseph Markson and Sweet Briars.

Joe finds Katie sat deep in thought in the fireside chair, 'Hey, you're miles away, Katie, are you feeling any better?' he asks, 'I'm afraid Lily is so exhausted she's fallen asleep on the sofa, maybe she'd be better off in bed,' he suggests.

Katie smiles, 'You're right of course, Joe. Bless her, she's had such a busy and exciting day, thanks to you. If you wouldn't mind warming a drop of milk for her, I'll give her a wash and get her changed, then perhaps you would carry her up to bed for me?'

He grins, nodding, 'It will be my pleasure, Katie.'

Conscious that in less than two weeks his mate will be calling for his order of wood, he explains that he'd neglected his work for too long, asking if she would mind if he went to work tomorrow, adding if she didn't feel well enough, he would be happy to put off his work for another day or so.

Feeling guilty, Katie is embarrassed, she knows he's obviously thinking of earlier when she'd collapsed. 'Why of course you must go Joseph, we'll be fine,' she insists brightly, 'besides, we have plenty to do here!'

Unconvinced, Joe shakes his head, 'I'm not so sure about that, when you collapsed this afternoon... it really worried me. What if it happens again and I'm not here?'

Not feeling able to confide in him the very personal reason why she'd collapsed, she has to think on her feet, 'I can assure you that it won't happen again, Joe, I was baking in the hot scullery all morning and then working out in the sun, it all got too much, I promise I'll take it easy, so please don't worry about me.'

In order to avoid any more of his probing questions, Katie declares she is tired and needs an early night and says goodnight.

Disappointed, Joe has been looking forward to their time alone this evening, reluctantly he bids her goodnight and settles himself in his fireside chair. Deep in thought, at the back of his mind, he still has the unsettling notion that she might possibly be pregnant.

After completing his early morning tasks, he returns to find Katie is up, Lily's sat at the table and the breakfast is ready.

'Are you sure you'll be all right, if I go to work today Katie?' he asks as they share the washing up.

Katie insists she'll be fine.

Very well then,' he sighs, 'I'll go, but I'll pop back at lunch time, to make sure you're all right,' he warns her, as he pulls on his jacket and steps into his boots, 'Oh, and one more thing Katie, before I go I want you to promise me that you'll take things easy, get yourselves out of the house, maybe sit in the garden, with Lily,' he says, his expression serious.

Knowing that if it happens yet again, she'll be forced to explain to him the real reason why she keeps passing out, she readily agrees. 'We will, Joe, please, don't worry about us.'

As he closes the door, he hears Katie scolding her daughter, 'Lilibeth, you really shouldn't have told Joe that Mammy keeps fainting, that's a private matter, between you and I.'

Now he's convinced more than ever that she was with child, and it troubles him deeply.

The next ten days fly by. All three happily settle into a comfortable routine, getting to know each other, each enjoying the other's company.

Joe went to work every day and Katie and Lilibeth relaxed, feeling more comfortable and settled in their new surroundings.

Katie deliberately organises a routine, doing the necessary household chores, including the washing and cooking, but now she's taking great care not to overdo things.

In the evenings, with Lily safely tucked up in bed, they would sit and unwind together in the parlour, both enjoying each other's company, with affable conversation about their day.

'If you don't mind my saying, you look tired tonight, Joe,' Katie comments. 'You work too many hours. After all, you're up and out working before dawn and you're outside in all weathers.' she points out.

Smiling, Joe nods his head in agreeance, 'You're probably right but I'm afraid it's a necessity, the animals need tending to, come rain or shine,' he says, adding, 'Huh, it's not just me you know, you work far too hard yourself, so I think it's time we all had a break, a nice relaxing day out together.'

Sitting bolt upright Katie panics, 'A day out, but where?'

'Hey, calm down, I was only suggesting I show you around the place, I thought we might take some food with us, there's a lovely shady spot down by the stream, we could eat there, it's so peaceful, I know you'll both love it. So, what do say Katie?'

Saying nothing Katie stands, collects the cups and takes them through to the scullery. Joe follows behind her.

Stood by the sink she starts to wash the cups, Joe stands close behind her, 'Katie, what's up, why don't you want to go out, don't you trust me?' he whispers, 'You know I'll look after you both.'

She swallows, for some strange reason his closeness and soft husky voice stirs butterflies low in her stomach, and she feels dizzy, she can feel his warm breath close to her neck.

'Come on Katie, be sensible, what harm can it do?'

Unable to justify a good reason as to why they shouldn't go out, she turns to face him, noting the mischievous glint in his eyes and the hint of a smile dancing on his lips. Katie gulps, 'Um… I don't know, maybe we could have a nice picnic in the garden?' she suggests tentatively.

Shaking his head, Joe shrugs he can understand her reluctance to go far, 'If that's what you really want, then the garden will be fine, I guess.' But he doesn't move.

Trembling she turns back to the sink. Sensing he's still stood so close behind her she's becoming flustered, the colour rising in her cheeks. She dries her hands on her pinafore, 'Um… I'm um… it's getting late, Joe, I think I should get off to bed, I'm tired,' she says, not daring to stay in his company any longer.

Disheartened he shrugs his shoulders, 'Oh? As you wish,' he sighs, 'fair enough, I'll say goodnight then Katie, I'll see you in the morning.'

'Yes, goodnight, Joe.' she croaks shakily. Convinced he'd noticed her flushed face and trembling hands, she needed to distance herself and escape to the sanctuary of the bedroom.

As she lay in bed staring at the ceiling, she pictures Joe and her heart lurches. It's uncanny, one look from him seemed to dispel all her misgivings of men, she resolves there and then to get a grip on herself, and forget her fanciful thoughts, or they might well find themselves homeless again.

To Katie's relief, they come down to an empty scullery, a pan of porridge is left simmering on the stove and the table laid for breakfast.

After a quick tidy, she washes and hangs out the sheets, next she sweeps and scrubs the floors and polishes everywhere, Finally Katie and Lilibeth have a bath and change their clothes.

Mindful that Joe would be home soon and expecting a dinner she decides to fry last night's left-over potatoes and greens to make bubble and squeak, to accompany the remainder of yesterday's chicken. Lilibeth helps by laying a blanket on the grass outside and set out the cutlery along with a jar of Katie's chutney.

Sat at the table, Lilibeth watches as Katie plates up the dinner.

Joe enters and beams at Lily, 'Hello little lady,' patting her on the head. 'Mmm, that smells good Katie, I'm starving. I um, I'd better go outside and have a wash,' he tells her, grabbing a towel and taking the bowl, 'won't be long.' he says disappearing outside.

'Here, you'll need this, Joe,' she calls after him, handing over a freshly laundered shirt.

Carving the chicken on the draining board Katie glances out of the window, she gasps, for a fleeting moment she catches sight of Joseph, stripped completely naked, he's stood shaving. She drops her head and closes her eyes, her pulse is racing as an exciting, tightening, grabs her, low in her stomach. Totally distracted, the knife slips and slices into her finger, she cries out.

Seeing the blood, Lilibeth starts screaming, 'Mammy! Joe! Where are you? Mammy's bleeding!'

Hearing Lily's distressed cry, he grabs a towel, hastily wrapping it around his hips and runs inside, 'Christ Katie, what have you done? Here, let me see,' he inspects the cut and breathes a sigh of relief, 'You're very lucky, it's not too deep,'

Katie recoils, quickly withdrawing her hand, bowing her head in modesty, closing her eyes.

It dawns on him that Katie is shocked at his state of undress, 'Um, oh bloody hell, I'm so sorry about this, I won't be a minute.' He dashes outside and pulls on his trousers.

Returning to the scullery he fills a jug with water, adds some salt and plunges her hand into the jug, 'Keep it there Katie, I'll find something to wrap it.'

Bandaging her finger, the closeness of his naked torso makes Katie tremble and her heart pounds uncontrollably, try as she may, she can't erase the sight of him stood completely naked in the garden.

He picks up on her awkwardness, 'There we go, all sorted. Hey Katie, you're shaking,' he points out, he's concerned, 'You're not going to faint again, are you?' he asks softly.

Breathing rapidly Katie tries desperately to compose herself, she shakes her head, 'No, no. of course not.' she stutters, 'Um… thank you for bandaging my finger, Joe.' She attempts to stand, 'I… I must see to the bubble and squeak, it's… it's st-starting to burn,' she stutters, anxious to distance herself, from his close proximity.

'Oh no you don't young lady,' he says firmly, 'I'll do that. Get yourself outside in the garden with Lily, I can dish up the food.'

Grateful when he brings out the food, Joe has put on his shirt, Katie tries to calm herself down, but she's still shocked and try as she may, she can't get the vision of Joe, stood stark naked in the garden out of her head, it makes for an uncomfortable mealtime.

Realisation that Katie had almost certainly spotted him naked through the window he curses himself for being so careless. It's obvious he'd embarrassed her. It was the last thing he intended, he makes up his mind to apologise to her when Lily is in bed and assure her it will never happen again.

He does his best to divert their conversation to more trivial and mundane matters. 'You're a wonderful cook Katie,' he says. 'You must tell me when we need more supplies, we must be running low.'

'Yes, well I'm afraid that's the last of the butter, Joe. In the past I had a churn at my disposal,' she explains, keeping her eyes lowered from his gaze.

'Humm, your wish is my command, my dear,' Joe declares, smirking. 'For what it's worth, I just happen to have a butter churn, so if you'd accompany me tomorrow morning, I can show it to you, mind you, it must be three years since my mam used it, but if it's any good I'll bring it back here.'

Katie looks at Joe and nods bashfully, 'Lovely, that will be a great help, thank you.'

Half an hour after Lilibeth had been settled in bed, Katie finds herself sat alone with Joe in the parlour.

No matter how hard she tries, she simply cannot erase the sight of him in the garden completely naked, she's unable to look him in the eye. Somehow, that moment had stirred uncontrollable feelings, emotions that she had never felt before, it's all so confusing. She knows it isn't embarrassment that she feels, but a strange, overwhelming feeling of longing, an outlandish feeling of desire for him. She had to distance herself. Licking her dry lips, she announces she is tired and needs an early night.

'Before you go up, I really need to talk to you Katie,' he says softly, leaning towards her, he knows they should talk about the situation.

Panicking she stands abruptly, 'I'm really sorry, I must go.' She says, her face bright red, she flees up the stairs.

All too aware that he'd needlessly embarrassed her earlier, he curses himself, 'Shit, how could I have been so bloody careless?' he mumbles, the trouble is, he's just not used to having company, let alone a woman. Now he's frustrated that he'd lost the opportunity to apologise for embarrassing her. Adding logs to the fire, he washes and shaves.

With his ablutions finished, he retires to his bed, his thoughts turning to earlier, to Katie and her reaction to seeing him naked in the garden, regretting he'd been so thoughtless.

After tending the animals, Joe enters the scullery. 'Morning girls,' he greets them cheerily, 'Any chance of a quick cup of tea before we go out Katie?'

Avoiding his gaze Katie nods and makes a fresh pot of tea.

'Is we going somewhere then?' asks Lilibeth.

'Yes, little lady. We're going to find my butter churn so that we can make some butter. Have you finished your breakfast?'

Lily rubs her tummy, 'All gone, I had porridge with some of my mamma's lovely jam.'

'Good,' said Joe, 'never mind the tea, we'll get off.'

Lily sits happily on Joe's shoulders as he guides them through the grounds, past the vegetable garden, through a sheltered walled garden until they reach yet another sprawling unkempt garden.

Katie's pleasantly surprised, there must be at least a dozen or more various fruit trees, she notes that they are heavily laden with young fruit.

Partially hidden by tall weeds and brambles she spots several clumps of rhubarb, a large patch of mint, some parsley and other useful herbs.

At the top corner of the garden there's a dilapidated old shed with the door hanging off and the tin roof partially caved in. For a fleeting, sickening moment she catches her breath, it reminds her of the workers' cottages at Penfold Grove, she shudders, letting out a long sorrowful sigh.

The laughter from Lilibeth and Joe quickly brings her back to the present.

'Look at me Mamma, Joe carried me to the shed, come on, hurry up!' Lily calls out excitedly from the top of the garden.

'Hey, mind the brambles and stinging nettles Katie!' Joe yells, 'Stay where you are, I'll carry you.'

Picking up her skirts Katie looked up haughtily, 'There's no need, I can manage, thank you very much,' she calls back, as she cautiously begins to pick her way through the spiteful undergrowth.

Watching her painstakingly stepping through the brutal weeds, Joe can't help but notice her slim legs and trim ankles. 'Be very careful Katie!' he warns.

The warning comes too late, Katie cries out in agony as a vicious rambler encircles her ankle, ripping into her skin.

Setting Lily to the ground, Joe made a dash to Katie's side, ignoring her protests he carefully untangles her leg and scoops her up in his arms, carrying her to join Lilibeth at the shed.

'Hell's bells, I'm so sorry Katie, it was stupid of me to bring you here.' he apologises profusely. 'Here, let me take a look.'

Recoiling, as he stoops to lift the hem of her skirt to inspect the injury to her ankle, the colour drains from Katie's face, her knees buckle, and Joe has to move quickly to catch her in his arms. He shakes his head.

These persistent fainting bouts cannot be ignored any longer.

As he supports her, he can hear her rapid breathing and feel her body trembling, 'I'll carry you home Katie, enough is enough,' he tells her firmly. 'I'm gonna ride into Holdean and fetch the doctor, Lily can sit with you in the cottage whilst I'm gone,' concern is written all over his face.

'No, Joe, please, it's not necessary!' she says breathlessly as he gazes into his eyes, 'Please, I'm fine, I'm not ill at all!'

Shaking his head with frustration he sighs, 'I'm sorry Katie, I'm not convinced. You shouldn't keep fainting all the time, you really must see a doctor.'

Letting out a long, drawn-out sigh, Katie knows the time had come to be honest. 'Please Joseph, no. The truth is… I do have a problem, but I don't need a doctor,' she finally admits quietly, glancing at Lilibeth and back at Joe, she lowers her voice to barely a whisper, 'I know I owe you an explanation, Joe, I promise I will tell you, but it's very personal. I would prefer to talk to you alone if you see what I mean,' she says looking back nervously at Lilibeth.

Realising what she means he nods, 'That's fine with me, we'll wait until a certain someone is tucked up in bed,' he agrees quietly, somewhat relieved that at last she will come clean, and hopefully put his mind at rest.

'Can you put me down now please, Joe?' she asks, clinging to his neck.

'If you're sure you are okay, certainly,' as he cautiously lowers her to the ground.

Katie nods her thanks and straightens her skirt, anxious to change the subject from her fainting bouts. 'Now we're here, I'd really like to see the butter churn,' she tells him.

'Fine, we'll have a quick look then we must get back and clean up that leg of yours.' he agrees. 'Now let me see, it's in here somewhere.'

The shed proves to be a veritable Aladdin's cave, strewn across the floor, piled on top of each other in a haphazard fashion are a variety of useful things. There's an array of flowerpots, seed trays, a huge ball of string, a pickaxe, garden forks, spades, rakes and a riddle and lots of various gardening implements, many of which are hung on the walls. On the right side of the shed, tucked away are several wooden crates filled with dusty bottling jars and their accompanying lids.

Joe rummages around, 'Right, let's see what we've got here.'

In the gloom, partially covered by a tarpaulin, Katie can just make out the revolving butter churn, covered in dust and cobwebs. Next to it is what looks like a pile of hessian sacks, above them is a seed box, overflowing with grubby muslin cloths.

'There it is, Joe,' Katie points out excitedly, asking him if he can bring it up to the house as soon as possible.

'No problem, I'll bring it up and put it in the dairy,' he tells her. 'Mind you, it will have to be cleaned first, it's not been used for quite a while.'

'Dairy, what dairy?' asks Katie looking puzzled.

Grinning, Joe stands with his hands on his hips, 'Across the yard, in the outhouse, the top building, to be precise. I'll show you later if you like,' adding, 'That is, after we've bathed and bandaged your leg and we've eaten dinner. I'm absolutely starving.'

'That reminds me,' says Katie, 'if I don't get back soon the food will spoil. Would you mind bringing Lilibeth back to the cottage for me, Joe? I've got to dash.'

Grasping her wrist, he scowls, 'Just you hold on, young lady, you've got to stop all this rushing about, we'll come with you.'

The minute they return home, Joe ushers Katie into the parlour, 'Sit down, I'll boil some water and find something to use as a bandage,' he tells her firmly.

On tenterhooks, Kate sits waiting.

'Here we go, a bowl of freshly boiled salty water,' he says, setting it at her feet, 'and I've torn up a pillowcase to make a bandage. Now let's take a look at that leg,' he says rolling up his sleeves.

Hastily drawing her feet back beneath her skirts, the colour rises in her face. 'Please, Joe, I can manage, really I can, but thank you anyway,' She protests nervously.

Shrugging his shoulders, he stands and huffs, 'Fair enough, have it your own way Katie, but make sure you clean it well, we don't want it getting infected,' he warns. 'Anyway, I'll go and have a wash in the garden whilst you're doing that. Call me if you need me,' he says, leaving her to it.

Out in the garden he chuckles to himself, he should have realised that Katie was prim and proper and far too embarrassed to allow him to bathe her leg. It disappoints yet amuses him, he'd never encountered a girl with such modesty in his lifetime, though he had to admire Katie's restrained sense of propriety.

Returning to the scullery washed and freshly shaven he finds Katie stood on one leg at the sink trying to scrape the potatoes. 'Oh no you don't, I can do that,' he tells her, taking the knife from her hand, 'Get yourself in the parlour with Lily and put your feet up.'

Katie readily does as she's told; she has been finding it increasingly difficult to mask her mystifying feelings when she's alone in Joe's company.

Katie tells Lilibeth a couple of stories to pass the time before Joe calls them for dinner.

As soon as they've eaten Katie announces it is Lilibeth's bedtime.

'But the dairy?' Lilibeth points out, 'Joe said we could go and see it after dinner. Can we, Mammy, please?'

Knowing it would put off the time she would have to explain her fainting bouts she agrees, 'Very well, but then it's your bedtime Lilibeth.'

Together they inspect the dairy, Kate is surprised and highly impressed. It is a large cool room with a flagstone floor and all the equipment you could possibly need for producing cheese and butter.

He shakes his head, 'I'm afraid It's not been used for a while so it's going to have to cleaned from top to bottom,' he explains.

Surveying the dust and cobwebs Katie is excited, with a butter churn and everything needed for making cheese she knows there is good money to be made when she gets it up and running. 'No problem, Joe, I'll soon have it all spick and span. It's a beautiful dairy. If I recall, there was a box of muslin in your shed, I'll need them for the cheese making, once I've cleaned up the dairy,' she adds enthusiastically. 'We could make a lot of money from the butter and cheeses, Joe. I also noticed there are a lot of pickling jars in the shed too.'

Huffing, Joe shakes his head, looking stern, 'Oh no you don't Katie, you are doing far too much already!' he says firmly, 'You need to be patient, cleaning out the dairy is men's work, so you'll just have to wait, and as for the stuff in the shed, I'll fetch it up, all in good time.'

CHAPTER 5

Lilibeth tugs at her mother's skirt, ''Mammy, I feel sick, my head hurts.'

Gently picking her up, Joe carries her back to the house and sets her down on the sofa. 'She feels very hot yet she's shivering Katie,' says Joe, his hand on her brow, 'she looks quite pale, yet her cheeks are red and hot too. Look after her Katie, take off some of her clothes to cool her down, I'll draw some cold water from the well,' he declares and dashes outside.

Soaking the corner of a towel in the cold water, Katie holds it to Lilibeth's brow. 'What's wrong with her, Joe?' she asks anxiously.

'I'm pretty certain she's got heat stroke,' says Joe, 'my mother had it a couple of times. The doctor said she'd been out in the sun too long, if we can cool her down, I'm sure she'll be fine.'

Taking it in turns they cool Lily with the dampened cloths until Joe is satisfied that she'll be all right. Between them they take her up to bed, sitting on the bed, staying with her until she falls asleep.

Joe is in the parlour deep in thought, piecing together all the different information that Katie had given him in their several conversations so far. He'd worked out that if she was nine months younger than Edward it meant she was only sixteen when she was forced to leave Sheybourne. He frowns, so young to be left completely alone. He recalls her previous employer, Sir Barton-Smythe, who'd told her he had found her a new occupation, she would be living on a small holding as a housekeeper, to a man who had just lost his wife and infant in childbirth. Then there was Katie's vivid description on meeting her new employer. She'd said she was terrified of him, describing him as filthy, obese, uneducated, and an uncouth permanent drunkard.

Putting it all together, suddenly it all seemed to make sense, he sits bolt upright, hoping he is wrong.

It was no good, he had to ask.

Creeping downstairs, Katie finds Joe sat in the parlour looking pensive, 'How's Lily?' he asks.

'Fast asleep thank goodness. I've opened the window and covered her lightly with just a sheet, as you suggested,' she answers as she sits opposite him, beside the fireplace.

Looking serious Joe leans forward and takes Katie's hands, he licks his lips, 'Please I don't want you to get upset, but need to ask you something,' he says quietly, 'I'm sorry Katie, but I have to ask, this man you were running away from,' he hesitates momentarily, 'was his name Soames, Albert Soames, by any chance?'

Mortified, Katie's body stiffens, 'You... you know him?' she asks, her eyes widening in fear, 'Oh dear God no! You know him, Joe...? Do you know him well? Is he um... is he a friend of yours... a neighbour?' she asks. Standing abruptly, she begins pacing the floor and wringing her hands.

Her reaction appals him, his suspicions are confirmed. He takes her hands and pulls her towards him, 'Hey, calm down Katie,' he says, wrapping his arms around her, holding her close. 'Hush now, please, try and calm down.'

Panicking Katie pulls away, 'No Joseph, we must go, straight away!' she cries out.

Grabbing her shoulders Joe lifts her chin with his finger to look into her eyes, 'Katie, stop. Listen to me please! You're not giving me chance to speak.' He sits her on the sofa and takes her hands in his, 'Look Katie, yes, it's true I know of Soames, but believe me, he is no friend of mine. I happen to be choosy about my friends. To be honest, I merely know of him by his foul reputation, and vague recollections of him when I used to attend the market years ago, always staggering blind drunk around the market, he was often violent and thoroughly abusive towards everyone, including his constant filthy attempts to try it on with so many pretty young girls. It was your description of him that finally gave it away Katie.'

'Are you quite sure, Joe?' she whispers warily.

'Yes, of course I'm sure, believe me, Soames is an obnoxious man and a friend to no-one. So, you can put that idiot right out of your head, you have nothing to fear Katie, you are both safe here with me. I promise

I will always keep you both safe,' he says, gently holding her closer to alleviate her fears.

Filled with relief Katie breathes a massive sigh and rests her head against his shoulder and closes her eyes, as his husky soft voice whispering in her ear, reassures her over and over, that they would always be safe with him.

Eventually he feels Katie's body relax, lifting her face he looks into her eyes, 'Hey, do you feel better now?'

Gazing into his eyes Katie gulps, she feels strange, butterflies are fluttering crazily in her stomach. His eyes are looking directly into hers with such compassion, she gulps again, her heart seems to somersault, his closeness is so comforting yet disconcerting, she has never experienced such emotions before, part of her wanting to stay in this moment forever. For the rest of the evening, they sit together, quietly sharing pleasant, idle chit chat. All the while, Joe's soft voice seems to mesmerise her, as he tells her of his future plans for Sweet Briars. Keen to change the subject of Soames, Joe tells her he is considering taking on a hired hand next year, to ease his workload and expand the business side of the market gardening, plus his intentions for the provision of an internal washroom, before winter comes. He also tells her that by agreeing to stay, they had changed his life for the better and he appreciates all that Katie contributes towards making the house a very happy, well run family home. 'In fact, I couldn't wish for anyone lovelier to share my home and my life with,' he says, sounding sincere.

At his last statement, the colour rises in her cheeks, she closes her eyes, help, the butterflies are creating havoc below her waist. Opening her eyes, she realises Joe is holding her hands and looking deep into her eyes with a look of…? taking a deep breath she swallows nervously. Not daring to stay in his company a minute longer, she decides she must distance herself and go to bed, or she wouldn't be able to conceal her feelings any more. Hastily she withdraws her hands and politely excuses herself, telling him she should be with Lilibeth, just in case.

Smiling almost knowingly he nods, 'Hum, very well, good night Katie. I'm sure Lily will be fine in the morning.' he tells her, 'Keep an eye on her, if you get any problems or you are worried about her during the night, please, don't hesitate, just call me.'

The following morning Katie comes downstairs with Lilibeth, to find the scullery empty, the window open, and the door propped ajar, allowing a pleasing breath of fresh warm air to sweep through the scullery.

Katie's thankful he isn't around; she'd had a disturbing night. As she'd lain in bed, Joseph had occupied her restless waking moments. When sleep finally comes, she was dreaming of Joseph, a vision of him stood before her, like a replica of the large statue in the vestibule at Sheybourne, his naked, muscled sculptured body stirring her, driving her crazy, his soft husky voice filling her mind with an unfathomable desire.

Somehow, she has to pull herself together, try to get the inexplicable, outlandish thoughts out of her head, it is disconcerting, all these feelings and thoughts are so confusing and overwhelming, she doesn't know what it all means or how to deal with it.

After filling the boiler, they sit quietly eating breakfast. Without her conscious bidding, her thoughts stray to Joseph.

Seeing him stripped naked had had an intense effect on her. A vision that she simply can't erase from her mind, instigating exciting thrills to pump round her body, crazily creating mixed feelings of both pleasure and trepidation. Everything is fast flying out of her control, for his statue-like, golden physique had undoubtably shocked her to the core.

The more Katie thinks about the exciting feelings she feels seeing Joe in a state of complete undress, the more confused she becomes. How could she possibly consider Joseph in that way? She must be losing her senses, after all, her only intimate experience with any man in her entire life had been seven long, tortuous years at the hands of her vile depraved husband and when she'd finally escaped his clutches, she had vowed there and then, that never again would she allow any man to get near her. With the memories of the despicable acts that she'd been forced to endure creeping into her mind, haunting her, the very idea fills her with revulsion. And yet...? Wasn't her dear friend Margo forever bragging about how rewarding and exciting her sex life was with Stan, and Margo's constant insistence that not all men were as vile and depraved as Albert. It keeps running around in her head causing conflict.

Now, despite her head warning her to steer clear of him, she finds her heart is crying out for him. So, what makes her think Joe would or could be any different than Albert? she asks herself. As far as she had been concerned, all men were the same, revolting and only after one thing, filthy self-gratification! There again… perhaps it was Margo's advice but… she is finding it so hard to fight the feelings Joe is creating within her.

Finished with his daily chores, Joe returns, he pours himself a cup of tea, joining them at the table, studying her, Katie looks deep in thought, he's wishing he knew what she was thinking

Realising Joe is there, watching her, the torrid heat rises in her cheeks, she tries to get a grip on herself, clasping her hands firmly together she sits rigidly on the chair, staring at the table, trying desperately to marshal her thoughts elsewhere, praying that he hasn't noticed her highly flustered state, she knows she would die of sheer embarrassment if he actually knew what was in her head.

Intuitively, Joe picks up on this feeling of… well of course he couldn't be certain but somehow, Katie looks awkward, ill at ease and kind of agitated, she's avoiding his gaze, her cheeks are rosy, red, and she's trembling, he suspects his thoughtless state of undress might have embarrassed her. Hum, was it that, or maybe it was something else? Whichever, he decides there is a need for them to talk again, alone. For a start, a few rules regarding his washing routine had to be decided to make for a harmonious household. He sighs, they had to talk, privately.

To do that he needs the young child out of hearing range, but canny Lily is sat watching them both intently, with a quizzical expression on her face. 'Humm, I tell you what Lily,' he says as he sweeps the remnants of the crumbs from the table onto a plate, 'why don't you take these outside, feed the birds in the garden, they want their breakfast too.'

Scrambling down from the table, Lily certainly doesn't have to be asked twice.

Left without Lilibeth for a chaperone Katie would have given anything to accompany her daughter into the garden but she knows if she stands her legs won't carry her, so she sits at the table, fearing what is to come. What did he want now? What is he going to say? Would there be repercussions after she'd foolishly divulged most of her past sordid history to him last night?

Excitedly feeding the birds in the garden, Lily is safely out of earshot, so Joe slides his chair closer to Katie. 'What is it Katie, what's wrong, are you feeling ill again?'

By moving closer, he serves to heighten her uncontrollable excitement, she feels strangely uplifted as thrilling sensations excite her beyond belief. She remains tight-lipped, fearful that she might give her embarrassingly foolish thoughts away, admitting her innermost feelings towards him. All the while, his closeness and his seductive eyes are making her tingle from head to toe, contradicting the vow that she had made that after Albert, she would never again allow any man to take liberties with her. Her head is throbbing. Rationalisation of the inbuilt fear of what might happen if she were to succumb to him, mixed with the conflicting, undeniably overpowering, prolific urge for the need of him, are all fighting a war in her head, she sits silently, wringing her hands.

Taking a fleeting glance at Joe she notices the intense yet tender caring look in his vivid blue eyes, she swallows nervously, wondering it isn't her fanciful imagination that somehow, he seems to feel the same way about her. Oh help, could she possibly be right?

Anxious to break the silence and speak to Katie before Lily returns, he places his hand over Katie's. 'Look, if this is about the washing business,' he says, 'I'm so sorry I embarrassed you. Don't worry, the back of the shed is fine with me, I'm tough, and the fresh air will do me good.'

Katie plucks up the courage to look him in the eye, but as their eyes meet, she's overwhelmed with an uncontrollable feeling of longing. Under his concerned gaze, for no explicable reason, she burst into tears. 'It's nothing t...to do with that,' she sobs, 'truly it's not, it's me, I um... oh dear, I don't think I can tell you.'

Joe frowns, wiping her tears away with his thumb, he's forced to second guess. 'Oh, I get it, last night. Katie, I do understand. God only knows you've been through a living nightmare, but it's all behind you now, buried in the past, it'll take time I know, but the memories will fade in time, I promise you,' he says, to reassure her, 'Soames is out of your life for good now, I swear.'

Meeting his gaze, his sincere compassion is encouraging, she shakes her head, knowing in her heart it isn't fair to mislead him. Struggling to regain a modicum of composure, she pats her eyes with her hankie and gulps, 'No Joseph, you're so wrong, it has nothing to do with "him" finding us either, it's not that at all. It's just... it's just me, you see I um... I can't...' It was no good, she loses her nerve, 'Oh God, I'm just being stupid and foolish,' she flushes becomingly and lowers her head.

Joe smiles and pats her hand, 'You're a lot of things my dear Katie, but you're neither foolish nor stupid. You're a truly wonderful mother to Lily, a brilliant cook, an outstanding homemaker and the best company that any decent man could possibly wish for, but foolish... stupid... never?' It was all he could do to stop himself adding, sweet, irresistibly beautiful and so very, very desirable too. Oh, Katie my love, if only.

Despite her tear-swollen eyes and pink nose, Katie smiles a smile that melts his heart. 'You're such a kind... sweet man Joseph, your generous thoughtfulness has brought sunshine into our lives, and for that I... we, will be indebted to you forever, thank you.'

However, Joe is still none the wiser as to what lays behind Katie's mood swings and numerous fainting bouts, though worryingly, he was almost certain that she is expecting a baby. I guess I'm just going to have to be patient, get to know each other better, and hopefully in time... he sighs, deciding, if indeed she was with child, it would become obvious soon enough anyway. He shrugs, 'Oh well, if you're happy, then I'm happy,' he says, winking knowingly.

'You got something in your eye again, Joe?' pipes up Lilibeth.

Joe spins around; they hadn't heard her return from the garden. 'Lily... um yes, as it so happens, I have,' he chuckles.

Lilibeth's eyebrows shoot up, 'Huh? What you got in your eye then?'

Getting up from the table he picks her up and twirls her around, 'Yep, it's my eyeball!' he teases then adds, 'And the sight of the two prettiest young ladies I've ever clapped my eyes on in my entire life!'

Lilibeth is delighted with his flattery, but poor Katie's stomach is all of a flutter again, suddenly she feels lightheaded, she licks her lips, her mouth dry, sitting in such close proximity, face to face, doesn't help matters either.

Excusing herself from the table, she tries to busy herself tidying away the dishes, she's so relieved that Lilibeth had come bounding back in when she had, because her daughter's sudden reappearance and natural curiosity had helped to mask her strangely disquieting feelings, giving her the opportunity to gather herself and hide her ridiculously fanciful thoughts. Though it doesn't help matters when Lilibeth goes t back outside into the garden, busily playing with her doll.

Just as she calms down and back in control, Joe creeps up behind her, resting his hands on her waist, whispering in her ear, 'Katie, we'll all have a day out, the three of us, tomorrow, what do you say to that then?'

Her legs turn to jelly, she grips the edge of the sink for support, she can feel his warm breath on her neck and immediately, to her horror, the stirring excitement returns, surging through her body, her cheeks flush. Flustered, she turns her head, 'Oh dear, I don't think we should, we um…' she tries to protest.

Grasping her shoulders, he spins her round, 'Excuse me, what's to think about? You know there's nothing wrong with a bit of happy relaxation spent in good company. All work and no play and all that,' he tells her, then adds, 'Look, if I'm honest, I feel guilty Katie, you really haven't stopped working since you arrived here, cleaning, cooking, washing, scrubbing, polishing, the list is endless. You're like a whirlwind sweeping through the place!' he grasps her hands, 'It's not that I'm complaining, definitely not, but you're doing far too much and to be perfectly blunt with you, if you don't mind my saying, yet again, you're not exactly in the best of health, are you? Now I happen to think that a nice relaxing day out together will do all of us the power of good, so what do you say?' Joe can hardly believe the words that come tumbling out of his mouth. When was the last time he'd felt the need to shirk his work on the whim of spending a lazy day out? There again, when did he have such wonderful company as Katie and Lily to idle his precious time away with?

Katie shakes her head, her mind is working overtime, what would he think of her? If she didn't suppress her ridiculously fanciful thoughts then she could well end up rendering them both homeless again, she must try to get a grip. 'I was going to say that you have your work, and so, for that matter, have we,' she points out, trying hard not to make her lame excuse sound as if she is ungrateful for his all too tempting offer.

'Besides,' she adds, 'I think we've disrupted your life enough already; we wouldn't want to become a burden to you, Joseph.' At least the last part of her statement is true.

Shaking his head, he tuts, insisting, 'Now that's complete and utter nonsense. Oh Katie, of course you're not a burden, nothing could be farther from the truth my dear.' he squeezes her hands, causing her body to tingle.

Whilst he's talking, his smooth voice is enchanting her, with such a silky intimate tone he's making her feel strangely euphoric, sending frenzied shuddering waves up and down her body. Oh help, for the first time in her life she has found a man that she feels a longing for, it just doesn't seem right. She gulps, 'But we can't, there's so much work to do today,' she protests weakly. Somehow, she knows she must curb these feelings towards him and stop the foolish notions going on in her head.

Exasperated he throws up his hands in frustration, 'Oh blow flipping work, I don't expect you to run around after me all day long. You've both been through so much in your short lives, you deserve to have some fun!' he says firmly, then adds, 'Listen to me Katie, this is your home now, you don't work here, you live here. Don't you see? I want you both to relax and enjoy life! A good meal at the end of the day, and two contented, happy girls for company is all I ask of you,' he lifts her chin with his finger until their eyes met, 'My dear Katie, please, say yes.'

Katie feels weak at the knees, how can she refuse him? He's so persuasive and besides, if she was honest, it would hardly be against her wishes.

'Well?' he presses her persistently.

Katie feels he must have hypnotised her for she hears herself saying, 'Oh yes, yes Joseph, we'd love to, I shall make us a picnic to take with us.'

A look of pleasurable satisfaction says that he'd won, 'Right, good, well that's sorted,' he declares, 'now I suppose I should get going, work to do,' he picks up his cup, finishes his tea, then smiles, 'so that's a date then, we're all off out tomorrow.'

Now he had actually persuaded her to go out for the day he can hardly wait, but it was painfully obvious to him that regardless of the assurances he'd given her, she was obviously fearful of leaving the confines of Sweet Briars and terrified of visitors. So, with the distinct possibility of his pal turning up unannounced any day soon, to pick up his wood order, he intends to get down the spinney this afternoon, load the wood on his cart ready to deliver it to his pal really early tomorrow morning, knowing full well that it would delay Stan's following visit for at least another month or more.

The truth is, he would have dearly loved to have taken Katie and little Lily with him, but right now he's having difficulty getting her to walk the countryside close to his home, let alone travelling all the way to Fennydown. Still, when he considered all that she'd been through, and the terrible time spent with that degenerate bastard Soames, it's all perfectly understandable, the bile rises from his stomach as he thinks of her forced to live with a perverted reprobate like Soames.

It's his intention to keep his trip to his mate a very brief visit, he doesn't want to be away from his house guests a minute longer than he has to, for since their arrival, he had found that his everyday work and chores were taking a back seat in his normal list of priorities. Both Katie and Lily, now take over his every waking thoughts, he wants, or is it needs, to be with them and in order to do that, he knows he must keep his impromptu visit to Stan from Katie, he also has to keep his pal in the dark so that the solemn promise that he has made to Katie would be kept. No one would find out from him that they were living at Sweet Briars. He figures the least people know about his house guests the better, so he resolves to say nothing, not even to his lifelong friend.

Pulling on his boots, Joe turns to Katie, 'Well that's definite then, we're all off out tomorrow, I reckon I can be finished with the chores and stuff well before midday,' he declares triumphantly, 'let's hope the weather stays fine for us tomorrow.'

Katie nods in agreement, carefully avoiding contact with his vivid penetrating eyes.

With the prospect of spending a relaxing day out in their delightful company, Joe's spirits soar, 'Anyway, no good me standing here doing nothing. I'd best be off to work; I've got a busy afternoon ahead. Are you quite sure you two will be all right whilst I'm gone?' he asks, reaching for his jacket.

'We'll be fine,' she assures him, 'but if you're going to be out all day, you'll need something to eat so I'll pack you a lunch, it won't take me a minute.'

Joe isn't about to argue with an offer like that, he sits in the chair beside the range, taking great pleasure in watching Katie flitting about the scullery preparing his food.

Coming in from the garden, Lilibeth sidles up beside him, slipping her plump little arm around his neck and together they watch contentedly, as Katie prepares his lunch.

'Here,' she says, handing him a small basket, 'this should keep you going all day and we'll have a good meal ready for when you get home.'

'Mmm, thanks, I could definitely get used to this, you're spoiling me,' he smirks. 'Now please, don't spend all day cooped up in here working, get yourselves out in the fresh air, put some colour in your faces.,' he orders, then with a twinkle in his eye, he winks at Katie, making her blush, 'There we go, I can see colour in your cheeks already.'

Katie tries to smile, but her heart is thumping, her face turning an even deeper pink, she's forced to look away to hide her embarrassment.

To Lilibeth's utter delight, Joe scoops her up in his arms, 'Be a good girl and look after your mammy for me today sweetheart, I won't be too long.'

'All right, are we all really going out together for a picnic tomorrow?'

'Yep, the three of us, well four if we count your Daisy, sweetheart,' he says. Straightening his jacket, he looks back over his shoulder to Katie, and smiles, 'I'll be back by teatime, see you later Katie.'

Lilibeth follows him into the yard and waves as he strides away, she feels warm inside, Joe had called her sweetheart, oh she did like Joe, 'Bye, bye, Joe!' she yells after him, 'see you later, byeeeee!'

'See you later Lily!' he calls back, waving vigorously.

Freshly boiled sheets and pillowcases billow on the line and several jars of pickled eggs and beetroot stand in orderly rows on the pantry shelf before Katie, not wanting to risk another fainting bout, decides to take Joe's advice to rest and take in some fresh air.

The pair set off to explore the gardens, Lilibeth with a basket and Katie carrying a pail.

Yet again the day proves exceptionally warm, there's not a cloud in the sky, the heat made just about bearable by the gentle westerly wind. It feels invigorating after the heat of the stuffy scullery.

They walk along the crunching gravel paths that lead from one garden to another, each garden very different to the last and all having their own purpose.

The first had obviously been a pretty flower garden, perhaps his mother's garden? Sadly, recent months of neglect had obviously allowed the weeds to flourish, now they were competing for space with the flowers and by the look of it they were easily winning the battle.

Gardening is one of Katie's favourite pastimes, in fact when she lived at Penfold Grove it was the one thing that she could do that gave her any sense of pleasure or freedom at all. It wouldn't take much, she could easily restore this garden to its original splendour, she decides. So, she makes up her mind to broach the subject over dinner tonight. If Joe has no objections, then she would soon have it neat and tidy again, besides, there is good money to be made from such a selection of flowers.

From the flower garden the path meanders through an archway into a high-walled, sheltered, cobbled yard, again overgrown with an abundance of healthy-looking weeds, the path covered in lush, downy green moss, which proves slippery under foot.

Partially hidden beneath a sheet of rusty corrugated iron she discovers a perfectly serviceable mangle which she decides could be put to better use if it was back in the scullery and makes a mental note to mention it, along with the flower garden, to Joseph that evening.

The sound of clucking chickens entices them through the next opening in the hedge, Lilibeth runs on excitedly. 'Mammy look, it's the chickens, Joe brought me here before, can we get some eggies for tea?'

Inside the tall neatly wired pen, a grand old colourful cockerel is perched high, proudly lording it over numerous noisily clucking hens.*

'I don't see why not darling, let's see if there are any eggs in the nesting box.'

Half a basket of eggs later, Katie stands and stretches her aching back. 'Would you look at all these lovely eggs Lilibeth, and so many of them, you know, Joe could sell them at the market and make lots of money.'

There's no reply.

Katie looks about her, her daughter is nowhere to be seen, panic stricken she stands, 'Lilibeth!' she shouts, 'Oh no, Lilibeth, where are you?'

'Here I is,' calls Lilibeth, from somewhere behind the hawthorn hedge, 'I found some Billy goats.'

Leaving the eggs, she runs through a gap in the hedge. Lilibeth is stood on a wooden gate grinning wildly. 'Billy goats, Mammy, I found Billy goats, look.'

'One is a Billy and the other's a Nanny goat to be precise darling, and don't you ever go off without me again, do you hear me!' she scolds, sounding really cross, her daughter's disappearance had given her a terrible fright.

'Me won't do it again, but I did find the goats for you, Mammy,' she answers by way of an apology.

Lilibeth considers she has two pretty, pet goats to admire and talk to, but Katie sees goats' milk, perfect for cheese making. 'The black one stood on the old table is the Billy goat, and this one here is the Nanny goat,' she points out, 'now let's see if she will let me milk her, where's the pail darling?'

'Um, by the chickens, I'll fetch it,' Lilibeth offers, about to turn tail and dash off.

Katie grabs her arm, 'Oh no you don't young lady, I'll go, you will wait here for me, and no running off!' she orders. 'You are not to move; do you hear me? '

Fortunately for Katie, the goat turns out to be quite affable, grateful to be relieved of her milk and in no time at all, she has almost a quarter of the pail filled with rich creamy milk. 'Now all we've got to do, is carry everything back to the cottage.' As the egg basket is by far the heaviest and most fragile, Katie opts for carrying the basket, 'do you think you can manage to carry the pail without spilling the milk, darling?' she asks.

Offended Lilibeth frowns, 'Course I can, Mammy, look,' she grasps the handle with one hand and her doll in the other and speeds away through the garden at a pace in the direction of the cottage, as fast as her little legs can carry her.

'Mind you how you go, those cobbles are damp. Careful, don't spill the milk!' she calls after her, 'slow down child!' she warns.

Full of excitement the child hears nothing and before Katie can call out again, she's reached the walled garden.

In the shade, the damp moss covering the cobbles is still moist from the morning dew, proving slippery underfoot. As she dashes beneath the archway she slips, down she goes, spilling the entire contents of the pail everywhere, including over herself.

Looking a sorry sight, tears flow as Lilibeth sits bedraggled in the puddle of wasted milk. 'Aw I'm sorry, Mammy,' her bottom lip is quivering, 'Ouch, my leg. Look, my leg is bleeding.'

'Oh dear, up we get,' says Katie, lifting her to her feet, 'Here, let me wipe away those tears and I'll have a look at your poorly leg.'

'W-will, Joe be cross with me for spilling all the milk, Mammy?' she sobs.

'Joe, cross? I wouldn't think so Pet, he's such a lovely man, he'll probably say something daft like it's no good crying over spilt milk or something,' says Katie, 'Come, let's get you home and get it clean and bandaged. Now let's see if you can manage to walk.'

Dejectedly, Lilibeth does her best to hobble home.

'I'm being very brave, isn't I Mamma?'

Smiling down at her daughter's tear-stained face, Katie nods, 'Yes darling, very brave,' she tells her as she gently cleans the dirt from her knee.

Washed and dressed in a clean set of clothes plus the addition of a satisfactory makeshift bandage covering her bruised and bloodied knee, Lilibeth soon returns to her usual sunny self and the rest of the day the cottage is a hive of activity and endless cheerful chatter as she willingly helps her mother with the household chores. By the late afternoon, the cottage shines, a tall, neat pile of freshly ironed sheets are now sat on the dresser and the dinner gently simmering on the stove. Both are feeling weary, so a cup of tea and plate of freshly baked biscuits are taken through to the parlour for a well-earned break.

Lounging in Joe's chair beside the fireplace, poor Lilibeth is desperately fighting the onslaught of sleep, but the minute she hears the door latch lift, she springs into life and makes a dash to meet Joe.

Before he has the chance to hang his jacket, he's greeted by Lilibeth running up to him with open arms crying out to be picked up.

A request incidentally, to which he happily obliges, in return he's rewarded with a large wet kiss planted firmly on his cheek along with a spontaneous hug.

'Hello sweetheart, have you had a good day Lily?'

'Ooo no, I hurt myself badly, on my leg,' she says, hoisting up her skirt to reveal the improvised bandage covering her knee.

'Oh dear, you poor thing, how did that happen?' he frowns.

'I found some goats,' she explains, 'Then Mammy wanted some milk to make cheese, but I fell over and spilled it all and then I hurt my leg badly, and it bleeded and bleeded. I cried and cried, coz all the milk got spilled over me everywhere, and I'm so sorry, Joe, I didn't mean to spill it,' she gasps, in desperate need of catching her breath.

'Hey up, there's no need to be sorry sweetheart, just as long as you're all right, that's all that matters,' he says, suppressing his amusement, 'Hey, it's no good crying over a drop of spilled milk you know, there's plenty more, so don't worry your pretty little head about it, my dear.'

Lily stops crying immediately she blinks in amazement, 'Oooo, my mammy said you'd say tha.' she says, 'Oh you are a clever, Mammy.' She turns back to Joe, 'and my mammy said you was a very lovely man too.'

Katie is wishing the ground will open and swallow her.

He turns to Katie and smiles, 'Oh did she now? Mmm, that's nice.'

Katie turns away to hide her blushes.

'We been washing and baking today. Mammy made biscuits and scones, and I did make more jam tarts, just for you,' explains Lily.

'Hum, I like the sound of jam tarts,' he says, just about managing to get a word in edgeways. 'But first things first, young lady, what about that old leg of yours, is it still painful?' he inquires.

'I haven't got an old leg,' she retorts indignantly, 'coz I'm six, and it doesn't hurt, coz my mammy fixed it up and mended it, it's all better.'

'I think Joe's pulling just your leg pet,' suggests Katie, fighting to keep a straight face.

'He won't pull my leg, will he, Mammy?' she asks, tugging down the hem of her frock.

Katie smile broadens, 'He'd better not, or he won't get his dinner.'

Joe does a good job of pretending to be heartbroken at the prospect of missing his dinner, after an extremely busy day, he's starving.

'Aw don't worry, Joe,' says Lilibeth holding his hand, 'you can have some of mine.'

'Well blow me down with a feather! That's generous of you Lily.'

Lilibeth looks puzzled, 'What blew you down?'

'Just a feather,' he grins.

'How can a fever knock you down?' she asks innocently, 'it's only little.'

Both Katie and Joe fall about laughing, which in turn sets Lilibeth off too.

Wiping the tears from his eyes, he gives her a hug, 'Oh you are a one, young lady. You're such a joy to have around.'

Gazing up at Joe in awe, she studies him, 'Is my mammy a joy to have around too?'

Looking directly at Katie, his eyes shine, his voice velvety and sincere, 'Oh yes, she certainly is Lily.'

Could she feel more embarrassed? 'Enough Lilibeth, no more bantering!' Right now, she's wishing the ground would open up and swallow her again.

'What's bantering?' asks Lilibeth.

Turning his head, Joe slips a crafty wink in the direction of the perpetually curious, loveable child.

Lilibeth screws her eyes closed, trying to wink back, but fails miserably.

'He's shutting his eye again, Mammy,' says Lilibeth, telling tales.

'I expect he's winking,' Katie suggests, supressing a smile.

'What's winking, Mammy?' Lily persists.

Irritated Katie scowls at her daughter. 'I said that's enough, isn't it, Joseph?' she repeats herself, looking to Joe to back her up.

'Your mammy's right, best we get on with our dinner and stop nattering.'

'What's nat...?' pipes up Lily.

135

Joe puts his finger to her lips, 'Er not now Pet, we can't let our dinner spoil,' he whispers, then he winks at her yet again, 'later Lily.'

Shrugging her shoulders, she grins, 'Aw all right, Joe.'

'Mmm, now here's a sight for sore eyes,' he says, looking longingly at the mouth-watering fruit pie for afters.

Concerned, Lilibeth stares at him, 'Why have you got sore eyes?'

Exasperated, Katie glares at her daughter, 'Lilibeth, we are at the dinner table. Remember your manners, please!'

Secretly, Katie is thoroughly enjoying the pleasant happy atmosphere. Somehow, Joe and Lilibeth have built up a rapport of quirky, jovial conversations between them, she finds it heart-warming and highly amusing too. However, she had always tried to instil good manners in her daughter, and she was not prepared to allow her to start taking liberties, despite the unusual circumstances. Oh, this is the way life should always be, simply perfect, she thinks wistfully.

At long last, Lilibeth, with her tummy full, falls silent, happy to sit and listen to the conversation between Joe and her mother.

Resting his hand over Katie's, his eyes meet hers, a little gesture that Lilibeth notices, but unusually, makes no comment about.

'You're looking flushed Katie, I don't suppose you had a rest today, like I told you, did you?' he asks.

His touch made her heart race and the heat rush up to her cheeks, to her horror she can feel her hand trembling beneath his. Hoping that he hasn't noticed, she withdraws her hand swiftly out of his reach. 'Oh, but we did, we went off to explore the gardens.'

'Mmm, I thought you had some colour in your cheeks,' he comments, his lips curling teasingly.

There's a wicked gleam in his eyes that Katie can't help but notice, his comment makes the colour rise in her face even more, nervously she swallows and licks her dry lips.

Lilibeth's eyes roam back and forth between Joe and her mother, totally fascinated. The novelty of a happy conversation of any sort, at the table, is an entirely new phenomenon to the small child and she's thoroughly enjoying every minute of it. It had never happened at her old home.

'We found the chickens and collected the eggs, and as you heard earlier, we also found the goats too,' Katie tells him, as she pours the tea.

He nods, 'Oh the goats and chickens, yes, well, I know it's a waste, but I've been throwing most of the cows and goats milk away, and most of the eggs too, for that matter, no need for them when you're on your own, in fact I was on the point of getting rid of most of the cattle and some of the chickens until you both came along,' he slaps his hands on his knees making Lilibeth jump, 'but now, with you and Lily here, well they can all earn their keep. I guess we can make good use of them.'

'You work very hard, and you get up so early, look Joseph, I'd be happy to milk the goat,' Katie offers. 'In fact, I don't mind feeding the chickens, collecting the eggs and milking the cows for that matter, if it helps you out.'

Exasperated, he rolls his eyes, 'Hum, you can collect the eggs and maybe milk the goat if you really want, but you should leave milking the cows to me, my dear.'

Lilibeth smiles to herself, Joe keeps calling her mammy 'dear'.

Noticing Katie looks put out by his last comment and about to protest, he jumps in again, 'They're used to me, I milk them around four thirty to five o'clock every morning, regular as clockwork, three hundred and sixty-five days of the year, there's no point in changing the habits of a lifetime. Besides just look at what you're doing now! No, I'm sorry Katie, it's too much for you, best you leave the cows to me.' He leans a little closer and pats her hand making her heartbeat even faster, 'You know you simply can't do it all Katie,' he says and winks, 'I'm sorry, I won't let you, my dear.'

Katie's lost for words; Joe's nothing like Albert. He hadn't raised his voice in anger, he hadn't been aggressive towards her either, his tone was calm, seemingly he is only being considerate towards her welfare.

The caring attitude that he has shown towards her is a completely new experience and it would take some time to get used to. Perhaps, whilst in the middle of an amiable conversation she could bring up the subject of the mangle and her plans for the flower garden.

A minute's silence passes, Lily smiles to herself, Joe has called her mammy 'dear', yet again.

'Joe, while we're on the subject of jobs to do, I wondered if it would be possible to bring the mangle up here, it's in the walled garden. It would be very handy, especially when winter comes.'

'No problem, consider it done, anything else, my dear?'

'Thank you, um yes, one more thing, I hope you don't mind my pointing out, but the goats' milk, chickens, eggs, and cows' milk, could all be sold at the market along with the excess fruit and vegetables too.'

He shrugs, 'Uh huh, I know, we used to sell it all at market in the past, well until my mother took ill…' he sighs.

Seeing the sadness in his eyes her heart goes out to him, he strikes her as being a wonderfully caring and sensitive man, someone so incredibly special.

Unusually for Lilibeth, throughout the adult conversation, she remains completely silent, her chin sat cupped in the palms of her hands with her elbows resting on the table. It's such a novelty watching grownups talk so pleasantly without it all erupting into screaming and violence. Patiently she waits, her eyes still looking back and forth between them, waiting for them to resume talking.

Her mother is first to oblige. 'The flower garden at the side of the house, Joe, it's really beautiful, but I hope you don't mind my saying, it's in desperate need of weeding and pruning,' she points out cautiously.

'Ah yes, the flower garden, all my dear mother's handy work,' he explains, 'it was her pride and joy.' He sighs deeply, 'Tch, now it's going to wrack and ruin. Time and inclination, that's been my problem,' he says sadly.

Katie sympathises, 'I can understand that. You know Lilibeth and I would be only pleased to work on it for an hour or so each day, we both love gardening. Besides, you could get a good price for the flowers at the market, fresh cut in the summer and dried in the winter,' she tells him enthusiastically.

Joe seems miles away, he looks so sad, as if lost in memories of the past.

Interrupting his thoughts, Katie takes the liberty of carrying on the subject, 'Joe, what I'm trying to say is… now that you've got two more mouths to feed, the money you could make at market would come in very handy for all the extra food, I'm sure.'

Lilibeth's eyes turn from her mother to Joe.

He's shaking his head, his eyebrows raise and his face breaks into a lovely smile, 'All very enterprising, my dear, you seem to have thought of everything, but…' his smile fades, 'you're not at all well. Now you can't deny it Katie, all these fainting bouts…' Although she's still very slim, he's now convinced even more that she is pregnant.

Lilibeth's eyes revert to her mother.

Acutely aware that she and Joe's every word is being scrutinised by her astute daughter, Katie leans forward, lowering her voice, 'Really, Joe, it's nothing, nothing at all,' she pauses for a second or two and bites her lip, why is she still lying to him? 'No, I'm sorry Joseph, that's not completely true,' she confesses, 'there is a problem, I'll admit it, but it's um…' glancing anxiously in the direction of her daughter, 'this is so very difficult for me to talk about. I want to explain to you, but um… please, not right now,' she whispers. Katie sits back, looking worriedly at Lilibeth and back to Joe again.

Nodding knowingly, he says nothing but mouths, 'We'll talk later,' then a hush falls once more.

Unable to resist, Katie steels a few furtive glances at Joe. His glorious sensual eyes seem to penetrate her very soul, stirring her. Oh no, not again. She's engulfed with confusing feelings of helplessness as he sends shivers down her spine, making her head spin, it's as if he's putting a spell on her, making her lose control of her emotions.

If she is honest with herself, she can't deny her feelings any longer, she knows exactly why she feels this way and right now she's grateful for the fact that he can't read her thoughts, for he'd surely think that she was being ridiculous, that she was mistakenly taking his simple acts of consideration and kindness as something much more than that, but deep down she knows it isn't just gratitude she's feeling.

Joe hands her a cup of milk, his hands seemingly lingering on hers longer than is necessary, she gulps, is he just teasing her? She can't be sure. Oh dear, she feels so confused.

Distraction, yes, that's what I need, she focuses on the open window, and the remainder of the washing billowing wildly on the line outside, oh anything but to meet his bewitching gaze.

Disappointed that the easy-going chit chat has stopped, Lily looks expectantly at Joe as if to cue him to speak, just as she's about to open her mouth to prompt him, he duly obliges.

Rising up he collects the dishes, 'Right, well I say we all muck in with the washing up. I've got a real early start tomorrow.'

The three of them set to work washing the dishes. 'Dinner was really appreciated Katie, thanks, now it's my turn to do something useful,' he tells her, 'I won't be long.'

He goes outside, returning within minutes carrying an enamelled jug full of milk. 'Goats' milk,' he explains, 'I'd best put it in the pantry to keep it cool.'

Out he goes again, this time he returns carrying two sacks.

Naturally Lilibeth is curious, 'Ooo, what you got, Joe?'

'Hah, wouldn't you like to know little one?' he teases.

The first sack is emptied onto the tabletop, out tumbles an assortment of vegetables. 'And I brought these,' he says tipping out the contents of the smallest sack.' Lilibeth jumps back startled.

Out slides two large olive trout with shiny, silver bellies. 'I had an hour to spare, so I did a spot of fishing,' he tells them, 'I was right lucky too, the fish were biting a treat.'

Lilibeth steps cautiously away from the table, 'Ooo, do fishes bite then?' her face full of surprise.

He chuckles, 'Not that sort of bite sweetheart, what I mean is, the fish bit the bait on my fishing line,' he explains patiently.

Thinking for a moment, Lilibeth looks up at Joe, 'Good job the fishes don't bite you, or Mammy would've had to bandage your finger, just like Mammy did to my poorly leg.'

Her comment turns his chuckle into a belly laugh.

The fish are dispensed onto a plate, covered and put onto the cool marble slab in the larder, whilst Joe replenished the log supply.

Filling a bowl with hot water, he picks up his razor and grabs a towel, 'Just gonna get cleaned up, sit yourselves down in the parlour and when I'm done, I think three mugs of nice warm milk will go down a treat. Off you go, put your feet up and relax by the fire, I won't be long,' he says then disappears outside to the back garden.

Lilibeth snuggles down on her mother's lap, with her doll held tightly in her arms.

Katie is gazing into the fire grate, deep in thought. It is unbelievable, in such a short space of time her miserable life has been completely turned upside down, it's all so surreal, and right now, she is counting her blessings, surely it was fate that brought them to Sweet Briars.

A shudder runs through her body, wondering what might have become of them if it hadn't been for Joseph. It was like a miracle, as if someone somewhere had been watching over them, steering them towards the safe haven of Sweet Briars cottage and dear Joseph.

A picture of her mother fills her mind and a tear falls, she's convinced her dear mother had been watching over her and answered her prayers.

There was no doubting that from day one, Joseph had been the perfect gentleman, he'd asked nothing from them in return for taking them into his lovely home. Mmm, Joseph, he has such a wonderful way with Lilibeth too, he has drawn her out of her shell and made her laugh for the first time in her short life. Katie can find no fault in Joe, she smiles to herself. True he had this weird kind of witty conversation that Lilibeth had merrily fallen in with, but that could hardly be construed as having a weakness of character, quite the opposite in fact. Lilibeth clearly loves him, besides; he has a remarkably calm manner and a gentle way of always putting them both at their ease. Which makes her wonder why such a handsome and considerate young man, should be living alone in the middle of...? Wherever it is he is living. How far had they walked? What distance lay between them and Albert Soames? Would he still be out there some-where, searching for them? Katie is confident he would be. A cold shudder runs through her body.

'Here's your milk Katie,' offers Joe, bringing her back to the present.

Katie, startled from daydreaming, looks up, 'Oh, I'm sorry, Joe, you were saying?'

'I said, here's your milk, blimey, you were miles away.' he hands her the cup, 'You're looking worried again Katie. Listen, I hope you're not having second thoughts about our afternoon out, are you?'

'No, it's not really that, but now you've mentioned it, Joe... um, you know our circumstances, if you he was to find us...' her voice trails away.

'You can put that man right out of your head, don't even think about him. I mean it. You're both safe here with me. Trust me Katie,' he says firmly.

Leaning forward she says in a hushed voice, 'You know we are both incredibly grateful to you Joseph.'

'Huh, you're grateful? You know you've only been here a short while, and already you've both totally transformed my life!' he tells her honestly, as he settles himself down in his chair opposite Katie with his drink and pipe, 'Do you know Katie, it's hard to describe, but somehow you've sort of woken me up and I'm gonna tell you why,' he says as he makes himself comfortable.

Lilibeth cuddles down on Katie's lap, content to give in to sleep.

'As I told you briefly before, I've lived here all my life, in fact I was born here,' he begins. 'This place has been in my family for many generations. Sadly, I really can't remember my father at all, he died when I was very young. After Father died, my mother took over the entire running of the place along with Will, our hired help,' he tells her, pausing to finish his milk, he places his empty cup on the tray then takes a couple of minutes to light his pipe, 'As I was saying,' he continues, 'it's the family business and we've managed a pretty good living out of it too. My mother, bless her heart, worked day and night, raising me and working the spinney with Will. We kept all the animals going, the cows, goats, a few sheep and chickens, we grew and produced all our food, and my mother even managed her flower garden too. Will worked mainly down in the copse and the reed beds with me, a real hard grafter was Will, worth his weight in gold and more, despite his liking for the odd tipple or two.'

Pausing again, to re-light his pipe, he gazes at Katie through the wisps of smoke then carries on, 'Of course I used to go to market with Will. We'd stay over for a couple of days mainly because Will was partial to the odd drink. His meagre wage always used to burn a hole in his pocket.' He chuckles to himself, at his recollection of days gone by. He also recalls the many pretty young girls and the intimate relationships he'd had, over the years, but he omits to mention this fact, he's sure Katie would not want to hear about those.

Fascinated, Katie sits silently, listening to details of Joseph's past life.

He takes a quick draw on his pipe sending up a spiral of smoke then he continues. 'Soon as he'd drunk it all away, we'd set off home again, his thirst quenched. Well not counting the odd cask of ale he'd stashed away on the cart that is.' Joe frowns, 'then one evening, he didn't come back for his dinner, in fact he didn't come home at all that night. I wasn't too bothered, he often stayed out tending the animals,' he sighs. 'Anyway, early the next morning I was out and about searching for him and eventually I ended up in the spinney, and that's where I found him, sat against a tree trunk, his cap askew over his eyes and an empty bottle gripped in his hand with a smile on his face. He was dead, God bless him.'

Frowning, Joe tuts, shakes his head and draws fruitlessly on his pipe that had gone out, yet again, 'Poor old Will, after that it was all down to me and my mother. We tried to replace him, but who in their right mind would want to work out here in the sticks for a pittance? Nope, it was a case of roll up our sleeves and get on with it, and that's the way it stayed, until just over three months ago.' He pauses sighing laboriously, 'Suddenly, my mother got really sick, she took to her bed and within three weeks she was gone. God rest her sweet soul.'

Reaching across for a little framed photograph, he hands it to Katie, 'My mother, a wonderful beautiful, woman, I miss her so much.'

The photograph is of a woman stood outside the scullery door in a high-necked frock and crisp white pinafore, dark hair framing her extremely attractive face. 'Why she's beautiful Joseph, I can see where you get your good looks from,' she tells him, handing the precious photograph back.

As he takes the photograph, he clasps her fingers firmly, just for a second or two.

Cursing herself for making such a blatant statement, she recoils back in her chair, what must he think of her, saying something so personal?

'Do you think so Katie? That's a nice compliment, thank you,' he says smiling with a smile that reaches his eyes, 'You know my mother would have adored you and Lily,' he chuckles, 'she spent the best part of my adult life trying to marry me off, bless her, she always said that this place was meant to be filled with a family, a big, happy family, and you know what? I reckon she was right.' Clearing his throat, he continues, 'Sorry, I digress, look, what I'm trying to say is, you and Lily, you've both filled this place with joy and happiness. It's what this cottage has been crying out for, so when I say you've both transformed my life, yes, indeed you have and I swear, I couldn't be happier.'

It's on the tip of Katie's tongue to ask why he had never married, he had after all, practically presented her with the opportunity to ask, but before she can utter a word he stands. 'Would you listen to me rabbiting on, look, Lily's sound asleep bless her. I'll carry her up to bed for you.'

'There we go little chatterbox, sleep tight,' he whispers softly, as he gently tucks her into bed. He turns to face Katie, 'I think perhaps we should call it a night,' he suggests, 'after all, we've got a busy day tomorrow, and you Katie, need to rest.'

Moving towards him Katie rests her hand on his arm, she needs to explain to him about her fainting bouts, 'I, I... really wanted to talk to you, there is something that you should know Joseph.'

Placing his hand over hers, he says softly, 'No need Katie love, not tonight. Besides, now you are both staying, I'm hoping there will be all the time in the world for talking.' His smile is wry and his eyes shining brightly in the candlelight.

The effect of which seemed to make her feel weak at the knees. 'I do too.' she confesses.

Stretching his back, he yawns, and Katie follows suit with an unavoidable compulsive yawn too.

Joe can't help himself, he grins, 'There you see, you're tired too. Why don't you get off to bed, we can talk again tomorrow night,' he suggests nonchalantly, not daring to stay in her company any longer. He's becoming aroused, he's so tempted to take her in his arms. He desperately wants to hold her close.

Although exhausted, she can't deny feeling of pang of disappointment. 'Yes, I suppose I am, it's been an exceptionally long day,' she agrees, stifling yet another yawn. Smiling she tries to give him the impression it doesn't matter, but inside she feels deflated, frustrated that the close, warm intimacy of the evening has been broken, she adores being in his company, besides, it would have been a golden opportunity for her to enlighten him with the truth about her fainting episodes, but somehow the matter would have to wait for another day.

'Aye, I guess we're both tired,' he agrees, 'and I'll be up by first light tomorrow,' he reminds her as he turns to leave the room, 'I'll get all the morning chores and the other jobs done really early so we can set off out before lunch'.

Katie nods, 'Sounds exciting, Joe,' she sighs, 'I'll say goodnight then.'

As he closes her bedroom door she sighs again. Tonight, when she'd sat alone with him in the parlour, she'd felt completely relaxed and at ease in his company. Joe is so easy going and they had talked comfortably all evening, she had learned a lot more about him too, though there was no mention of anyone special in his life, either past or present. Her only regret is that she hadn't got around to confiding in him, explaining what he called her fainting bouts, but like he said, they have all the time in the world. Katie smiles to herself, such a lovely prospect.

Stripping off, Joe lays back, naked on his bed. Little does Katie know that Joe too, had regretted ending their evening, but maybe, he decides, the way he feels towards her, told him that it was probably for the best that the evening had ended when it had. Oh Katie, dear sweet Katie. Oh, how I wanted you tonight. There were so many times when he felt sure, that the feelings he had for Katie might be mutual. Could he be wrong? Oh Katie, he sighs, such a young, intoxicating, beautiful, mysterious young woman, he'd only known her for such a short time, yet she had rendered him totally smitten and now she held him uncontrollably captive. Joe hand slides down and grasps his manhood, with a blissful vision of her in his mind he relieves himself. Katie, sweet, beautiful Katie. He comes quickly, laying relaxed and satisfied. It's going to be a long night. He frowns, wishful thinking man, why would a stunner like Katie, be interested in someone like himself? If she knew what was in his heart, she would probably run a mile. But I can dream, he thinks wistfully. 'My dear sweet Katie, sleep tight, my beloved,' he murmurs under his breath and slips into a deep contented sleep.

Unbeknown to Katie, Joe plans to be up long before dawn, it's his intention to drop off the wood for his mate in Holdean, he wants to ensure that he won't turn up at Sweet Briars unannounced.

Although exhausted, sleep also eludes Katie, she lay in bed, but restful slumber just won't come. There's an element of anxiety concerning tomorrow, she would have to try to distance herself from Joe on their excursion, somehow, she had to try and curb the strong feelings she feels for him. After all, she is a married woman with a small child, and they are merely his lodgers, she is only his housekeeper. But there's no respite, the re-occurring vision of Joe stood completely naked keeps her mind working overtime. Besides, he makes her feel safe. He is so considerate, softly spoken and undeniably extremely handsome too, she can feel her heart pounding, she's getting carried away again. Then her thoughts turn to Lilibeth, the transformation in her daughter since they'd arrived here was astounding. She had blossomed into a happy-go-lucky, carefree child, all of which, she directly attributes to Joseph, the man that had offered them a very comfortable, safe sanctuary without any obligation, for that fact alone, she would be eternally grateful. Slipping out of bed she creeps downstairs, the very least she can do is pack Joe a decent meal for the morning.

CHAPTER 6

The following morning, the girls come down to an empty kitchen.

Sat warming on one side of the hot stove is a pot of porridge, the empty log basket had been refilled and the boiler topped up.

She smiles to herself, the food that she'd prepared for him has gone.

Over breakfast Katie and Lilibeth chat. 'Mammy, is we gonna have a picnic with Joe today?'

'Yes, darling, so eat your breakfast, we've got jobs to do and must be ready when Joe finishes his chores.'

In the meantime, Joe's day had begun, long before daybreak, working with a degree of urgency, the cows and goat had been milked, he'd also collected eggs to give to Stan's wife Margo, and all on account that Stan had told him that he would be calling in for more wood supplies within days, and that was the last thing he wanted, today of all days. So, with the wood already loaded on the cart the previous afternoon, all he has to do is hitch up the horse and be off.

The basket of food that Katie had left for him, plus four dozen eggs and a churn of milk is loaded on the cart for his pal, it's time to make a move, for he intends to return home as soon as is physically possible.

The sun is just rising in the sky as he sets off, it's a good two-hour trek along a well-worn track that he, his father and his father's father had walked, driven cattle and rattled along in the cart over so many years. Thankfully, his horse knows every inch of the journey blindfolded, so his concentration on negotiating his way along the eroded track isn't needed, his mind is back at Sweet Briars.

Preoccupied, his thoughts are revolving around the pretty young woman and her delightful child that had dramatically and unexpectedly entered his solitary life and made such an impact on him in such a short space of time. Yes, it had been a huge shock, but he couldn't deny that it was a turn of events that he was rapidly coming to terms with. He knows only too well that he, Joseph Markson, a lifetime bachelor, was enjoying his newly adopted, instant family, Katie and little Lily.

Though a vision haunts him, the awful memory of when they had first met in his yard. He could still picture Katie stood frozen to the spot like a trapped animal, a bowl of milk in her trembling hands. Then there was poor little Lily, terrified and clinging to her mother's skirt, both scared witless as to what could or would happen to them. He also recalls Katie's story, a happy childhood spent with her mother on the Sheybourne Estate. Then the trauma of her dear mother's passing, immediately followed by the callous and heartless stance, Sir bloody what's his name had taken towards Katie's future well-being. Quite literally dumping her unceremoniously, at the mercy of one Albert ruddy Soames, of all people, only to be cruelly beaten!

A shudder runs through his body, the very thought makes him want to vomit. No wonder they had fled for their lives from Soames, a good for nothing, filthy drunkard. Inside he feels a compulsion to do everything in his power to make them both happy and eradicate those vile memories.

'Whoa there Horsey! Mornin', Joe!' Stan yells, over the noise of the wheels grating on the track, he yanks on the reigns to stop his horse colliding with Joes.

Joe's startled back to reality, 'What's that? Oh, Stan Mate, how you doing? I'm just on my way over to yours, as it happens.'

'Huh, obviously better than you Mate. Yer was bleedin' miles away?' Stan grumbles, 'if it hadn't been fer me horse, I would've been in the ruddy ditch!'

'Believe me, you don't want to know,' answers Joe, 'Anyway, how's your Margo and Freddie keeping?' he asks politely, changing the subject.

'Aw fair ter middlin', fair ter middlin' ta Mate,' he says, clambering up alongside Joe on his cart.

'So, what brings you out here?' Joe inquires, 'I wasn't expecting to see you today.'

Stan lifts his cap and scratches his head, 'I reckon yer got a peg loose boy. Didn't I tell yer I was askin' fer more wood? Didn't I say I'd be back ter pick it up?' he playfully punches Joe's arm 'Come on, Joe, what's up, somefin' wrong boy?'

Joe shrugs, 'Like I said Mate, you wouldn't want to know.'

Stan stares at Joe, puzzled, 'Huh, is that right?'

Joe says nothing, he'd been well and truly caught on the hop, what with the shockingly unexpected business of Katie and little Lily turning up at Sweet Briars out of nowhere, and in such strange circumstances and all that had followed, it was little wonder that his actual arrangements with Stan had just gone clean out of his head.

'Well, I reckon yer brain's addled boy. Anyways, turn yer cart round and we'll head up ter Briars and load up me wood,' suggests Stan.

Joe frowns, what about Lily and Katie back at the cottage? He was forced to do a bit of quick thinking. One thing was for sure, if he was to turn up with Stan, he didn't want to think of the consequences. He knew Katie would be packing up and fleeing in blind panic with Lily in tow. Besides, he couldn't let her down, he had made her a promise and there was nothing on earth that would make him go back on his word. His mind's working overtime, searching for a solution, he knows she would never forgive him, and he couldn't live with himself if that happened.

'Hah, no problem Mate, I was on my way to yours anyway. I've got all your wood loaded on my cart, I've even got milk and eggs for Margo on board. We might as well load it all on to your cart here and now, so if you give me a hand, we can get it swapped over in no time.'

Removing his cap, Stan scratches his head, 'Well if yer say so boy, come on then, let's get started.'

Both men strip to their waists, spit on their hands and makes a start, transferring the wood.

Toiling away for more than an hour, Stan plonks himself down on the grass, he's a good few years older than Joe, and was beginning to feel his age, so he rests whilst Joe finishes shifting the last of the wood. 'I don't s'pose yer gotta drink wiv yer, have yer, Mate? I'm fair parched and I's right famished and all.'

'As it happens, I've got a couple flagons of cider on the back and I got some food in the basket and all,' Joe tells him.

With a rumbling belly and eager to quench his thirst, Stan goes to the rear of the cart to find the basket and set it down on the grass.

Stan is about to open the lid. 'No, leave the basket Stan!' shouts Joe, jumping swiftly down from the cart, 'I've got two flagons of cider here.'

Joe's harsh voice surprises Stan. 'Bloody hell, what's up wiv yer?' retorts Stan, looking mystified.

Steady on, Joe reprimands himself, take a deep breath, think what you're saying, or you'll give the game away, he's annoyed with himself for reacted by raising his voice so sharply. 'Sorry Mate, ahem, here, have a drink,' he says handing over a flagon of cider. 'I've probably got a bite or two in my basket.'

Secretly he's delighted that they'd bumped into each other, it would cut his trip to Fennydown by almost three hours or more and he could return home to the girls much earlier than expected.

With both horses free to graze, and Stan quenching his thirst, Joe tentatively lifts the cover on the basket, sat on the top are sandwiches filled with an egg salad. 'There we go, Stan, these should help to fill your belly.'

Loading his cart had built up Stan's appetite and he devours his sandwiches in no time, 'Got anyfin' else boy?'

Beneath the sandwiches are some buttered scones and three jam tarts. Joe considered it to be well worth the sacrifice just to send his mate on his way home, 'Here, a jam tart and a scone Stan,' he says, handing them over, but Stan had spied the rest of the contents of the basket. His curiosity is aroused.

Normally Joe would have been chattering nine to the dozen with Stan, who, for the past few months had been Joe's only source of conversation and contact with the outside world.

Stan couldn't help but notice Joe's strange tight-lipped silence. 'Here yer go Mate,' says Stan thrusting the cider into Joe's hand, 'Maybe that'll loosen yer tongue boy.' he jokes, waiting for a response, but Joe seems miles away, so he gives him an encouraging nudge in the ribs with his elbow, 'Hey up, yer don't seem ter be yerself terday, what's up, Joe?'

The sharp dig has the desired effect, 'Sorry Stan, you were saying?'

Stan tuts, 'Gawd, yer ruddy quiet. Yer ain't sickenin' fer nowt, are yer?'

'Eh, me sick Stan, nah, nothing like that. Here, have a some more to eat,' says Joe, uncovering the basket.

Stan's eyes open wide, 'Cor, would yer look at that bleedin' lot!'

'Help yourself,' offers Joe.

Stan grabs a chunk of crusty bread, 'Now yer ain't gonna tell me yer made this lot yerself, are yer?' he chuckles, 'I mean, would yer look at that pie in there, it looks mighty tasty.'

Smiling wryly, Joe isn't about to give anything away, 'Something wrong with the food then Stan?'

'Nay lad, nowt wrong at all, in fact it's all bloomin' lovely,' he replies. He might have an inquisitive nature, but he's also ravenous, so his questions are put on hold momentarily as he gratefully tucks in.

Annoyed with himself, Joe curses under his breath, he should have been more careful with the contents of the basket.

Interrupting Joe's thoughts, Stan frowns, 'So is yer gonna tell me what's been goin' on?' he asks, wiping his mouth on his sleeve and helping himself to another jam tart.

Jo shrugs, 'Dunno what you're on about.'

But Stan's brain is working overtime, baffled he takes another bite of the jam tart, it suddenly dawns on him, 'Blimey, Joe, I reckon yer been and gawn and got yerself a woman at long last, yer crafty bugger.'

Ignoring Stan's questioning Joe takes a long swig of the cider and changes the subject. 'This cider's good, I had loads of windfalls in the orchard last year, I'm hoping to get a good crop again this year,' he says handing the drink back to Stan.

Adjusting his cap, Stan nods, 'Cheers, Joe, I 'preciates this Mate.' He swallows down a hearty gulp, 'so who's this new woman what yer got then?' he persists like a dog with a bone.

'Huh, there's nothing to tell Stan, honest,' says Joe sounding vague.

Stan polishes off his food with gusto, washing it down with the last of the cider, but he isn't about to be fobbed off, he knows Joe's hiding something and it's eating away at him, 'Git away wiv yer. Come on, lad, spit it out, I ain't a ruddy daft, yer know.'

Joe is struggling with his conscience. He's desperate to confide in his friend and the more he thinks about it, the more he's convinced that he can trust his pal. On the other hand, he had made a promise to Katie, and he is a man of his word. Still, maybe it wouldn't hurt to make a few general enquiries, including Soames, after all, there were plenty of questions that he feels sure Stan could answer.

Another sharp dig in Joe's ribs disturbs his thoughts. 'Ouch, hey Stan, what do you keep doing that for? '

'Cos I'm talkin' ter meself Mate, I told yer, I ain't ruddy daft, Joe. So come on, spit it out, who's the lady yer got livin' wiv yer?'

Ignoring him, Joe shrugs his shoulders again, he wants answers from Stan,

'Forget it, you're barking up the wrong tree Mate,' he tells him, 'Stan, I erm… I was just wondering, how's things are going at market?'

Stan scowls, 'Alwight, have it yer own way, fer now,' says Stan huffing, clearly annoyed that he's being fobbed off, 'Huh, same as always, the markit's quite busy, trade's fairly good.'

Joe nods, 'Hum, that's good, and how is Mick and Edna doing?'

'Fair ter middlin', Jed and Joanie's 'specting their first in a monf or so. Our Margo, Edna and Verity been clackin' away wiv them ruddy knittin' needles fer monfs. It drives yer bleedin' mad, and as fer the ruddy wool all over the bleedin' place!'

Joe laughs, 'I can imagine Stan, is… is your Freddy still playing the field with all the young girls?'

'Aye, there been a quite a few, though he seems ter be sweet on his latest gel. A pretty liddle fing, her name's Verity.'

'Oh, really Stan?' said Joe, feigning interest, 'And erm, and what do you know about Soamesy, the old drunkard? Hah, is he still around or has he drunk himself six feet under yet?' he asks, trying to inject some humour, yet doing his best to sound casual?

Stan's taken aback, he stops chewing, his bushy eyebrows shoot up, 'Soames! Do yer mean Albert bleedin' Soames of Penfold Grove?'

'Aye, that's him,' confirms Joe nonchalantly.

If it had been anyone else poking his nose and asking, Stan would have told them to mind their own business, because other country folks affairs were their own concern round these parts, but this is Joe asking, someone he'd known man and boy, a good life-long pal.

Stan's curiosity is aroused even more, Joe had set him thinking. Eyeing the freshly baked bread and scrumptious looking remnants of the delicious chicken pie with the golden pastry crust sat in the basket, slowly a notion crept into his mind, 'Joe, mate, about this new woman of yourn.'

'Woman?' says Joe, looking pensive and offering no explanation.

As realisation hits Stan he almost chokes on his pie crust, 'Christ all bloody mighty, it can't be! I don't ruddy believe it. I reckon I knows who made this lot!' he blurts out.

Joe gnaws on his lip, his expression deadly serious.

Agitated, Stan leaps to his feet and glares down at Joe, 'I fink yer better start talkin' boy!'

'Please Stan, we've known each other a lifetime,' says Joe, 'and I'm desperate, there's things I need to know first before I say anything. But you must understand, our conversation must go no further, not even to your Margo.' His tone is forceful and his expression deadly serious. 'Please Stan.'

Shaking his head, Stan frowns, 'I'm right, yer ruddy well knows I am, yer got yerself a new gel. So, tell us who she is! What's her name?' he demands forcefully, he couldn't sure, but in the back of his mind, Katie had sprung to mind. Who else could bake food like this?

Looking a tad nervous, Joe frowns sombrely, 'I mean it Stan, I want your word before I say anything!'

Stan thinks about it. In all the twenty-five years he'd known Joe, forceful aggression was something he had never seen in him before, yet here he is, all fired up. It was obviously important to him, he holds up his hands, 'Okay, calm yerself down Joe, but I'm tellin' yer, it's me what's gonna want answers when yer done, so what exactly does yer want ter know?'

Wrestling with his conscience, Joe knows Katie will be mortified, but he has to talk to someone. He also knows he'd be foolish to think that they could go on living together at his place for ever, sooner or later it was bound to come out, should he keep quiet, bide his time? As much as he wants them there, he knows in his heart it can't possibly work, she couldn't live at Briars, never leaving the boundaries. No, like it or not, it was his duty to set her free, after all, if there was anyone in the world he could trust, it was his good mate, Stanley Hooper. Sighing, Joe is now positive that as his closest friend, he wouldn't betray his trust. However, the fact remains, he has questions that needed answers first, but he wants Stan's promise before he's prepared to say another word.

Deep inside something is driving Joe, he wants Katie to feel that they can be free of that bastard Soames forever, and by God, he was going to make it happen one day soon. It had pained him to sit and listen to Katie pouring out all the misery she'd been forced to live through and if Stan could fill him in with more details, maybe it could help him to alleviate her fears, sparing her further distress. Maybe he could wipe the slate clean for her so that she would be able to get on with her life, no more looking over her shoulder in constant fear.

'When yer ready, Joe, I say when yer ready boy,' prompts Stan, waiting impatiently, anxious to get his own questions answered as soon as possible.

'Do what Stan...?' Joe's mind is fixed back at the cottage.

'Yer miles away agin, come on, Joe, snap out of it, now tell us, why's yer askin' about ruddy Soamsey?'

'Before I say anything, do you swear our conversation will go no further, not even to your Margo! Do you?' Joe demands.

Affronted Stan scowls, 'Aw come on now, Joe, how long have we been friends? If I says I won't blab then I ruddy won't!' Stan insists, he's sorely aggrieved that after all the years he'd known him, Joe was taking his distrusting attitude towards him.

'Thanks Stan, I'm grateful. Remember, I'm putting my trust in you. Now tell me what you know about Soames,' he prompts again, 'I've not seen or heard about him since I stopped going to market with Will. So, tell me what happened after young Brodie and her infant died?'

Stan draws on his pipe, pushes the brim of his hat up, sighs deeply then obligingly agrees to talk. 'Alwight then, Joe, have it yer own bleedin' way. Young Brodie, ahem, yes well after she died, Soames found himself anover young gel. Gawd knows where she came from but...' he stops for a moment, 'look, Joe, afore I tells yer any more, there's somefink I really gotta know. '

Despite being painfully aware that he's betraying Katie's trust, Joe persists, he's determined to get all the facts and he isn't prepared to put up with Stan's shilly-shallying any longer, 'First things first Stan, tell me all you know about Soames after Brodie.' Joe's face is growing dark, his frustration taking over, 'For pity's sake, come on man, out with it, I have to know!' he demands, fiercely agitated.

Taken aback by Joe's uncharacteristic outburst, Stan holds his hands up, 'Okay, okay, but I'm tellin' yer, it ain't a pretty story, and yer might well be sorry yer asked and all.'

To Joe's frustration Stan pauses, again, relights his pipe, then rests back against a tree trunk. 'Like I was sayin,' this new gel what Soamesy got, we didn't know where she came from, she just started turnin' up at the markit wiv him. Aw a right lovely gel, a real stunner, she was, so very young and well-spoken wiv real nice manners and all,' says Stan, 'a quiet, very pretty young thing who wouldn't say boo to a goose. Monf after monf, they came ter markit. Each visit, she brought more and more stuff ter sell. Lovely bakin'. Crusty bread, pies, cakes, jams and bottled all sorts,' says Stan, glancing into the basket of food, 'Anyway, our Margo got talkin' wiv her, she wanted jars fer bottlin' stuff and jams like, so our Margo swapped some jars fer some of her bread, pies and lovely grub, they struck up a real friendship.'

There's a brief pause for breath then Stan carries on, 'After a while Margo and Edna got ter be real good pals. It wasn't difficult mind, coz everyone liked her. I s'pose we all felt sorry fer her too, being lumbered wiv an old drunk like him. I mean, she was makin' the money and he'd just drink it all away. Anyway, she soon learned to buy all her supplies a bit sharpish, afore he came back fer her takin's, poor love. Our Margo and Edna took her under their wing, so ter speak.' Stan pauses taking a deep breath, sighs and looks at Joe,' Look Mate, I dunno if yer want to hear any more, yer ain't gonna like it, believe me.'

Passing the second flagon of cider to Stan in the hopes of loosening Stan's tongue, Joe waits whilst Stan quenches his thirst, until exasperated, he clenches his hands, 'Come on Stan, please, I gotta know!'

'Alwight, don't say I didn't warn yer. Here goes then. Wivin a couple of monfs, the gel changed from a stunnin' beauty ter a pale skinny fing,' he says shaking his head. 'Ruddy tragic ter see it were, she was sort of jumpy and nervy like. Our Margo was worried, we all were, we could see all the cuts and bruises, then she got really sick. Anyway, my Margo said she had her suspicions that Soamesy was not only knockin' her about, but takin' real dirty liberties wiv her if yer catch me drift. Next markit, Margo and Edna took her aside fer a chat. Our Margo reckons she were a pure innocent, didn't know bugger all about men, sex and all that stuff. Anyway, they talked to her, woman ter woman and by gawd, they got the shock of their bleedin' lives! Turns out the first time he had her was when the filfy bastard came home early and caught her in the tub, starkers like, and he um, er... he dragged her out of the tub and forced himself on her.'

It's as if someone had stabbed Joe in his belly. 'You mean he raped her? Dear God, no!'

'Yep, he raped her alwight, in fact he started doin' it regular. Dear Lord, he was brutal wiv it and all, so Margo told me. Well, our Margo and Edna talked ter her, private like. I can tell yer, they were ruddy shocked. Turns out she were not only pregnant, but she were pregnant, and didn't even know it! Anyway, Soames came staggerin' along, blind drunk and afore me and our Freddie could knock hell out of him, she takes one look at him, and she passes out at our feet!' Pausing briefly, he gulps down more cider. 'My Margo never said nuffin' about the baby, she told him in no uncertain terms Katie was comin' back home wiv us coz she was sick. My gawd, Joe, were he mad, but yer should've seen our Margo, bless her, faced up ter him like a good un. She told him the poor gel were so sick she was comin' back wiv us, and that was final.' Stan looks at Joe and shakes his head, 'I tell yer, Joe, me and Freddie was ready fer him, but he didn't so much as put up an argument. Margo reckoned he didn't want Katie if she were sick, coz she'd be more of a liability than of use ter him. Huh somehow, he crawled up on his cart and left her wiv us, making his way home alone. Katie, gawd bless her, was scared rigid.'

Confirmation at last, Stan had named her. Katie, yes, the sweet innocent young woman that followed in poor Brodie's footsteps was "his" Katie. He's incensed, eaten up with revulsion and hatred, vowing there and then, that he would make Soames pay for his evil ways, by God he would! but the harrowing story proves too much. He gives out a long heavy groan, clenches his hands into taut white knuckled fists, after listening intently to Stan's every word, he feels sick inside with the whole sorry story, bile rises from his stomach, he's physically sick.

Stan turns to face Joe, 'Is yer alwight Mate. I reckon you've heard enough.'

Bewildered, Joe gawps at Stan, 'Enough! You can't mean there's more?'

Stan nods, 'Aye, Joe, lots more.'

'Keep going Stan,' Joe urges, through clenched teeth, 'I've gotta hear it all.'

Stan shrugs his shoulders, 'Alwight, Joe, if yer insistin'. As I was sayin', we kept Katie wiv us fer about a fortnight. She were in a right state, scared silly she was. Our Margo took her time, explainin' that she was expectin' a little baby as a result of him raping her. Jesus, she were so innocent our Margo had ter explain about sex and gettin' pregnant, poor kiddie, she had no idea at all, bless her.' Sighing he shifts, 'Eventually she came around to the idea. Then, wiv no good reason, she comes out and says she wants ter keep the baby, she's gonna tell Soames she's expectin', and they'd have ter get wed.' Stan's shaking his head with disbelief, 'We could hardly believe it, Joe! Her wantin' ter bloody marry him!' Stan looks at Joe and shrugs his shoulders, 'Our Margo, Edna, Mick and me, we all tried to talk sense into her, we really did, even our Freddie put in his two pennorth, but there were no talkin' her out of it. My Margo said Katie desperately wanted someone ter love. Her own little baby were gonna fit the bill. Gawd love us, she was prepared ter live wiv that filfy rotten bastard Soames so that she could give the child a name, and have a roof over their heads, she said it were the respectable fing ter do.'

Lifting his cap, Stan scratches his head again, he tuts, frowning, 'We loved Katie, just like our own, but she weren't havin' none of it. Anyway, ter cut a long story shorter, we took her back ter Penfold. We stayed wiv her while she told him she was pregnant. Oh, you should have seen his horrible ugly mug, he just sat gloatin'. He knew he had a hold on her.' Stan clenches his fists, 'Katie insisted she'd made her mind up.' Stan shifts again, he's feeling uncomfortable with sitting so long, he was also upset at having to relate Katie's tragic life history to Joe.

Without Joe's encouragement Stan continues, 'Next markit day, they got wed, we was all there, givin' Katie our support. Me, Margo, Edna, Mick, our Freddie wiv one of his new gels. Huh it took all of ten minutes fer them ter wed then he was gawn, orf ter get himself blathered. Poor gel, she didn't have a clue what was happenin'. Anyway, the damage was done, and she was married fer better or worse. Come markit days, Margo and Edna did their best ter help her frew her pregnancy. Bloody Soames weren't no bleedin' help, that's fer sure. She carried on workin' her fingers ter the bone and him bloody well lettin' her do it!'

Stan, sighs long and hard, sadly the cider jar is now empty, so he's obliged to carry on with a parched throat, 'Four weeks later, markit was just finishin' and Katie started wiv baby pains. Albert were nowhere ter be seen, so we got her ter our house on me cart. Poor love, she had a real bad time, it went on fer over two days, Margo said it were touch and go fer quite a while. Course the baby were weak and as small as yer'd never believe, bein' born so early like, but by gawd, she was a little fighter. Margo took it in turns wiv Edna, lookin' after them both and somehow, they pulled frew. Katie had a little girl, called Lilibeth, an unusual name it's true. Lily was after Katie's late and most treasured mother Lillian, and the Beth bit come from an old friend's name, Elsbeth. Such a pretty little fing was Lilibuff, she obviously didn't take after him, fank gawd.'

Stan stops to wipe his brow, 'Yer know, Joe, it took Soames four ruddy days ter sober up enough ter miss her. Then he came stormin' over ter fetch them, he thought he could take them home right there and then. Course me and our Margo told him they were far too weak ter travel, and Katie and the baby could die. We said Katie would be back when she's good and ready. I tell yer, Joe, he got right stroppy, so I told him straight, yer might chuck yer weight around when it's a woman, but if yer wants ter take on me, along wiv Mick and our Freddy then he only had ter say. I also told him young Brodie might have died along wiv her baby, but it weren't gonna happen ter Katie. Bleedin' coward, we sent him home wiv a flea in his ear. Anyway, Katie stayed wiv us till the next two markits had passed, then she went back ter Penfold Grove wiv him, and that, more or less brings us up ter the here and now, Joe boy, 'cept the grizzly details of the filfy pervert, forcin' her ter do such God-awful dirty things and carryin' on where he left orf wiv her as soon as they were back at Penfold. Poor sweet soul, coz of him she had several miscarriages yer know, but I ain't gonna go inter that stuff,' concludes Stan, 'it's a tragic story,' he says shaking his head. 'Such a bloody tragic story. He looks at

Joe, his face ashen and grim, 'I'm sorry Mate, but yer did ask me ter tell yer.'

Joe sits, maintaining his silence. Shock, anger, pain, fury, sadness, it is all churning around inside him, his heart goes out to Katie. It explains everything, her nervousness and shyness, why she was so wary of him, and who the hell could possibly blame her?

'Now I been real patient like, I reckon yer got somefin' ter tell me, ain't yer?' says Stan quietly.

Joe is trying to think. He trusts Stan with his life, and from what he'd heard, Stan and his family had been more than good friends to Katie. They were the nearest to a family she had now.

'Well, Joe? I's waitin' Mate.'

'It's true Stan, they're with me at Sweet Briars. I took them in a while ago,' he confesses

Euphoric, Stan stands, throwing his cap in the air, 'Gawd almighty, I was bleedin' right! What a ruddy relief, we were beginin' ter fink the bastard had done them in, Joe! We've searched high and low fer them. How are they? Are they alwight? Right, I gotta see them, now!'

'No wait Stan! You can't go barging up there yet, we've got to talk about it! Just sit down a minute.' The raised tone of his voice makes it obvious that it's more of an order than a request.

Stan looks puzzled, he huffs, 'Why the hell not? I gotta see them.'

Joe hands Stan a second piece of pie to placate him, 'They're fine Mate, I swear. Stan, listen to me, please. They just turned up at Sweet Briars out of the blue, they were both in a terrible state when I found them. The weather was foul, and they were both soaking wet. At first, I thought Katie was a filthy dirty tramp, she looked so bad,' he tells Stan, 'I think they'd been living rough in the fields. When they turned up, they'd apparently been living in my barn. Poor Katie was battered and bruised, and they were both scared witless, so I took them in.' He shakes his head. 'It was obvious they were running away from someone, they were both terrified, so I offered them a safe sanctuary at mine. I had no idea who they were, and I certainly had no idea that they were running away from that bastard Soames. How could I?' he sighs once more. 'They were in a desperate condition when I found them Stan, soaking wet, battered, bruised and filthy. Since then, I've spent all my time trying to calm them down, trying to make them feel safe Mate. It wasn't easy, but I think the girls trust me now. Stan, I also made Katie a promise that no one would ever know they were living at Sweet Briars and I'm not about to let her down now.'

'But we're her friends, Joe!' remonstrates Stan.

'I understand what you're saying and of course you want to see them, it's only natural, and you will, but I have to talk to Katie first, explain why I confided in you.'

'I dunno,' says Stan, scratching his head, 'we all been worried ter deaf about them. We knew they'd gawn missin' coz bleedin' Soames came ter ours, and damn me, he's been back every day since. He even searched our house; he was bloody sure we were hidin' them. Christ, our Margo will be so ruddy happy. Joe, we're right grateful ter yer fer helpin' them out, but I want ter see them, take them home wiv me, then me and Margo can sort fings out.'

All of a sudden, someone else wants to take over. Now, Joe's protective role is about to be snatched away from him and he's struggling to get his head round it. He considers the trauma that Katie and Lily have lived through. True, he now knew they had real friends who obviously cared for them both deeply, good loyal friends, and Katie undoubtedly needs their support, he knows he can't deprive them of that. But Margo, Stan and their son Freddie, Edna and Mick and their three sons, are his friends too. Maybe Katie and Lily should be with them, but can he let them go? Also, there's still that bastard Soames to consider. He doesn't even bother to think about it further, 'I'm sorry Stan, but I need time, time to explain to Katie why I broke my word to her. I don't want her to lose her trust in me,' he says grimly. 'Yes of course you must see them Stan, all of you. But we're old friends and I'm asking you to trust my judgement and wait a bit. Let me talk to Katie first, break the news to her gently. I must explain to her ... I need to tell her that through a chance conversation, I discovered that we both share the same, pretty wonderful, mutual friends.' He looks directly at Stan, appealing to his better judgement, 'Aw come on Mate, you've no idea what sort of state they were in when I found them!'

Stan is shaking his head, 'Sorry Mate, I'm not sure I can see yer logic, what harm can it do fer me ter see them?'

Joe pauses for a minute and comes up with what he thinks is a good compromise. 'Perhaps it would be better if you and Margo come to Briars to see them. My point being, Soames has already visited you, looking for them already, so there's nothing to say he won't come back again, is there?'

Uncertain, Stan shakes his head, 'I dunno know, Joe, our Margo's gonna be livid, if I leaves them both at yours.'

Rapidly losing his patience, Joe is becoming visibly distressed with Stan's obstinate reluctance to agree. 'Right Stan, let's say Soamesy turns up at your place and finds Katie and little Lily there, he'll cause havoc. You give him a good pasting, but you won't gain anything Stan, except bruised knuckles and a sore head, and him? He'll take Katie, his legal wedded wife, and his child, back to Penfold Grove for a lifetime of unimaginable misery. Like it or not, they are married for Christ's sake! The truth is the law is on his side. Is that what you want to happen to Katie and Lily? You must know he won't let them go Stan, ever!' He points out, sounding a grim warning. 'And there's Katie's welfare and feelings to consider. Aye Stan, Katie's petrified of him and so is little Lily, and with fucking good reason, according to what you've just told me.' He grasps Stans shoulders, 'Believe me Stan, the girls have been through pure hell. Think man, where's the safest place for them to be right now? Soames would never think of coming to mine in a month of Sundays.' Joe relaxes his grip on Stan. 'Please Stan, leave them both with me for the time being. At least you know they'll be safe and well cared for.'

Thinking long and hard, Stan agrees 'Hmm, since yer put it like that, then I'll go along wiv whatever yer fink is best Mate. So, what's yer proposin' for us ter do then?'

'Just give me a few days, let me speak to Katie in my own time, surely you owe me that much,' he finishes, throwing himself on Stan's mercy.

Ground down and won over to Joe's way of thinking, Stans grim expression breaks into a broad smile, he grabs Joe's hand and shakes it, vigorously. 'Alwight I agrees Mate, yer got four days.' Stan holds out his hand, 'give it here Mate, I gotta fank yer fer takin' them in and lookin' after them, I knows our Margo'll give yer a smack on yer kisser too,' he quips, still gripping and shaking Joe's hand. 'We'll be over this Friday then, come dinner time, if that suits yer boy?'

'All right, Friday it is Stan,' says Joe, relieved that at least he had earned a reprieve. 'We'd best finish up here then you can get off home. Tell Margo that they're both safe and well, put her mind at rest. But Stan,' he adds soberly, 'you must make Margo understand that it's in Katie's and Lily's best interest that she shouldn't breathe a word to anyone. I mean it! Tell her from me, in a few short days we will all sit down together and work out what to do for the best.'

As soon as Stan had given in, it felt like a ton weight had been lifted from Joe's shoulders, he sighs a long sigh of relief. 'So, what are you waiting for Stan, the sooner you get home and tell Margo the better.'

'Aye yer right Mate, I reckons I got plenty of wood ter get on wiv anyway,' says Stan, all fingers and thumbs in his haste to re-harness his horse, he's anxious to get back to Margo and impart his incredible news.

They shake hands, 'Time fer me ter be makin' tracks,' Stan declares 'Gawd, I can't wait ter tell our Margo I've found them. She'll be tickled pink when I tells her that they ain't only safe, they're at Sweet Briars wiv Joseph Markson! Bloody hell, she'll be delirious.' He shakes his head, 'Been out of her mind wiv worry she has, we all has.'

Flicking the reigns, he calls to Joe, 'See yer Mate, give the gels me love, tell them we'll see them Friday dinner. Hey up Horsey, homeward!' Overjoyed, Stan heads home to Fennydown, anxious to impart his sensational news to his good lady wife.

Joe climbs aboard his cart and steers homeward, as he does, he mulls over the best way to break the news to Katie. Perhaps he should come straight out with it the minute he arrives home. He frowns. There again, maybe, at the very least, they can have this afternoon out together first, or maybe he should wait until Lily's in bed tonight, or even wait and tell her tomorrow? Oh hell, it had been his intention to give them a happy relaxing day out, but by opening his big mouth he had put the kiss of death on what would have been a beautiful relaxing day out, spent in their company.

He curses himself for confiding in Stan. Now his stupid curiosity means that one way or another they would soon be gone, gone out of his life just as quickly as they had entered it, a day he was dreading with all his heart.

You don't miss what you've never had, he tells himself. Huh, bloody ironic that. How wrong can you be?

Perhaps he should wait and tell her tomorrow? He ponders, or maybe even spend a second day out with them. He knows he has to tell her sometime, but selfishly, he wants to keep them to himself for at least two more days, two wonderful days of fulfilling and rewarding domestic bliss spent with Katie and little Lily, before he breaks the news that he had blabbed to Stan. After all, Margo and Stan wouldn't be here until Friday. He has four whole days to spend with them in the meantime.

Determined to make their day a special day to remember, he finally makes his mind up. His decision to tell Katie about Stan could wait. They would have a couple of wonderful days out together, then he would break the news tomorrow evening, hoping that she might find it in her heart to forgive him.

CHAPTER 7

'Joe!' Lily squeals, as he opens the door.

Sweeping her up in his arms she gives him what was fast becoming a warm, customary welcome home hug, followed by the usual convivial wet kiss on his cheek.

'Now that is what I call good timing.' Katie says, greeting him with a beautiful smile, 'Sit yourself down and put your feet up, I'll make you a cup of tea, you can have a rest before we set off, I've made the picnic and we're ready to go.' Katie's looking radiantly happy, Joe does his best to conceal his heavy heart. 'I'm afraid I raided the basket this morning, I was starving, there's not much left,' he confesses.

Katie shrugs, 'Not to worry, there's plenty more here.'

'Never-the-less, it was very thoughtful of you to take the trouble to make it, I want you to know that I appreciated it, I really did,' he insists. 'I'll just go and clean myself up in the garden before we go. 'I won't be long.'

When he returns, Joe is riddled with guilt and feeling uncomfortable, to say the least. Maybe he should tell her about Stan now. His train of thought is distracted by Lily. 'We been in the dairy all morning,' she tells him. 'We made some butter, see,' she says, pointing out a pat of golden butter in a dish, 'and Mammy said we're going to make some cheese one day, very soon. So, is we all going out, coz I been a good girl, all day? And I helped Mammy do all the housework, everywhere.'

He grins, wondering if she might faint from lack of breath.

The scullery falls silent. Lilibeth seemed to have run out of conversation, for the present at least.

Thanks to Lilibeth, her momentary silence means Katie can manage to get a word in, 'Everyone ready to go?'

'Yes please!' comes the chorus.

The afternoon is kept simple, a picnic in the meadow, idle chit chat, watching rabbits bobbing about and making daisy chains ensue, but sadly, all too soon it is time to head home.

Six thirty, Lilibeth is strip-washed in the scullery and dressed for bed.

'There we go Pet, all ready, come on, let's say goodnight to Joseph,' says Katie, carefully brushing her daughter's hair.

'Someone in there want a lift up to bed'? enquires Joe, popping his head round the scullery door, 'I'm ready when you are Lily.'

'Wheee! I'll get my Daisy,' says Lilibeth, obviously delighted that he'd offered to carry her up to bed himself.

'Right, piggy-back for two it is then,' he says and carries her up to bed.

'Lilibeth, say thank you to Joe for the lovely day out, we both really loved it, thank you Joe. We thoroughly enjoyed ourselves.'

Lily responds with a hug. 'Thank you, Joe, nighty night.'

'Nighty night sweetheart,' he says, gently stroking her rosy-red cheek.

At last, the cottage is blissfully quiet, Lilibeth is sleeping soundly upstairs.

Joe and Katie sit either side of the fire in the parlour, quietly enjoying their hot milk.

She studies Joe as she sips her drink, 'I'm sorry about Lilibeth, she can be so noisy and boisterous at times,' she says apologetically.

Shaking his head, he smiles, he'd grown really fond of Lily. 'Please, don't apologise Katie, little Lily has brought life to this old place, you both have, and I've thoroughly enjoyed every moment.'

At this point, he wonders if he should come clean and tell her about Stan, but just as he builds up the courage to confess, Katie leaps to her feet, startled.

'What's that noise!' she exclaims.

'It's okay, I'm pretty sure we've got a fox hanging around outside,' he tells her, 'I'll have a look.' Stood by the window he peers outside, 'There he is, come and have a look, quick Katie!'

Joining him at the window, they stand side by side, Joe slips his arm around her shoulders, they watch the young fox, slinking around the yard in the moonlight.

'Beautiful, isn't he?' whispers Katie.

'Hum, sly, more like, 'he says scowling, 'I reckon I'm gonna have to keep a closer eye on my chickens.'

Reassured, Katie returns to her chair.

'What a lovely home you have Joe, it's so peaceful and quiet. The cottage is really comfortable, and the countryside around here is beautiful, I can see why you love this place,' she says stretching her legs, sighing contentedly, 'Who could ask for more?'

Intoxicated by her beauty he gazes at her, the soft, flickering light from the oil lamp, lighting up her gorgeous auburn hair and putting a sparkle in her beautiful clear blue eyes. Her voice is sweet and soft, he could sit and listen to her for hours, indeed he wishes he could spend all night with her, but Stan's words are echoing around in his head. We'll all see you Friday. He has just three short days left to share with them.

'About tomorrow,' he says, breaking into her thoughts, 'I reckon the weather will break soon, so let's make the most of it and take a picnic again, maybe we could even do a spot of fishing. What do you think Katie?'

Apprehension flickers over her face, 'Oh, I don't know Joe, we won't go far, will we?' she asks, still not sure about leaving the safe confines of the cottage and gardens. 'Only, we would be more than happy to stay here.'

Joe rolls his eyes, in exasperation, 'Is that so? Well let me tell you something, my dear Katie. As it happens, I own all the land around here, acres and acres, so we won't meet up with a living soul,' he assures her. 'Besides, you really seemed to relax today, it did you a power of good, you look beautiful. You deserve a break, and it's my way of repaying you for all that you've done for me,' he insists. 'As I told you when you first came here, you will always be safe with me,' he leans towards her, lowering his voice, 'and I have my pride too, you know. So please, allow me to say thank you for all you've done here. Besides, I've promised Lily, we can't let her down, so come on Katie, let's all have some fun together.' His eyes fixes on hers, pleading with her, willing her to say yes.

Dear Lordy, how can she resist him? With his powerful persuasive declaration easily winning her over, breathlessly she finds herself surrendering, 'Thank you, Joseph. It sounds wonderful.'

'That's settled then,' he says, relieved to have secured another, possibly last, glorious day in her wonderful company. After a long memorable day, he rests back in his chair, unable to suppress a yawn.

'You look all in,' she tells him, yawning herself, 'You get up so early and work so many hours.'

There was no denying he'd had an exceedingly long, eventful day. 'Yes, I suppose we could call it a day.' He yawns again. Too long in her company and he might be tempted to spoil everything and confess about his fateful meeting with Stan, or even worse, declare his feelings for her.

Katie follows suit by yawning again, 'Oh help, it's catching.' she giggles.

Joe's sad face breaks into a bright smile, 'Oh it's so good to see you so happy Katie, you have such a beautiful smile,' he tells her 'You both deserve a lot more happiness in your young lives,' he says sincerely.

Gulping, Katie turns away. How embarrassing, Joe is so free with his compliments, and she doesn't know how to deal with them. In danger of succumbing to his charms, she lowers her eyes and stutters, 'I th-think I should s-say goodnight, Joe.'

Disappointment shadows his face, it's not what he wants, but at least there's tomorrow. 'Sleep well, my dear, I'll see you later.'

'Yes, bright and early, good night, Joe, and thank you for today, it was wonderful.' To his surprise, she leans over and presses a light kiss on his cheek.

Lying in bed he strokes his cheek where she'd kissed him with her soft lips, closing his eyes, picturing her today, happy, carefree, relaxed with the sun shining on her burnished auburn hair, he relieves himself again.

All three are up early the next morning, though Joe had hardly slept, his conversation with Stan had haunted him. But today, he had resolved to put those thoughts behind him, well, at least until tonight.

'Joe,' Lily pulls at his shirt sleeve, 'Don't you like your breakfast?'

'Huh? Sorry ducky, I was miles away,' he says, looking at his stone-cold porridge, 'Lily, what do say to a nice picnic today?' he asks. 'The cows and goat are milked, the chicken fed, all the eggs collected, the horse is happy, and the logs are nicely stacked up next to the range, so how about it?'

'Oh yes please, is we going now, Joe?' she asks excitedly bouncing up and down on her chair.

Their chattering brings a broad smile to Katie's face, hum, rabbiting on, it would seem, is a pastime shared by both her daughter and Joseph.

'Can we, Mammy, I love picnics with Joe, we can take Daisy, coz she likes picnics too, please, Mammy, please?'

'I think it's a splendid idea,' says Katie. 'Mind you, I'll need a hand to prepare the food, any offers?'

Both Lilibeth and Joe eagerly answer in unison, 'I will!'

Katie chuckles, 'Oh my, a pair of Polly parrots, and a prize pair at that.'

Delighted, Lilibeth claps her hands, 'Ooo, isn't my mammy lovely, Joe?'

'Oh yes, she certainly is,' he agrees, looking directly at Katie, his dark blue eyes filled with longing.

It was either the way his eyes met hers, or his comment, that sends Katie scurrying into the safety of the larder, to hide her enchantment and regain a degree of calmness.

'Anything I can do. Katie?' he calls.

'Um, no thanks, I'm um, looking for the jam,' she calls back.

Sat watching Katie as she slices the bread and adeptly prepares more food, there is admiration in Joe's eyes, for the transformation in Katie over the past few months has been nothing short of a miracle. She had changed so dramatically from the day they both met. The haunting look of fear and despair had vanished. Now she had a smile that could melt your heart and take your take your breath away.

'There, that's it!' she announces, wiping her hands, 'all done and dusted, time to go.'

'We didn't do no dusting today mamma,' Lilibeth points out.

'No, and you're not going to either,' Joe chips in, 'today we're going to have a really enjoyable day out,' he tells her, 'because today, we are all going fishing for our tea!'

Lilibeth's face is a picture worth framing.

'I'll just fetch the rods from the barn,' says Joe.

Lilibeth is beside herself, 'I'll come with you,' she says, taking his hand.

Katie smiles, 'You two get off and fetch the rods, it won't take me five minutes to pack the basket.'

Lilibeth is out of the door in seconds, Daisy in one hand and Joe, being tugged along, with the other, 'We won't be long, Mammy!'

In no time at all, the basket is on the table, bursting with an enviable feast, including one of Katie's raspberry jam pies and a jar of goats' cream.

Determined to make the most of the day, Joe breezes into the scullery, 'Are we ready?' He's accompanied by Lilibeth, two fine fishing rods, a couple of sacks and a keep net.

'Almost. I've just got to put this milk in a jug. There, that's it,' says Katie, removing her pinafore, 'I think that's everything.'

Joe lifts the basket, 'I do hope so, this weighs a ton. Off we go then,' he says, closing the door behind them. 'Hum, just what the doctor ordered, a beautiful warm sunny day,' says Joe, inhaling a deep lung full of air.

'Are you sick then, Joe?' asks Lilibeth frowning.

'Sick, who's sick?' queries Katie.

'I think Joe's sick, Mammy, he said about a doctor.'

'I think he's pulling your leg again sweetheart, says Katie stifling a chuckle, 'Take no notice.'

'Oh no, not my legs again,' says Lily pulling her hemline down to protect them.

As is becoming the norm, Lilibeth's incessant, habitual and witty repertoire, has the effect of setting them all laughing. The air is filled carefree laughter until they finally reached the riverbank.

'Well, what do you think?' he asks Katie, setting down the basket and laying out the blanket on the grass.

Sitting on a large boulder Katie looks around. The riverbank is lush and green, the bright sunlight flickers through the weeping willow dancing on the rippling water. 'Oh, Joe it's simply beautiful here,' she sighs in awe.

Jumping to his feet, Joe yells, 'Quick Lily, here, grab hold of the rod, we've got a bite!'.'

Quick as lightening Lilibeth grabs the rod, 'Me got it, quick, Joe, quick!'

'Hold on, don't let go Lily!' he shouts, 'I'll try and land it in the keep net.' Tugging a little too enthusiastically, Lily pulls on the rod, loses her balance and slips.

Katie, who is keeping a close eye on her daughter, leaps to her feet, snatching Lilibeth back from the edge of the bank, beating Joe by seconds.

Too late to stop himself, Joe dives into the water, surfacing, only to find Lily, safe in her mother's arms, they're both laughing hysterically at him.

Climbing out he stands wet, bedraggled, and roaring with laughter.

'Oh no, Joe, look at you, you're soaking wet.'

Looking skyward, Joe breathes a sigh of relief, 'Oh Katie, I'm sorry, I didn't think, I'm not used to little ones, are you all right Lily?'

'I'm all right, did we lose my fish?' asks Lily, apparently not the least bothered by her near fatal escapade.

'Er, nope, the fish is still here. Thanks to your mammy, everything's all here. You, the rod, and this blooming great fish, he says, proudly holding up their handsome catch on the end of the line. 'Wow, I don't think I've ever caught such a big fish in my life!'

Clearly shaken, the smile fades from his face, 'I'll tell you what though, young lady. Your mammy and me, we nearly had kittens, so I think we should move away from the water and find somewhere else to eat our picnic,' he suggests, 'I'll put the fish in the keep net for later.'

'I had a lovely kitten,' says Lilibeth wistfully, 'we left it with my papa, didn't we Mamma? '

Sadness clouds Katie's face, 'Yes, I'm sorry darling, I'd forgotten about Bella.'

'Papa will look after my Bella, won't he Mamma?' she asks anxiously.

The mood had suddenly changes, it has turned sombre.

It pains Joe to see the little one so sad, he throws off his sodden shoes, socks and clinging wet shirt. he challenges Lilibeth, 'Race you to the oak tree over there!' and without waiting for her to answer, he takes off across the field.

Lilibeth runs after him as fast as her little legs will carry her.

He feigns a fall, rolling head over heels.

'I won, I'm first!' calls out a jubilant Lilibeth, 'I'm the winner!' she yells to her mother and waves.

'Best of two, I'll race you back to Mammy!' he offers, tripping clumsily over his feet, to ensure that Lilibeth gets a head start and beat him fairly and squarely.

'I won, I'm first again!' puffs Lilibeth, jumping onto her mother's lap.

Joining them he lays on the grass, resting back on his elbows, bare chested, studying the sky.

Lilibeth promptly lays beside him, 'What are you looking at, Joe?'

He looks up again, 'The clouds, sweetheart.' Lying flat, he put his hands under his head, 'Look up, look at the big cloud right above us, what do you see?'

'Just a big white fluffy cloud,' she answers truthfully.

'Look again Lily,' he says, 'there's a big woolly sheep right above us, do you see it?'

Lilibeth looks skyward, squinting her eyes, trying hard to fathom out what he's talking about.

'So, do you see it now, sweetheart?' he asks again.

Shrugging her shoulders, Lilibeth frowns, 'No, just a big fat cloud.'

He gives her nose a playful tweak, 'Look harder, look at the shape of the cloud, do you see, there, right above us.' He points to the large voluptuous cloud immediately overhead, 'the cloud is a funny shape, it looks just like a big fluffy white sheep, now can you see it?'

Wrinkling her little nose and squinting her eyes she inspects the cloud again. 'Where?'

Moving his head closer to Lily he points directly at the cloud formation. 'Look at the shape, see, that's his big fat body, and there, that smaller bit in the front is his head, he's got four short little legs too, and look, there's even a tufty little bit at the back for his tail.'

'Oh, I can see it!' she says excitedly, suddenly cottoning on. 'Mammy look, a big fluffy sheep!'

Opening her eyes, Katie peers skyward, to examine the shape of the supposed sheep. With careful studying she can make out what looks like it could be a head, and yes, a fat oval body with a small wisp at the back that could be construed as a being a lamb's tail, but as far as she could make out, if it was a sheep, it only had three legs. 'Well, I suppose with a good bit of imagination you could be right, Joe, but how come he only has three legs, he's a funny sort of sheep,' she points out chuckling. She glances across at Joe, his bared torso is very muscular and lean, his flat stomach has rippling muscles, she swallows, feeling guilty and quickly averts her gaze. Laying back on the grass, she closes her eyes, her mind is working overtime. In her mind's eye she is shamelessly visualising the sculptured vision of his body, so close beside her. She pictures his tanned, muscle-bound naked torso and immediately her heart begins to race, and butterflies begin to take flight in her stomach. With her head full of fanciful, impossible thoughts she drifts to sleep.

Above them, the high winds continue to blow southward, blowing and re-arranging the shape of the clouds, naturally evolving and altering them yet again.

'Your mammy's quite right Lily,' he tells her, 'but that's the beauty of cloud watching, you see old Mother Nature constantly surprises us all by blowing up a high wind and swapping and changing things around us. Yep, she keeps us guessing every day. Do you see that smaller cloud over there, Lily? Look at the shape of it. Now that one looks like a small fat duck,' he points out. 'You know, it's all down to dear old Mother Nature. Now take the trees for example.'

Lilibeth stares at him bemused. 'Trees?'

'Yes trees,' he grins. 'All through the winter when it's freezing cold, the branches are plain and bare of leaves, along comes Mother Nature and dresses them up with snow and ice, making them look really sparkly and pretty whilst the tree sleeps. Then when spring finally comes, she warms up the weather nicely, stirring the trees from their sleep, they open new buds so that the trees will be covered with fresh green leaves throughout the summer. With the warm sunshine and rain, they grow taller and stronger. Autumn follows summer and Mother Nature gives everyone on the land a grand finale when the leaves turn spectacularly red, yellow, orange and brown, before they fall to earth.' He looks at Lily, 'Mother Nature takes care of everything for us. You know there's something new and wonderful to see every day. That's why we should open our eyes to the beautiful world about us.'

Fascinated admiration is written over Lilibeth's face. 'Tell me another story, please Joe.'

'Really? Hum, well maybe later, my dear,' he tells her.

All three, lay quietly side by side in the warmth of the sun, relaxing and absorbing the peace and tranquillity of the surrounding countryside.

He inhales a long appreciative breath and sighs contentedly. Today, he decides, is as near to a perfect day as it could ever be, he also wishes with all his heart and soul that it could never end.

The tall grasses surrounding them swish and sway like fans in the gentle breeze and high above, a lone kestrel hovers, skilfully scanning the ground for mice and voles.

Carried along on the warm whispering winds, the sweet singing of a song thrush can be heard, accompanied by a background of the monotoned harmony of caw cawing from at least a dozen or more rooks that are circling above their nests, high up in the trees.

Joe rolls his head to the side, where Katie lays beside him.

Her eyes are closed, her thick long lashes resting in her sun-kissed face, she appears to be sleeping. He studies her fine features.

The warm sun is bathing her beautiful face, giving her pale flawless skin a radiant glow, he suppresses a groan, dazzled by her beauty. He can't help himself, his eyes wandered lower to Katie's profile, he couldn't help but notice her pert breasts and protruding nipples, lightly swathed with fine cotton, leaving little to his imagination as her chest rises and falls with her every breath, he's uncomfortably aroused. Her glossy auburn hair tumbles over the grass, tantalisingly, within an inch or two of his fingertips. His heart lurches and deep inside he feels an overwhelming urge to take her in his arms and hold her close. Oh, my dear sweet Katie, in just two days you will be gone, out of my life forever, my sweet precious love. A shadow blocks the warm rays of the sun from his face, disturbing his wayward thoughts.

Lilibeth is stood above him, her hands clasped together. 'I got a little beetle,' she says, as her hands gently open, 'see?'

Rising up on his elbows he takes a look, 'Why it's a ladybird,' he explains, 'I can tell you how old she is, if you want.'

Lilibeth frowns, 'Oooo, how you do that then?'

He grins, 'By counting her spots, look.'

Lilibeth cautiously unfurled her hands a little more, 'Go on then, how old is she?' she challenges him.

'One, two, three, four, five, that makes her five months old... I think, or is it five years old? Nope, I'm sure it's five months. Humm, I know a rhyme about a ladybird, do you want to hear it?' he offers.

'Oooo, yes please,' she says, sitting down, making herself comfortable, and as close as she can beside him.

'Okay, well it goes something like this. Ladybird, ladybird, fly away home, your house is on fire and your children alone.' Gently he opens her cupped hand, blowing softly into her palm, the ladybird flies away. 'Off you go, home to your children ladybird, quickly.'

'Straight home now, bye,' said Lily waving, enthusiastically running off in search of more ladybirds.

Gazing longingly once more at Katie, Joe's becoming so aroused, he's obliged to roll onto his stomach to hide the prominent bulge in his trousers. To try and focus his mind elsewhere he begins to search in the grass

'What are you looking for?' asks Lilibeth returning, laying down, copying Joe and rolling onto her stomach.

'Looking for a lucky four-leaf clover, sweetheart,' he explains patiently.

Lily frowns, 'What's them then?'

Amused by her cute inquiring expression, Joe grins, he plucks a piece of clover, 'Now this is clover, see, it's got three fat leaves? One, two three,' he counts. 'Now sometimes, if you look extremely hard, you might find one with four leaves. They're supposed to bring good luck to the finder, and not only that, if you are clever enough to find one, you can even make a wish.'

Never a one to be outdone by a challenge from anyone, her tiny fingers search eagerly through the grass, 'Is this one, Joe?'

'Um, one, two, three,' he counts, 'Nope, afraid not, try again.'

Though her eyes are closed, Katie isn't sleeping, but listening to her daughter and Joe, both interacting happily together. It warms her heart, she's filled with admiration for Joe's wonderful, natural gift of communication with a child so young. She concludes that he is most definitely a very rare breed of man, a man who is blessed with the patience of a saint. It is little wonder that Lilibeth had grown so very fond of him, just as she had too?

She inhales a lungful of the sweet air, overcome with a warm feeling of contentment and tranquillity, at last the fears and tensions that had previously plagued and tormented her mind seems to have dissolved away completely, leaving her feeling strangely serene and totally at peace. Oh, if only life could really be like this, always, she wishes, wistfully.

After much searching, Joe manages to find a four-leaf clover and discreetly places it close to Lilibeth's fingers.

'Yes, I got one!' she squeals, 'Mammy, Joe, look!' and she holds it up triumphantly.

'Hum, I think I'd better check it Lily. Now let me see. One, two, three, four!' He counts, 'Hey, it really is a four-leaf clover! Oh, you're a clever girl. You know you can make a wish if you like, but you must close your eyes first,' he tells her, 'Go on, close them or it won't come true.'

Lilibeth squeezes her eyes tightly shut, 'I wish, I wish... I wish we can stay here with my Joe, for ever and ever!'

Both Joe and Katie exchange fleeting glances, their eyebrows raise in surprise, they smile at each other. Though Joe's outward smile masks a deep-rooted feeling of morose sadness and foreboding. If only little one, if only. He sits up and pulls on his shirt, now dried by the sun's warmth.

'Anyone hungry?' asks Katie.

'Meeee!' squeals Lilibeth, 'and Joe, and my Daisy.'

The sight of Katie's cooking laid out on the tablecloth is a sight to behold, 'Mmm, would you look at all this Lily,' he says, licking his lips, 'Fit for a king. You know you're right. Your mammy really is the best cook in the whole wide world, and that's official.'

Looking smug Lilibeth grins, 'I told you she was, didn't I.'

He nods,' So, you did, my little one.'

The long stroll back to the cottage that evening is deliberately slow and unhurried. Lilibeth, completely tired out, is sat on Joe's shoulders, fighting the onslaught of sleep. He carries the blanket and the basket, now containing the fish, Katie follows behind carrying the fishing rods and keep net.

'Thanks for deciding to come Katie, it's been a really lovely day all round. I for one, have thoroughly enjoyed every single minute,' he tells her as they amble home.

'Oh, so have I Joseph, I'm so pleased you talked us into going, it's been absolute heaven,' she agrees.

Later that evening, all three are sat weary but happy in the parlour, the cottage bathed in a pleasant, tranquil atmosphere.

Washed and ready for bed, Lilibeth is curled up on her mother's lap, she yawns, 'Can you tell me a story, before I go to bed, please.'

'All right darling, just a short one,' agrees Katie.

Lilibeth fidgets, 'Oh no, Mammy, I want Joe to tell me a story,' she states adamantly.

He glances helplessly at Katie, who merely shrugs her shoulders, 'I think you're the favourite tonight, you've done all right so far today. Give it a go,' she suggests smirking.

'Hum, I don't know,' Joe clears his throat nervously, 'Ahem, I'm not sure that I know any stories that are suitable for young children,' he says with a wry smile.

Sliding down from her mother's lap, Lilibeth edges up to his chair, 'Of course you do,' she says, looking up at him expectantly with her big blue eyes. To her, it was inconceivable that he didn't know stories. 'Please, Joe.'

He smiles, 'Tch, how can I refuse? Aw come on then, up you get,' he says, patting his lap, 'But I'm going to have to put my thinking cap on.' He looks to Katie for help, but she just smiles sweetly and shrugs.

Whilst Lily settles down, he wracks his brain for something fittingly appropriate for a young child. As a life-long bachelor and an only child, he is totally inexperienced as far as telling children's stories go, so he's forced to plumb for the tale about the magpie. He clears his throat, 'Are you ready sweetheart?'

Lilibeth nods and snuggles down on his lap.

'Oh well, here goes. One beautiful spring morning, a long, long time ago, a lovely lady called Violet was doing the washing in the scullery. She took off her ring and put it on the windowsill for safe keeping. All morning she was busy, and when at last, the washing was hung out to dry, she returned to the sink. Now where's my ring? she says, searching on the windowsill, but to her dismay, it was gone. Poor Violet was dreadfully upset because the ring was very precious to her. Jack, her dearly departed husband, had given her the precious ring on their wedding day. For several days, Violet and her son, searched high and low, but the ring had vanished.' Briefly pausing, Joe shifts Lily to make her more comfortable, then carries on.

'A week later, Violet was busy baking in the scullery, her son was sat at the table eating his dinner. A magpie perched brazenly on the windowsill pecking furiously at a mirror, Violet clapped her hands. Go away, shoo, go on, shoo! The magpie screeched her protest, flapped her wings, and flew up into a tree. That gave her son an idea. Has the magpie done that before mother? he asked. I'll say, Violet told her son. Wretched bird, he's always doing it. Well, the next morning, he opens the window wide and lays the small mirror flat on the sill to catch the sun rays, then he waited outside in the garden. After a while, the magpie flew inside the window and started pecking at her reflection in the mirror. Again, Violet shooed him away, but this time, her son was waiting outside. As the magpie flew off, he followed as it took flight. He watched her land in a tall tree, disappearing into her nest. Although the tree was high, somehow, he managed to climb the branches and reach the nest. The magpie squawked at being disturbed and flew off. Well, you'll never guess Lily, there in the nest, he found an array of sparkling trinkets, shiny glass beads, and little pieces of tin and amongst them was his dear mother's ring. Violet was so delighted to get her ring back that she cried tears of joy. So, little Lily, it proves that you can never trust a magpie with anything that shines.'

Katie was extremely impressed with his storytelling, 'What a lovely story Joseph, but sadly, somewhere along the line, Lilibeth has fallen asleep,' she points out.

Joe looks down at the cherub like features of the sleeping child that lays cradled in his arms and tuts, 'What a pity, bless her. Oh well, at least I sent her to sleep. You know Katie, that was a true story. Violet was my dear mother, and the lad was me.' He gazes fondly at Lily, he sighs, there was no doubt he would miss her endearing, innocent charms, she's so beautiful, just like her dear sweet mother. 'Oh well, I reckon it's time for your bed, little one.' He whispers.

'I'll take her, Joe,' says Katie standing up.

Tonight, could almost certainly be one of the last times he would have the pleasure of tucking her into bed, he shakes his head, 'If you don't mind Katie, I'd like to carry her up, you can tuck her in,' he replies, 'Deal?'

'Deal,' says Katie smiling sweetly.

Pulling back the covers, they tuck Lily in the bed with her precious doll. 'Today has been absolutely wonderful, it really has,' she whispers, 'A beautiful day that I will never forget. Thank you, Joe. '

'Believe me, I enjoyed every single minute of it myself,' he says truthfully. Then his smile fades, his heart sinks, in a couple of days this wonderful day will be no more than a treasured memory.

The moment that he'd been dreading has come. Now he would ruin everything and tell her about his meeting with Stan. 'Katie, we need to talk dear, shall we go down to the parlour?' he suggests.

Exhausted but happy, Katie yawns and stretches, oblivious to his melancholy expression, 'If you don't mind, I could do with getting to bed myself. I can't remember when I've had so much fun, but I am tired, really tired. Can it wait until tomorrow?'

In his heart, he knows that he shouldn't put off the inevitable and prolong the agony but, she does look tired and if he is honest, he is too. He figures tomorrow would come soon enough anyway, so what was the point of spoiling what had been the perfect day?

Opting to take the coward's way out he agrees, 'Of course Katie, we'll talk first thing in the morning. I'm really glad you enjoyed yourselves. I did too. Sleep well Katie. Goodnight my dear.'

She smiles, 'Good night, and Joseph, thank you again for today, it was perfect.' Without thinking, impulsively she reaches up and kisses him lightly on his cheek.

Joe looks directly into her eyes and takes her hand. 'Mmm, yes, today was really special, thanks Katie,' he plants a kiss on the back of her hand then reluctantly lets her go.

At this point, Joe should have retired to bed himself, he is genuinely exhausted, he'd been up well before the cock crowed this morning, milking the cows and the goat, collecting the eggs and bringing up the logs. Followed by his extremely eventful, yet harrowing trip, meeting up with Stan and all that ensued, it all weighs heavily on his mind, in total contrast to the most glorious afternoon spent with Katie and Lily. The final seal on a perfect afternoon is that she'd kissed him goodnight. His fingers touch his cheek, he can still feel her warm soft lips. His brow creases, morning would come soon enough, and then...?

Despite his tiredness, the bed that beckons him with the promise of a good night's sleep looks cold and uninviting, so he goes back down to the scullery. After stoking up the range and filling the boiler from the well, he pours himself a generous measure of brandy, lights his pipe and settles in his chair.

Sat deep in thought, he curses himself for not telling her tonight, then he curses himself for being stupid enough to break his promise to Katie in the first place, now his loose tongue and pathetic curiosity has spoilt everything.

In spite of their memorable, happy afternoon, he now feels as if a black cloud of doom is hanging above him, and as if it couldn't make matters worse, there was so little time left. Stan and Margo would be here by midday, the day after tomorrow, just one and a half short days away.

He tries to console himself with the knowledge that if he is to trust his judgment then perhaps it was all for the best. Incredibly, by sheer coincidence, he had learned to his astonishment, that Stan and Margo not only knew Katie, but were apparently very close to her. He's confident that they will stand by the girls, but on the downside, they would almost certainly, and rightly so, take them home with them to Holdean. He tries to imagine the cottage silent and empty once more. He shudders, it really doesn't bear thinking about.

When Stan had walked into the parlour and announced that not only had he had found Katie and Lilibeth and confirmed that they were both not only safe and well, but more incredibly, they were actually staying at Joe Markson's place, Margo had practically collapsed with relief, laughing and crying hysterically and demanding answers to a million and one questions, not giving Stan a second to get a word in edgeways.

'We must go now!' she'd insists, removing their partially cooked dinner from the oven and putting on her coat.

Fortunately for Stan it's their son Freddie coming in, that eventually calms her down.

'Mam, what the hell's goin' on, why have yer got yer coat on, and why's me dinner not on the table?' He looks to Stan for an explanation.

Before Stan can open his mouth, Margo jumps in, 'Oh, Freddie lad, yer never gonna guess. We found them, Katie and Lilibuff, they're alive! Can you believe it? Your father's been and gawn and found them! Oh, my gawd, Katie and Lilibuff are safe! It's a bloody miracle. Oh, thank gawd!' As she speaks her voice becomes more and more shrill until she's almost beside herself with relief.

In the end, Freddie has to resort to raising his voice and shouting before he gets finally through to his mother, 'Mam, fer gawd's sake, sit down, just shut up, will yer? Let me old man speak!' he bawls in exasperation at his mother's uncontrolled hysteria.

Margo blinks, staring at her son indignantly, 'Freddie! Just who does yer fink yer shoutin' at? Stanley 'ooper, tell him he can't speak ter his mother like that!' she demands, then slumps back in her chair, exhausted. No one yells at her like that, not even her hubby, but the shock of her son having the audacity to raise his voice to her has the desired effect, she clams up and puts on her best sulking face, she's rendered temporarily speechless.

Inwardly, Stan chuckles to himself, after all these years, his misses had at last, met her match in his son, Freddie.

Putting the kettle on, Freddie slips the pan of roasting potatoes and meat back in the oven and beckons his father to join him at the table along with his mother.

'Right, nice and calm now,' says Freddie coolly, 'You first Pops, what the hell is me mam babbling on about?'

About to interfere, Margo opens her mouth to speak but Freddie lifts a commanding finger to silence her, 'Oh no, yer don't, I said keep it buttoned Mam, let me old man talk first.'

Looking wounded at being chastised and put in her place by her only son, Margo huffs and pouts, folds her arms beneath her breasts, reluctantly agreeing that Stan should enlighten them with the full story about how he had found Katie and Lilibeth, just in case she had missed something, she sits back in her chair and purses her lips.

Miraculously, Stan manages to go through the entire events of his day without a single interruption from Margo, an occasional, stern hard look from Freddie kept her in her place when she was tempted to do so.

Eventually, after Stan has finally filled them in on all he knows, Margo ventures to speak up, 'Why can't we go to get them now Stanley?' she whines, her voice practically pleading.

Stan shakes his head, 'First orf there's me cart, it's loaded ter the hilt wiv all me wood, it'll take me and Freddie at least an hour or more ter unload it and stack it in me yard, and I can't expect Horsey ter go all the way back to Sweet Briars agin, not ternight. Besides, it's ruddy dark and they'll be in bed by now. And last of all gel, coz I gave Joe me word we'd visit on Friday, and I certainly ain't gonna break it,' he said firmly. 'Look, I wants ter see them as much as anyone, but we'll go on Friday, like what I promised Joe, and that's the end of the subject.'

Freddie pats his mother's hand, 'The old man's right, Mam, at least we knows they're alive and safe wiv Joe,' he says softly. 'Hey, look on the bright side, that vermin Soames ain't caught up wiv them, they are safe, and he ain't ruddy likely ter find them there, is he?'

'Yes, well... alwight,' she sighs, she knows she's lost the argument, 'but we's definitely goin' bright and early Thursday mornin' mind, and I really means early, and I ain't gonna take no fer an answer Stanley 'ooper!' she says as a begrudging compromise.

Desperately hungry, Stan gives in and nods, 'Aye alwight, we will, me old love. Glad yer seein' sense. Now what about me dinner?'

Joe doesn't bother to go to bed, he's simply not tired, he knows, come morning, he will have to pluck up the courage and tell Katie that he had betrayed her trust. Instead, he'd sat in his chair miserably trying to visualise life at Sweet Briars, without Katie and Lily, it doesn't bear thinking about.

After milking the cows and goat, just before dawn, Joe returns to the scullery with a cart load of logs, he strips, has a good wash and shave then gratefully sinks into his chair with his mug of tea, topped up generously with brandy. Before he finally gives in to sleep, he decides that he cannot put off the inevitable a moment longer, Stan and Margo would be here tomorrow, he would have to tell Katie about his meeting with Stan, immediately after breakfast.

When Katie and Lilibeth come down the next morning, they find Joe sleeping, uncomfortably straddled in his fireside chair, one leg over the arm of the chair, his head tilted to one side and his shirt wide open, exposing his muscle-bound chest, his boots stood soldier like, drying in front of the glowing range.

A basket of eggs sits on the table, plus there's a churn of milk stood beside the larder door.

'Don't wake him darling,' says Katie in a hushed voice, tip toeing around the scullery. 'Poor thing, he must be completely exhausted.'

But the minute her mother's back is turned, Lilibeth being Lilibeth simply can't resist the temptation. 'Is you sleeping, Joe?' she whispers softly in his ear.

He opens one eye, then the other, and grins. 'Nope, just shutting my eyes for forty winks Lily,' he lies.

He stands and stretches his aching body, causing Katie to take a sharp intake of breath as his shirt parts with his trousers.

Quickly she turns away, 'You know it won't do you any good sleeping there, Joe.' She's already busy preparing the breakfast, 'You need a proper night's rest, you work far too many hours as it is.'

Joe doesn't answer so she turns to look at him, 'Oh dear, you look very pale, Joe, are you all right?' she asks, handing him a mug of tea.

Lilibeth is stood gazing out of the window her attention apparently engrossed in something out in the yard.

Here's my opportunity, he decides, oh well, here goes. 'Thanks for the tea. Don't worry about me, I um, I'm fine,' he clears his throat, 'Ahem, look, take a seat, please Katie, I've erm...' It was no good, his mouth is dry, his nerves are getting the better of him. Taking another mouthful of tea, he steels himself to confess. 'Katie, I have to tell you something...' but before he can utter another word, Lilibeth lets out a shrill scream and flees out the door, into the yard.

Alarmed, they both run to the door.

Lilibeth is tearing down the yard, both arms waving frantically, screaming, 'Uncle Stan! Aunty Margo!'

For a moment, Katie stands dumbstruck in the doorway, then she yelps, lifts her skirts and takes off, following swiftly in her daughter's footsteps.

There's whoops of delight, hugs and tears, kisses and more hugs.

Stood at the top of the yard, Joe is watching from the door. If anyone bothered to look back, they would see the look of utter despair on his face. Stan had promised they would come tomorrow lunch time. What the hell happened? What went wrong? He feels as if he'd been stabbed through his heart. Watching the joyous reunion, deep down, he grudgingly knows he has done the right thing in confiding in Stan. He sighs soulfully, friends reunited with friends, just as it should be. A lump comes to his throat, he shakes his head, sighing, the time has come, he tells himself. Turning he retreats inside. Oh hell, get a grip man, he rebukes himself, doing something practical, filling the kettle to put on the range.

Minutes later the little scullery is bursting at the seams, the air is buzzing with so much excitement and chatter you can hardly think.

Stan slaps Joe heartily on the back, 'Mornin', Joe, sorry we caught yer so early Mate. Well, yer know how it is, our Margo just wouldn't wait till termorrer,' he explains. 'Aye but it's right good to see our gels safe and well, all thanks ter you Mate,' he declares, shaking Joe's hand, 'I'll tell yer somefin', yer a ruddy hero Mate.'

Then it's Margo's turn, she flings her arms around Joe's neck plastering kisses all over his face, 'Oh, Joe, ta ever so much lovey, thank gawd it were yerself what found them. Gawd, love us, we was beginnin' ter think we'd never see them again, we thought he'd done them in! We been worried ter death, we all have.'

Stan's son Freddie intervenes, grasping hold of Joe's hand like a vice, shaking it until his hand goes numb, only to be rescued by Mick and Edna, each shaking his hand in turn and patting his back, hard enough to take his breath away.

Fortunately for Joe, the humble kettle turns out to be his saviour, it's hissing loudly and spouting clouds of steam, he excuses himself from the melee, setting out a tray with a pot of tea and a plate of Katie's biscuits.

The cottage is immediately flung into total mayhem, suddenly, Joe is surrounded. Everyone is helping. Stan has brought a cooked ham from home, and Freddie begins slicing it, whilst another starts cutting Katie's fresh crusty bread, someone else does the buttering. Margo emerges from the larder with a cake, followed by a pot of jam and a plate of scones, it's total bedlam.

Within fifteen minutes the table is groaning, 'Come on, get stuck in!' announces Margo excitedly. 'Fill yer plates up, we'll eat in the garden, it's a beaut'ful day.'

It doesn't escape Margo's notice, that Stan had magically produced two jars of cider, but what the heck, she decides, today is a celebration. In fact, with all the hullabaloo and excitement, Margo quite forgets that she doesn't really drink and when they've all eaten, she drinks three full beakers of cider. As a consequence, tiddly, she ends up with an uncontrollable fit of the giggles, much to everyone's amusement.

Skipping over to Joe, Lily takes hold of his hand, 'Him's my Uncle Stan, and that nice lady there with the green frock and red hair is me Aunty Margo,' she points out. 'And him over there is our lovely Freddie, and them two there, eating all the cake, is Uncle Mick with my Aunty Edna.'

'Well, I'll be blessed,' says Joe forcing a smile, what a lot of relatives you've got sweetheart. My, you're a lucky girl. '

Giggling, Lilibeth runs back to join Freddie.

Looking around for Katie, he sees her sat momentarily, apart from the others, he can see her euphoric smile had disappeared, she's nervously ringing her hands, looking terribly upset.

Seizing the opportunity, he approaches her, stooping down, he whispers in her ear, 'Katie love, can we go inside for a minute, we must talk, now.'

Shrugging her shoulders, she nods indifferently, so he helps her to her feet and leads her indoors, 'We'll talk in the parlour if that's all right with you,' he suggests softly.

Katie shrugs her shoulders, nodding in half-hearted agreement.

Sitting her in the chair by the window, he drags a chair across so that he can sit facing her, seeing the fear in her eyes he frowns, he can't understand it, he thought she would be happy.

'How, Joe, how on earth did they find me?' she asks tearfully, 'If they can find us so easily, then so can Albert. We're not safe here anymore. Oh Joseph, I just know he'll find us.' Tears stream down her face.

Joe grasps her trembling hands in his, 'Oh my dear Katie, I am so deeply sorry, but you see, this is all my fault. It was me,' he confesses, 'I told Stan you were here. Oh, Katie love, I know I swore I wouldn't say a word and I wouldn't have, honestly, except...' he sighs, 'there were a few chance remarks from Stan, when he collected his order of wood. That's when I discovered that you and I share the same mutual, honest, trustworthy friends,' he explains. Shaking his head, he sighs deeply. 'Katie, I swear, I genuinely believed that you'd want to see them. It was stupid of me, unforgivable. I'm so sorry, if only I could turn back the clock.'

Her face brightens, her tears stop flowing, 'Stan, you say it's Stan that collects your wood?' she says in amazement.

Looking thoroughly dejected, Joe nods, 'Yes, I'm so, so sorry.'

Leaning forward she hugs him with relief, 'So that's how they knew we were here. If only I'd known. Oh Joseph, thank you, thank you for bringing them to me, I've missed them all so much.'

'Does that mean I'm forgiven then?' he asks, bewildered.

Her eyes sparkle, 'Why of course you are.'

Again, her pretty blue eyes melts his heart, he pulls her up and holds her, wrapping his arms firmly around her, drawing her close.

Willingly she stands, her eyes closed, revelling in the warmth and security of his arms.

'I swear I'd never do anything to hurt you Katie, never!'

'Oh Joseph, I'd forgive you for anything,' she whispers snuggling her face into his chest, 'Mmm, hold me in your arms, Joe, hold me tight.'

'You hoo! You hoo! Where the devil is yer both?' calls Margo.

The blissfully, intimate moment is shattered.

Immediately they part. He takes a couple of strides towards the door, coming face to face with Margo.

'There yer both is,' she says, as she dramatically sweeps into the parlour, 'What yer both doin' in here?' Without waiting for an answer, she grabs Katie's hand, 'Outside the pair of yer, we've gotta talk, make plans.'

A reluctant Katie is led out into the garden.

Joe, filled with mixed emotions, follows close behind, his head bowed, and his hands thrust deep in his pockets. This is the point when they say they are taking them home, he thinks sadly.

'I reckon yer should get yer stuff packed and we can all head orf home, ducky,' says Stan, putting on his jacket and adjusting his hat.

'Aye, we don't want ter leave it too long, it'll be dark soon,' adds Freddie.

Both Katie and Lilibeth stand side by side, holding hands, looking lost and bewildered.

It's all happening far too fast for Joe's liking; they are acting in haste without considering what's best for Katie and Lily. He groans.

Deciding to speak up, Joe raises his hands and clears his throat, his expression sombre. 'Ahem, for what it's worth, I reckon you'll be making a really big mistake,' he announces.

Immediately the chattering stops, all eyes turn, staring at Joe.

'Sorry folks, but I don't reckon you're all thinking straight,' he repeats.

'What d'yer mean Mate?' asks Stan, lifting his hat and scratching his head then plonking it back on his head.

With the possibility of Katie and Lily about to disappear from his life forever, Joe isn't in the mood to argue, he decides it's time for some straight talking. Glancing at Katie, he says quietly, 'Look Katie, I'm really sorry, I don't want to frighten you, but I think this has to be said.' He looks around at everyone, 'It's pretty obvious to me that Soames isn't going stop looking for them, is he? So please Margo, all of you, I'm asking you to think about this. I've already spoken to Stan about this once, and I'll say it again. If Soames finds them at yours Stan, he'll insist on taking them back to Penfold Grove,' he points out. 'Don't forget, Katie is still his legal wedded wife and because of that fact alone, I guess he'd be well within his rights to take them too. You all know Soames isn't about to give up looking for them, is he? I mean, where's the first place he's gonna look for them? Yours Stan,' he says, answering his own question. He turns to Katie, 'I'm sorry, I don't want to frighten you, but…' he shakes his head, 'I'm asking every one of you to just stop, think for about what I've just said.'

Stunned by his bold statement they look blankly at each other then back at Joe. Mick is the first to respond, 'I reckon, Joe's makin' a lot of sense. Ruddy Soames's been sniffin' around ours, and your place Stan. We all know what he's like.'

Edna nods in agreement with her husband, 'Aye, we all know he ain't gonna stop searching fer them, is he?' she echoes her husband's sentiments.

Reluctantly Freddie agrees, 'I s'pose I gotta agree wiv Mick and Edna.'

Up goes Stan's hat and he scratches his head again, 'So what's we gonna do about it?'

Joe stands tall, hands on his hips to address them all, 'Regardless of whatever anyone else thinks, and this is crucial, this has got to be Katie's decision entirely, her choice of course, but I'm suggesting they both stay here, with me. You must know Soames would never think of looking here in a million years, they'd be safe out here with me.'

Nodding slowly, Stan voices his opinion, 'Yer may well be right Mate, I mean, the bloke's ruddy evil. I ain't never seen a man so murderous. Like Joe says, I reckon we has ter think of what's best for our Katie and Lilibuff.' He lifts his hat and scratches his head to think, 'Nah, I reckon Joe's right, it ain't worth the risk of takin' them back home wiv us,' he concludes.

Wrapping her arm around Katie's shoulder, Margo says quietly, 'Katie, it's up ter you gel. Look, we've known Joe all his life and a right good, kind man he is. Meself, I fink yer'd be safer here wiv him, at least till all this has been sorted with that bloody husband of yourn. So, it's whatever yer wants to do ducky.'

Joe steps closer to Katie, 'And if Katie chooses to stay here with me, you know that you are all welcome to come visiting, anytime you like.' he says, hoping to sway their decision, adding, 'but at the end of the day, it's really up to Katie to decide what she wants to do. What do you say Katie, would you like some time to think about it?'

Katie, who up until this point, had remained completely silent, speaks up at last, 'I um... my dear friends, I want you all to know that since we arrived here, Joe has been really wonderful to Lilibeth and I, and I can tell you all now, without his help and generosity, the fact is, we'd have both been found dead in a ditch for certain,' she tells them, 'Without a doubt, we owe him our lives. Since Joe took us in, he has been kindness itself,' she turns to Joe, 'and for that Joseph, I thank you from the bottom of my heart. We feel safe here with you, so if your very kind offer still stands, I... we, would prefer to stay here, with you at Sweet Briars.' she leans sideways and whispers to Joe, 'That's if you're quite sure, it's all right?'

He grins, 'Oh yes, most definitely,' he says quietly as a lump comes to his throat.

Katie smiles to herself, she had deliberately omitted to tell them that the deciding factor is Joseph himself. He's so kind, considerate and thoughtful, the list is endless, and she's hardly going to tell them that he was so mind-blowingly fit and sexy, that when he speaks to her, he sends thrilling shivers down her spine, like no man had ever done in her entire life. She suppresses her pleasure, thinking about his beautiful, intense, blue seductive eyes every time he looks at her, the eyes that seem to have the power to look into her soul, exciting her beyond belief. All that aside, Joe is so protective of her, and yes, she feels so comfortably safe with him. Ooo yes, she not only needed to be with him she wanted him too.

'Does I take it that that's sorted, yer won't be comin' home wiv us then gel?' asks Stan interrupting her thoughts.

'Thank you, for your kind offer Stan, but no, we'll be staying here at Sweet Briars, I'm sure it's for the best.'

Joe looks skywards, God bless you Mother.

Katie stands beside Joe, who now has Lilibeth perched on his shoulders as they watch their friends pile up on their cart, preparing to head off home to Fennydown.

'Hang on folks, a couple of things before you go Stan,' says Joe, 'I know it probably goes without saying, but, first, and most important... absolutely no-one must ever mention that they know where Katie and Lily are. You've not seen her, agreed?'

'Agreed!' they all chorus, simultaneously.

'Now I know I said that you are all welcome to visit anytime, but please, always make sure you're not being followed here,' Joe tells them, looking deadly serious. 'Finally,' he adds, 'I should give you a list for my next order of supplies Stan, I reckon I'm going to need a fair bit extra, now there are three of us to feed.'

'No worries, Joe. We got markit in a couple of days so me and Stan'll bring yer supplies over Monday,' Margo explains, 'and don't worry about no list, I reckon I knows what Katie wants fer her larder, don't I Lovey?'

Katie smiles, 'Thank you, Margo, and thanks to all of you. I'm so happy. It's been really wonderful seeing you all again.'

With a sharp flick of the reigns from Stan, the horse and cart turns in the yard, the large heavy metal rimmed wheels grate over the gravel as they disappear into the lane.

'Are you happy you're staying here with me, Lily?' asks Joe.

Lilibeth grasped her hands around Joe's head firmly, 'Oh yes, Joe, lovely,' she replies beaming.

Relief swells his chest, 'Come on girls, let's go home.'

Tea is a relaxing affair, Katie poaches eggs to go with some of the ham that Stan brought, whilst Joe slices and butters the bread.

Lilibeth does her bit by laying the table. 'Wasn't it lovely to see Aunty Margo and everyone today Mamma? Are they coming to see us again?'

'Yes darling, of course,' she answers, 'they'll be back, so we're going to have to do some extra baking.'

'Are we making more pies then?' asks Lilibeth, 'Coz Uncle Stan likes your pies the bestest.'

'Yes darling, and we'll bake some more bread and scones too,' Katie, turns to Joe, 'Um, would you mind if I give Margo and Stan some butter and some of my baking?'

'Good Lord, of course not.' He chuckles, 'My mother always used to give them stuff, you know, eggs, butter, cheese, milk and other bits and bobs. Margo's a fine needlewoman and they'd swop stuff between them, all the time.' he tells her smiling good naturedly. 'Who'd have ever thought that we both share the same mutual friends,' he comments, shaking his head. 'Aye, an unbelievable coincidence.'

Lilibeth's ears prick up, 'That's cos I found a four-leaf thingy, and now we can stay here forever, with my Joe.'

Subtle glances and smirks are exchanged between Joe and Katie.

'Would you really like to stay here always, Lily?' he asks, deeply touched that the little one should make such a touching statement.

'Of course,' She answers in a manner that questions his need to ask her in the first place.

Comfortably settled beside the fire, Lilibeth, ready for bed ambles over to Joe, 'Tell me a story before I go to bed, please, coz me and Daisy likes your stories?' she asks sweetly.

'Oh dear, I'm afraid I'm a bit short on stories Lily, I can't think of any offhand,' he tells her honestly.

'You can tell me the magpie story, coz me and Daisy likes it,' she suggests clambering onto his lap in anticipation.

He grins, 'Hum, as it's the only story I know, then the magpie story it is then. You comfortable sweetheart?'

Lilibeth nods and snuggles down.

Resigned, Joe begins the tale about the thieving magpie, all over again. Just as before, Lilibeth is sound asleep before he'd even reaches the middle of the story. 'Huh, not having a lot of luck, am I Katie?'

She giggles, 'On the contrary, you've done very well, she's sound asleep, shall we take her up to bed?'

'Good idea, she's had a pretty long day, one way or another.' Gently he carries the sleeping child upstairs in his arms.

'Lily should sleep well tonight, bless her,' says Joe, as they settle down together in the parlour.

'Yes, it's been a very enjoyable and exciting day, it meant so much to Lilibeth, me too, for that matter,' she says wistfully. 'And as for Margo and Stan and the others, the truth is I never thought I'd ever see them again. They're the nearest we've got to a family. I love them all dearly.'

Frowning, Joe fidgets uncomfortably, 'While we're on the subject, I um, I must apologise, again.'

'What for? '

'For breaking a confidence. You do know that it will never happen again? I want you to feel that you can trust me completely Katie.'

'Well, I can't deny it was a shock at the time,' she tells him, 'I was upset, it's true, but only because I thought that if they could find us so easily, then I thought Albert could find us too. Joe I've been scared to death that Albert would turn up and force us back to Penfold. As it turns out, well, I'm incredibly grateful to you, and yes, of course I trust you, implicitly.' Katie pauses then adds shyly, 'you know Joseph, I thought for one awful minute they were going to make me go back to Fennydown.'

'As long as you are here Katie, no-one will ever make you do anything you don't want to do, ever again.'

Gazing around the cosy little parlour, she looks at Joe and smiles, 'I feel so happy here Joseph, thank you, for everything.'

He grins, 'Like I said before if you're happy, then I'm happy.' Unable to stop himself he yawns.

Giggling, Katie's lovely pale blue eyes seem to come alive, 'Ooo, don't start me off with your yawning, you know it's catching.'

'It's so good to see you so happy Katie, and I hope your future is full of fun and laughter,' adding, 'You know Katie, you have a really beautiful smile.'

Swallowing, Katie suppresses her pleasure at his compliment, she feels the need to change the subject, his gaze is stirring butterflies in her stomach, 'Um, we've all had a very, long day Joseph. I'm tired, surely you are too? '

Smiling tenderly, he leans towards her, 'You know you really ought to learn to take a compliment my dear. I mean it, you light up the room with your gorgeous smile.'

Self-conscious and not used to compliments, Katie squirms, averting her eyes to the floor.

Smirking he shakes his head. What a day it's been, at the start of the day, he had been resigned to the fact that they would be leaving Sweet Briars and probably out of his life forever, but in the space of a few short hours, it had been Katie herself, that had decided she wanted to stay, to him it was a heart-warming comfort.

Covering her mouth with her hand she feigns a yawn and stands.

The corner of his lips curl, he knows what she was doing and why, 'Okay, have it your own way,' he tells her smirking. 'Get yourself off to bed, I won't be far behind, I'll bring your bowl of water up shortly.'

'Thank you, Joe, I can honestly say that today really has been amazing. The lovely picnic with our dear friends in the garden, your lovely home, and you of course, oh everything. I can't remember when I've had such fun.' Impulsively, she leans forward and pecks him on the cheek, 'Thank you, Joseph, thank you for everything.'

Leaning closer he looks into her eyes and says, 'And you, my dear Katie, are an unbelievably beautiful young woman.,' he whispers huskily. 'You won't regret deciding to stay, I promise you. Today is the start of a new adventure, for all of us.'

A flurry of butterflies take off her in her stomach, she blushes. With a shy smile, she reluctantly bids him goodnight.

CHAPTER 8

'Hey up, did yer notice, Stan?' asks Margo, snuggling up to her hubby on the front of the cart as they travel homeward.

'Notice what gel?' he says, flicking the reins to hurry the pace of the horse.

'The difference in our Katie and Lilibuff,' she replies.

Stan nods, 'Not half, young Katie got some colour back in her pretty cheeks, and maybe put on a little weight too.'

'Aye she looks a different gel already,' agrees Edna.

'That's coz she's got away from that bastard Soames,' says Freddie, who's sat on the back of the cart with Mick and Edna, 'Let's hope he never finds them,' He adds solemnly.

Stan pushes the front of his hat up, 'Aye yer right there boy. Now don't ferget, yer all gotta keep quiet about where they're livin'. But I'll tell yer somefin', me and Joe's decided we're gettin' tergether ter see if we can do somethin' about Soamsey. I dunno what, just yet, but Soamsey's gotta be sorted, once and fer all.'

'Aye, I'm wiv yer there, Pops.' says Freddie, 'I reckon it's about time someone sorted him out, we should've done it years ago.'

'Aye, well yer can count me in,' chips in Mick, 'The women round these parts ain't safe with that ruddy drunken pervert on the loose. It's right tragic the way that dirty bastard treated poor Katie.'

'Yep, and don't ferget poor Brodie and her little baby and all,' adds Stan. 'Now the thing is, this is men's talk only, we ain't gotta let on ter Katie that somefin's afoot, Joe were most particular about that.'

'There ain't no reason fer her ter find out nowt, is there?' says Freddie, rubbing his hands together, relishing the thought of sorting Albert Soames out, once and for all!'

Stan, sporting satisfaction on his face grins, 'Right then, next visit I'll have a serious talk wiv Joe. Now listen ter me Margo, no blabbin' ter no one, and if yer don't mind me bein' blunt Edna, not a word between yer, no offence gels, but it's our Katie's and Lilibuff's safety what we gotta fink about.'

Looking indignant, both Margo and Edna sit up scowling haughtily, 'What do yer take us fer, a couple of gagglin' fish wives? We won't say nothin' ter no one. We ain't no gossips, we'd do anyfin' fer our Katie and Lilibuff, wouldn't we Edna?'

'Aye, course we would,' agrees Edna, affronted to think Stan would suggest they would tell anyone.

That night as they snuggled up in bed, Margo turned to Stan, 'I was finkin', our Katie could do a lot worse than settle down wiv a good, honest, handsome man like Joseph.'

Stan raises his weary head from the pillow, 'Do what Margo? Humm, I dunno about that, she been through a lot with that bleedin' pervert Soamsey, and after all those filthy goin's on wiv him, I can't see the poor gel wantin' ter settle down wiv any man, not even our Joe.'

Margo slides her hand under the covers and gives his cock a squeeze and smiles, 'Stan love, a man needs a good woman, and a woman needs a good man. Yer don't notice nothin' do yer. Didn't yer see the way Joe kept lookin' at Katie, and how he went all protective over them when we wanted ter bring them back here?'

'Nah, get away wiv yer.' he chuckles dismissively, 'He just wants ter do what's best for the gels, so he does.'

Margo smiles knowingly, 'I don't know Stan, sometimes yer can't see what's in front of yer ruddy nose. Joe and Katie looked so comfortable and at ease wiv each other,' she points out. She had spotted the many looks and glances between them, 'Well, like I said afore Stan, every man needs a good woman, and every woman needs a good man, you mark my words if I ain't right,' she tells him, her hand gripping him, rousing him.

Slipping his hand between Margo's thighs, he tells her softly, 'Yer speak wise words, my sexy saucepot. I hope yer right, but I don't hold out no hope fer poor Joe. I reckon Katie's suffered far too much at the hands of that bleedin' reprobate Soames, she's probably been damaged fer life, and who can blame her? Still, while we're on the subject of, lovin' my little sexpot,' his eyes glow lecherously.

'G'morning you two, sleep well?' Joe greets them cheerily, he's in the scullery preparing breakfast, in a contrasting mood to the previous morning he's grinning broadly, looking decidedly bright-eyed and full of the joys of spring.

'We certainly did,' says Katie, 'I'll cook breakfast?'

'No need,' he says, 'I've already made the porridge, cut the bread and buttered it, the scrambled eggs are nearly ready, so up to the table. I've made a pot of tea.'

Katie feels guilty, she'd never had anyone wait on her in her entire life. 'You should have called me Joseph. I would have done this,' she chastises him.

'I thought you'd need some extra beauty sleep,' he teases.

Lilibeth feels left out of the bantering session, so she chips in with her two pennorth, 'My mammy is beautiful, she's the most beautifulest mammy in the whole world!'

Glancing at Katie, his eyes twinkle wickedly, 'Well I certainly wouldn't argue with that fact, sweetheart,' he agrees, playfully tweaking Lily's button nose. He looks back at Katie, her face is a delicious shade of rose pink. 'Why my dear Katie, I do believe you're blushing. Mmm, I wonder why?' he comments, smiling broadly.

Katie gulps.

Still grinning ear to ear, he finishes his meal, 'Well, do have you any plans for the day Katie?'

'I've got some baking to do, but that won't take long, then I thought that Lilibeth and I could carry on in the dairy. What about you?'

He feels a strong urge to blurt out something rash like, spend every single minute with you, but using every ounce of his willpower, he manages to bite his tongue, 'Just the logs to bring up for the fire and draw more water from the well, everything else was done first thing, whilst you were both tucked up in bed, sleeping,' he tells her smirking. 'Anyway, I won't be long, I'll catch up with you both in an hour or so.' He butters the last slice of toast and hands it to Lily, 'Are you going help your mammy today sweetheart?'

'Course I am,' she tells him, spreading a liberal dollop of jam on her third slice of toast.

'I don't know where you put it all,' He jests, shaking his head, 'Little half pint like you, I reckon you've got hollow legs.'

'Ooo mam, he's on about my legs again,' reports Lilibeth to her mother.

Katie tuts. 'I don't know, what am I going to do with the pair of you?'

Joe laughs, his eyes twinkling, 'I don't know either, so I reckon I'd better get off to work before I get myself into deep water.'

Lilibeth looks up to him puzzled, 'Does you want Windy Wills wellington boots then, Joe?' she asks with an expression so serious that he struggles to keep a straight face.

'It's just a figure of speech, sweetheart,' Katie explains.

Lilibeth frowns, waiting for his answer.

Joe grabs his jacket; he's still grinning like a Cheshire cat. 'I think I'll leave the explaining to you Katie, or I'll be here all day.'

He looks at Lilibeth, who was apparently still waiting to hear why, if he was in water, he wouldn't want the boots, her funny puzzled expression turning his broad grin into fits of laughter and despite all Katie's efforts to keep a straight face, she finally succumbs, doubling up with laughter too.

'Right, that's it,' says Katie, patting her eyes dry on her pinafore, 'We've all got work to do.'

'Too right,' he agrees. 'By the way, I've put another chicken in the larder for dinner Katie.'

'Thank you, I'll pluck it later, hum, I think I'll use some of that lovely ham that Stan brought, maybe I'll make some chicken and ham pies. Then we must get over to the dairy.'

'I'll be along later, he says, carelessly slinging his jacket over his shoulder, 'Now don't get overdoing it. Bye for now, you two.'

Lilibeth runs to the door, stands on her tip toes and pouts her lips, 'Kiss?'

'My pleasure,' he says, picking her up and duly obliging.

Marching up to Katie, she puts her hands to her waist and with a very straight face says, 'Joe's going to work now, Mammy, so you give him a kiss bye-bye too.'

Katie turns scarlet, 'Lilibeth, behave!'

With his eyes twinkling, Joe beckons Katie forward with his index finger, 'Come, don't let's disappoint little Lily, please.'

Cautiously she steps forward and kisses him lightly on his cheek.

As she does so, he catches her arm and briefly kisses her softly on her lips.

Stepping back startled Katie blushes, 'Ooo Joseph, I um... oh dear, I'll see you later,' she croaks.

Joe grins from ear to ear, 'Mmm nice, I'll see you both shortly.' He winks at Katie and closes the door behind him.

A couple of hours later, Joe turns up at the dairy, 'How's it going girls?'

Katie had been hard at it for the best part of the morning, finally running the blades through to separate the curd, she feels hot and weary.

He rolls up his sleeves, 'Here, I'll scrub up, I can do that, sit down and have a rest, you look all in Katie.'

More than grateful to accept his offer she takes a seat, despite the temperature being a great deal cooler inside the dairy, it is still laboriously hard going, carrying countless heavy pails of water from the well to wash the muslin cloths, and scrubbing every cheese mould scrupulously clean, she'd found it exhausting. By the time she had sliced and separated the curds from the whey, Katie was beginning to struggle. Now was not the time for one of her fainting bouts. So, with her energy completely drained, she sits gratefully on an upturned barrel beside Lilibeth, watching him working.

It's pretty obvious that Joe has done plenty of cheese making in the past, he drains the whey into a large tub, then lines the moulds with the cheese cloths, finally he packs the cheese into the moulds and stands them on a rack, within no time at all, over two dozen small cheeses are lined up and the vat had been thoroughly scrubbed clean.

'I'm thirsty,' declares Lilibeth.

'Me too,' says Joe, slipping her a wink.

'We're finished here so we might as well go indoors and get a cold drink and something to eat,' suggests Katie.

'Race you home, Joe!' says Lily, who immediately dashes off, giving herself a good, healthy start.

Joe likes the 'home' bit, he sprints after her, only to be beaten to the door by a respectable yard or two.

'Phew, you win again,' he gasps, 'I reckon I'm getting too old for this game.' Putting his arm out he blocks Lily's path, 'Hang on sweetheart, you first Katie,' he says, swinging open the door and moving aside.

Just two steps inside the door Katie stops, taking a sudden intake of breath, astounded at sight before her. Every available space in the parlour is filled with freshly cut, sweet smelling flowers. She stares at Joe, speechless.

'For you m'lady,' he says bowing low.

'Ooo, Mammy, lovely flowers,' says Lilibeth, 'lots and lots of flowers, everywhere!'

Stunned, her mouth drops open. 'F... for me, Joe? I um... don't know what to say,' she stutters.

An abundance of flowers filled every surface of the parlour, 'Oh Joseph, they... why they're beautiful, all of them!' she says, impulsively standing on tip toe and planting a peck on his cheek.

Beneath his golden tan, Katie sees a hint of blushing that matches her own, as she steps back his eyes met hers, they spark an exciting powerful connection between them.

'Just a little something to brighten your first permanent day here, in your new home,' he explains sheepishly, 'Pretty flowers for a very pretty lady,' he whispers in her ear.

Katie's pulse begins to race erratically, the colour in her face deepens.

His highly unusual, surprising gesture makes for a very pleasant, relaxed evening all round. Joe keeps looking at Katie with a distinct look of yearning that makes her tremble.

It had been a long day, Lilibeth is so tired that she'd asked to go to bed as soon as they'd eaten dinner and without her usual request for a story.

'What time do you reckon Stan and Margo will arrive tomorrow?' he asks, stretching his legs and warming his toes in front of the smouldering fire.

'Early if I know Margo,' she giggles, 'I've done some extra baking, they all have enormous appetites.'

He rises from his chair, 'Well then, I've got a little job to do, I won't be long,' he says, grabbing his jacket and stepping into his boots.

Katie sits alone in the parlour, the cottage peacefully still and quiet.

Surrounded by the array of flowers, she's deep in thought. The flowers were such an unexpected, thoughtful surprise, she decides Joe is like no other man she'd ever met before, he's so thoughtful. Sighing, she remembers the callousness of the so called 'gentlemen', Sir Edwin Barton-Smythe and his son Edward, who had unfeelingly deserted her when she needed them most, the term 'gentleman' appears to be a more appropriate title for a man like Joseph Markson. A true gentleman in every way. He'd surprised her with this room full of flowers, obviously putting a great deal of thought and effort into his grand and chivalrous gesture, it tugs at the strings of her heart. He's so sweet.

She finds it hard to believe that just a few short months ago she was trapped, like a prisoner, in a living hell. Married for life to an obnoxious filthy drunkard of a husband, suffering from his incessant mental and degrading physical abuse, a world apart from the serenity and safety that she has found with the extremely handsome, caring Joseph Markson.

Did she have any regrets about running away from her husband, and taking her daughter with her? Dear God, absolutely none!

From the day that she'd arrived at Sweet Briars, she felt she was living a dream, but if it was a dream, she didn't want to wake up... ever!

Right now, she felt genuine peace, confident that the days with Albert Sebastian Soames are firmly behind her.

Half an hour later, Joe returns with a sack of full of fruit and fresh vegetables. 'Tomorrow's dinner, and extra for our visitors,' he explains. 'We can't have our guests going hungry.'

Whilst strolling down to the vegetable patch, Joe thought about the past few weeks and the extraordinary turn of events that had been thrust upon him without a hint of forewarning.

The same old things keep revolving round and round in his head. Katie and Lily turning up like two desperate, filthy, pitiful urchins, clean out of the blue. Then there's his friends Stan and Margo. How could he have possibly known, when he met Katie that she would form a circle with Stan and Margo and one extremely obnoxious Albert Soames? Now, by chance of an inexplicable coincidence, he had found himself woven into the centre of it all. He could barely believe it was all happening! He smiles to himself, so much had occurred in the past few months, when his mundane but seemingly contented life had been turned well and truly upside down! After twenty-six years of living the life of a supposedly carefree bachelor, meeting Katie had dramatically changed his expectations in life in an instant. If he'd thought he was happily resigned with his lot in life before their arrival, he'd been hugely mistaken, because from the very first moment his eyes met hers, he had been absolutely smitten.

Recollections of the numerous girls he had courted in past come to mind. Lovely, young girls that had taken his fancy. Some were much more experienced than others, and they taught him so much that now he proves to be an adept thoughtful lover. But, if he was honest with himself, there was not one that he had any desire to spend the rest of his life with. That was until the day that Katerina entered his life.

His heart races at the very thought of her, he feels sure that there are times when he'd sensed that she felt the same way as him. Not for the first time she had kissed him, perhaps it was just gratitude, but there were so many times her eyes told him a different story. Yet despite all this, in the back of his mind, he can't help but think that maybe he was running ahead of himself. He knows Katie is extremely vulnerable. Just a short while ago she was living with her deranged brutal husband. His heart sinks. Soames, her 'husband', like it or not she was married. A shudder runs through his body at the very thought. The sickening revelations that Stan had furnished him with, regarding the gut wrenchingly obscene things that Katie had been forced to endure at his mercy, is laying heavily on his mind.

After his talk with Stan, he'd decided that he should conceal his feelings, he certainly wouldn't try to take liberties either, he had far too much respect for her. He had to give her time, plenty of time to re-adjust and settle down to a 'normal' life. She is carrying terrible scars that in time, with care and patience, would hopefully fade, until one day she would accept and embrace a new way of life, maybe even to earn to love.

He wants her so badly, but at the end of the day, it has to be Katie that comes to him, he had to know that she was willing on her part. As for that bastard Soames, that was a matter he intended to deal with, all in good time.

As he saunters back to the cottage, he wonders what his mother would have thought about all this business if she'd still been here? He was certain she would have fallen in love with them both, welcoming them with open arms.

A smile comes to his lips, he chuckles, it's funny, until Katie and Lily turned up, the only noise around Sweet Briars was the cows mooing and the birds singing, now it's full of happy conversation and laughter, his cottage now bursts at the seams with contented family life. But, right now, with the chickens shut away for the night, he wants to get back to Katie.

Whilst Katie sits waiting for Joe to return, she considers what could happen tonight when they are alone, the prospect thrills her, she's convinced that he feels the same way as she, it's the things he says, the look in his eyes when he looks at her, she sighs contentedly, counting the minutes till his return. Mmm, Joseph, even thinking about him excites her beyond belief. She sits in excited anticipation of his home coming. Could she dare to heed Margo's advice, did she have the courage to follow her heart?

But when the door opens and he steps inside, what does she do? Like an idiot she panics, asking him to excuse her, giving him the pathetic excuse that, although it's early evening and the light only just beginning to fade, she's lost her nerve, declaring she's tired and needs an early night. The minute she'd said it she felt stupid, even young Lilibeth could have come up with a more plausible excuse than that, but fear and doubt had taken over. Her indecisiveness is fighting a war in her head.

Eyebrows raised, Joe smiles knowingly, it was as if he could read her mind and understands her reluctance to stay, 'Hum, if that's what you want my dear, fine. You go up, I'll bring your water up later.'

Katie's heart is thumping so loud that she's positive he can hear it beating, 'You... you don't mind, do you?'

'I can't deny I would have enjoyed your company, but if you're tired...?' he's smiling wryly, 'it's best you get off up to bed my dear.'

Katie swallows, part of her is questioning why she'd done that, but she would have to go now, or her resolve would weaken, 'Umm yes, well, I think I'll say goodnight then, and Joseph, thank you again for the beautiful flowers. I really appreciate what you did, you are so thoughtful,' She thanks him shyly, she turns, climbing the stairs to bed.

Although up at the crack of dawn the next morning, Katie comes down alone, to an empty kitchen. An empty mug, knife and plate sat beside a cold teapot on the draining board. The log basket is stacked high and the range fire glowing. She sees that Joe's jacket is gone from the door peg.

Deeply regretting losing her nerve last night she busies herself with the chores. Flinging open the windows and doors, the sweet sound of the birds whistling a cheery good morning, lifts her spirits, bringing a smile to her lips. A fresh breeze flaps the curtains, waving their greeting to yet another warm day, and wafting the perfume from the masses of flowers that dress the parlour permeating throughout the entire cottage, she smiles dreamily, Joe is certainly right about dear old mother nature. She sighs, but this time for the first time in so many years, she sighs a truly contented sigh.

Setting to, she stokes the boiler, keen to take advantage of a good drying day, the flour is brought out to make the bread and pastry for the pies. Whilst the dough is set aside to rise in the warm kitchen, she decides to check on Lilibeth, she is unusually quiet. Upstairs Lilibeth is taking a nap, 'Hey, wakey-wakey sleepy head, up you get darling, there's lots to do.'

'Yoo hoo! Anybody there?' calls Margo up the stairs.

Surprised, she shakes Lilibeth, 'Come darling, Aunty Margo's here! We're coming Margo!' she calls back.

They both run down to the parlour, where hugs and kisses are exchanged all round, 'Hello Margo, I thought you were coming tomorrow!' says Katie, a little surprised by their impromptu visit.

'Couldn't wait ducky. Just had ter see yer both again, check yer both settlin' in nicely,' says Margo

Stan comes marching in carrying some of their supplies. 'Alwight gel?' he asks, as he sweeps pass her with a huge sack of flour perched somewhat precariously on his shoulder.

'Here, Stanley, come in the parlour. Take a look at this lot!' calls Margo, entering the parlour and staring open mouthed at the masses of flowers adorning the room.

Peering over Margo's shoulder, Stan's eyebrows raise, 'Gawd love a duck, what the bleedin' heck is this lot in aid of?' he looks to Katie for an explanation.

Predictably the colour rises in Katie's face, 'Aren't they beautiful, Joe did it, to cheer me up, you know.'

Margo slips a wink at Katie, 'Hum, I told yer, thoughtful and kind is our Joe, a right gent, bless his heart.' Then adds, 'I can't fink of the last time our Stanley gave me flowers, in fact I dunno if he ever did!' she chuckles.

Entering the scullery with two large sacks slung easily on each of his broad shoulders, Joe realises that everyone is staring at him quizzically, he stops and grins, 'What?'

Grateful for Joe's timely arrival, Katie's hoping to be spared any more embarrassing questions.

Stan gives him a sly nudge and says quietly, 'Nice flowers, nice touch boy,' giving him a knowing wink.

Joe glances at Margo and bites his lip, he can tell by the wicked look in her eyes she's about to pass one of her suggestive comments. 'Yes, well, I thought I'd make her feel at home. Erm… Katie, that's all the supplies in the larder,' he explains, interrupting Margo's probable line of frank and suggestive innuendos, thus saving Katie any further embarrassment. 'I've got to get some more wood for Stan and load it onto his cart, so I thought when we're done maybe we can take a picnic down to the stream, make a day of it, what do you think Katie?'

Lilibeth jumps up and down, tugging on her mother's pinafore, 'Oh can we, Mammy, please?'

'We'd love to, but the dough has risen and about to go in the oven and there's washing to finish and hang out too,' she answers.

'I'll help yer, lovey,' volunteers Margo rolling her sleeves up, 'It shouldn't take long wiv the two of us.'

'I can help,' interrupts Lilibeth, prompting another round of collective laughter.

'So how long do you think it'll take? Only I'm thinking, if me and Stan load up the wood now, we should be done in about an hour or so.'

Margo nods, 'Aye, that'll be plenty of time.'

'Don't be long, Joe,' says Lily.

Joe ruffles her hair, 'We'll be as quick as we can sweetheart.'

Lilibeth grins running up to him with open arms, 'Me kiss?' she offers her pouting lips. To her delight, Joe picks her up, only too happy to oblige.

Guiltily, Katie beats hasty retreat into the larder, just in case her daughter suggests that she kiss Joe too, just as she had the last time.

Lilibeth's cheeks glow as she runs to the open door, 'Bye-bye, don't be long, Joe, Bye-bye Uncle Stan, byeeeee!'

Margo grins at Katie, 'I see yer all gettin' on like a house on fire. I don't fink I've ever seen young Lilibuff so happy, and I must say yer lookin' pretty chipper yerself Katie lovey,' she tells her with a hint of suggestion in her voice. 'Oh, by the way, tell, Joe, our Freddie managed ter get some more tea, a bottle of that French brandy and some baccy (tobacco), on the quiet, no questions asked ducky,' she says winking.

Parking herself at the table, Margo drinks the freshly made tea and munches her way through a few biscuits. 'Now the men are out of the way and Lilibuff is in the garden, tell me what happened wiv that bastard Soames and how yer ended up here, wiv Joe, of all places.'

Tears well up in Katie's eyes, 'Oh Margo, you've no idea what a nightmare we've been through' she tells her, 'I was petrified. Albert was so drunk, he said he wanted to... he tried to force me to... oh you know what sort of filthy things he made me do. I couldn't Margo, I just couldn't. It was only a few weeks since I'd lost the last baby, but he just wouldn't take no for an answer. He smashed up the furniture, punched and kicked me until in the end I must have screamed out loud, because Lilibeth came running in...' Katie bit her lip nervously, 'God forgive him, he was so demented he actually raised his hand with a belt, to strike my Lilibeth! Oh Margo, poor Lilibeth was rooted to the spot, terrified. I had to stop him somehow. His trousers were wrapped around his ankles, and as he went for Lilibeth I grabbed his waistband to stop him and he stumbled and knocked himself out on the marble washstand, blood was seeping from his head on the floor. Margo, I really thought I'd killed him.'

Katie's voice is so quiet, Margo moves her chair closer, putting a comforting arm around her shoulder. 'Dear God, so what did you do?'

'I had no choice, we had to get away. If we hadn't left when we did, he'd have killed us both!' She buries her face in her pinafore, remembering that night as clearly as if it was yesterday. Taking a deep breath, she continues, 'So, we fled in the dead of night. We slept rough to start with, but then the weather turned on us, we were forced to hide in the barn. Then Joseph found us... he took us in.'

Scowling, Margo hands Katie her handkerchief, 'Drunken, filfy bastard,' she murmurs. 'It ain't no surprise ter me gel. That Soames is worse than a wild beast, didn't I tell yer, yer should've left him long ago?'

A shudder runs through Margo's slim body, recalling how horrified she'd been when Katie told her of the sick debauchery Albert Soames had been inflicting on her. Margo sighs, sweet innocent Katie, she actually believed Soamesy's sick perverted sexual demands were an everyday occurrence between normal folk! How many times had they begged Katie to leave him? Hundreds! If yer must stay wiv him, let him drink himself silly, at least he'll be too drunk ter do anyfin' and he'll leave yer alone gel, she'd told her repeatedly. Margo sighs again, shaking her head. It was good advice that had fallen on deaf ears. Sadly, Katie was utterly petrified of him, she would never stand up to him.

'Look, Katie. All I'll say is, yer fell on yer feet, landin' here lovey,' Margo consoles her. 'Now, let's dry them tears ducky, we don't want ter upset our Lilibuff, does we?'

Katie sniffs and wipes her eyes, 'Do you know Margo, Joseph has been really wonderful, we can never repay his kindness.'

'Good gawd, he wouldn't expect yer to, he's got a heart of gold, he has!' says Margo, 'Believe me gel, you couldn't have happened upon a kinder, nicer bloke, and I'll tell yer somethin' else gel, he's a real catch he is too. Believe me, he ain't nothin' like that bastard Soames and his filfy dirty ways,' she appends for good measure.

Leaning back, Katie stares wide eyed at Margo, genuinely shocked, 'Margo! I can assure Joseph has been the perfect gentleman and he, I... we wouldn't!'

Shaking her head, Margo's obliged to put her hand over her mouth to hide her smirk, she thinks that Katie protests too much.

Despite living with Soames, Katie was surely still as innocent, or was it ignorant now, as the day she was born, she really had no idea at all just how wonderful a normal, loving sexual relationship could be.

Frustrated, Margo scowls, 'Oh gawd Katie, ain't I taught yer nothin'? Look, I ain't sayin' yer had a bit of lovin' wiv Joe, fer gawd's sake! All I'm sayin' is yer got yerself a lovely safe house here, and a real fine man ter protect yer both. Nothin' more, nothin' less.' Margo sighs, 'Look, Joe's a very special, honest bloke, salt of the earth he is.' Finishing her tea, she stretches her back and tuts, there's a glint in her eye, 'I fink we'd better have another talk gel. Yer know Joe's grand, a real catch and he deserves a good woman, and there ain't a finer woman than what you is. Fink on what I's tellin' yer gel.' Then adds, 'Yer know, there's young Lilibeth ter fink of and all, her needs a decent, proper daddy.'

Flustered, Katie licks her dry lips, her face turning bright red.

Nothing gets past Margo, she grins, Katie is looking uncomfortably guilty, 'Mind gel, yer can't deny, Joe's a right sexy bloke all round, ain't he? Coo er, what a lovely body he's got. Cor, wiv them golden bulgin' muscles and all. Mmm, ruddy perfect I'd say. I wouldn't mind findin' him in me bed, I tell yer gel, if it weren't for my Stanley.... Oh, if only I was a few years younger!'

Outraged and mortified Katie's mouth drops open. 'Margo!'

Throwing her hands up in frustration Margo shakes her head, 'Now look here gel, there's nowt wrong with a bit of special lovin' Katie, I told yer afore, wiv the right bloke it can be so good it'll make yer cry out wiv joy and beggin' fer more, believe me. Take it from someone what knows.' She wags her finger at Katie, 'Yer never know, yer might be lucky enough ter find out for yerself, if yer brave enough gel.'

Breathing rapidly, Katie is wracked with guilt, does Margo know how Joe makes her feel, can she read her mind? Does she know how much she wants him?

Margo interrupts her thoughts, 'Oh happy days. Me and my Stanley still has plenty of sexy lovin' in us, anytime, anywhere,' she said dreamily, her eyes sparkling, her face glowing.

'Margo, enough. Please stop! I don't want to hear!' she protests, jumping in to prevent her forthright pal divulging any more highly intimate revelations. It's so embarrassing.

Until now, Margo had grinned brazenly throughout the entire conversation, but when she thinks of Katie, living with Soames and the filthy way he treated her, her mood changes. 'Look ducky, I'm gonna tell yer somefin' and I wants yer ter listen and take it in,' she says looking very serious. 'Now don't yer go judgin' all men by yer rotten no-good husband, he's a filfy dirty bastard and he's sick in the head, the lowest of the low. Now I know yer ain't askin', but yer knows me well enough gel, so I'm gonna give yer a bit of advice, so listen ter what I'm tellin' yer,' she says.

Ignoring Katie squirming with embarrassment and protesting wildly, she carries on regardless, 'Don't ever be frightened ter give in and let yerself go. Accept him willingly and yer can find out fer yerself, what a really wonderful feelin' it is ter share yer beautiful body wiv someone so special,' she sighs yet again. 'Oh, Katie love, trust me, it's such a sexy, excitin' feelin'. Believe me gel!'

Keeping her eyes lowered, Katie whispers, 'But Margo...' she's close to tears again, she stutters, 'I... I'm s-sure you're right, but...'

'No buts ducky,' intervenes Margo, 'just remember what I told yer. Yer won't never regret it,' says Margo firmly. 'yer a special young woman and yer deserves ter be loved, proper like.'

Katie nods timidly, giving nothing away. Margo is the dearest friend she'd ever had, and close enough to talk about all sorts of private, personal things, she couldn't say she was comfortable with it, but she respects her advice and opinions. Her mind fills with thoughts of Joseph, once more.

'Right, that's it gel!' said Margo slapping her thighs and taking charge, 'We'd better get on. Git the bread out of the oven Katie, I'll finish puttin' the clothes on the line. Lilibuff!' she yells upstairs, 'Come down here, yer can help me wiv the pegs. Come on, hurry up child!'

Margo's incessant bossing brings a smile to Katie's face, dear Margo, always so good with organising and ordering people about, she's in her element.

At last, the remaining items of washing are hung on the line, and with Lilibeth in the garden and out of earshot, Katie whispers, 'Margo, I um… I need to know, have you heard any more from Albert?'

'Albert? Why goodness me no!' she lies. Her Stan had told her not to tell Katie that Soames had been around daily, demanding Katie returned to Penfold Grove, and even worse, threatening to kill her if she won't go back to him. Stan had said he was going to talk to Joe instead, put him in the picture, so to speak, sort something permanent out. 'Yer gotta put that bastard Soames out of yer head gel. You know he ain't never gonna find yer livin' here wiv Joe,' she reasons.

Katie smiles a half-hearted smile, 'I'm sure you're right.'

Sighing, Margo gives her a reassuring squeeze, 'It's alwight gel, we're all here ter look after yer. Yer both safe wiv Joseph.'

In the meantime, down in the spinney, Stan enlightens Joe to the persistent daily enquiries and the current threats from Soames, then backs up the gravity of the situation by proceeding to give him even more graphic details of the horrific sexual demands that were regularly forced upon Katie.

Poor Joe's tanned face turns ashen, his blood runs cold. All logical conversation deserts him, it's way beyond his comprehension, he retches and is physically sick.

'The bastard's a dangerous, a menace, and I'm tellin' yer now. He ain't about to give Katie up,' warns Stan.

Shaking with rage, Joe breaths deeply, 'You know what Stan, we gotta put a stop to this, once and for all,' he says through clenched teeth.

Puffing on his pipe, Stan nods, 'Aye, just what I was sayin' ter our Freddie and Mick. Yer do know we is all wiv yer, all the way, me old mate. Our Freddie and Mick'll be right alongside us. In fact, we can round up a couple of our Freddie's strappin' mates and Mick's three boys and all, if we need them.'

'Thanks Stan, you're a pal, but we're gonna have to think this through, make proper plans.' Then a thought strikes him, Katie, 'Bloody hell Stan, Katie will be devastated and scared silly when she finds out that he's still searching for her!'

'Ain't no reason why she should know nothin',' says Stan, smirking, 'I told our Margo ter keep quiet. What our Katie don't know can't hurt her, can it?'

He pats Stan's back, 'Cheers Mate, I'm really grateful. I'll give it some careful thought, and when I come up with a constructive plan, we'll talk again. But this conversation is for us alone, not a single word to Katie or Margo, right?'

Stans face is grim, 'Not a word, Joe, I swear.'

Having made his mind up that Soames should be dealt with, good and proper, Joe's thoughts return once more to Katie. Slapping his hands on his knees he stands. 'Right then, come on Mate, let's be off, or the women will be wondering where we've got to.'

As he strolls back with Stan, he deliberately lifts his spirits, for Katie must never know about any possible plans that he might have for Soames. 'I hope the girls are ready, a good day out will do us all good.'

'I couldn't agree more Mate,' Stan agrees, 'and I just happens ter have a bottle of Freddie's brandy on me cart, to chivvy us along,' he says touching the side of his nose and winking. 'I might even get our Margo to have a drop or four. Aye a right frisky filly she was, when we got home that night, I can tell yer,' he says with a massive grin on his face.

Joe can't help but laugh out loud. For all their years, Stan and Margo kept the intimate side of the marriage going as strong as ever, neither of them making a secret of the fact that apparently, they regularly enjoyed every minute of it too. 'She's a good woman, your Margo,' comments Joe, 'You're a very lucky man, make no mistake.'

'Aye yer ain't wrong there boy,' says Stan giving Joe a nudge and a knowing wink, 'Yer know, Joe, our Margo says what young Katie needs is a kind and gentle man. Someone decent ter cherish her, like what she deserves.'

Joe choses to ignore his comments saying nothing, but he's thinking, if only Stan, if only. Though he can't help wondering. After the shocking revelations that Stan had furnished him with, he now doubts that poor Katie would or could, ever trust or love any man, let alone intimately, ever again. God help us, who could blame her?

His decision is made, their future together, if there is to be one, has to lay in Katie's hands alone.

As he enters the scullery rubbing his hands together, Joe grins, 'Are you girls ready to go?'

'We is, there's two baskets on the table, one fer you Stan, and that's one's fer Joe. Me and Katie'll carry the blankets.'

'What about me?' asked Lilibeth, vexed she's being left out.

'You, little lady,' says Joe thoughtfully, 'have the most important job of all, because you are carrying one of the empty baskets, so we can collect the eggs for Aunty Margo and Uncle Stan to take home, all right?'

Lilibeth plonks Daisy in her basket, grinning happily, 'all right, Joe, deal.'

The afternoon turns out to be a thoroughly enjoyable, light-hearted occasion. They all laughed and joked together, appreciating Katie's fine picnic, and indulging in a few ciders followed by a couple of brandies. Afterwards, the empty baskets we are filled with various vegetables.

Lily helps Joe and Stan to feed the chickens and collect the newly laid eggs, all the while, happy carefree conversations and merriment fills the warm afternoon air.

'Aye, it's been a right grand day.' says Stan, 'We'll be back the day after next markit, and I'll bring some more brandy, tea and baccy, and whatever extras our Freddie can git fer yer Joe, along with yer supplies, of course.'

'Thanks Stan. Tell Freddie I'm grateful, and I've still got a few casks of the old cider, the strong stuff, if you need it,' he replies, shaking his hand and grinning.

'Hah, the more the merrier,' says Margo to Stan with a twinkle in her eye and a lopsided grin.

Stan laughs raucously, his plump belly wobbling so much he almost loses his balance as he climbs onto the cart, indeed his uncontrollable laughter is so infectious that one by one they all join in.

It occurs to Joe that it has been many a year since there had been such fun and happiness around his neck of the woods, and he, along with everyone else he was enjoying every minute of it.

'We'll be over the day after next markit,' Margo informs them. 'We'll bring Mick and Edna wiv us next time. We'd bring our Joanie, but she's gettin' nearer her time wiv the baby. Gawd love us, she's as big as a house, she is. I reckon it could be twins! Anyway, Jed says it's best they don't travel far, and I don't blame him.'

'I can't wait for your next visit,' giggles Katie, 'I'd better start baking now!'

'A couple of them tasty meat pies and a crusty loaf or two would be welcome gel,' says Stan licking his lips and patting his well-fed belly.

Margo playfully cuffs her husband round the ear, 'Yer cheeky blinkin' devil, Stanley 'ooper,' she scolds.

Leaning down she gives Katie a kiss and a hug, 'Oh well, time ter be makin' tracks, or it'll be gettin' dark afore we know it. We'll see yer the day after markit.'

'Hey up Horsey, walk on!' said Stan, flicking the reigns, 'See yer later folks!'

As the cart trundles down the lane, they can hear Margo's squeals and shrieks of laughter.

'What a pair.' says Joe shaking his head and smiling, 'Pity everyone can't be like that.'

Peering up at him through her eyelashes, Katie nods shyly in agreement.

CHAPTER 9

That evening, with Lilibeth tucked up in bed, they retire to the parlour. Joe has drawn the curtains to cosy the room, lit the fire and the two small oil lamps.

'Oh, it's been wonderful today Joseph, I've really enjoyed myself,' she says putting her hand to her mouth to stifle a yawn.

'It has indeed. Margo and Stan are the salt of the earth and great friends too,' he yawns.

Katie follows suit and yawns again, 'I think an early night might be a good idea. I've got so much to do tomorrow. Butter to make, shallots and tomatoes to pickle, oh, and now we've got more salt I can bottle the runner beans, we can't have anything going to waste?'

Joe frowns, 'Tch, no wonder you're always tired. Now listen to me Katie, you're doing too far much,' he scolds. 'How many times have I got to tell you, my dear, it isn't necessary.'

'Joe, there are three great loves in my life, first and foremost is my precious daughter, the next is cooking and the third is cleaning, all give me enormous pleasure and satisfaction,' then she adds, 'I've also got my pride so it's my way of repaying you, for all you've done for us.'

Glancing at her he expels a long breath, I wish I could be her fourth love, he thinks wistfully. 'Hum, highly commendable Katie. Your skills are a credit to you and believe me, I'm an incredibly grateful recipient, but, if you don't mind my being blunt Katie, you're not as strong as you think you are. I've seen your fainting bouts for myself, it really worries me Katie, and to be perfectly frank with you, it's getting beyond a joke. I know you're not well, and to be honest, I think you should let me take you to see the doctor in Holdean. I've got plenty of money.'

Avoiding his eyes, she gulps, 'Please, Joe, I'm not ill,' she gnaws her bottom lip nervously, 'but there is a reason though,' she admits. Taking a deep breath, she looks at him apologetically, 'I'm so sorry, Joe, I owe you an explanation.'

For all his pushing, he wasn't sure he wanted to hear what she has to say.

'The fact is…' she swallows and looks at Joe, he's frowning, looking uneasy. 'the truth is,' she falters, 'I um, in the past I've had several… oh dear, this is very personal, Joe… I don't think I can bring myself to tell you.'

Concerned he leans forward and squeezes her hands, 'Now you've got me really worried. Are you ill? Or dare I say… maybe you're pregnant?' he suggests softly, holding his breath, not sure if he wants to know.

The colour rises in her face, she withdraws her hands, 'Oh no, Joe, I'm not ill, and I can assure you I'm most definitely not pregnant either. The truth is…' Her breathing becomes shallow, 'Oh dear, this is so hard for me to tell you this. The truth is… in the past I've had several early miscarriages, the last one only a few months ago,' she blurts out. There, she'd said it.

Leaning towards her with genuine compassion in his eyes, he speaks softly, saying, 'Katie, my dear, 'I'm so, so sorry, I really had no idea.'

Flustered, she backs away, 'Please, Joe, don't, I'll be fine, in fact I haven't fainted for quite a while, I'm feeling so much stronger, thanks to you,' she confesses.

He takes her hands in his once more, 'I'm so sorry Katie. What you need is plenty of rest and I'm gonna make sure you get it, my dear,' his gaze is caring and sincere.

Relieved she isn't pregnant, her honesty is a revelation to him, he admires her bravery, confiding in him about something so personal. However, Stan had already enlightened him to the disgusting way she had been so badly abused, though at least he knew she wasn't pregnant by Soames, so he could be grateful for some small mercies.

If he'd been angry about Soames before, it was nothing to what he's feeling now, and today, after his chat with Stan, he had been left in no doubt as to the macabre fate of poor Brodie and her new-born infant. Undoubtedly Brodie had been forced to suffer the same fate as Katie, to endure unspeakable sexual torture at the mercy of that despot Soames. He's incensed with rage and consumed with so much hatred that it twists and strangles his gut until the pain is almost unbearable, when he thinks of the violation, degradation of rape inflicted on both sweet, innocent Katie and Brodie. How, on God's earth, he wondered, could any man treat a woman so badly? His clenched knuckles whiten. But he deduces, Soames isn't just any man, in fact he isn't a man at all! He's sick and evil and by God, he would make him pay for his reprehensible acts! Something had to be done about him, before yet another innocent, unsuspecting young woman is trapped in his lair. He had to think, come up with a plausible, practical and permanent solution, and fast!

Sighing, unwillingly she withdraws her hands, stands and makes a move towards the scullery.

'Where are you going Katie?'

'Milk, I thought we could do with a mug of hot milk before we go to bed.'

'Good idea, but you can sit yourself down, I'll make it,' he says firmly.

Her mouth falls open, she's about to argue, when he gets to his feet and smiles, 'Hey, I'm a big boy and quite used to warming a drop of milk,' he teases, 'Now put your dainty little feet up, and no arguments.'

Alone in the scullery, he wrestles with his conscience. Intimate knowledge of her sufferings, all mixed up with the strong carnal desire for her has him perplexed. He's finding it increasingly difficult to be alone in her company, his feelings for Katie are so compelling and arousing that he desperately wants to get closer to her. However, after her last shocking admittance regarding her miscarriages, he decides he should avoid the situation completely.

They drink their hot milk, affably chatting about Margo and Stan. Both, it would seem, deliberately avoiding eye contact with each other. But every minute that passes in Katie's company is drawing him closer to her, his desire overwhelming him. It's no good, it was up to him to take control of the situation. Stretching his torso, he fakes a yawn, 'I think I'm going to have to call it a day.' he says apologetically, 'Early start again tomorrow.'

Hoping to conceal her disappointment she reluctantly agrees, 'Yes, I suppose it is late.'

Whether it is the excitement from the day, the talk with Margo, or the relief of sharing her personal divulgences that evening, she doesn't really know, but Katie sleeps a lot later than is normal the following morning.

A sharp knock at her bedroom door wakes them both from their sleep with a start. 'G'morning girls, your breakfast is out here when you're ready,' he calls through the door.

Sliding from the bed and wrapping a shawl around her shoulders, she peers gingerly round the door.

Sat on the mat is a tray with hot buttered toast, a pot of jam, two mugs, one of tea and the other of hot milk, all accompanied by a small vase of fresh flowers. 'Oh Lilibeth, look what Joe's done for us darling, isn't that thoughtful?'

'Mmm, nice,' says Lilibeth getting stuck in.

Despite feeling guilty at receiving room service, they thoroughly enjoy their meal, she'd never had her breakfast in bed in her lifetime, she couldn't wait to see Joe and thank him.

If she was expecting to see him when she carries the tray downstairs, she's to be disappointed, the scullery is empty, and his jacket gone from the door peg.

Of course, she understands that he has to work, but she wanted to thank him for the breakfast treat. Never mind, it'll keep till later, she decides.

No matter how hard she tries to dismiss him, Joe seems to permanently invade her thoughts. The only solution is to occupy herself, so for the best part of the day they scrubbed and polish every room in the house.

Late afternoon, Katie's about to dish up the dinner when there was a sudden huge crash and rumble of thunder that sends Lilibeth scurrying into her mother's arms. 'Naughty thunder, I don't like it banging!' she whimpers, clinging to her mother, shaking like a leaf.

'It's only big fat rain clouds bumping into each other darling,' Katie explains, making light of the storm, 'Don't worry, it will soon go away. 'As she speaks the room darkens and she's obliged to light the oil lamps.

A sudden flash of blue lightening momentarily lights up the room, quickly followed by another loud crash of thunder, startling them both.

'Oh no, it looks like we're in for a bad storm,' says Katie.

Right on cue, huge raindrops rattle and pound at the windowpanes, and within minutes, water is running down the yard in torrents.

Terrified, Lilibeth looks up to her mother, 'Ooo, Mammy, what about poor Joe, he'll get very wet.'

As if by command, the door flings open, Joe rushes in the door, completely drenched from head to foot.

'Lilibeth, run upstairs and fetch a couple of towels for Joe, quickly, now!' she urges.

Obediently she runs up the stairs.

'Phew, what a storm, I'm like a drowned rat!' he kicks off his sodden boots and shakes his head, spraying her with droplets of water.

Giggling she puts his boots in front of the range to dry. 'You must get out of those wet clothes, or you'll catch your death.'

Shivering, he removes his dripping coat, about to hang it on the door peg when she takes it from him. 'It won't dry hung there, here,' pulling a chair in front of the range, she drapes his jacket on the chair back. 'There, that should do the trick, now where's Lilibeth got to?' She's about to holler up the stairs when Lilibeth returns, carrying the towels.

'Thank you, darling, give them to Joseph,' she says, putting the kettle on the range. 'I um… I think I should take Lilibeth in the parlour whilst you dry yourself off and change your clothes, then I'll make us a nice cup of tea,' she says shyly, hurriedly ushering her daughter out of the scullery, though not before she catches a delicious fleeting glimpse of Joe's naked, muscled torso. Her heart skips a beat, sending a thrilling shiver through her body. His physique certainly compliments his good looks, she decides, she smiles wryly to herself.

Lilibeth is sat telling her Daisy a story, Katie is sitting mesmerised by the rain running down the windowpanes, her emotions running riot. She's consumed with a bewildering mixture of anticipation, or maybe it's apprehension? Both blending together with an excitingly strong feeling of both want and desire, yet at the same time, she's scared stiff. Her mind is in turmoil, she had never experienced feelings like these, ever. But with Joseph she feels this heady kind of excitement that makes her pulse race, dare she admit to herself that she wants him? In the back of her mind, she can hear Margo giving her advice, 'Believe me Katie, not all men are like that filthy ruddy husband of yourn.' It's certainly giving her food for thought, could she...?

'Mammy, dinner's ready, wake up!' Lilibeth's tugging at her arm.

'Hah, I don't know where you were, but you seem miles away,' says Joe chuckling, 'Come, I've dished up the dinner.' There's something about his gaze as he looks down at her thrills her, for some unexplainable reason Katie feels tongue tied, her mouth is dry, she seems to have lost her power of speech.

Taking her hand, Lilibeth leads her mother to the table.

Leaning forward, with his elbows on the table, Joe clasps her hands, 'Katie, is there something troubling you?' he whispers. His large hands gently encompassing hers. Not daring to look into his eyes she focuses on her plate.

He frowns, 'Look at me Katie.' Lifting her chin with his index finger he looks directly into her eyes.

His intense blue eyes seemed delve into her soul and for a fleeting moment she weakens, feeling she might even faint from sheer pleasure. Quickly she averts her eyes, fearful that he might read her thoughts, but try as she may, it's no good, his eyes hold her captive, she steals another glance. It's hard to explain, it's like they can talk to each other intimately, through their eyes.

He continues to look deep into her eyes, his thumbs brushing over her knuckles, she gulps, she can plainly see he shares her feelings, she gulps again. 'Oh Joseph,' she murmurs.

'Katie,' he purrs softly, sensing her responding to him, 'I think perhaps we should talk my dear,' he says softly and glances at Lily, 'Umm, privately... perhaps this evening?'

Lilibeth by now, has finished her pudding and is curious as to why Joe keeps whispering to her mammy, she slides from her chair to join him. 'What's you whispering for, Joe?'

'Erm, nothing much little Lily,' he says, tearing his eyes from Katie and marshalling his thoughts elsewhere, 'Well... I was um... asking your mammy if it would be okay for you to help me build a proper swing for you.' The old swing had been there since he was a boy, a single thick rope is now green and rotten, with a piece of broken wood tied to the bottom to sit on. 'I thought we could put it in the back garden, right outside the window if you like, that way, your mammy can watch you on the swing.' He suggests, adding. 'Is that all right Katie?' he asks, unable to take his eyes off her.

Somehow, his husky voice is sending shivers down her spine and butterflies fluttering low in her belly, she swallows, purses her lips and blows a silent whistle to compose herself, nodding her head, giving her approval.

'Ooo, a proper swing, just for me…?'

'Yep, just for you Lily,' he tells her.

'Oh, thank you, I'll get up very early tomorrow, then I can help you make it,' she promises eagerly.

Sensing the atmosphere has changed between them, he's desperate to talk with Katie alone, maybe this is his opportunity, 'Well I'd really appreciate your help Lily, but if you're getting up so early then perhaps you shouldn't stay up so late tonight,' he suggests.

To their amazement, Lilibeth readily agrees, 'I can go to bed now,' she offers, anxious to please him.

'Hang on young lady, not so fast, you've got to have a proper wash first. In the scullery, please,' orders Katie.

At last, they're alone.

Joe tends the fire, adding a couple of logs and lights the oil lamps before he makes himself comfortable in his chair opposite Katie.

He leans forward, 'Do you fancy a cup of tea or something?' he asks.

Katie shakes her head, fidgeting, 'No, not really, thank you,' she stutters, right now she's wishing that she had gone to bed with Lilibeth.

He leans forward, his eyes meeting hers, 'I um, I think we need to talk Katie, don't you?' he suggests in a tone that is soft, yet undeniably sensual.

She doesn't mean to, but she lets out a long sorrowful sigh, how on earth can she possibly tell him that inside he's making her tremble with excitement?

Taking her hands in his, he looks deep into her eyes again, 'It hurts me to think that you might be unhappy. Talk to me Katie, please, what is it? '

Joe's closeness fires up all her emotions and for some inexplicable reason, she burst into tears, hiding her face with her hands.

'Oh Katie, please don't cry,' at a loss for offering words of solace he stands and opens his arms, 'Hey, come to me Katie, would you like a cuddle?'

Impulsively, without a second thought, she stands, willingly accepting his comforting embrace, clinging to him, burying her head in his chest, so close she can hear his heart beating. 'Don't let me go Joseph,' she says, in a voice that's barely an audible whisper.

His strong arms encompassed her reassuringly, 'Please don't cry Katie, everything's going to be all right now, relax, I've got you,' he murmurs softly.

For a while they are locked silently together. 'Better?' he asks taking a couple of steps back, resting his hands on her delicate shoulders.

Katie looks up at him with sad doleful eyes, she sniffs and nods.

Against his better judgement his heart rules his head, unable to resist, he cups her face in his hands and tenderly kisses away her tears, 'Please don't cry Katie, I can't bear to see you so unhappy.'

Looking directly into his darkening eyes, Katie stammers, 'You're going to th-think I'm being silly Joseph, but… I'm not sad at all.'

'But your tears?' He's bewildered.

'I don't think I can tell you, Joe, I know it sounds ridiculous but… '

Feeling an overwhelming desire to comfort her, he moves to the sofa and invites her to join him, 'Katie, come, sit with me.'

Surprisingly, she does.

'Can I hold you again?' he whispers tentatively.

There was no sign of protest from Katie, so he gently wraps his arms around her, drawing her closer. Comfortably at ease with each other, not a word is exchanged between them, somehow it doesn't seem necessary. It's a feeling to savour, but, holding her so close is his downfall, he's becoming highly aroused and there's nothing he can do to control himself, he's forced to let her go, for fear of where it might lead. 'Katie love, it's late, I'm sorry, but I think perhaps I should send you off to bed. I don't want to, believe me, but I respect you Katie, it's what is right.' In his heart he desperately needs her, aches for her, but he has to be strong, now was not the time to take liberties.

Groaning inwardly, she sighs, 'I suppose you're right.' her voice betrays her disappointment, she wants desperately to stay in his arms.

Begrudgingly he releases her, he lifts her face and tenderly, kissed her lightly but briefly on her lips, 'Goodnight sweet Katie, sleep well, I'll see you in the morning,' adding softly, 'I'll always look after you.'

Neither sleeps well that night.

Katie lay cradling her pillow, as over and over again, she relives the wonderful moment when he'd held her close to him and kissed her lips, so lightly yet tenderly, oh how she wanted more. Joseph, Joseph, his name keeps going around in her head, at that moment, everything had felt so right.

The magic spell is broken, when nightmare thoughts enter her mind, nasty tortured memories of her life with Albert, a violent man that was completely devoid of feelings or compassion. Dear God, there were so many times she had wished she was dead, indeed, if it hadn't been for her beloved daughter Lilibeth…? She leaps from the bed, retching until she's sick in the bowl. For seven long years, all she had ever felt was complete revulsion at the very thought of intimacy.

Laying back on her bed, the haunting evil memories slip easily to the back of her mind as thoughts of Joseph creep in and take over her once again.

Could it really be so different with someone else? With Joseph?

Hadn't Margo assured her that consenting intimacy was a beautiful thing, when two bodies lovingly shared and enjoyed their coming together? Try as she may, she just can't imagine it. Love and joyful willing intimacy, it would seem, is something she knows absolutely nothing about, and yet… her body quivers with anticipation, aching for him. So, what, or who, had now erased those terrifying memories with Albert? Awaking these wonderful feelings of willing desire, creating emotions that she'd never even knew existed…? It was quite simple, one man… Joseph.

If Katie had difficulty sleeping that night, then Joe had fared no better.

Despite the lack of sleep over the past few weeks, every time he closed his eyes she was there. He could picture her as vividly, as if she lay beside him. Her provocative pale blue eyes that had held him in a spell since the day he'd first met her. Dear sweet Katie, her long silky auburn hair is a perfect frame for her delicate, pale face and fine features.

She's so beautiful, and then tonight…? Tonight, he had held her body so close that he could feel her heart beating. When he felt her shapely body pressed to his… He's becoming uncontrollably aroused, dear God, he wants her, so badly he's so painfully hard, he pushes back the covers, closes his eyes and with visions of Katie filling his mind he relieves himself.

Waking with a start, he sits bolt upright, he's drenched in sweat, his heart is hammering. He grimaces as vague recollections of his horrifying nightmare creeps into his mind. Flashes of vivid sickening scenes of Soames and the disgusting way he had so cruelly abused her, it had shaken him to the core, it had all been so real.

Jumping out of bed he rushes downstairs for a glass of water.

Sitting at the table, his mind is working overtime, maybe he should face the fact that even if she was free, perhaps she might never learn to trust a man enough to share love, let alone give herself to anyone, and yet… he closes his eyes, when he'd held her so close, he was absolutely convinced that he wasn't mistaken, he was certain that she felt the exactly the same as he.

Daybreak comes as a relief to both of them.

With Lilibeth still sleeping, Katie slips a shawl about her shoulders and creeps downstairs.

Joe is sat at the table, gazing blankly into his empty mug of tea.

'Good morning, Joe, reading your tea leaves?' she asks flippantly.

'Hah, wouldn't know where to begin,' he chuckles, 'Edna reckons she can. My dear old mum used to swear by Edna's readings.'

Katie joins him at the table, 'Here we go, one fresh pot of tea, shall I pour?'

He looks up, and those beautiful enticing blue eyes are looking straight at him. 'Did you sleep well?' he enquires, his mouth dry.

Katie sighs, 'Not too bad, I suppose,' she answers, shrugging her shoulders. She's about to ask the same question of him, but they both reached for the teapot at the same moment and their fingers touch.

The effect is like a bolt of lightning, sending tingling shivers through them both simultaneously. As if it was the most natural thing to do, their fingers entwine, and their eyes meet again.

His eyes darken, he whispers huskily. 'Oh Katie, my dear sweet Katie.'

She gulps, 'Oooh Joseph.'

Their fingers tightened as he leans over the table and draws her hands to his lips, 'Dearest Katie.'

Barely able to breathe she licks her dry lips, 'I'm sorry I went to bed Joseph, I really wanted to stay…'

'Is we making my swing now, Joe?' Asks Lilibeth as she breezes into the scullery.

Startled, they withdraw their hands them like guilty children.

'Tonight?' he mouths to Katie.

Feeling awash with anticipation Katie smiles shyly, 'Oh yes, yes,' she mouths.

A tug at his sleeve brings him down to earth with a bump.

'My new swing, Joe,' Lily reminds him, 'is we going to make it now?'

'Er swing? Hum, oh yes, right, let's have breakfast first, then we can get cracking.'

Throughout the day, Joe works with Lily's enthusiastic assistance, directly in line with the kitchen window.

Stripped to the waist, he keeps glancing through the open window, to see if she's there.

Katie manages to spend the best part of her time, washing and working by the open window. Intimate glances are exchanged frequently between them, as endless supplies of drinks and snacks ensure that their fingers frequently touch, more glances and silently mouthed messages are passed back and forth, all apparently unnoticed by Lilibeth.

'Mammy, Mammy, see me!' calls Lilibeth.

Katie looks outside, Lilibeth is sat on the swing, Joe is gently pushing her back and forth.

'Higher, Joe, higher!'.' Lily squeals, 'Wheee! More Joe, wheee!' Her little face is beaming.

'Not so high, Joe!' Katie warns, as she dashes outside.

'Let my mammy have a go,' says Lilibeth, putting her feet to the ground to stop the swing.

'Oh no, I couldn't, I'm far too heavy.'

Her excuse makes Joe laugh, 'Rubbish, tiny little thing like you, here, hop on,' he says, holding the seat steady for her.

It's many years since Katie has sat on a swing, but she remembers the fun she'd had at Sheybourne, 'Well all right, but not too high,' she warns.

Joe bites his lip, his fingers tingling, holding his breath as he slips his large hands around her tiny waist. Pulling her back he whispers softly in her ear, 'Tonight Katie, tonight,' before he lets her go.

Stood watching, Lilibeth claps and jumps up and down, 'Oooo, push, Joe, push Mammy higher!' she yells, hopping up and down excitedly.

Gently he pushes her back and forth.

Exhilaration runs through her body, 'Oh my, this is fun Joseph, I've not been on a swing for years,' she giggles.

'Higher, Joe, push Mammy higher!' shouts Lilibeth, egging him on.

'Oh no, enough!' Katie cries out, 'Stop, oh please stop, Joe, the swing will break!'

'Never!' he laughs, enjoying her pleasure, 'It'll take a lot more weight. Here, let me show you,' he says as he moves round to face her.

Before she knows what's happening, he'd picks her up, sits himself on the swing, then holding her close on his lap, wraps his arms tightly around her. 'Do you feel safe with me Katie?' he murmurs in her ear.

'Oh, I do,' she whispers.

For a few moments they swing gently back and forth, 'Mmm, tonight, sweetheart,' he whispers huskily in her ear.

Scuffing the ground, he swings them gently back and forth, his arms firmly around her waist, his chin resting on her shoulder, her close proximity turning him on big time. 'Mmm, oh Katie, Katie, Katie, I can't wait until tonight, just the two of us, alone.'

'Please, Joe, not so high,' she begs, as he gets carried away, swinging them even higher. 'Oh, help, stop!' she pleads, though she's giggling uncontrollably.

Feeling her body relax he ignores her protests and hugs her closer, throwing back his head and laughing with her.

Squealing excitedly, Lilibeth stands by, watching the proceedings, clapping her chubby little hands, chuckling with glee. Full of mischief she goads, 'Go higher, Joe! Swing Mammy higher!'

It can't be denied, Katie is enjoying herself, it's written all over her face, she's laughing and pleading with him at the same time. 'Oh, Joe, stop, let Lilibeth have a go, oh please,' until eventually, he bows to her wishes. 'Tonight sweetheart,' he whispers, before reluctantly letting her go.

Taking a seat on the bench, Katie sighs contentedly, her gaze ambles around the enclosed walled garden, a deliciously warm, very private, well-protected sun trap. The midday sun shines and flickers through the row of tall silver birch trees, their dappled shade giving welcome respite from the unforgiving heat of the summer sun, the birds are singing and the air smells sweet with the heady perfume of the flowers. The wonderful sound of Joe's laughter mixed with her daughter's infectious giggling is incessant. Katie sighs serenely, she feels completely safe from the vileness of the outside world.

Watching Joe pushing Lilibeth on the swing she marvels at his relentless patience. Thanks to him, the transformation in her daughter has been undeniably dramatic. Lilibeth is revelling in her new-found freedom, chattering away nine to the dozen with him, as he obligingly, pushes her backwards and forwards, making her shriek with delight.

Sat staring into space, Katie's thoughts turn to Joseph. Mmm, dear Joe, such a fine figure of a man, and undoubtably the most handsome man she had ever seen. Just being in his presence makes her feel calm, safe and secure. His temperament is always genial and so laid back that absolutely nothing ever sems to faze him. More than that, he actually seems to appreciate her company. Not since she'd left Sheybourne, had she had a decent conversation with anyone, it was a real novelty. Joe is so easy to talk to. He also appears to be genuinely interested in whatever she has to say too. Soames never talked, just barked out his orders and filthy demands.

Quietly observing Joe interacting with her daughter, she knows she can no longer ignore the fact that that he is having a powerful effect on her. She feels alive in his presence, especially when he looks at her with his sensually deep blue eyes that always seem to sparkle, often mischievously playfully and sometimes, oh so sexily. Oh help, he makes her flesh tingle, she feels alive, and dare she admit to herself, he excites her! She'd loved it when he'd held her in his arms last night, she was desperately hoping that he would do it again. With colour rising in her face, she excuses herself and returns to the scullery, filled with a stirring feeling of anticipation with the prospect of being alone with him tonight. Right now, she can't wait for Lilibeth's bedtime.

The whole day turns out to be not only an enjoyable and fun packed day, but an exhausting one for Lilibeth, who by the time they've finished tea, is so weary that her mother has excused her from helping with the dishes, instead she sits on a rug in front of the fire in the parlour, playing quietly with Daisy, until it's her bedtime. To their surprise, not even a story is asked for. Just a hug and a kiss from Katie, then Joseph as they tucked her in bed. Lilibeth gives into sleep almost as soon as her head meets the pillow.

'Ahem, I asked if you would like one?' Joe asks again.

'One what?' says Katie staring vaguely into the flickering flames in the hearth.

'Tea,' he repeats, 'I was asking if you wanted a cup of tea. Er, what else?' there was a hint of a teasing smile dancing on his lips.

Glancing up at him, Katie sees his eyes darkening, is it amusement, or something else? She fidgets, 'Oh, um tea? Um, I don't know. No, no thank you Joseph, I won't,' she mumbles, suddenly overcome with acute nervousness.

All day she had waited, counting every minute until they would be alone, but now the time had come she was feeling decidedly anxious. It was all very well being flirtatious with Joe when Lilibeth was around, but now? Now they were alone together, she suddenly feels out of her depth, he seems so, so experienced. What does she know about these things, nothing?

Then there's all the small talk. It isn't easy to make trivial conversation on mundane matters, when all the while, his soft, husky voice is stirring her, and his sexy eyes continually taunting her with tempting promises of… oh help, he sends her concentration clean out of the window. If only she could pluck up the courage to talk to him, be honest with him and tell him about the wonderful way he makes her feel, that she was wishing with all her heart he would take her in his arms again, kiss her and… she shivers in anticipation.

Sat opposite Katie in his chair, Joe's quietly observing her. He's concerned, he can't help but pick up on her unease, he'd also notes her long, drawn-out sighs, it is disconcerting. 'Katie, what's troubling you?'

As she looks into his eyes, her heartbeat quickens, it's on the tip of her tongue to blurt out the truth, but stubbornly she bites on her lip and manages to keep her thoughts to herself, determined to admit nothing, for fear of making a fool of herself.

Unconvinced and looking pensive, he wonders if perhaps, he'd offended her by being too familiar. Dear God, if she only knew what I was thinking, she would probably take fright and run a mile, he thinks to himself.

Still, no matter how hard he tries, he can do nothing about the way he feels, other than show restraint and hide his deep longing for her. 'What's worrying you Katie, can't you tell me?' he repeats. Sitting back, he waits for her to reply.

Drawing on his pipe, his whole being aches with an overwhelming desire to hold her close and kiss her soft lips again, and who could blame him? There wasn't a woman alive that could hold a candle to Katie, she's so stunningly attractive, sweet and innocent. Yes, he's sorely tempted, but the doubts are there, hovering in the back of his mind. Katie is different to all other girls he'd ever known; it was a matter of his utter respect for her that is holding him back.

As the minutes of silence drag by, he's beginning to wonder if he could have possibly read the situation all wrong, he is forced into soul searching. Maybe she felt he was putting pressure on her, or even worse, that he was taking advantage of her vulnerability? He cringes at the thought. If that is the case, then perhaps it would be for the best if she went back to Fennydown with Margo and Stan on their next visit, though that was the last thing he wanted.

This time it is Joe that lets out a long soulful sigh, all these ifs, buts and maybes could easily drive a man insane. On top of all that, there's also the thorn in his side, Albert Soames. Regretfully, he's still part of the equation too. All this wondering and presupposing is tormenting him, driving him crazy, he'd felt certain that she felt the same way, but now he was having serious doubts. It's no good, there's nothing to be gained by sitting in silence, he had to know where they stood.

Tapping his pipe on the fire grate he leans forward, taking the liberty of taking her hands in his, 'Tell me Katie, is it me?' he asks gravely, 'If I've said or done anything, anything that offends you I'm sorry,' he shifts closer. 'Because if you don't feel the same way, you must tell me.'

She gulps, his impassioned gaze undoubtedly stirring her, her naturally inbuilt fears and reservations are fast fading into oblivion. Trying to control her shallow, rapid breathing she closes her eyes. Can't he tell that she wants him, and why on earth should he think he'd offended her? Surrendering to her innermost feelings, she plucks up the courage, blurting out, 'But Joseph, you've got it all wrong. No, of course it's not you, and no, you haven't offended me at all. In fact, nothing could be further from the truth,' she confesses breathlessly.

His spirits rise, though cautiously he still holds back, it's imperative that she is sure she's doing the right thing. It had to be her decision and hers alone.

Waiting, his heart pounds, but she makes no attempt to enlighten him, so to break the deadlock he stands and holds out his arms, inviting her to come to him of her own free will.

Hesitating for a second or two, she smiles timidly, stands and moves slowly towards him, 'Hold me, hold me close Joseph,' she says in a hoarse whisper.

Elated he gasps, 'Oh Katie, Katie,' he gushes, drawing her into his arms, relishing at last, the thrill of holding her lovely body against his own. Though he realises that a simple embrace with Katie can have its pitfalls. With the feel of her slender body pressed against his, he's instantly aroused. Somehow, he feels obliged to restrain himself before things go too far. No easy task, for he's coming perilously close, almost too close to stop himself, he's forced to search his conscience. He sighs deeply. Oh hell, we can't, it's too soon, he decides. Weighing everything up, the dilemma facing him is taken out of his hands, it's his respect for her that is the overriding factor.

Reluctantly he releases her from his arms and cups her face in his hands. Looking deep into her eyes he shakes his head apologetically, 'Oh Katie, you are so incredibly special. I wish I could hold you in my arms all night, but…' his head falls, his voice barely audible, 'I'm so sorry Katie, I think perhaps, you should go back up to Lily.'

Horrified, she steps back, as a wave of disillusionment engulfs her. She wanted him to hold her and never let her go. More than that, she needs him. But now, it seems, he's merely playing with her. When it came to it… he doesn't want her at all!

Instantly he picks up on her obvious distress, the mortified look on her face tells him so, he's plunged into wrestling with his conscience. Yes, it was true she'd appeared more than willing to walk into his arms, but if he was honest with himself, when he thought of the way she had been so violently abused and taken advantage of by Soames, he feels riddled with guilt, he feels obliged to question his motives. What right did he have to even consider a serious, intimate relationship with Katie, after all, she was a married woman with a child! Recalling her many miscarriages, he bites his lip, the last one, Stan had told him, a few months ago. I can't, we mustn't. His decision is made.

His brow furrows, 'I'm so sorry Katie, you've been through so much, please believe me, I want you, but it just wouldn't be right, my love.' Now he is struggling to try and control his urges, no easy task when, through her flimsy cotton dress he can feel the warmth of her shapely body against his own.

Before he can explain himself, she gasps and cries out 'Oh no, Joseph! How can I have been so stupid? How humiliating, I thought you wanted me! Oh, dear God, no, no!' she spins round and swiftly flees up the stairs.

Alone with just his thoughts, he wanders aimlessly around the scullery, washing the dirty crockery and generally tidying up. Finally, he strips naked, washes, wraps the towel around his waist and shaves, all with a heavy heart.

The large bottle of brandy on the dresser catches his eye, a temptation that he can't resist, he pours a small measure and sits beside the range, he needs time to think.

Lighting his pipe, he settles back in his chair, remembering the desolate look of disillusionment Katie had directed at him when he'd drawn back from her, the hurt in her beautiful eyes when he had rejected her, sending her off to bed. He gulps a swig of brandy.

Until the circumstances of his dear mother's ill health had halted his regular fortnightly trips to the market, he had been like any other red blooded adolescent male, filled with curiosity, with an eye for a pretty girl. His good looks and fit body always ensured that, come market day, there was never a shortage of nubile, willing young women that could tempt him, and indeed, many had done so, he certainly wasn't without carnal knowledge of women. But this business with Katie was so very different, she was so special, there was an aura of a fascination about her, but... the situation is complicated. He sighs. He wanted her and she appeared to want him, so what was his problem?

Realistically, it wasn't just a physical attraction, a game of reckless lust. Oh no, he'd experienced that with many a young girl in his time, but Katie? She's so different, no matter how much he yearns for her, he is also driven by an even more compelling urge, to spend every minute of his time with her, cherish her, protect her and make her happy.

Solemnly he sighs, tops up his drink and gulps the brandy down, his mind in turmoil. Just half an hour ago she had willingly fallen into his arms of her own volition, and what had he done when she'd come to him? He'd rejected her, cruelly sending her away. Oh Katie, Katie, sweet Katie, what are you doing to me? Why did I push you away?

Frustratingly, when he'd held back and sent her to bed, he knew instantly, by her reaction, that he had made a huge mistake. Damn and blast it. Why hadn't he called her back?

Swallowing the rest of the brandy he refills his glass. Could we have? Would she have? Or more importantly, should we have?

Legally she is married, he reasons. Mind you, seven long years wed to that bastard Soames maybe, but surely it must have been a living hell, a prison sentence rather than a marriage. That's why she'd left him, ran away. But facts were facts, and he should surely face them. Knowing of the living hell she had been forced to endure at the mercy of Soames, what gave him the right to expect her to respond to him? Oh hell, he wishes with all his heart that he'd had the backbone to sit her down and tell her that if she couldn't face the intimate side of a relationship, it didn't matter one jot to him.

With all the soul searching going on, his head is beginning to throb. Grimacing his thoughts turns to Soames and the depraved sexual demands that Katie had been forced to submit to. A cold shudder runs through his body. Then another worrying thought occurs to him. God forgive him, was it possible Soames was the only man that she had sex with? She had told him of her past and there had been no mention of any other relationship, he cringes as the truth dawns on him. Sweet Jesus, he's right. Was it any wonder that she was so frightened of intimacy, scared to death of any male? Indeed, it would explain everything.

Staring into the bottom of his empty glass, he huffs, even an idiot could tell she was naïve. Anything remotely sexual always seemed to send her scurrying into her shell. Seemingly she had an inbuilt aversion to anything that was remotely sexually orientated, and after being married to Albert Soames, who the bloody hell could blame her? And yet, she didn't shrink away from him tonight. He emits a long, drawn-out sigh. If only he could have talked it through with her.

Bitterly regretting his actions, he shakes his head, he knows he'd been a stupid, inconsiderate fool. If it wasn't too late, he needed to apologise and explain himself to her, at the very least.

After raking out the fire, he shuts down the damper, and extinguished the oil lamps, with a heavy heart he carries Katie's wash basin up upstairs.

In hopeful anticipation he taps lightly on her door then waits, straining his ears for any sign of movement but, to his disappointment, everything appears quiet and still.

Anguished and racked with despair, he curses himself, it's too late now, he'd even lost the opportunity to explain himself, and even worse, how could he possibly face her in the morning?

Just as he's about to set the bowl down on the landing, he hears the latch being lifted, the door slowly opens.

The sight before him takes his breath away, he gasps. From the glow of the candlelight, Katie's naked figure is silhouetted through the transparency of her flimsy nightdress, tantalisingly accentuating the shape of her slim, yet shapely body.

Aghast, he stands dumbstruck, clutching the bowl, 'Katie, I um,' his mouth gapes open, he can't help but stare in awe. He swallows, exhaling a lung full of air, 'I've brought up your um… washing bowl,' he explains feebly.

Katie's body holds him spellbound, creating an intense stirring of deep and pleasurable longing coursing through his veins, for the first time in his life, a woman holds him both captive and speechless.

Clearly flustered, he takes a step forward, setting the bowl down on her tallboy, looking genuinely distressed, 'Kate, about tonight. I'm so very sorry, I wasn't saying I didn't want you,' he says quietly. 'Look, would you erm… can we talk, downstairs, please?' He holds out his hand.

Glancing warily over her shoulder towards her sleeping daughter Katie takes a tentative step towards him, then another.

Without thinking he sweeps her into his arms. His breathing heavy and laboured as he lightly brushes his lips against hers, to his delight, she responds, offering her lips, her hands clinging to his arms.

His kiss is soft and tender and his hold, oh so gentle, 'Katie, oh Katie, I'm so sorry about tonight,' he tells her. 'Please, forgive me.'

With the trace of a smile, she rests her head to his bare torso.

Holding her close, he hears her contented sigh, 'I wonder… would you agree to come downstairs with me Katie?' he asks, 'Just to talk, give me a chance to explain myself, please.'

Though her face holds a hint of apprehension, she nods, 'Um, yes, Joe, I think I'd like that.'

Relieved to be given the opportunity to explain himself, he turns to lead the way, but three steps down he pauses looking back, she is still stood on the landing, visibly shaking. 'Just to talk Katie. Come, take my hand,' he says softly.

Her trembling hand slips into his, she gulps, not out of fear, but because of the nervous anticipation that's still bubbling inside her.

With the fire now reduced to glowing embers, the temperature in the parlour had dropped, a chill, hangs in the room. Grabbing a shawl, he wraps it around her shoulders, ushering her to a chair, 'Here, sit close to the fire, I'll build it up, it won't take me a minute.'

After lighting the oil lamps, he stokes the fire, adding logs until he's satisfied with the licking, greedy flames.

Turning he looks down at Katie, sat illuminated in the firelight, she's smirking. Why?

It dawns on him, he is clothed in just a small towel around his waist, 'Oh Christ, Katie, I'm so sorry about this. I'll get my trousers, I won't be a minute,' he says as he turns, hastily leaving the room.

Katie is all of a dither, she can't help being highly impressed with what she'd seen, for the towel hid very little, dare she admit to herself, she feels a pang of disappoint that he's going to dress?

Joe returns wearing his trousers, though still bare-chested, he sits opposite her, 'Katie, about tonight, I'm so very sorry, believe me, but you left before I had a chance to explain myself,' he says quietly. 'What I said... it came out all wrong. I'm so sorry, I didn't mean to hurt you.'

Despite the thrill of him sitting before her half naked, her look of regret remains from his earlier rejection. Lowering her eyes, she shrugs nonchalantly, mumbling almost apologetically, 'Please, don't apologise, it... it really doesn't matter.'

'But it does matter Katie, it matters to me,' he jumps in. 'I upset you and that was the last thing I intended, please believe me,' he sighs, his face filled with regret, 'Katie, I think perhaps it's time we talked, get things out in the open, there's so much that needs to be said.'

Her response is an unconvincing nod, it's all right for him to say they should talk, but she feels out of her depth. The words are there, but somehow, she can't bring herself to say them out loud.

Trying to lighten the mood, Joe smiles, 'What's up Katie, has the cat got your tongue?'

Looking up at him with troubled eyes, Katie shrugs again, she looks lost.

Seeing her sat there looking uncertain he has to do something. Unable to resist, he stands, 'Katie?' he says offering her his open arms.

A little wary, Katie rises to her feet.

Trying to conceal his delight, he gently wrapped his arms around her, drawing her close, but his joy is short lived when she begins to whimper and shake. It's hardly the response that he'd expected. 'Katie?' his seductive voice grows lower, 'Look, if you don't want to talk... if you don't want me to hold you, if you want to go back upstairs, then I'll quite understand,' he says gently.

'No! No Joseph, please, don't push me away again, I want you... I really do.' her voice is shaky, sounding almost desperate, 'It's just... you must understand, I don't know what I have to do, I'm no good at...' her feeble voice trails away.

With his finger her lifts her chin, gazing into her eyes, his lips close to her lips, 'Katie? you don't have to do anything you don't want to. Perhaps if we talk it might help,' he sounds genuinely concerned.

Bless him, Joe is being so patient with her, she feels frustrated, 'But I told you, I...' she wrings her hands, 'Oh it's so hard for me to explain.' Her voice wavers, 'I um, I'm not very good at talking.' Her chest is tight, she feels panicky, until this moment she'd found even the thought of sex with any man utterly repulsive, but now...? Now she had to find the guts to talk to him, be honest, and tell him why she was finding this all so difficult. She knows if she doesn't tell him, he will, almost certainly, push her away again and she simply couldn't bear for him to reject her, sending her back upstairs alone, oh not again. Not now, when they were so close.

Joe's brow creases, his tanned face taking on a paler hue, 'I don't understand. Is it me?' An horrific thought occurs to him as Soames creeps into his mind, 'Oh dear God Katie, do I frighten you?'

Shaking her head vigorously her response is lightening quick, 'Oh no Joseph, it's not you at all!' she insists, averting her eyes from his puzzled gaze, she lowers her voice, 'It's not you, it's me, I'm so sorry, Joe what I'm trying to tell you is, umm, I don't seem to be able to put my feelings into words as easily as you. I feel so stupid,' she says, as her voice fades, and she sinks back down in the chair, looking distraught.

Exasperated they are getting nowhere, he looks down at her shaking his head, someone has to start talking, he has the feeling that if he waits for Katie, they will wait forever. Lifting her face, he says softly, 'Look at me Katie, please. I can't bear it when you're upset.' He pauses, 'Can we talk openly Katie? Perhaps it's me being foolish, I don't know,' he sighs. Frustrated, he pauses to think, 'Katie, would it help if I had my say first?'

Although she says nothing, she doesn't object to his suggestion, so it is down to him to start first.

If nothing else, throughout his life, he was always honest, he decides if ever there was a time to be honest, this was it, regardless of the consequences. He kneels before her, lifts her chin so he can look at her.

'Katie, I'm gonna be straight with you,' he moistens his lips, wishing he had another very large brandy at hand to give him courage, 'there's something I need to tell you, though I suppose confess would be more accurate.'

She opens her mouth to interrupt, but he's started now, and he's determined to tell her exactly how he feels, 'Please Katie, hear me out.' His heart begins to pound, 'Look, I've never met a woman like you before, I find you utterly intriguing. You are an extremely beautiful young woman, but more than that, you're so very special. Do you know, from the very first moment I saw you, I was totally captivated?' he says quietly, a hint of a smile dancing on his lips.

Holding her breath her eyes widen and her heartbeat quickens.

'Maybe it's wrong of me, I don't rightly know, that's up to you to decide,' he resumes, 'though I feel I should be honest and tell you how I feel. You see, I just can't help myself, you're not only an extraordinarily attractive young woman, but I also find you irresistible. Somewhere deep inside, I feel that I have found my soul mate in you.' He looks directly into her eyes and clasps her hands, saying, 'You occupy my every waking moment, if I close my eyes, you're there, if I'm away from you I feel you're near me. You know Katie, I can't even sleep without seeing you in my dreams?' He swallows, 'I adore you, Katie.' Mindful of the disgusting way Soames had used her, he adds, 'But I want you to know that I would never ever hurt you, I swear.' Then finally he says softly, 'Listen to me Katie, if you don't feel the same way, or if I have offended you, then I apologise profusely for being so blunt and forward.'

Katie looks stunned, her mouth is opening and closing without a sound coming out.

Now he'd started his words flow freely, 'Hear me out before you say anything, please Katie. Look, I don't want to give you the wrong impression. Please believe me, I want you to know that I'm not out for what I can get from you, a mad moment of sex and passion or a sordid affair, I wouldn't do that to you. I want you to know that I have every respect for you. I would never take advantage of you either. It's not about that at all, I'm just trying to be honest with you, tell you how I feel about you.'

234

Taken aback she blinks, letting out a sharp gasp, 'Oh Joseph, do you mean it?' she asks, searching his face, hoping with all her heart that his words are truthful and genuine.

Although she'd been shocked by his frank admission, she's deeply moved, what he'd told her struck a chord in her heart, he looks and sounds so sincere. Lifting her head her eyes met his, 'Tell me, Joe, do you really mean it?'

A smile spreads over his face, he beams, 'Oh yes Katerina, believe me, every single word.'

Her breathing shallows, there was no mistaking the fact, she had heard it with her own ears, he'd actually told her he adores her!

Joe's forthright declaration strengthens her resolve to be just as honest with him, it was imperative that she pluck up the courage and be truthful. Somehow, she had to make him understand the way that she feels. Throwing caution to the wind she gulps and stammers shyly, 'I have to admit... I don't know how it happened, but... I um, I feel the same about you.' Closing her eyes, she lowers her head to avoid his gaze

Stunned by her reply his eyes widened, 'You do? You mean... I haven't been imagining it?' he lifts her chin to look deep into her eyes again, 'Really, Katie?'

Inhaling deeply, she closes her eyes, and when she opens them again, she smiles shyly, 'Yes Joseph, I'm quite sure.'

Filled with elation he takes her into his arms, a feeling of euphoria binding them together.

Knowing that that their feelings are mutual, his confidence lifts, perhaps now it was time to be completely honest with her and declare everything. 'My dear sweet Katie,' he swallows, 'I want to tell you. No, I have to tell you.' he corrects himself.

Concerned, she gazes at him, 'Tell me what?'

Taking a deep breath he grasps her shoulders, 'Oh what the hell,' he mutters, then blurts out, 'I know we've only known each other a short while, but Katie, what I'm trying to tell you... the fact of the matter is, I can't help myself, I've fallen hopelessly in love with you!'

Apprehensively he sits back on his heals, holding his breath, waiting for her response, searching for her face a reaction. Though somehow, his unexpected, sweeping statement seems to have rendered her temporarily speechless.

His brow furrows, 'Katie...?' he prompts nervously, 'Say something.'

It seemed an eternity before his declaration registers in her brain, 'You say you love me, oh Joseph,' she gulps, 'Can it be true.'

Pleasure dances in his eyes, straight faced he repeats, 'Yes, I adore you Katerina, I'm madly in love with you,' he whispers, 'I love you so much it physically hurts me.'

Happy tears fill her eyes, she lifts her face, offering him her lips.

At first, he holds her tentatively, planting several light teasing little kisses on her lips, his gentle hands pressing her body closer. As a result, an exciting tension builds between them, as her impassioned reciprocation grows more and more eager.

Spurred on by her response, his desire heightens, and his kisses grow more intense. Nuzzling his head in her hair he says softly. 'I truly love you, Katie.'

Breathless she looks into his eyes, 'Say it again, Joe,' she murmurs

Holding her tenderly he looks down at her and whispers, 'My precious darling, I love you, with all my heart.'

Spurred on by her willingness he kisses her hungrily, one hand grasping her head, the other at the small of her back, pressing her against his growing erection, 'Oooh Katie, what are you doing to me?' he moans as he begins to harden.

'Oooh Joseph,' she gushes, 'I'm so very happy! But...' she peeps up at him through her thick eyelashes, her bottom lip quivering, 'Joseph,' she asks, her voice muted and wary, 'You won't hurt me, will you?'

There's no denying her question shocks him to the core. Lifting her face to his, he kisses the tears from her eyes, 'Dear God! No of course I won't hurt you, darling, I love you.' He shakes his head, he knows she is thinking Soames and the abominable way he had abused her, he must allay her fears, 'Katie, you must realise, Soames is a very, very sick man, what he did to you wasn't making love at all. Sadly, what you were forced to endure was for his own horrific, sexually sadistic gratification. Oh, my love. I swear I could never hurt you darling, I'll always be gentle with you, you're so very precious to me.' He frowns, 'Look, if you don't trust me and you want to stop, then of course I will.'

'No Joseph, please don't stop! I want you to love me,' she says clinging frantically to his arms.

'Hush, sweetheart, relax darling,' he murmurs, holding her close he kisses her tenderly on her lips.

Her lips are pliable and hungry, he moans with pleasure as he relishes the stimulating taste of her willing mouth, 'I want you Katie,' he purrs. 'I want to make love to you.'

Katie shudders, responding by whimpering breathlessly as her desire and need for him heightens, she can feel his warm heavy breaths as he nuzzles into the nape of her neck, gently kissing her, stirring and building her desire.

Cupping her face in his hands he looks deep into her eyes, 'Be honest with me Katie, do you really want us to make love, or shall I stop? You know you only have to say, darling.'

Reaching up, she wraps her arms around his neck, 'Please, Joe, of course I want you…' She replies, sounding breathless, almost desperate as her voice trails away.

An expression of concern spreads over his face, 'I'm sorry Katie, I'm not entirely convinced. I feel I might be pushing you into this, I know I have no right.'

Alarmed at his possible rejection, she shakes her head, 'No, no, you're so wrong!'

'But you're trembling. Is… is it me then Katie?' he asks softly.

Still shaking her head, she lowers her eyes, 'Oh no Joseph no, it's not you at all. It's me,' she confesses shyly, 'It's just… I'm not really sure what you expect of me. What I'm trying to tell you is… I don't know what you want me to do.' Katie gnaws her lip.

Taken aback he cups her head to look her into her eyes, he smiles kindly, his eyes filled with compassion, 'What I, want you, to do? Oh sweetheart, if you… we… want to make love, it's easy. But only if this is what you truly want,' he tells her, tracing his finger over her soft tempting lips. 'But Katie, I have to know it's what you want.'

Albert Soames and his perverted demands come to mind, he recognises and understands her apprehensive reticence. 'Katie, I want to make something clear to you. Making love is not just about 'my' needs and 'my' desires. Oh God no, this is all about us, your wants, your needs too, do you understand what I'm saying? Look, perhaps you should take more time to think about this.'

His gentle touch and his sensuous soft voice, is driving her to distraction, this is all a totally new experience, and she can hardly believe what is happening. Even more surprising, she's desperately craving more of him.

Captivated, she gulps, this is all so different with Joseph, he's so gentle and tender, he has awoken strong emotions inside her, feelings she didn't even know existed, delicious feelings that she has absolutely no control over. Studying his face, she sees no leering or sick perverted lust in his eyes at all, just genuine, heartfelt love, he's so honest and sincere, 'I really do want you, Joe, please believe me.'

Bowing his head low he kisses her lips tenderly, 'I want you too, my darling but I certainly won't force myself on you, I won't take advantage of you, I'm not that sort of man. Besides, you might wake up in the morning and hate me for what we've done. So, if you feel you want to go back upstairs...'

Despairing, her reaction is instant, they've got so close, now he is going to stop, reject her and send her away, yet again. Panicking she tightens her hold on him, 'Oh no Joseph! Why on earth would I hate you? Don't you understand, I really want you. Please, don't push me away again!' Tears spring from her eyes, 'Don't you want me, Joseph?'

'Oh Katie, my sweet love, hush darling, please don't cry.' he says, hugging her reassuringly. 'Yes, of course I want you, desperately, but if you want to think about it... If you want to wait...'

She relaxes her hold on him. Dear Joseph, he's so patient with her, so unselfish and considerate, 'But I don't want to think about it,' she stutters, 'I don't want to wait either! Please Joseph.' her complexion is glowing, her bright blue eyes filled with desire, imploring. him.

'Then talk to me Katie, tell me what you are thinking.'

There's a long sigh from Katie, 'Well... the truth is... I want you badly, but... I'm not as experienced as you may think. You see this is the first time in my life I have ever felt I wanted to... you know... do it. I suppose I'm asking you to be patient with me,' she finally admits meekly.

There was no doubt in his mind she wants him, but she'd shocked him when she'd asked if he would hurt her, thankfully, now that she'd explained, he understood, she was obviously thinking of Soames and his perverted demands.

Burying his head in her hair he tells her, 'Thank you for telling me, it explains a lot. All I ask is you trust me darling.'

Safe in his arms, somehow, he gives her the strength to feel kind of liberated and daring. Desperate to encourage him, she throws caution to the wind, 'I truly want you, please,' she cries out, and boldly taking the initiative, takes his hands and places them over her breasts, 'Oh please Joseph, don't make me wait, I want you so much, truly I do!'

Genuinely taken aback by her forthright action, he gasps with pleasure. 'Mmm, oh Katie, are you sure this is what you want?' his calm, carefully controlled voice now a husky, silky smooth whisper.

His hands drop to his lap, his gaze to her bodice, her pert breasts heaving as her breathing increases.

Frustration is creeping in, what did she have to do to convince him? She's panting so fast she feels dizzy, of course she wants him!'. 'Oh please, I want you to love me!' She watches, a tad nervously, as his eyes fall on her nightdress again. 'Touch me Joseph, please. I want to be yours,' she whimpers.

His breathing is heavier, labouring, as his fingers untie the delicate little bows one by one.

Her heart thumps even harder, as anticipation surges throughout her quivering body.

As each ribbon loosens, he looks her, to make sure that she was still at ease and isn't having second thoughts, but Katie's eyes are alive with longing, her body shivering with thrilling expectation. Holding his breath, he tips up her chin and looks deep into the eyes, asking, 'Are you quite sure darling?'

'Yes, oh yes,' her eyes are pleading with him.

Chapter 10

Convinced that he won't be taking advantage of her, slowly he slides her nightdress away from her shoulders, her bodice slips to her waist. The sight of her breasts is overwhelming he expels a long, drawn-out gasp, 'Oh sweet Jesus... you're so beautiful.' Gently he cups her firm breasts in his hands, his thumbs circling over her nipples, overjoyed, he moans with pleasure as they harden and lengthen at his touch. 'Oooo Katie, my beautiful Katie,' he groans as he runs his fingers through her long lustrous hair, drawing her to him, skin against skin. Suddenly they are the only two people in the whole world.

Carried away, he kisses her with such passionate ardour that her lips part, allowing his tongue to explore her mouth, yet another new experience that is so intimate and stimulating Katie feels as if they are joined as one.

'Mmm, ah my sweet Katie,' he groans, 'I want to be inside you, I promise to be gentle, trust me darling,' he purrs.

His velvety voice stirring her, the years of inbuilt fears are readily and enthusiastically thrown aside as highly sexual, anticipating feelings rise uncontrollably inside her.

'Relax my sweet,' he murmurs. 'Easy, relax, nice and slow darling, enjoy our love making. Oooo, my sweet darling, I need you so much,' he croons so softly.

Closing her eyes, she whimpers, eagerly digging her nails into his back, drawing him closer, 'Oooo please, take me,' she pants, 'please, Joe!'

Grasping her silky hair, he pulls her head back and softly kisses the tip of her nose, her lips, her chin, then her neck, she's breathless as he lowers his head, Katie pants little cries of delight as he nuzzles into her breasts. He's creating feelings, so mind-blowingly exciting she cries out his name in ecstasy. 'Please, Joe, oh please, make love to me!'

Cupping her face, he gazes lovingly into her eyes, 'Tell me darling, are you quite sure about this?'

Tears of joy are running down her face, unbridled, she cries out, 'Oooo, yes, Joseph, hold me, touch me, I need you!' she pleads, as thrills radiate throughout her body, her breathing so rapid she's on a euphoric high. Right now, for the very first time ever, she has an uncontrollable urge to accept and absorb everything so deliciously intimate with him, oh Lordy she is desperate for him! 'Oooo, don't stop!' she begs, gasping for every breath.

Beneath his sensual touch, she writhes as his fingers wander all over body, gently caressing her, sending her into raptures way beyond her control.

His breaths turn to throaty needy gasps, his heart pounds heavily as his eyes met hers, 'Katie, I love you so, I need you.' They are both filled with a forceful, mutual bond of unadulterated, desperate need of each other.

'Oh, sweet Jesus, I want you so much, Katie,' his silky voice murmurs, groaning lowly with a hunger to take her now. He gasps, he's painfully hard and silently praying that she won't tell, him to stop.

There's no need for her reply, her hands slid down his back, grasping his buttocks, pulling him closer, she moans softly as he teases her, his lips and teeth gently toying with her hardened nipples.

She yelps, crying out, 'More Joseph, more!'

Kneeling between her legs, resting back on his heals, clearly unabashed, he unbuttons his trousers and his cock springs free, his seductive eyes, drinking in and savouring every inch of her flawless naked flesh.

Stood completely naked, he reveals his broad, sculptured chest, heavily muscled arms and unbelievably narrow waist and hips. Katie's eyes widen, she gulps, below his flat prominently muscled belly, she sees his willy is enormous. The only male that she had ever seen naked in her entire life had been that of her husband's ridiculously obese, flabby white body, that always stank of a dire, nauseating odour. But Joseph? Help, he reminds her of the large stone sculpture that stood in the Great Hall at Sheybourne. His body is so different, it is undoubtably a shock to her system. Most obvious is his manhood, so large and prominent, in comparison to Albert's little willy that was hidden by his gross overhanging belly. Katie gulps in awe, it is ramrod stiff from the base of his dark curly hair to the tip. Oh Lord help her, he is... the only words she can think of is, staggeringly beautiful!

But lurking in the back of her mind she feels a pang of apprehension, it is clearly obvious to her that he's extremely experienced in these things. What did she know of Joe's sort of lovemaking? Absolutely nothing! Somehow, she feels woefully inadequate, she just knows she is going to be a disappointment to him. A single tear runs down her cheek.

He sits back, looking guarded, 'What's wrong Katie, do you want me to stop?'

'No Joseph no, I'm... I'm just scared, scared I'll disappoint you.' she confesses.

He is stunned, 'Oh my darling Katie, how could you possibly disappoint me? Taking her hands in his, he kisses each palm, 'Hush my sweet love, we'll take our time, relax, enjoy this, if you're unsure sweetheart, then leave it to me, my precious. Put your trust in me, darling.'

His deep husky voice soothes and reassures her, she relaxes. Delicately his hands gently caress her body, running his fingers down her spine he grasps her buttocks, pulling her so close she can feel his hard erection pressing against her belly.

Enraptured she quivers, panting with anticipation, her lips part, overwhelmed and desperate to give herself to him, she cries out 'Love me Joseph... please!'

'Katie, Oooo... my sweet love.' he purrs, 'relax darling.' easing her up he slips her nightdress over her head, now she's completely naked. 'Oooh, Katie... my sweet love,' he groans deep in his throat, 'I want to be inside you. Can I...? Shall we?' he whispers softly, almost desperately.

Her reply is in her eyes, wide, alive and pleading him.

He kneels between her thighs, supporting his weight on his elbows he cradles her head in his hands and studies her, 'Katie, you're shaking, are you comfortable with this, sweetheart?'

'Yes, Joe, but um... I am a bit nervous,' she admits shyly, breathlessly.

His eyebrows raise, he smiles and gives her a squeeze, 'Don't be, darling, I won't hurt you, trust me Kate, I'll be gentle.'

They kissed tenderly, revelling in their shared intimacy, exchanging murmurs of pleasure as his fingers slide over her belly through her pubic hair, as his finger strokes her clitoris she gasps, her body jolts.

Enraptured with such sensations as he toys with her, she clasps her hands behind his neck eagerly pulling him down towards her until his entire body covers hers.

'Oh hell, I desperately want you Katie,' he groans as he fights to slow his burning ardour.

'Take me,' she pleads. Her beautiful eyes are shining with eager need, she had never known such gentleness and sensitivity. 'Take me now.'

Cupping her head in his hands he looks deep into her eyes, he is so ready to take her, 'Oh Katie, my love, I want to make you mine, darling I want to be inside you.'

'Joseph, please... don't stop,' she responds joyously. 'I want to be yours.'

Sweet Jesus, there was no way on God's earth he can possibly deny her the pleasure of experiencing the joys of love making, not now. Hugging her close he whispered softly, 'Trust me, relax darling.'

Cocooned beneath his heaving chest, Katie wraps her legs tightly around his hips, plucking up her courage she says very softly, 'I need you so badly.'

He savours the feel of her soft warm flesh against him, hugging her naked lithe body, 'Mmm, you feel so good.'

Moistening her lips, she looks into his deep blue eyes with an indescribable yearning, 'I love you, Joseph.'

'I love you too, my precious, beautiful Katerina.'

Glowing inside, she admits shyly, 'I've loved you for so long. You're so different to anyone and everything I've known in my life; you are so incredibly patient with me. Oooh... you have such a sexy body. I need to be loved by you. Show me how to love and be loved!'

He smiles and kisses her passionately, invading her mouth with his tongue, 'Are you ready darling?'

Her eyes ablaze with desire and barely able to breathe, Katie nods. 'Oooh yes... yes, Joe.'

'Relax, my sweet. If I do anything to you that you don't like, you must tell me and I will stop, immediately,' he promises.

Slowly tracing the contours of her face, lingering over her soft lips, then down her neck, Katie takes a sharp intake of breath as his fingers lightly traced over her breasts. Tugging each nipple in turn, he delights in their response, hardening and extending to his touch.

She whimpers, her body writhing beneath him.

'Oh, my beautiful, sweet darling?' he whispers. 'Is this nice?'

Katie pants breathlessly, 'Mmm yes. Oooh, so good.'

His muscle-bound chest looms above her, because now comes the moment that he will take her and make her his own.

Katie moans with delight as his hand glides leisurely, from her breasts, down over her thighs, she grasps his arms, crying out. 'Oooh help. Oooh yes, yes!'

'Oh Katie, my beautiful precious girl,' he murmurs huskily. 'Relax.'

Until this moment, Katie had been totally naïve and completely inexperienced in the exquisite delight that the pleasures of the flesh could give her, but cocooned beneath him, she relaxes, feeling no sense of fear or awkwardness, willingly she surrenders herself to him. It is such a very special, tender moment.

The depth of his love shows through, as expertly and competently he continues talking softly, rousing her until she is panting rapidly and begging him. 'Oh please! Please!'

Deliberately taking his time, comes the moment, his breathing is now deep and laboured, he's painfully hard. 'Are you sure you want this, my darling?'

'Oh please!' she cries out.

Expelling a throaty moan, he holds his breath, closes his eyes, savouring the exquisite tightness of her as slowly, he penetrates her until he's deep inside, revelling in the feel of her as she clenches around his cock, welcoming him.

Tightening her legs around him her breathing increases into short sharp pants as slowly he begins to move, in out in out. Digging her fingers into his back she cries out, 'Oh Joseph, Argh!'

Concerned he pauses 'Katie, am I hurting you?'

'No, no!' she gasps breathlessly, grasping fistfuls of his hair, 'Don't stop!' her voice demanding, , her big blue eyes shining bright and wild.

Taking his time, he gently makes love to her, caressing her, cherishing her, savouring her, encouraging her, constantly whispering reassuringly, relishing the joy of being inside her, giving her his love.

Suddenly he tightens his hold, giving out a long, drawn-out throaty moan, as his muscles stiffen, 'Oooh no... not yet...! Oooh dear God! Argh... I'm coming! I'm coming! Katie!' he calls out. Shuddering, he holds her tightly as he climaxes, expelling a long self-satisfying, soft groan in his throat as his semen fills her with his intense love. 'Oooh, sweet Jesus, Katie!' he moans, absorbing the euphoric pulsating waves throughout his body. 'Oh, shit, I'm sorry Katie, I just couldn't stop,' he rasps, 'Oh Katie, my love. Oh bliss. You're mine, all mine,' he utters hoarsely, as his breathing slowly returns to normal. 'Mmm, skin on skin. I love you so much darling'

She flinches as he withdraws from her.

Raising himself up he gazes adoringly into her eyes, 'Are you all right, my love, I didn't hurt you, did I?'

Tonight, Katie realised that dear Margo was indeed right about the act of sex and loving. For the first time, she'd experienced just how exciting and fulfilling, loving intimacy can truly be, with the man that she loves. 'I'm fine, more than fine. Oh Joseph, you were so gentle and yet it was all so... I don't know... life affirming, exhilarating, invigorating! I love what you did to me, how you made me feel.'

Closing his eyes, he groans softly.

Sated and feeling euphoric, she curls up in his arms, her head resting on his chest. They lay, their limbs entwined, lost in their passionate, shared love for each other.

They are rudely interrupted from their fulfilling contentment when the cock crows. Joe suddenly sits bolt upright, 'Christ Katie, the ruddy cows, damn and blast it! I'm late with the ruddy milking, and Lily, she'll be up soon!' he exclaims panicking.

Scrambling around, desperately picking up their clothes they stop, look at each other and burst out laughing. Holding her close, he lifts her chin and gazes lovingly into her eyes, 'My sweet, adorable Katie, I love you so much. That was so… special.'

She smiles dreamily, 'Mmmm, yes Joseph, it was so… thrilling, I swear I've never felt such love and happiness, ever,' she confesses, 'Somehow, I feel kind of… I don't know, liberated!' sliding her hands around his neck she pulls his him down so their lips meet.

Reluctantly they part, 'Oh hell, I'm sorry my love, but I really do have to do the milking, they simply can't wait.'

Giggling like a schoolgirl, her vibrant pale blue eyes shine as she watches him dress, he looks such a comical sight, hopping about on one leg as he struggles to pull on his boot, but sadly time has run out on them.

'Look, Joe, the milking, it's not a problem, if you put the kettle on, I'll run up and get dressed. I'll just check Lilibeth is asleep, but it is so early, I'm sure we've got ages. A quick cup of tea and we'll milk the cows together,' she says pulling her bodice together, covering her breasts from his admiring fixed stare, then bubbling with delight, she flies silently up the stairs to dress.

'Are you happy, my darling?' he asks as they sit side by side milking the cows.

'Deliriously happy,' she tells him truthfully.

'Are you quite sure you have no regrets about what we've done?' he asks looking wary.

Katie shakes her head,' Absolutely none at all, I really loved it, it was so… thrilling!' Gazing up through her eyelashes she lowers her voice, 'I love you so much Joseph.'

'Hum, I love you more, Katerina,' he says, planting a tender, light kiss on her soft lips.

Undeniably, the experience of making love with Joe had left her feeling insanely euphoric, she throws back her head and laughed, 'You couldn't possibly, Joe.'

His expression grows a little more serious, he stands and adjusts the front of his trousers, 'Oh believe me, I do, darling.' Reaching out he caresses her flushed cheeks, 'I want to make love to you again, I want you so much.' Frowning he bites his lip, he feels the need to apologise,

'I'm sorry, I feel you've been cheated, darling, you should have come, with me.'

Not understanding his apology, she looks up at him, her face glowing with colour, but this time, it's not through embarrassment, 'Oh help, I want more,' she squirms on the stool, 'I want to do it, again!'

His lips curl, his eyes flashing wickedly, 'Oh really, right now?'

She giggles, 'Oooo yes, most definitely, right now,' she says shamelessly.

Beaming, his eyes shine devilishly, 'What right here, right now?' he asks, playfully teasing her.

Katie swishes the hair over her shoulder and smiles radiantly, 'Yes, Joe, here, now, please!'

Ecstatic with her blatantly open response he knows for sure that miraculously she had put her understandable past abhorrence towards sex firmly behind her. She has allowed him to show her how wonderful, sharing loving intimacy can be. For so long he had secretly hungered for her, and now Katie had trusted him, willingly giving herself to him, now she was his, he loved her so much. 'Careful what you're saying, darling, you'd better not tempt me,' he smirks.

With an impish look on her face she giggles, 'Oooh, could I?' she asks, blatantly goading him, 'Really, Joe?'

'Absolutely, you do it all the time, so be warned my precious,' he declares with a burning licentious look in his eyes. 'Mmm, hopefully later?'

'Oooo yes please,' she grins.

Eventually the milk is finally delivered up to the house, when they'd enter the back door, they are greeted by nothing more than silence.

After checking that her daughter is still sleeping soundly, Katie lays the table and prepares breakfast.

Startled, Katie jumps, gasping as Joe creeps quietly up behind her, wrapping his arms around her waist drawing her against him. He groans softly as he nuzzles into her neck, planting several tender kisses, playfully nipping her earlobe.

She wriggles, crying out, 'Oooo help! You're doing it again Joseph!'

'Mmmm, believe me, I'd like to Katie. You are doing all sorts to me,' he purrs softly, Then, with his hands splayed flat on her belly he pulls her closer so she can feel his swollen erection against the small of her back.

Katie turns, smiling saucily, 'Mmm, I wish we could.' Oh, how she wants him again, right now!

Joe laughs, sweeping her off her feet and kissing her passionately, his silky voice full of emotion as he whispers, 'Oh I love you. I love you so much you drive me to distraction. Oooh hell, you're making me ache. Do you know what I'd love to do to you right now, sweetheart?' he says with a wickedly sexy look dancing in his vivid, dark blue eyes.

Smiling coyly, she giggles and shakes her head, 'No, but I do hope you're going to tell me.'

'I want to make sweet love with you, darling, I want to be inside you again. Mmm, my sweet, beautiful girl.' He sighs, 'Oooh Katie, Katie, Katie, I would give anything to have you in my bed, right now!' Gently he stands her down, pressing her body to his once more, so that she's in no doubt how much he needs her.

Exhilarating senses radiate throughout her body as she feels his swollen erection pressing hard against her belly.

It's clear to Joe that her naïve inhibitions have now deserted her completely, as shamelessly she slides her hand inside his trousers to his groin, grasping his penis, 'Oh God, it's so big!' she squeaks. Beneath her touch she can feel him throbbing as she caresses him. Loving the feel of him, boldly she squeezes tighter.

Closing his eyes, Joe moans with pleasure. 'Oh, sweet Jesus.' A low groan rises from his throat, 'Mmm. Oh, please, darling, you've got to stop! No sweetheart, we mustn't!' he protests. 'We can't, at least not here. Lily might come down,' he warns, reluctantly pulling her hand from his pants.

'We could go to your room?' she suggests, eager to prolong the intimacy between them.

The prospect of two badly fitted old wooden doors between themselves and Lily, seems like a bad idea to him, but Katie's face is so full of expectation, and so is he.

Inspired he comes up with a suitable alternative, 'Perhaps we could go down to the barn,' he suggests, 'Up in the loft, we would hear Lily if she were to come looking for us, and at least we'd be out of sight up there.'

Flushed with an excited fire in her eyes, she squeezes his hands, gushing, 'Oh yes, please Joseph.'

Anyone that had ever known Katie, would have been forgiven for thinking she had taken leave of her senses. In less than a few hours she had seemingly lost all her innocence and inbuilt fears of intimacy, now she would have flown to the moon if he'd asked her.

Incredibly, at the ripe old age of twenty-three, she'd experienced, for the very first time in her life, his love, his genuine tender love making. Joseph has awoken feelings and emotions within her that she didn't even know existed. It is a life asserting revelation that she now embraces unreservedly, now she's craving more.

'Are you comfortable my darling?' he asks, as he lays beside her in the straw.

'Mmm, very.'

'So, did you enjoy making love, my darling?'

Feeling brazen she slips her hand inside his shirt, through his chest hair, feeling the warmth of his skin, 'Oooh yes.'

'Shall we make love again sweetheart?' he asks softly.' You want it?'

Her heart comes up in her mouth, just the look in his sexy, darkening eyes is turning her on, 'Oooo yes, I want you,' she pants breathlessly, 'do it again, Joe, oh please.' Her eyes now shining bright with hunger.

He grins, 'Er, do it? Tell me what you want Katie? Say it, darling, tell me what you want us to do,' he teases, his sensual eyes shining with a heady combination of heartfelt love and deep, lustful longing.

Her breathing's erratic, 'I want to make love Joseph, I want to feel you inside me again, please.' Completely uninhibited, she shocks him by laying back, boldly untying the ribbons on her bodice exposing her breasts. 'Please I want more!'

Leaning over her he grasped her head in his hands, 'Oh Katie, my sweet love, you are so beautiful.' He groans a long throaty groan. 'Relax my darling,' he urges softly, 'This time, I want you to come with me.'

He purrs, as his hand cups her breast, 'Mmm, Oh I love your gorgeous breasts, darling, I can't leave them alone,' his fingers adeptly tug and roll her nipples, his tongue toying with them, arousing her. She groans loudly as he sucks hard on each nipple in turn, sending her into raptures of passionate deliriousness. 'Do you trust me, darling?' he whispers.

She nods enthusiastically. 'Yes. Yes, I do,' she pants.

Over the years, through his many past experiences, he had perfected the art of prolonging his lovemaking with foreplay, so that he could truly satisfy a woman and himself completely, he had always been capable of taking his time and pacing himself to make it last so much longer, but it's no good, Katie's enthusiastic response tips him over the edge. 'Dear God, I want you so much,' he exclaims, as skilfully, his fingers caress her. He sighs a soft, guttural groan in his throat, it isn't easy to control himself, when Katie is proving to be so readily receptive to his slightest touch. Slipping his hand between her legs, he stimulates her clitoris with his fingers, rousing her higher. 'Do you like this, is this good?' he whispers sexily. 'Do you want more, darling?'

Eyes shut tight, enthralled with his sensuous ministrations, her body writhes beneath him, 'Mmm. Oh yes, yes,' she coos. 'More!' she cries out, both her hands grabbing fistfuls of his hair, as she absorbs the intense feeling he's creating inside her. Overwhelmed, she cradles his head, running her fingers through his hair crying out sweet moans of satisfying rapture as he takes her higher. 'Please, oh please Joseph!'

It proves to be a very intimate moment for both of them. Lost in each other, no one else exists.

Undoing his fly to release his impatient cock, he takes her hand in his, encouraging her to grasp him, already he is throbbing and hard. 'Mmm, hold me, play with me,' he slides his hand over hers, showing her how to pleasure him, 'Like this, not too tight, darling. Oh yessss, gently,' he coaxes her into a satisfying rhythm. 'Oooo yes. Mmm, that's so good, darling,' eyes closed he moans. 'Oh hell, Katie you've gotta stop or I'll come!' he beseeches her, 'Please Katie, stop. I need to be inside you. I want you to come for me.' Breathless he is desperate to be inside her.

Reluctantly she withdraws her hand, 'Mmm, oh Joseph,' she moans softly, as he climbs between her legs, his knees spreading hers wide. 'Are you ready?' he asks, in a silky husky purr.

'Oooh yes!' she cries out, fisting her hands in his hair, pulling him closer.

It's a mutual feeling of shared euphoria as he gently guides his cock, pushing inside her, oh so slowly until he is deep inside.

Groaning loudly, he relishes the tight feel of her, as her body clenches around his throbbing cock.

Overcome with passion they are lost in their own little world as gradually he pushes in out in out, gradually increasing his pace, driving her wild.

Biting his lip, he's forced to pause, giving his overly eager erection a chance to subside a little, he was almost to the point of no return, but he desperately wants to give her a mind-blowing orgasm.

Stilling, he drinks in the beauty of her flawless body. He purrs, 'Oh my darling Katie, I love you, you have such an exquisite body, you turn me on just looking at you. You drive me wild.'

While his fingers delicately trace over the contours of her flesh, thrills run riot through her body, and if she were to admit the truth, she would do anything to please him.

She moistens her lips, her breath racing frantically as she closes her eyes, loving the feel of his firm golden flesh against her own. Possessively he increases his rhythm, faster and faster, deeper and deeper, filling her with his passion and love.

Simpering, her body writhes uncontrollably beneath him, her head flaying side to side as his pace increases, taking her higher and higher. 'I want you to come,' he urges breathlessly, 'Come Katie, Come. Come for me now!'

As if on command, Katie shrieks his name, 'Joseph! Ah!' her body stiffens, her head thrown back, suddenly her body shudders as an intense, convulsing feeling of euphoria engulfs her, radiating pulsating thrills throughout her body, consuming her as she comes. 'Ooooh Joseph… Oooh, Joe!' she screams wildly, her rigid fingers clawing into the flesh of his back.

Simultaneously, Joe's muscles ripple and tighten, he exhales a long throaty groan, his orgasm overtakes him as she clenches him in the throes of her climax, loudly he cries out, 'Yessss. Sweet Jesus…! Oooh yessss, oh Katie!' He stills, filling her with his semen and his loving adoration.

Panting heavily, Katie licks her dry lips. With Joe still spasmodically pulsing inside her, wide-eyed and full of wonder she gazes up at him, 'Oooh Joseph. What happened?' she asks breathlessly, highly flushed, she gasps for breath as the feeling of unbelievable ecstasy rushes wildly throughout her body, 'Oh Joseph, can you feel it too?'

Tenderly he smiles down at her, softly moaning, 'Mmm... oh yes, my sweet darling. And you?'

'Mmm. Oh yes! It was... it was... indescribably exhilarating!' her eyes ablaze, still absorbing her enthralling orgasmic high.

Completely satiated he sweeps her hair away from her delightfully pert breasts, kissing each nipple in turn. 'Mmm, oh yes, perfect, this time we both climaxed together,' he purrs with pleasure, as his fingers lightly travel down her spine, grasping her firm buttocks, savouring the feel of her body still holding him inside her. As reluctantly he pulls out of her, she flinches. 'So, was it a good orgasm, darling?'

Frowning, she looks puzzled, 'Orgasm...? I don't understand, what do you mean?'

'Oh, my sweet love, it means we both culminated our lovemaking at the same moment,' he tells her with a satisfied smile on his face. 'When I came inside you, you came too, we climaxed together,' he explains gently.

'Mmm, such a powerful, all-consuming feeling. I can't believe what happened...' she says, still not understanding.

He chuckles, 'It was mind-blowing. Mmm, oh the joy of filling you with my love, darling,' he declares, 'I love you so much.' Then her question sinks in, could it be that it was her very first orgasm? Disbelieving he shakes his head. 'You know Katie, for all that you've been through, you're a still a pure innocent, so inexperienced, bless you.' He frowns, he has to ask, 'sweetheart, are you telling me you've never experienced an orgasm before?'

Katie frowns, shaking her head, 'Orgasm...? No, no, never, ever. Oooh I loved it! Can we do it again?'

Tenderly he smiles, her first orgasm. Really? 'You know, it will be like that every time we make love, darling. Oh God Katie, I love you so much.' He props himself up on his elbows to playfully suck and nip each nipple in turn again.

'Joseph!' she shrieks, 'Oooh help!' she is still in the throes of such a high, her fingers grip his taut muscled biceps, 'You mean we will always have that incredible thrill every time we make love?' she pants. 'Mmm... I loved it; I want more!'

'What? Now? Phew, Katie you're insatiable! But believe me, I'm not complaining at all,' he grins. 'In fact, I'm loving every minute of it!' Looking serious he takes both of her hands, 'Listen to me Katie, I can't help but worry about you, you must tell me if I hurt you. I... I didn't, did I?'

All smiles she shakes her head, 'No, not at all, it was just so incredibly... I don't know... um... exhilarating. I loved it! I want you to do it again!'

Joe tuts, grinning from ear to ear 'Oh my sweet love, you're turning into a nymphomaniac, my beautiful sexy girl.'

Unaware of what he means, she frowns, 'Oh, is that bad?'

Raising his eyebrows, he chuckles, 'Good grief, my sweet love, believe me, living with a nymphomaniac is every man's wildest dream come true! Making love, twenty-four hours a day? Oh yes, it means that I'm the luckiest bloke alive!' he declares. 'Don't ever stop wanting to make love with me, my precious.' He curls his arms around her, drawing her close. 'Oh, my sweet Katie, I want you next to me, naked in my bed, your glorious hair spread out on my pillow,' he purrs, 'tonight, tomorrow night, and every night from now on, my precious.'

Snuggling into him she sighs. 'If only we could Joseph,' she says wistfully.

A shaft of sunlight shines through crack in the wall, reminding them that time is passing. Helping her to her feet he holds her close, 'You know our Lily will be up soon, we really should get back to the cottage.'

Expelling a long, contented sigh, Katie daringly strokes his erection, the light isn't very good in the barn, but she can feel it is stiffening from her touch. 'You are so sexy Joseph, I love you inside me, it's so intense. Can we make love again, soon? Say yes, oh please, Joe, I want more?' she asks, searching his eyes, pleading with him.

'Mmm, I would say tonight sounds good to me, darling, when our Lily is tucked up in bed, of course,' he says with a boyish grin.

'Oooo, I can't wait Joseph. I need you again,' she murmurs.

Fortunately, when they return home, they find the scullery empty and the cottage quiet and still.

After a quick check, Katie is relieved to find Lilibeth is still sleeping.

Whilst Katie prepares breakfast, Joe, strips to the waist and with the sun on his back, is out in the garden, whistling as he splits hefty logs with ease, glancing every few minutes, into the scullery window and smiling lovingly at Katie.

Porridge is simmering on the stove, toast and jam, sat on the table. 'Joe, I'm just going upstairs to bring Lilibeth down for her breakfast,' she calls through the open window.

Joe, his tanned body glistening with sweat, rushes into the scullery and steals a passionate kiss and slips his hand up her skirt.

Her body jerks as his finger toys with her clitoris, emitting several little yelps and gasps of joy, 'Mmm, that's to keep you going till tonight, my sexy darling. I can't wait,' he whispers, 'I want you so much Katie.'

They are joined at last by a bleary eyed Lilibeth, who has been rudely awoken from a deep sleep by her mother, insisting on her having a good wash before she can come down to eat her breakfast. For a change all is quiet at the table. Apparently Lilibeth had awoken with a good appetite and more interested in her breakfast than conversation, she is totally engrossed in emptying her plate as soon as is possible.

'Love you,' Joe mouths across the table, whilst Lilibeth concentrates on spreading jam on her toast.

Katie smiles, 'Love you too,' she mouths back.

'Want you,' he mouths soundlessly.

'Need you,' she replies just as silently, wriggling on her chair.

Finishing his tea, he looks out of the window. 'Hum looks like another nice day,' he comments, still grinning at Katie, 'We won't get many more days like these. We've been more than lucky with the weather so far. After an unusually long warm spring, followed by a hot dry summer, the weather has been kind to us, but we desperately need rain for the vegetables and fruit.' Studying the clouds through the open window, he frowns. 'Huh, having said that, I reckon we could well be in for a drop of rain before the days out, if we're lucky.'

Katie rises to clear the table, 'There's plenty for us to do indoors, are you going to help me, Lilibeth?'

'I can't Mamma, I'm playing on my swing with Daisy, coz she hasn't been on it yet,' she replies.

Joe shrugs his shoulders, 'Nobody going to ask what I'm doing then?'

Lilibeth giggles, 'What are you doing, Joe?'

'A few jobs around the house Lily, and when you've finished playing on your swing you can give me a hand, if you like.'

'Ooo I'd like that, what is we doing?'

Joe smiles down at her, 'Winter will come soon enough, so I thought we might all benefit if I make a proper lean-to, outside the back door,' he tells her.

'What's a lean-to?' asks Lily.

His brow creases as he tries to come up with a simple description for the perpetually inquisitive child. 'It's like a corridor, linking the back door to the toilet, it'll keep us dry in the winter when we need use the lavatory,' he explains. 'I've got plenty of wood, I should have a spare door and hopefully a glazed window or two somewhere in the barn.'

He turns to Katie, his smiling eyes twinkling, 'If you weren't so busy Katie, I'd take you to the barn and show you,' he says cheekily and winks.

Glancing at Lilibeth, Katie turns bright red, whispering, 'Why Joseph Markson, I hope you're not being saucy!'

He smiles cheekily and leans closer, 'My dear Katie, so what if I am?'

She swallows, moves even closer and whispers, 'I think I like you being saucy,' she tells him shyly.

'I certainly wouldn't mind you being saucy with me. Hopefully tonight, my love,' he whispers in her ear.

Coyly Katie blushes. 'I think I'd like that too.'

He smirks, 'Right, well, when the lean-to is finished, I'd like to do something about my mother's old room, next to the parlour. Any suggestions Katie?'

'It looks like it was someone's bedroom,' she comments, 'I found it when I did the spring cleaning.'

'Aye, and so it was,' he says reflectively, 'It was Will's room for many years, then after he died it became Mother's bedroom, her joints were playing up and she couldn't climb the stairs any longer.'

Lilibeth's bored with the conversation that doesn't seem to include her. 'All gone!' she proclaims, cleaning the last smears of jam from her plate with her fingers. Sliding down from her chair she makes a quick dash for the back door.

Katie frowns, 'Lilibeth, come back here, right now! Please, remember your manners child? Just look at your sticky hands.'

To her disgust, and despite a lengthy protest, Lilibeth is forced to endure a second scrub of the morning with the soap and a flannel before she can finally go outside and play on her swing with Daisy.

Enjoying a second cup of tea and precious time alone together, they sit opposite each other at the table, their fingers entwined. 'Oh God Katie, I love you so much,' he says in his velvety sexy voice. 'You're so very special to me.'

Her eyes close for a second, cherishing his words, 'I love you too Joseph. Oooo, I want more.'

Suddenly she's in his arms. 'Tell me, tell me again, my sweet,' he says, holding her close.

Her face looks up to his, 'I love you so much Joseph, I want you, I really loved it when you came inside me. It's so exhilarating, you made me feel... I don't know, I feel complete, as a woman!'

'Say it again Katie.'

'I love you, Joe, I want you to make love to me, again!'

'About that Katie, I have to ask, you've no regrets, have you, darling?'

Gripping his hands tightly, she answers him truthfully. 'None at all, I wanted you then and I want you again, right now, this minute. I love you, Joseph Markson.' From her throat she emits a long soft sigh of genuine contentment, 'Mmm, it was all so different to what I imagined. I loved it. Oh Joseph, I want more.'

'Me too, darling.' All too briefly their lips meet, but sadly, with Lilibeth outside the window they are forced to part, he sighs, 'Hell Katie, it's no good, I want to hold you in my arms forever, darling, but I won't get a thing done if I don't make a start on the lean-to.'

As is his habit, come rain or shine, he takes his coat from the door peg, 'Have a think about my mother's room, I have a few ideas myself, we can have a chat about it when I get back. I should only be about an hour or so,' he tells her.

Katie notes the wicked glint in his eye and flutters her eyelashes.

'Tonight, my sweet love,' he says softly kissing her lips, 'Mmm, tonight,' then he's gone.

True to his word, in less than an hour he returns, the cart creaking under the strain of its heavy load of wood and tools.

Sitting on the grass, Lilibeth is completely engrossed in her own little world of make believe. She has an enamelled bowl, full to the brim with sudsy water, apparently giving her beloved doll Daisy a bath. A lone, single voice seems to be having an interesting conversation, 'This is a nice bath, isn't it, Daisy? Yes Lilibeth, lovely. Nice in the pretty garden, isn't it, Daisy? Yes Lilibeth, lovely flowers. Do you want to go on my new swing when you're dry? Ooo yes please Lilibeth.'

Joe shakes his head, chuckling to himself and leaves her to it, he'd never understand the child's world of make-believe.

Joe finds Katie in the parlour, bent over the little side table polishing, it's an opportunity he can't miss.

Sneaking up behind her he grabs her hips pulling her back against his swollen erection. 'Did you miss me, darling?' he asks and spins her round to face him.

'Every single second you were gone,' she says as she reaches up, flinging her arms around his neck offering her lips. As his tongue pushes into her mouth she reciprocates, toying with his tongue and exploring. A long intimate passionate kiss holds them together, which leaves them both grinning and gasping for air.

'Whilst Lily is in the garden Katie, I want to talk to you about the back room, my mam's old room, I have an idea that I'm hoping you'll consider.'

Katie, at the age of twenty-three and newly awoken to the rewarding joys of sex, feeling the love and his mutual passion, slides her hand to his groin, to be repaid with a low throaty groan from him. But with the sound of Lilibeth's voice coming in from the garden, he knows that if they stay alone in the parlour, he won't be able to control himself and tells her so.

Drawing her close he chuckles, telling her that she would almost certainly be a whole lot safer if they were in the scullery, away from temptation. Already aroused, he threatens to take her there and then if they stay alone a moment longer.

Pouting she reluctantly agrees they should go in the scullery.

Katie's eyes positively shine as she sets too, making a pot of tea and a plate of assorted sandwiches, well aware that Joe's greedy eyes are following her every move.

Lilibeth, when summoned to come in for lunch, stays put, protesting, 'But Mammy, I'm busy, I'm playing with Daisy.'

Joe dashes out the door and sweeps her up in his arms, 'Hey up, little Lily, lunch first, play second, and if you are really good, I'll let you help me finish making the lean-to after we've eaten. Deal?'

Lilibeth beams, 'Oh all right, deal.'

Katie smiles to herself, he'd certainly got the measure of young Lilibeth.

Lunch doesn't take long, or at least in Lilibeth's case it doesn't. Much to her mother's disgust, she bolts her food and is back outside in no time.

Alone once more, Joe and Katie show restraint by remaining respectfully seated opposite each other at the table, his eyes full of longing, 'Oooo 'I love you.' his voice lowering to a sensual husky purr. 'You're so beautiful, I want you. Tonight.'

Gulping, her cheeks flush a fetching rose pink, 'I want you too.'

'Humm,' he smirks. 'Well, that's easily arranged, darling. Sweet lord, I can't keep my hands off you,' he sighs a long needy sigh. Stroking the palms of her hands his eyes penetrate hers, filled with love and desire. 'Christ, I'm getting desperate,' he tells her, adjusting the prominent bulge in his trousers for the umpteenth time, in an effort to hide his urges.

'So am I,' she tells him, wriggling on the chair, 'me too.'

Beaming he squeezes her hands, 'So tell me, my sweet love, what exactly would you like me to do about it?'

Leaning forward she boldly whispers, 'I want you to hold me in your strong arms and make love to me, I want you to make me come again.'

Joe's Adam's apple rises and falls, 'Christ, oh yes please,' he smirks. 'Oh hell, I think we should change the subject, discuss my mother's old room, before we get ourselves into trouble, sweetheart.'

She looks puzzled, 'Your mother's room?'

'Uh huh, sadly we're not married Katie, so we always have to consider what's right and proper where Lily is concerned, do you agree?'

'Why of course I do,' she answers, wondering where he's going with this.

'So how do you think she'd feel about having her own bedroom, all to herself?'

'Well, she had her own room in the past,' Katie replies, 'Why do you ask?'

'I dunno how you feel about this... but I want to sleep with you Katie, and I don't mean hiding up in the barn, or on the floor for an hour or two when Lily's gone to bed either, that's kind of sordid, juvenile stuff.'

Katie grasps his hands, 'I could sneak into your room when Lilibeth is sleeping.'

'I can hardly wait, but the old doors upstairs don't close properly, you can hear everything through them. If, my darling, we share my bed, you... er we, would almost certainly wake Lily with our lovemaking, if you get my drift,' he points out diplomatically.

Katie's eyebrows raise and her face flushes, 'Oh help, well if you put it like that, then you're right of course, so what can we do about it?'

'Well, this is where my mother's room comes into it.'

Looking quizzical Katie leans forward, 'I don't get it.'

'As we're not married sweetheart, in the name of decency, for you and Lily, I thought Lily could have your present room all to herself, and I, of course, will retain my own bedroom upstairs, for appearances' sake, because it's what Lily is used to. But, if I turn my mother's room into a double bedroom, we could tell Lily that it is your room, but in truth it would actually be 'our' room and little Lily will be safely out of earshot and none the wiser when we make love and sleep together.' He explains, 'So what do you think, darling?' adding, 'Katie, if it's what you want, if you agree to these changes then I suggest you speak to Lily, test the water, so to speak.'

The very thought of sharing the same bedroom with Joe is giving her goose bumps, causing her pulse to race in anticipation at the prospect. After a brief discussion, she readily agrees to the arrangement, they mutually decide that Katie will broach the subject with Lilibeth, as soon as possible.

Throughout the rest of the afternoon, Joe continues building the lean-to. He's so eager for Katie to sound out Lily's opinion, Joe prompts her, 'Come on Katie, talk to Lily.'

'Um, can I hang Daisy on the line to dry?' asks Katie emerging into the garden.

'Yes, please, Mammy.'

'There, she'll soon dry swinging in the breeze, would you like me to push you on your swing, sweetheart?' offers Katie.

Enthusiastically Lilibeth nods again.

Joe looks at Katie smirking, giving her a nod of encouragement.

Whilst pushing Lilibeth back and forward on the swing, they chat. 'Do you remember having your own bedroom and your own bed at the old house, darling?' asked Katie as casually as she can.

'Me and Daisy? Yes, Mammy,' replies Lilibeth, looking a little unsure of Katie's question.

'Well, Joe says that he can make the front bedroom really pretty, just for you and Daisy. What do you think of that?'

'But where are you going to sleep, Mammy?' she asks matter of factly, 'You going to sleep with Joe then?'

Mortified, Katie is taken aback.

A small smile comes to Joe's lips, he has been eavesdropping. Bending down he whispers in Katie's ear, 'Hey, take no notice, she's a child, it's just an innocent remark, bless her. She has no idea of such things. Don't worry, tell her about the downstairs room, tell her it will be your bedroom.'

Katie swallows, 'As you know, Joseph has his own bedroom, across the landing, remember?'

Seemingly no longer particularly interested by the conversation, Lilibeth shrugs nonchalantly and bites into her biscuit.

'The thing is, darling, to give us all more space, Joe said he'd turn his mother's old room, downstairs, into a bedroom for me, so we'll all have a bedroom each. Isn't that nice? So, what do you think Lilibeth?'

'I've made something very special to go in your own bedroom,' Joe interjects. 'Well actually it's for Daisy,' he explains, by way of an incentive-come-bribe to Lily, who up until now, appears not to be bothered either way.

Joe's mysterious statement has caught her attention, now she's intrigued. Curiosity getting the better of her, she asks, 'For my Daisy. What is it then?'

Giving Katie a wink he grins at Lily, 'Wait here with your mammy, I won't be long, sweetheart,' he says, and he disappears down the yard in the direction of the barn.

Joe seems to be gone an age, bored with waiting Lilibeth returns to her swing.

'Hey, Lily, do you want to see your surprise?' Joe calls through the open scullery window.

Any interest in her swing is instantly lost as she dashes inside, her natural inquisitiveness now her priority.

'Where's Daisy's surprise then, Joe?' she asks, scanning the scullery.

'Close your eyes, sweetheart,' he says, picking her up in his arms.

Shaking with excitement, she tries to close them, but simply can't resist peeking, so Joe covers her eyes with his hand and carries her up to the front bedroom.

Equally curious, Katie follows behind them.

'Ready Lily? Do you want to see?' he teases, prolonging the agony.

'Oh please,' she begs, barely able to contain her excitement.

'There you are,' he says setting her down on her bedroom floor, 'So, what do you think, Lily?'

Beside the bed is a beautifully crafted little wooden rocking cradle, 'For your Daisy,' he explains, 'Do you like it?'

Lilibeth's face lights up as she inspects the new cradle, then holds out her arms to Joe. Obliging, he scoops her up in his arms, she hugs him, 'Oh thank you, Joe, thank you, is it really for my Daisy?'

He smiles, 'Of course it is sweetheart. If you have your own bed, then I thought Daisy deserves one too.'

Lilibeth shrieks, 'I want my Daisy, she wants to go in her new bed!'

Obligingly, Joe runs downstairs to fetch the doll from the washing line, whilst Katie put a pillow in the base of the cot to serve as a mattress adding a pillowcase for a cover. 'Oh, my darling, the cradle is beautiful, you're a very lucky girl Lilibeth. You know, Aunty Margo's coming to visit us tomorrow, shall we ask if she can make some pretty bed covers for Daisy's cradle?'

'Oooo, my Daisy would like that,' she replies.

Leaving Lilibeth to acquaint Daisy with her new cradle they go down to the scullery.

Joe is warming milk, 'Humm, Lily seems perfectly happy to be in there on her own,' says Joe, 'What do you think Katie?'

Sat resting in the chair with her feet up, Katie agrees, 'I think the cradle sealed the deal. You are so full of surprises. It's really handsome, when on earth did you make it?'

He shrugs, 'Over the past couple of weeks, an hour or two here and there,' he explains, 'I think she likes it.'

'Likes it? Joe, it's perfect. Oh, you're so thoughtful and clever.'

He grins, squats down and takes her hands in his, 'My pleasure, darling,' he says giving her a quick peck on the lips. Lowering his voice, he whispers, 'I must confess that up until now, I've never had dealings with little ones. But your Lily, well, I'm really very fond of her.'

'Yes, I know, and Lilibeth is extremely fond of you, Joe, and who can blame her? You are simply wonderful with her.'

Shaking his head, he smiles, 'Well now, who'd of thought it, me, a lifelong bachelor, acting like I'm a real dad!'

Looking serious, she tells him, 'You'd make a truly wonderful father, you're a natural Joseph.'

Gripping her hands, he looks deep into her eyes, 'Oh I'd like to be Katie,' he says, his voice low and sincere. 'Now, we should do some serious planning, Margo and Stan are coming tomorrow,' he reminds her, 'so perhaps we can rearrange the rooms the following day? I've made a start distempering the walls already, I'll light the fire, to air the room thoroughly before we move in together.' His hands encircle her waist, 'I love you so much.'

Inching closer, Katie whispers, 'I love you too Joseph, very, very much.'

Elated, Joe's eyes fill with mischief, he cups her breasts, squeezing her nipples lightly between his fingers and thumbs, but enough for her to cry out, 'Oh Joseph, ouch. Oooh, help!'

'Hush, darling, Lily will hear you,' he warns, kissing her lips to silence her. 'Oh my, your breasts are so perfect, and your nipples are so responsive, darling. I love that they are all mine, I want to see them and play with them, constantly.' He groans, 'Oh sweet lord Katie, you turn me on so easily. Still, not long to wait now, darling, I love you so,' he whispers huskily, turning her on and making her squirm at the very prospect.

Reluctantly he stands and takes a deep breath, 'Oh bloody hell, I'm sorry, darling, I can't trust myself to stay here with you. I've got to get on with the lean-to. I'd really like to get it finished before Stan and Margo arrive tomorrow.' Highly aroused, he adjusts his trousers yet again, to hide his very obvious erection, he sighs, 'Oh Katie, my love, you have no idea what you do to me.'

'Oooo, I think I do,' she giggles, reaching out and stroking the prominent bulge, making him groan with pleasure.

The air fills with the intense desire between them.

'Mmm… Oooo er, I think perhaps I'd better go, or we might get caught.' He says, gnawing his bottom lip.

'I'll bring you some tea later,' she offers by way of poor compensation.

Picking her up in his arms he swirls her around, kissing her passionately, 'I'll look forward to that, darling, I love you so much Katie.'

Throughout the afternoon Joe happily works away with a smug smile on his face. The haunting fear in her eyes when they first met are long gone, now her beautiful powder blue eyes shine with vitality, radiating her obvious love and need for him. Miraculously she has emerged from her dark sordid past into an exciting new future, their future. His heart is bursting with happiness.

Lilibeth, content to be the centre of what she now feels is a very new, and happy family trio, busies herself between her mother and Joe, feeling happy and content, their future is now secured.

Just as the last nail is seated home, and without any notice, there's a startling almighty crash, followed by a flash of lightening and the heavens open. Just in time, Joe manages to close and bolt the door to shut out the torrents of driving rain. 'Phew,' he says, removing his shirt and shaking the rain from his hair, 'it's all finished and just in the nick of time, how's that for timing Katie?'

With a saucy look in her eyes, she hands him a towel, daring to pinch his nipple, she jumps back giggling, but Joe is too quick for her and grabs her wrist, pulling her into his arms, he's grinning, 'Ouch, I'll get you back tonight,' he whispers his delicious promise.

'Ooo er... I think I should join Lilibeth in the parlour, give you privacy,' she suggests, not bothering to disguise the longing in her eyes.

Grinning, Joe's eyes twinkle salaciously, 'Mmmm... what a pity, I'd have liked you to stay,' he murmurs softly. 'It looks like we could do with somewhere more private to bathe too, I'd better put that on my list.' Smirking, he winks at Katie. 'Tonight, my precious love.'

That evening, the rain continues to lash ceaselessly against the windowpanes in the parlour, With Lilibeth upstairs in bed sleeping soundly, Katie is sat on the floor facing the cosy fire. With his legs splayed open, Katie sits between them, her back resting against his chest. Joe is cuddled up behind her, his arms encircling her protectively.

Resting his chin on her shoulder, he's sucking and grazing her earlobe, whispering in her ear, sending shivers up and down her spine. 'Are you happy, my precious?'

The warmth of his breath against her neck is as exciting as a kiss itself, she sighs contentedly, 'More than you'll ever know, Joseph.'

'I expect Stan and Margo will bring the tribe with them tomorrow,' he comments, souring the intimate moment.

For some strange reason she feels a pang of disappointment, for no matter how much she loves them and how much she enjoys their company, the realisation hits her, that at long last she has found her own little world of love, peace, and contentment, she desperately wishes that she could keep Joe all to herself.

'What time d'you think they are likely to get here?' he asks, breaking into her thoughts again.

'Early, if Margo has her own way,' she tells him giggling.

'Humm, with a bit of luck they will be gone before teatime,' he says, as if he can read her mind. 'The nights are beginning to draw in and it's a fair old trek back to Fennydown' he points out, gently planting several light kisses on her neck. 'Just think, darling, I'll never have to send you up to sleep with Lily after tomorrow. We can be naked and make love as much as we want, any way we want, in the privacy of our own room.'

'The room's almost finished Joe, so I thought that maybe we could make love in there tonight,' she suggests with a ring of hope in her voice.

Craving his touch, Katie pulls his hands down inside her bodice to her breasts, she had been thinking about it for most of the day and thought it might help if she were to give him an incentive.

Groaning he murmurs, 'Oh my darling, your breasts are heavenly,' he says cupping them, 'Mmm, I love your nipples,' playfully he tugs them making Katie squeal, 'they're so very tempting.' Peering over her shoulder, he watches as she slowly unties the ribbons, exposing her breasts so that he can hold and caress them.

'Mmm, they're so firm,' he groans, 'Oh God, look at them, I can't resist, I can hardly wait until you lay next to me in our bed, naked.' His hands skilfully encourage her nipples to harden and protrude with his fingers.

Revelling in his touch she pants breathlessly. Behind her, she can feel his erection hardening.

With his fingertips, he rolls and tugs her sensitive nipples, talking to her, whispering against her ear, 'Is it turning you on, darling? Oh lord, , I want you so much,' over and over.

Feeling desperate she pouts, 'It's not fair Joseph, you're teasing me, are we going to make love?'

He moves back a little so that she slides down on the rug, climbing between her legs his broad chest arches above her, holding her head he gazes deep into her eyes, 'I love you so much Katie.'

Eagerly, her fingers dig into his back, pulling him down, 'Ooo, Joseph please,' she pants frantically, 'make love to me!'

'Katie, my love,' he says looking serious, 'I need to tell you something before we make love. I want you to know that the love I feel for you is totally different to anything I've ever felt before, I'm deeply in love with you.' He clears his throat, 'I'm not sure if you want to hear this, but we must be frank, share our innermost thoughts and feelings, as it were.'

Taking a fortifying lung full of air, he tells her, 'Katie, my love, I need you to know that I accept that 'in law' you are married. That, my dearest love, is sadly a fact, and there's nothing I can do about it. But the way I see it is, it's all finished and buried in the past, darling, what I'm trying to say is, I need you, I want you to be mine. I want to share my entire life with you, my bed, my body, my soul with you. I love you so much,' his voice drops lower. 'Believe me Katie, it's not easy for me to say this, but I think we should be careful, for a while. I can't come inside you again, at least, not yet. And yes, before you say anything, I do know what I'm asking of you, the truth is, I'll struggle myself, but the truth is, I need you healthy and strong before we start making babies.'

Staggered at his unexpected suggestion Katie gulps, 'Babies? You want babies. Oooo, really, Joe?'

His look tells her he is deadly serious.

'Of course, sweetheart, I love you and I want us to have lots of babies, Lily needs brothers and sisters, we don't want our Lily brought up all alone in this big old house, do we?'

Joe has stunned her, when out of the blue he declares he wants babies, their babies. Her hand reaches to stroke his cheek, she's about to voice her concerns as to whether or not she would even be able to carry a baby for nine months, when she remembers her wedding ring, stuffed in her pocket, taking it out she throws it into the red-hot flames of the fire, the last reminder, with the exception of her precious daughter, of her horrendous marriage to Albert Soames.

Lifting her face, he looks into her eyes, 'One day, my precious, I will take you to church, you will wear my ring and become my wife,' he says solemnly. 'Tell me, darling, if you were free, would you marry me?'

Overwhelmed she flings her arms around his neck, 'Yes, yes, oh yes, I would marry you right now, if I could!' though in the back of her mind she can't help but fret, what about all the babies she'd lost, could she give him the children he so obviously wants?

Joe hugs her even closer, 'Who knows, darling, he might even drink himself to death, if we're lucky,' adding, 'Katie, I swear right now, I'll not wait a minute longer than I have to. I'll take you to church and put my ring on your finger and make you my wife just imagine, Mrs Joseph Markson.'

Katie looks at him lovingly, 'I'd love that, Joseph.' Hoping against hope that it isn't going to be just a pipe dream.

'Hey… I wonder what Stan and Margo will have to say tomorrow?' he asks, playfully nipping and tugging her nipples.

'Oooo, help!' she shrieks, then her eyebrows shoot up. 'Hold on, y-you're not going to tell them about us and what we've been doing, are you?'

He frowns, 'Is there any good reason why I shouldn't, you're not ashamed of us, are you?'

Her reply is instantly a tone of indignance, her head, 'Good grief no, of course I'm not!'

'Perhaps you've changed your mind then?' he asks warily.

'Oh, heavens no, no! It's not that, I'm just thinking of Lilibeth, don't you think we should tell her first?'

His body relaxes, his relief evident, 'Lily, phew, is that all? For a minute I thought you'd got cold feet. Look, of course we should talk to Lily, explain things to her.'

'But not yet, not with Margo and Stan coming tomorrow, I want her to get used to the idea first.'

He looks offended. 'Katie, darling, I swear I will love Lily as if she's my very own flesh and blood,' he assures her. 'I love her dearly.'

Squeezing his hand, she tells him, 'I have no doubts about that Joe, but it's a big step for Lilibeth, she's only six. I'm not quite sure how she'll react. I know she loves you, Joe, but we should take our time, pick the right moment, maybe even do it together. Give her chance to accept it, before we tell Margo and Stan, or anyone else for that matter.'

'Of course, darling, Lily will always come first. But I'm warning you, I can't keep it to myself for forever, I want to tell everyone that you are mine,' he kisses the tip of her nose. 'So, when exactly do we tell Lily?' he asks with a wry smile.

'Soon Joseph, very soon, I promise.'

'All right, I'll leave it for to you to decide, but I like the idea that we'll tell her together, then who knows, one day, hopefully in the not-too-distant future, you'll marry me, and we can tell her that wonderful news together too.'

'Ooo, my sweet Joseph, you make me feel like a child again, carefree and so blissfully happy,' she giggles.

Spreading her legs, he kissed her passionately.

'Mmm, oh Joseph,' she purrs, 'I love you, so very much.'

'I love you more than life itself, my love. I'd die for you,' he whispers as he closes his eyes, absorbing the tight feel of her as he pushes deep inside.

As the embers of the fire die down and the room chills, Joe shifts, 'I'm sorry, darling, it's getting late, and Stan and Margo are bound to turn up early tomorrow.'

Sitting up she sighs. 'I suppose so.'

They stand together on the landing, 'I love you so much, my sweet, sweet Katie. I can't imagine my life without you now, and I don't intend to, either.'

'I love you too, Joseph.'

'Sleep well, darling.'

'I'll try,' she replies.

He sighs, 'Me too, my sweet love.'

'See you in the morning then,' she says half-heartedly.

Grinning broadly, he pulls her closer, 'I can hardly wait. In just two nights we become one, my sweet, then I will show you how wonderfully exciting sex and making love can really be,' he tells her, before they reluctantly part and go to their separate beds.

CHAPTER 11

By the time Stan's cart rolls into the yard, Joe had completed his chores and made a good start on his mother's room.

Both Katie and Lilibeth have prepared plenty of food to feed their guests.

Margo's in the door first, her arms filled with a bulky, brown paper parcel. 'Mornin' Katie, how's yer gettin' on Ducky?' Stopping dead in her tracks her mouth falls open, spotting the table as she walks through to the parlour, 'Well bless my soul. Here Stanley, feast yer eyeballs over this lot!'

Stan blinks, 'Good gawd Katie, what's this lot in aide of?'

Trying to mask her guilty conscience with her constant thoughts of Joe, she fights unsuccessfully, to quell the colour rising in her face. 'I've baked your favourite cake Stan,' she points out, seeking a diversion.

Stan, whose belly takes priority over everything, with the exception of good frequent loving with his beloved wife, is easily distracted. A staunch supporter of Katie's delicious baking, he's in his element with the enviable choice of food, he grabs a large slice of cake and sinks his teeth into it, which earns him a sharp slap on the wrist from Margo, 'Stanley 'ooper! What yer playin' at, anyone would fink I don't feed yer. Where's yer bleedin' manners?'

Stan's cheeks are ballooned out like a hamster. 'Sorry, me old love, I just couldn't help meself,' he says, playfully squeezing Margo's rump with his cake free hand.

Highly amused, Joseph, his frame leaning against the wall with his muscle-bound arms folded across his broad chest grins sideways at Katie, who is looking decidedly ill at ease at Stan and Margo's forthright affection in front of herself and her young daughter. 'I dunno, what are we gonna do with the pair of them?' he whispers in her ear.

Standing really close to Katie, Joe turns his head and whispers discreetly so no-one else can hear. 'I love you so much, I'm looking forward to tomorrow night, my sweet lover,' he chuckles.

Horrified he might be overheard Katie gasps, turning bright red, she could see the wickedly sexy look in his eyes and whispers so low, that only he can hear. 'Oh hush, please Joseph, they might hear you!'

'Oh no! What's wrong with poor Freddie?' asks Lilibeth, pointing to Freddie.

All eyes turn to Freddie, who is sporting a very obvious painful, shiny black eye.

Stan shoots his son a warning glance that doesn't go unnoticed by Joe.

Gnawing his lip, Freddie shrugs, 'Aw it ain't nuffin', I hit me ruddy head on the old man's cart, that's all.'

Joe smells a rat, 'Huh, a likely ruddy story,' he mutters.

'Cider Mate?' jumps in Stan.

'You what?' asks Joe frowning.

Stan shifts uneasily from one foot to the other, he raises his hat and scratches his head, 'Erm, yer cider, Joe, yer promised me some of yer cider, the strong stuff. And I wouldn't mind goin' and gettin' it, now,' he says nodding his head towards the door.

'Really Stan? I thought you still had plenty,' then he twigs that Stan wants a quiet word. 'Oh right, no worries Mate.' Joe shrugs his shoulders, 'I've still got a few flagons left in the barn.'

'Well, I fink we should get some, put it on me cart, right now,' says Stan, sounding weirdly persistent. 'Coz I don't want ter ferget them when we go home.'

Bemused Joe looks at Stan, 'What, right now, this minute?'

Stan hoists his trousers and readjusts his hat, 'Aye, well there ain't no time like the present, and our Freddie will give us a hand, won't yer boy?'

'Yep, right, Pops, let's get on wiv it,' agrees Freddie. Perhaps a bit too readily for Joe's liking, he deduces that something serious is afoot.

'But you've only just got here, what about the food?' Katie protests.

'Ain't nuffin' on the table what can't wait fer a bit,' says Margo, steering Katie towards the parlour door, 'Come on Ducky, I been and gawn and brought yer a few fings, they're in here.'

Pouting, Katie reluctantly leaves the scullery.

Joe turns to Stan, 'What the ruddy hell's going on Stan?'

'Whisht, outside, Joe, come on Freddie,' says Stan manhandling them both outside.

Out in the yard, Joe is uneasy, he knows Stan of old, he can definitely smell a rat, he wants answers, and he wants them now. 'Stanley Hooper, I'm waiting!'

Stan glances back at the door then takes hold of his elbow, 'Keep walkin', Joe, we gotta talk.'

Joe glares at Stan, 'It's that bloody Soames, isn't it? Come on, out with it! What the hell's happened? Tell me!' he insists forcefully.

Safely out of earshot from the girls, Stan lowers his voice, 'Aye, yer right, Joe. Yer should know, Soames is still on the bleedin' war path.'

Joe frowns, looking at Freddie's eye, 'I see, so it was Soames that did that.'

Freddie shrugs his shoulders and smirks, 'Nah, course not. I told yer, I scuffed me eye on the old man's cart.' He grins, 'But yer should've seen bloody Soamsey, he fell ter the ground like a dollop of fresh cow pat, splat!'

Exasperated, Joseph stands, hands on hips and legs astride. He's in no mood for Freddie's shilly-shallying or jesting, 'So, are you gonna tell me what the hell happened then Stan?' he asks again.

'Soamsey turned up at markit, drunk as a bleedin' skunk he were.' begins Stan.

Joe clenches his fists taut, 'And…?' slowly Joe is failing to control his temper.

'First orf, Soames was tryin' ter git booze.' Continues Stan, 'Course no one would sell him none. As yer know, he's been banned from the drinkin' houses coz he gets so violent. Anyway, then he gits real nasty, askin' everyone if they knows where Katie and Lilibuff is. Course one no one tells him nuffin' coz they don't know nuffin', then he starts makin' threats about what he'll do ter them when he finds them. Believe me Joe, he bleedin' means it and all. Then the dirty bleeder starts tryin' his luck wiv some of the pretty young gels, pesterin' them and not taking no fer a bleedin' answer. Well, yer know what he was like, Joe, he ain't never changed, he's still a dirty old bugger.' Puffing up his chest and looking proud, Stan sniggers, 'Hah, that were till our Freddie heard his new gel screamin' blue bloody murder. Our Freddie actually caught him in the act, pawin' and maulin' the titties of his new lady love, young Verity,' says Stan grimacing.

'Aye, soddin' dirty bastard!' chips in Freddie scowling, keen to brag about his prowess. 'Well, I weren't having none of that wiv my Verity! I dragged him orf her and punched his bleedin' lights out. I tell yer, I was that mad I wanted ter bloody kill the filfy bastard.'

'And that's when he gave you that black eye,' says Joe nodding.

'What? Huh, take more than him ter land one on my Freddie.' Stan jumps in, grinning broadly, 'Anyway, after Freddie punched him ter the ground, our Freddie stands up, all triumphant like, and catches his ruddy eye on me bleedin' cart, daft bugger.'

For the first time in his life, Joe feels murderous. 'Enough!' he snarls, 'That dirty pervert's gotta be sorted, once and for all. He's gotta be stopped, and I'm talking permanently!'

'Aye,' agrees Stan, lifting his hat and scratching his head again, 'and ruddy sharpish and all.'

'Hum, give me a few days. I'll think of something. But keep it under your hats for now lads. I won't have Katie finding out about this,' says Joe, rolling up his sleeves, 'Now let's get these jars of cider on your cart and get back to the girls or they'll be wondering where we are. I don't want Katie getting wind of this.'

Meanwhile, indoors Katie is opening the bulky parcel that Margo has given her. Inside is a practical small, thick winter coat, a sweet little frock, including petticoats and knickers, and a pair of leather boots, all for Lilibeth. Plus, two petticoats, a very attractive, light blue frock, with a lovely, knitted shawl to match, two camisoles, three pairs of knickers, and a pair of black leather boots for Katie. Margo points out that she and Edna had made them all, with the exception of the boots, of course.

Grateful, Katie flings her arms around Margo, 'Oh thank you Margo, it's just what we need, they're really lovely, thank you.'

'Well, we can't have yer going around the house starkers, can we gel,' she quips, playfully digging Katie in the ribs. 'Cor, just imagine, what our Joseph would fink of that? Coo, that'd turn him on wivout a doubt.' Margo winks, 'I bet he'd be like putty in yer hands, 'specially wiv a lovely little figure like what you's got. Yer know our Joe's always had an eye fer a pretty gel, and there ain't none prettier than you gel.'

Katie's shocked expression turns deep scarlet. 'Oh Margo, what a terrible thing to say!'

Margo throws her arms in the air in exasperation, 'Oh fer gawd's bleedin' sake Katie, I were on'y jokin' wiv yer! Tch, gawd help us! Yer don't ever change, it still don't take nothin' ter make yer embarrassed, do it?'

Gnawing on her lip nervously, Katie is now convinced that somehow, Margo knows about her and Joseph. 'Um, Lilibeth, you haven't shown Aunty Margo what Joseph kindly made for you yet,' she prompts her daughter, eager to change the conversation.

Margo is dragged up the stairs by Lilibeth.

'Look what I got for my Daisy,' says Lilibeth, standing proudly beside the cradle, 'Joe did make it for my Daisy. Isn't he clever?'

'Cor, you lucky little gel,' she said, patting Lilibeth on her head, she turns to Katie smirking, 'Seems ter me, our Joe's ruddy good wiv his hands and all. What do yer say ter that. Katie?' she teases, winking a sort of implicating crafty wink, 'Coo, he's gorgeous, he wouldn't have ter ask me twice. I mean, what a sexy body he's got. Phwor, yer know even his lovely husky voice is a turn on, all sort of low and sexy like, and his come ter bed blue eyes.' Margo was practically drooling nonstop, 'If on'y I were a few years younger, gel. I'd wouldn't have ter be asked twice, oh no, and I ain't the only woman what finks that either.'

The inuendoes from Margo are just too much for Katie, the blood drains from her head, her complexion turns to a pale waxen hue, she's perspiring profusely, yet at the same time feeling so lightheaded she feels faint, she totters back, landing onto the bed.

'Oh, my good gawd! Lilibuff, go and fetch Joe, quick child... run!' orders Margo, then somehow manages to drag Katie, who is protesting wildly, up the bed.

The three men were still discussing the future, or rather the lack of one, for Soames as they saunter back to the cottage when they hear Lilibeth, standing in the open doorway screaming hysterically, all three, break into a sprint. Joe scoops Lily up in his arms, 'What is it, darling, what's wrong?'

'Mammy!' she gasps, 'My mammy!' pointing to the upstairs window.

Striding two steps at a time, Joe flies up the stairs to find Katie laying propped up on Lily's bed, Margo sitting beside her, fanning her with a flapping pillowcase to give her air. Katie looks deathly pale; he notices her bodice is partially opened too.

'Margo, what the hell happened! What's wrong with Katie? Shall I send Freddie for the doctor? Katie, tell me what's wrong?' his voice is choked with anxiety. Margo notes his distress but keeps her knowing thoughts to herself.

Raising herself onto her elbows Katie forces a smile, 'I'm fine, please don't make a fuss, Joe, it's just Margo making a mountain out of a mole hill, as usual, it's nothing.'

Sitting beside her on the bed he holds her hand, 'Are you sure Katie? Should I send for the doctor Margo?'

As she rises from the bed, Margo pats Joe's shoulder, 'Nah, she'll be alwight now Pet, she's in safe hands wiv you.' she tells him, turning to find Stan, Lilibeth and Freddie, now stood peering through the open doorway. 'Here, what yer gawpin' at? Let's not make a fuss you lot. I reckon we should put the kettle on,' she says, taking command of the situation. 'Stan, take Lilibuff down ter the scullery. Come on Freddie don't stand there gawpin', yer can give me a hand wiv the tea, give them a couple of minutes alone,' she turns and winks at Joe. 'I'll make us some tea and I'll give yer a shout when it's ready, I reckon Katie's gonna be fine now, so don't worry lad.'

The second the door closes, Joe flings his arms around her, 'Oh Katie, are you sure you're all right, darling? Is it because of the miscarriages?' His concern turns to a frown as it slowly dawns on him that he might have hurt her when they made love, 'Christ, no! Is it because we made love? Did I hurt you?'

274

She squirms, highly flustered, 'No Joseph, I promise it was none of those. Oh, dear if I told you, you wouldn't believe me, honestly it was nothing. I'm fine, Joe, truly.'

Unconvinced he frowns, 'Are you absolutely sure?'

Putting her hand to her mouth she stifles a giggle, 'I'll tell you later, when we're alone. Please, don't worry, darling, I swear, I'm perfectly fine.'

'You promise?'

'I promise,' she assures him.

Just as he takes her in his arms and kisses her, they hear the shrill voice of Margo yelling up the stairs, 'Yoo hoo! Yer tea's ready!'

Assured by Katie that she feels fine, relieved to see her smiling and relaxed, Joe, blatantly ignoring Margo's call, draws Katie closer, 'Oh my sweet Katie,' he whispers, his voice low and silky, 'I love you so much, thank God you're okay, I don't know what I'd do without you.'

'I love you just as much,' she murmurs, 'but if we don't go down right now, Margo will come flying through the door at any minute.'

Joe grins, tightening his hold, 'Mmm, I can't wait to have you all to myself tonight,' he gushes.

'Mmmm, me too.' she purrs, running her fingers through his hair.

His eyes fall to her open bodice, 'Mmm, mine,' noticing her hardened nipples pressing against her flimsy bodice, he can't resist, opening her bodice he holds her breasts, his thumbs circling her nipples, making her yelp with pleasure. 'Ooh Joseph. Ooo help!' she cries.

Katie whimpers softly, cherishing the feel his warm panting breath as he nuzzles into her breasts. 'Ooh Katie,' he whispers, moaning softly, 'I want you, darling, oh how I want to make you mine again,' His lips bury into the warm flesh of her breast, sucking on her as if he is hungrily drawing the love from her.

Her arms draw him closer, her fingers running through his hair, 'Mmm... Oooo...! Help!' he playfully nips her nipple with his teeth, she cries out, 'Joseph!'

'Joe!' yells Margo up the stairs again, 'Katie!'

Alarmed, Katie clasps her hands to her mouth, 'Oh no, do you think they heard us?'

He's still grinning, poor Katie's flushed face is a picture of guilt, 'I guess we'll find out when we go downstairs, darling. Here,' he says, 'you'd better tie your frock if you don't want to give the game away.'

Katie looks down, on her breast are two deep red marks where his lips had been, 'Oooo, Joseph, what's that?'

Gently he kisses her pouting lips, 'A tenderly given love bite, from me to you, sweetheart.'

Her face flushes even deeper, 'But what if Margo sees it?'

'Best cover it up, if you're that worried,' he chuckles, 'But I'll tell you now, Margo's had more than her fair share of love bites in her time, and I've no doubt some were in some very strange places too, believe me.'

Katie hastily fastens her bodice and finger tidies her hair, 'Oh help Joseph, do I look all right?'

His hands encircled her tiny waist, 'Katie, my dearest beloved, you look perfect. Come, we'd best go down, I can't trust myself to be alone with you a minute longer,' he tells her, giving her a quick peck on the lips.

As they both enter the kitchen, all eyes turn upon them.

Katie does her level best to walk nonchalantly to the boiler to fill the sink with hot water.

Lilibeth is sat on Stan's lap, happily sharing an oversized portion of cake. Freddie is making short work of the chicken and potato pie.

Margo is sat at the table noisily slurping her second steaming hot mug of tea, 'That's better, I'm pleased ter see yer got a lot more colour in yer cheeks now gel. Our Katie's lookin' a whole lot better now, don't yer fink Stan?'

Joe grins, Katie gulps, blushing, she's forced to turn her back on them to regain a modicum of dignity. Standing in a daze, she slices the cake. 'There, help yourselves everyone,' she announces, setting the plate on the table and picking up her mug of tea.

'So, what's all this grub in aid of gel, is yer expectin' an army, or maybe somefin' else?' she asks, smirking at her.

Katie shoots a worried glance at Joe; he simply shrugs his shoulders and says nothing.

'Fer gawd's sake missus, leave the gel alone,' says Stan jumping in, noticing Katie's obvious discomfort, 'Take no notice of our Margo, she's like a dog wiv a ruddy bone. Anyway, yer lookin' a lot better now gel, yer got colour back in yer pretty cheeks alwight.'

'It's the tea, it's hot,' Katie proffers as a lame excuse.

Margo sniffs, 'Dunno why, when yer ruddy tea's gawn cold, I tell yer Stanley, she had plenty of colour when we got here. Her face was rosy-pink, then upstairs, somefin' suddenly made her go all faint and pale like. Mind you Stan, yer right, she's certainly got her colour back now, that's fer sure,' she adds for good measure, giving Joe a crafty wink.

It is chivalry on Freddie's part, that comes to Katie's rescue. After weeks of fruitlessly courting his lovely Verity, he can spot Katie's embarrassment a mile off, 'Aw come on Mam, stop yer teasin', leave the poor gel alone. Ain't she done us all proud wiv the tasty grub what she's made us?'

Looking like the cat that had got the cream, Margo has this sort of feeling in her water that there's something going on all right, she had spotted the way Joe keeps hovering around Katie, the furtive little glances between them, then there's the way he reacted when he'd found Katie upstairs on the bed thinking she was ill. There weren't any flies on her, she was also hoping her instincts were right. Well, she certainly wasn't about to spoil things by chasing the issue. But Margo being Margo just can't resist, 'Anyway, I'm glad yer feelin' better Katie, Joe obviously sorted yer out,' she says smiling wryly across at Joe.

'Mam, fer pity's sake, leave the poor gel alone!' Freddie orders annoyed at his mothers' persistence.

'Why Freddie, I'm sure I don't know what yer mean.' Retorts Margo, feigning a look of innocence, slipping another wink at Joe.

'Erm, nights are drawing in now Stan,' comments Joe, in an effort to guide the subject elsewhere.

'Aye, yer ain't wrong there, I reckon it won't be long afore we have ter get orf and makin' tracks.'

'I'll fetch your eggs and pack you a basket,' says Katie, springing to her feet, relieved they are about to leave, 'Did you get your cider Stan?'

'The what...? Oh, the cider, um... yep, we did gel, ta ever so, enough ter keep me and Freddie happy fer a while. I don't suppose yer got any of that chicken and onion pie what our Freddie was guzzlin' goin' spare, have yer lovey?'

'There's one put by, just for you Stan. Oh, and there's some biscuits, blackcurrant jam tarts, a dozen scones, oh, and a pot of jam and a few more of your favourites too, there we go,' she says, handing him the heavy basket.

Standing, Margo brushes the crumbs from her skirt preparing to leave, she has a mischievous grin on her face and a twinkle of suspicion in her green eyes. 'I gotta say Katie love, yer really knows how ter spoil a man rotten, yer gonna make some lucky bloke a very happy man one day, fer certain. What d'yer fink, Joe?' she says, unable to resist goading him one last time.

For the sake of preserving poor Katie's honour, he's obliged to drop his head to conceal the smile on his face, 'Mmm, yes, I'm sure she will,' he mutters.

'Mam, that's enough!' says Freddie wagging a finger threateningly at his mother. 'It's time fer us ter be makin' tracks.'

As they all pile onto the cart, Joe hands up two weighty churns of milk, Freddie shifts them into a corner as if they are as light as a feather, he also takes the eggs and Katie's basket. 'Oh, here, Joe, I nearly fergot, I brought yer a bottle of that French brandy yer asked fer.'

Handing him the cash, Joe takes it and thanks him.

'Margo, could you do something for me?' Katie asks.

'Aye, anyfin' gel, what is it?'

'Could you make some bedclothes for Daisy's new cradle please?'

'Aye, of course lovey, I'll bring them next visit. We'll see yer all on...' she turns to Stan, 'when is we comin' back Stan?'

'Hum, the day after next markit,' he replies.

'There yer goes, we'll be back afore yer knows it gel,' declares Margo. She snuggles up to Stan, 'Come on, me old darlin', let's get home ter that rug in front of the fire, I reckon yer needs some lovin'.'

Freddie's eyes roll skywards, 'Aw fer gawd's ruddy sake Mam, don't yer ever stop?'

Margo grins broadly, 'Huh, take no notice of our Freddie, he's on'y jealous, coz he ain't gettin' nowhere wiv young Verity, his shy new lady love.'

Shocked, Freddie scowls, there was no need for his mam to tell everyone of his failings, 'Mam! Shut up, will yer mam!'

'See you in a couple of weeks Katie love. Bye Lilibuff, bye, Joe,' says Margo smirking again.

Between them, Katie and Joe settle Lilibeth down for the night then retire to the parlour.

Joe takes her into his arms, 'I was beginning to think they'd never go.'

They kiss a lingering, loving soft kiss, their tongues entwining, stirring their need for each other.

Settling down on the rug together, Joe sits with his legs apart, Katie sat in front resting against his chest, his arms are wrapped tightly around her. Nuzzling his head in her hair he sucks on her earlobe. 'So, are you going to tell me what happened today, darling? You worried me to death., Christ, tell me it wasn't because we've made love?'

Katie shrugs her shoulders, 'No, I've already told you! To be honest, I can truly say I've never felt better in my whole life!'

'Well, something happened,' he persists.

Bashfully she lowers her lashes, 'I... I er I don't think I can tell you why.'

'And why not, darling?' he probes.

'Because it's highly embarrassing,' she whispers shyly.

To encourage her, he slides his hands inside her bodice and cups her breasts, 'Why don't you try, my love,' he suggests as he gives her an incentive, expertly reducing her embarrassment by tweaking and tugging her nipples, instantly turning her on.

Katie squirms, protesting, 'Oooo... Joseph, no... Oooh help, stop, you're not being fair.'

Never one to give in, Joe continues his assault, until she's writhing helplessly on the floor, 'Come on, darling, I need to know what happened, tell me, please sweetheart.'

Beside herself, she's putty in his hands, 'All right... stop! I give in, I'll tell you!' she pants, 'But promise me you won't laugh at me?'

'Good grief, of course I won't,' he says, grateful that it's beginning to get dark, and she can't see the smirk on his face.' Considering the way Margo had suggestively teased them all day, he was sure that Margo's forthright attitude regarding sex was probably the reason Katie is in such a quandary.

Taking a deep breath, she says in almost a whisper, 'I'm pretty sure Margo knows what we've been doing. She said things... you know, things,' she says bashfully.

Joe tuts, 'Oh dear, here we go again. You know...? Things...? I don't know what you're talking about sweetheart, that's why I'm asking. What sort of, things, and you knows are you on about?' he asks, trying hard to suppress his amusement, 'Can you be more precise?'

'Margo was saying things like erm... asking me what I thought about you being so g...good with your hands, as if she were inferring that you were... that we were... you know what, then there was all the food, she was asking me if I was expecting something... you know.'

He gulps, 'Good grief, she thought you were pregnant?' the thought hadn't occurred to him.

Biting her lower lip, Katie frowns, 'Then she was saying things like um, me running around the house in the... with um... no clothes on, in front of you!' she blurts out before she can stop herself. Katie sighs, 'I mean, as if I would. She knows full well that I wouldn't run around naked in front of anyone. Oh Joseph, Margo is so forthright with her implications. It's silly I know Joseph, but I'm sure she knows.'

'Knows what?' he asks.

'About us, making love,' she answers shyly.

'Seriously, darling? Surely it wouldn't be the end of the world if she did, would it my sweet?' he chuckles.

'I suppose not, oh dear, I feel pretty stupid now, all the drama and hints about us. You know she was watching us like a hawk all afternoon.' She shakes her head, 'Joe, I'm not used to this open talk. Margo's so outspoken, with her constant crude sexual implications.' While she's on the subject, she decides he ought to know about Margo. She swallows, 'And Joseph, there's something else you should know about Margo. I er... I happen to know that Margo fancies you, she keeps telling me she wouldn't um, kick you out of her bed, she says you've got a very sexy voice, come to bed eyes and she keeps saying how handsome and fit your body is too,' she adds timorously.

Throwing his head back he laughs raucously, 'Did she now? Well, she's out of luck, darling, she's got a heart of gold bless her, but she's old enough to be my mother. She's too skinny and has enormous breasts, not my type at all, sweetheart.' He tuts, 'Surely you're not jealous, darling. Hah, I think she's goading you with all her sexy talk and innuendoes, trying to embarrass you sweetheart, you know what she's like. Besides, she's madly in love with her Stanley.'

Katie nods in agreement, I'm sure your right, darling, of course she loves him, but her open talk of sex and stuff makes me feel really ill at ease, I'm just not used to it,' she confesses bashfully.

Sweeping the hair from her shoulder he plants several light kisses on her neck and shoulder, 'My sweet darling, you shouldn't be embarrassed. Despite your horrific experience with Soames, I'm afraid from day you were born you've led a very sheltered life indeed, you're just not used to all this frankness. But I do understand where you are coming from. But hey! now you mention it, darling, you have such a beautiful, sexy body, and the thought of seeing you running around here naked? Oooh, Katie, you're making me hard!' he says, pressing his erection into the small of her back.

Katie sniffs, 'Thank you, you're so understanding,' then it sinks in what he'd actually said, 'Joseph! Oooo, you're so rude, you're as bad as Margo!' Though she has to admit there are times she'd felt brazen enough to willingly strip naked for him, but oh no, not now in the cold light of day, she wouldn't, she just couldn't!

He'd thought it before and he was still of the same opinion, at twenty-three she'd experienced so much, yet knew very little about life. 'Me, rude? Never Katie, though I want you to know, my precious, that I have absolutely no objections whatsoever, if you have a change of heart and want to run around here naked, you're so sexy,' he tells her, still toying with her breasts.

Katie bites her lip and giggles as he nibbles her ear, 'Well... you never know your luck, Joseph. Maybe one day.'

He smiles to himself, with the prospect of her moving into their room tomorrow night, he figures he won't have to wait too long before he can enjoy the pleasure of seeing her stunning body completely naked. Christ, he wants her, now! 'Are you comfortable, darling?'

'Mmmm, yes, lovely,' she coos as she relaxes in his arms.

'Mmm… I love your breasts, darling, they're so firm, they're perfect and they're all mine,' he groans appreciatively. 'Is this nice, darling?' he asks as his fingers pull and roll her hardening nipples.

'Oooo… yessss, Oooo… Lordy. Oh help.'

Turning her to face him he buries his head into her breasts, gently suckling on each nipple in turn, making her coo with pleasure, 'Mmm, so Margo was teasing you about me seeing you in the nude,' he grins, 'Knowing Margo as I do, I shouldn't ask how that conversation came about,' he says trying desperately not to laugh.

'But it wasn't exactly like that, oh you know what she's like, going on about rude stuff, and in front of everyone!' she protests. 'Hey, you're laughing at me Joseph, you promised you wouldn't!'

'Darling, I'm not laughing at you at all,' he said trying hard to stifle a chuckle, 'Oh my sweet darling, you're such a rarity. You've led such an insulated life, you really are a pure innocent,' he lifts her face, his eyes shining and full of longing, 'But while we're on the subject of you being naked sweetheart. I don't think I can wait until tomorrow!'

'Oh help, not now Joe, it's still light outside. Oooo, I couldn't!' her breathing increasing so rapidly she could barely breathe.

Joe hugs her close, 'Hush my love, calm down. I've told you before, I will never ask you to do anything you don't want to do, ever? I was just hoping that you might have re-considered the idea, that's all.'

A tear or two rolls down her highly flushed cheeks, tears of frustration, her clasped fingers are twisting nervously, she shakes her head, 'You've got it all wrong again, Joe.'

He raised his eyebrows, looking bewildered, 'Have I? I don't understand.'

'It's all right for you Joseph, you're so… um, it's very obvious that you have had several… you know…' Taking a deep breath, she struggles to find the courage to come right out and say it. Clearing her throat, she blurts out, 'I was going to say that you've um… well you obviously know everything there is to know about making love, you're so good at it. It's plain to me that you've clearly had a great deal of experience with…' she gulps, 'lots and lots of girls!'

Cupping her face in the palms of his hands he looks straight into her eyes, 'My dear sweet darling, I'm twenty-six, so yes, there have been others. I'm sorry, darling, I can't deny it. But I wouldn't say that there were that many girls, and not one that was really special either. Besides, they are all way back in the past and long forgotten,' holding her close he kisses her lovingly, to reassure her. '

A pang of jealously stabs her heart. Others, he'd said, others, plural.

Frowning she stares at him, 'H...how many others?' she asks warily, not sure that she really wants to know, 'Were they all very beautiful and very um... sexy?' she hesitates for a moment 'Though I guess you wouldn't have wanted them if they weren't. Tell me Joseph, did you love them and um... did you do to them what we do, you know, make love to them, naked?' Immediately, she could kick herself for asking such a personal question. Of course, a handsome, virile, single young man like Joe was bound to have had the pick of any girl he wanted.

His eyebrows raise, she'd shocked him with her questions, 'Oh Katie, where did all that come from? What's this all about? Good grief, you're not jealous, are you?'

Of course, she'd have liked to deny it, but she can't, she also knows he's right, he's twenty-six, and so deliciously handsome and charming, it was obvious that there must have been so many pretty young girls, and who could blame them either, what a catch. He must have made them all go weak at the knees and only too willing to give their bodies to him. She sighs, feeling a sharp pang of jealousy towards all these girls. The idea of pretty girls laying naked with Joe, and even worse, Joseph making love to them the way he made love to her, the very thought makes her feel sick with jealousy. Her eyes fall to her lap. Margo had said he'd had an eye for a pretty girl. I bet he's made love to hundreds, she decides. The knot of resentment, at the thought of Joseph intimately sharing his beautiful body, making love with so many girls clenches and tightens a knot in her belly, she bites her lip, 'I'm sorry, I shouldn't have asked. I suppose I am jealous,' she admits.

'Oh sweetheart, it's a fact of life, boys grow into men, and you know how inquisitive adolescent young men are when they reach puberty, naturally curious about pretty young women and their bodies, and yes, a juvenile desire to experience sex.'

'I don't, as it happens Joseph!' she snaps, interrupting him sharply.

'No of course not, that was a damn stupid thing for me to say.' He wants to be honest, but he doesn't want to hurt her feelings either. 'All right Katie, you're asking so I'm going to try to explain the way it was. You see, as I matured into a young man, I was naturally inquisitive about women, and sex too, for that matter, it's only natural. Often sex was, shall we say… offered to me by a pretty young girl, and being a red bloodied male, I was curious, and eager to learn. Yes, I'll admit, I was more than willing to take every opportunity to experience sex and explore women's bodies for that matter. But darling, you must realise, it was all just part of growing up. It was just adolescent curiosity, never anything more. Look Katie, I swear I never loved any of them. Darling, you are my first and only love,' he sighs. 'Please believe me?'

Looking thoroughly miserable, Katie shrugs, staying mute.

'Look sweetheart, what's in the past should stay in the past.'

'Hum, I suppose,' she shrugs again, 'I'm so sorry, forgive my irrational jealousy, if I didn't want to hear, then I shouldn't have asked, I have no right.'

Relieved, he smiles, 'You don't know what that means to me, but darling, neither of us can change our pasts, good, bad or indifferent, but I do understand where you're coming from,' he admits. 'Sweetheart, I'm gonna be totally honest with you. I'm not exactly blameless myself, as far as jealousy goes. You know Katie, the very thought of any other man seeing you naked, apart from me, makes me jealous as hell. Even worse, knowing that Soames used your beautiful body and had sex with you, albeit against your will, the very thought of him actually taking his pleasure from you drives me insane!' he shudders. 'Yes, it hurts me badly. I admit I'm jealous of him, of course I am.' Tightening his hold on her to reassure her he whispers, 'As far as Soames goes, it was just cold, calculated perverted sex to satisfy himself. He used your body against your will, for his own gratification. But I do know it was one-sided, darling. Don't you see my love? Just like you, I am as jealous as hell, knowing that there was someone before me.' He sighs a long woeful sigh, looking thoroughly wretched, 'I guess I know exactly how you feel, my love.'

Joe's honest admittance concerning how he felt about Albert, was a reality check for her, Joe is so wise. She wants to explain to him that what Soames did to her and made her do to him was nothing to be jealous of, but there's nothing to be gained by discussing it more fully, except to maybe cause more hurt. When he'd said, what's in the past must stay in the past, he was so right. If they wanted to move forward it meant the past had to be accepted and more importantly, forgotten. Putting her arms around him she kisses him with fervour, there are tears in her eyes. 'Oh, my sweet, loving Joseph, you are the only man that I have ever loved or will ever love. I treasure every single precious moment I spend with you. I am yours and yours alone.'

'You're the only woman that I have ever loved, my darling, and I will love you till the day I die. The way I see it, you are here, with me now. Yes, we've both got a past, virtually everyone I know has a past, but now that we've found each other we can have a wonderful future. Fate dealt its hand and now life begins for us, right here and now. I love you so much. My precious darling, we will have a whole lifetime of our very own precious love to share, from today we can make our own wonderful memories.'

Tears trickle down her cheeks, 'Oh yes, I know we will.'

The atmosphere changes, his breathing becomes deeper, laboured, as his hands wander over her body, gently caressing her, 'Mmm, oooh, Katie, my own sweet Katie,' he moans as he nuzzles his head into her glorious hair, 'Ooh Katie, you drive me crazy. I love you with all my heart. I want to make love to you,' he murmurs softly.

His impassioned words instantly eradicate the morose thoughts of Joe and his previous conquests, filling her with love and desire, she loves and wants him so much. 'All this talking between us is so new to me Joseph, I love that we can talk so openly, it feels so right.' Looking into his seductive eyes, she strokes his erection, loving hearing him groan deep in his throat with pleasure at her touch. 'Let's make love, Joe.'

'Mmmm… oh Katie,' he murmurs, pulling her close.

Her hands circle his neck, 'Oooo, I need you so much, I want you now.'

Could he love her any more than now? A lump comes to his throat as he embraces her, his eyes glistening with tears, 'I'll always be gentle with you, my precious.'

Eventually he sighs, releasing her from his arms 'Katie, it's late, darling, this is the last time we sleep alone, this time tomorrow we shall make love in our bed, and I'll make you mine forever.'

Taking his hands, she holds them to her breast and says, 'Wherever you go I shall always be by your side. Oh, Joe, I don't think I'll sleep a wink tonight.'

Joe shakes his head and chuckles, 'I know I won't,' he tells her, adjusting the bulge in his trousers. 'After tonight we will never spend another night apart, my precious girl.'

Katie sighs wistfully, 'Till tomorrow.'

Joe grins a broad cheeky grin, 'I hope you get all the sleep you need sweetheart, because you won't get much sleep tomorrow night,' he tells her with lustful promise twinkling in his eyes.

Katie's hand covers her mouth, 'Oooo Joseph, I hope so too,' she giggles.

'I love you, my darling,' he whispers softly.

The following morning Katie wakes very early, she'd barely slept a wink. Lilibeth feels her mother getting out of the bed and pads downstairs to find her.

Joe is already in the scullery preparing breakfast.

'Morning Lily,' he greets her, sounding full of the joys of spring.

Lilibeth, looking tired and grumpy ignores him, instead she curls up in his chair beside the fire, rests her head on the cushion and promptly falls asleep again.

'Hum, 'I'll try again. G'morning Katie, did you sleep well?'

Rubbing her eyes, she shrugs, 'I found it hard to sleep, I kept thinking about tonight.'

'Mmmm, me too sweetheart. Breakfast is ready, what about Lily?'

With a smile on her lips, she admits, 'I think she's still tired, bless her, I guess I disturbed her sleep last night with my tossing and turning.'

Spotting the tin bath propped up against the door, she tip-toes to Joe, trying not to wake her daughter, whispers, 'We'd like a bath this morning please if that's all right with you.'

'Wow, we...?' says Joe, spinning round, with a salacious look glinting in his eyes, 'Mmm, I'm really liking that idea, oh my love,' he replies hoarsely in her ear. 'Yes please.'

'Joseph, ahem, I meant me and Lilibeth!' she scolds him.

'Oh well, you can't blame me for trying,' he says sighing. 'The water's already piping hot, let's eat breakfast then I'll fill the tub for you.'

Suddenly wide awake, Lilibeth sits up and stretches, 'I don't want a bath, I'm not dirty. Go on, Joe, you tell Mammy, I'm clean, coz I been in my bed all night,' she says scowling, looking to him for back up.

Smiling lovingly, he picks her up, 'A lovely warm bath sounds good to me, what could be nicer than sharing the bath with your dear mammy, sweetheart,' he glances at Katie and smirks.

'Oooo stop, Joe, you're getting too saucy,' she mouths.

Pouting her lips Lilibeth persists, crossing her arms, obstinately shaking her head. 'I don't want a bath, I want to go outside with my Daisy, coz it's sunny!'

Katie tuts, chastising her daughter for defying her, 'Now listen to me Lilibeth, I not going to argue with you. I said bath!'

'Come on, it will be fun Lily,' says Joe intervening, 'Mammy can wash your lovely hair for you and make your pretty curls nice and shiny.'

Still feeling tired and even more grumpy, Lilibeth continues to protest. 'Don't want a bath, you have a bath with Mammy instead!' she suggests stubbornly.

'Mmm, that's a real nice idea sweetheart,' he says failing to hide his grin, 'but I've already had my bath, long before you got up this morning,' he looks at Katie whose expression was one of horror, 'Out of the mouth of babes, darling, after all, she's only six. She takes after you, she's totally innocent,' he chuckles.

With breakfast finished they share the task of washing and drying the dishes, then Joe prepares their bath. 'Right there you go Lily, just right for you to jump in.' He sighs. 'Sadly, I suppose I'd better make a hasty retreat,' he looks at Katie with a yearning look in his eyes.

'Don't go, you can scrub my back, Joe.' Says Lily, holding up a flannel, 'my Daisy would like it too?'

Taking a deep breath his cheeks colour almost as deeply as Katie's, 'Sorry sweetheart, I've got so much to do today.' he proffers. 'Your mammy can do it. I'll love and leave you both to it.' He winks at Katie and quietly closing the door behind him.

Striding down the yard he sniggers, dear sweet innocent Lily, bless her. 'Mmm, share the bath with Katie? Oh well, I can always live, in hope,' he mutters to himself. He'd noted that at the time, although Katie had blushed at Lily's suggestion, she'd tried hard to stifle a giggle. At last Katie appears to be a lot more relaxed and at ease with the sexy talk and innuendos. Hum, just imagine, the pair of us stark naked in the bath together. Wow, what utter bliss! he chuckles. Mmmm, the prospect of privacy from prying young eyes makes his mind up. He decides to build another room specifically for bathing, and soon.

His mind wanders to tonight. Mmmm, my beautiful sexy Katie. Oooo, I can't wait! With that thought in his mind he enthusiastically knuckles down, cleaning the metal bedstead in the barn.

The day flies swiftly by, he has finished distempering the walls in their bedroom and brought up the bedstead from the barn, putting the double mattress from his old bedroom on top. Katie has washed and polished the floor, put up the newly laundered curtains and laid the bed with clean sheets, finally the pretty blue patchwork throw that she'd found in his mother's tallboy dresses the bed.

Removing a loaf of bread from the oven, Katie runs upstairs to fetch a couple of flannels, the wash bowl and jug, her nightdress and freshly laundered towels to put in their new bedroom.

Meanwhile, in the garden, Joe has a complete strip wash and shave. After working all day, Joe's ready for dinner, he feels the need to bolster his strength for their first whole night together, for he had no intention of sleeping.

Before going to bed, Lilibeth insists that Joe tells her the magpie story, all over again.

As soon as they had settled her in bed, Katie quietly asks if she can have a word with him in the parlour, concerning Lilibeth.

Worried, Joe sits beside her, wrapping his arm around her shoulder, 'So what's the problem with Lily? Talk to me, darling.'

'This is very awkward,' she explains fidgeting, 'I know you say Lilibeth is very young and innocent, she's only six after all, but I'm wondering if it's time I explain certain things to her, what do you think?'

Raising his eyebrows, he's curious, 'What sort of things, sweetheart?'

'Well, she seems to think it's all right to say things, for instance, like when she said I should kiss you when you went to work. Then she thought I would be sleeping with you, in your bedroom. Um... she even suggested you have a bath with me! Not forgetting Stan and Margo, they're so blatantly open and descriptive about um... loving and all sorts of innuendoes in front of her. Yes, you say she is innocent, Joe, but Lilibeth's not stupid, she is very astute and picks up on everything she sees and hears. She um... is also well aware that men are different to women.'

Alarmed at her statement he pulled her closer, 'What are you trying to tell me, darling?'

Katie shifts uncomfortably, taking Joe's hand, she looks up at him anxiously. 'I'm so sorry, but I need to explain how.' She gulps, 'This isn't easy for me, Joe. I don't want to hurt you by telling you how she knows, but it's the only way I can explain about the problem.'

Joe pulls her closer, 'Hey, we share everything, sweetheart, I won't be upset. I'm just pleased we can share our problems. Go ahead, you talk, and I'll listen, darling.'

Plucking up courage, Katie takes a deep steadying breath, her voice lowers, her face reddening. 'I'm sorry to tell you this, Joe, I feel so ashamed and embarrassed, but as I said, Lilibeth is well aware of the difference between a male and female, because...' she gnaws on her lip, 'I'm sorry Joseph... you see her father was never, shall we say um... discreet. He would um... bare himself, regardless of her presence, you know, when he demanded sex and...' Katie's voice wavers, 'um, other things, if you understand what I mean, Joe. That's how she knows, I'm mortified to admit it, but sadly Lilibeth has seen the difference for herself.'

Stunned, he stares at her, his mouth gaping open, barely able to comprehend what she's telling him.

Ignoring his horrified expression, red-faced, she continues, 'My point is, Joe, recently, Lilibeth has unwittingly, started to come out with lots of inappropriate things, albeit as you say, innocently. So, I'm wondering if I should explain about... you know, um... private things. What do you think, Joe, do you think she's too young for that sort of discussion?'

Horrified, he's momentarily struck dumb, his blood runs cold. It is inconceivable to him that Soames could be so depraved. It beggars belief that Katie and Lily had been forced to endure such atrocities.

Gently lifting Katie onto his lap, he holds her close. Hiding his revulsion, calmly he says softly, 'Oh, my poor sweet darling, I'm so sorry,' though inside he is incandescent with rage. Lifting her chin to look into her eyes, he says quietly, 'I think you are very brave for telling me all this, thank you, darling. Now, I want you to know that there's not a problem that we can't sort out between us. I just need to think for a minute.'

'Oh, Joe, I don't want her to grow up being pathetically naïve, like me, being totally innocent and ignorant of the facts of life.'

Inspiration suddenly hits him, 'sweetheart, there are several issues you've raised here. First, perhaps there's a simple way of explaining certain facts to her,' he suggests. 'I think mother nature might be the way to go. Yes, perhaps we could show her the facts of life.'

She gapes wide eyed at him, 'No, Joe, No! We couldn't possibly! Not in front of Lilibeth!'

'Whoops,' He clears his throat and grins wryly, 'Hey no sweetheart! I'm sorry, I don't mean that 'we' literally show her. Of course not. I'm thinking more of Mother Nature's way. Hum, how about we get some sheep and a ram, we can educate her nature's way, by letting her see how a ram takes the ewe and we get baby lambs in the spring. Keep it really simple,' he suggests. 'I've said it before, but you can't beat Mother Nature.'

Pondering, she gives the matter some thought, 'Oh I see what you mean,' she kisses his cheek. 'That's a wonderful idea, Thank you, darling.'

'My pleasure, sweetheart.' He kisses her forehead, pleased he'd come up with an acceptable solution, though the next issue was much more difficult. His expression darkens when he pictures sweet little Lily, forced to witness such abhorrent atrocities by her so-called father. Dear God, she was so young and innocent, the very thought makes his skin crawl. 'Katie, you probably won't want to discuss this, but there's a more difficult problem that I don't think we can ignore.'

'Oh, really?'

'Most definitely,' he lifts her chin so that he can look into her eyes, 'Katie, it sickens me to the stomach, when think of what Lily had to witness with Soames, what he did was so morally wrong. But to me, it's imperative that Lily should know that what he did wasn't normal or acceptable to abuse and treat women like that! We can't possibly allow her to grow up thinking what Soames did was right, or normal to behave that way, can we?'

Grimacing, Katie agrees, 'I know, you're right.'

'It's totally wrong and unacceptable Katie, so I think it's up to us, we must convince her that normal, good relationships are based on love for each other, giving love and sharing love, the way we do.'

'Of course, Joe, we must talk, work out how best to broach the subject.'

'Good, we'll talk about it tomorrow evening. Now back to the sheep. I've had sheep in the past,' he points out, 'So I'll get in touch with Henry, he'll sell me a few sheep and loan us a ram. All for educational purposes of course,' he adds, smiling and kissing her nose, 'So, how d'you fancy lamb for dinner, my love?'

Katie giggles, 'Mmm, nice.'

Holding her close he sighs contentedly, 'It's getting late, I'd better shut the chickens in, and when I come back, I'm taking you to bed, darling. We've waited long enough. I'm thinking your sexual education needs a great deal of broadening, my precious, and tonight's the night.'

As Joe marches down the yard, he's grinning from ear to ear. Tonight, with Katie completely naked he will explore every inch of her beautiful body, they will share their love in the privacy of their own bedroom.

Suddenly the peace and tranquillity are broken when there's a racket coming from the lane.

Stan's cart clatters noisily into the yard.

As it pulls up, Stan's poor lathered horse is snorting clouds of steam.

'What the bloody hell...? Hey, what's up Mate?' he calls to Stan.

CHAPTER 12

A breathless, agitated Stan clambers down from his cart, followed by Freddie, Mick and two of his sons, Jed and Tommy, all five looking gravely serious.

After drawing in enough breath to speak, Stan blurts out, 'Soames, the bastard, he's on his way here! We gotta git them gels out of here, Joe!'

Shocked, Joe grabs his shoulders and shakes him, 'Stan, get a grip, slow down Mate!' he turns to Freddie, 'What's he gabbling on about?'

Freddie's expression is equally serious, 'He's right, we reckon Soames was outside Mick and Edna's open winder and heard them talkin'. He went crazy when he heard they was living here wiv you. He reckons he's comin' ter get them back! By gawd, I can tell yer, he ain't none too happy wiv you neither, Joe, he reckons he's gonna blow yer bloody head orf! Mick, Jed and Tommy came ter our place ter warn us. He's on his way here, Joe! We're all here fer yer Mate, so what is we gonna do about it?'

In a split second, Joe's contented happy smile vanishes his expression is now one of disbelief, 'And you reckon he's actually on his way here?'

Stan nods, 'Aye, ain't no doubt about it. And Joe, he's not only blind drunk, he's got a loaded bleedin' gun wiv him and all. He reckons he's gonna kill the lot of yer if she won't go home wiv him. I'll tell yer now Mate, he bloody means it!'

Freddie rests his arm on Joe's shoulder, 'We ain't jokin' Mate. None of yer is safe here no more!'

'Shit! How long have we got?' asks Joe.

Stan lifts his cap and scratches his head, 'It's hard ter tell, as I said, he's drunk as a skunk, so I reckon it's all down ter his old nag how long afore he gits here.'

'He won't be too far behind us,' Freddie warns, 'maybe half an hour at most. So, what's yer plan, Joe? We're all wiv yer, yer knows that.'

Joe nods and shakes Freddie's hand, 'Thanks, I'm really grateful Freddie, to all of you.'

'Well, we can't have a bleedin' drunken rapist roamin' the countryside wiv a loaded gun, and there's Katie and her nipper to fink of,' adds Mick

'Aye,' they all chorus.

Joe frowns as the seriousness of the impending situation hits him, 'Shit! Katie and Lily.' He wracks his brain, 'It's too late to get them away from here now. Have you got your gun with you Stan?' he asks in a tone that denotes a matter of dire urgency.

'Aye lad, we all have, they're all under me seat on me cart.'

With no time to lose, Joe thinks quickly and takes control, 'Right. Tom, first I need you to see to Stan's horse and cart, take them up behind the cottage on the left, unhitch him and settle Stan's horse with mine, then get yourself over to the dairy, behind the door. Jed, fetch the guns, you can stand inside the barn door. Stan, I want you to cover the door of the lean-to, to cover the back entrance, Mick, if you could stand behind the side of the house over there, behind the water butts, and Freddie, I'm putting my trust you to take protect Katie and Lily for me. I want you to take Katie upstairs to the front bedroom. Lily's already there, sleeping. No lights mind, and no matter what, do not come down till I call you. Understand?'

They all nod in unison.

'Are you all happy with the plan,' he asks.

Again, they all nod.

'Anyone got any questions or suggestions or anything to add?' Joe asks.

They all shrug.

Freddie turns to stride off towards the cottage. Joe quickly grabs his arm, holding him back, there is the distinct possibility that Katie might not be decent, 'Here, hold up Mate, wait here till I've got them both safe upstairs, out of harm's way, then when I come out with my gun, you can take over, all right Freddie?'

'Course, Joe, no problem, but where's you gonna be standin'?'

'Front ruddy door Freddie, He'll have to kill me before he gets to my girls.'

Jed returns carrying their guns, to be joined by Tom a few minutes later. 'Right, that's the horse and cart sorted,' reports Tom.

Acutely aware that time is marching on, Joe takes charge again, 'Check your guns are fully loaded and ready lads,' he orders, 'and remember, none of us shoots first.' He turns to Freddie, 'Give me five minutes, then when I come out you can take over. You're to keep the girls upstairs and stay with them, and no lights Freddie. Guard them with your life!' he pats' his back, 'I'm relying on you to keep them safe Mate.'

'Freddie grasps both of Joe's arms, 'Don't worry, Joe, Soames will have ter get by me first, and there ain't a chance in hell of him doin' that!'

Joe nods, 'Thanks Freddie, you know I wouldn't trust them with anyone else but you.'

Stan is getting agitated, hopping from one foot to the other, 'Gawd love us, hurry up, Joe, he could be here any bleedin' minute!'

Lifting the latch of the front door, Joe tentatively peers into the parlour, 'Katie, are you decent, darling?' he asks. Katie is sat relaxing by the fire smiling, dressed in a blue dress, the stunning blue dress that had miraculously transformed her from a filthy dirty vagrant to his beloved sexy girl. Her glossy auburn hair is tumbling around her delicate shoulders, her pretty face lightly flushed with excitement. 'Yes, of course, Joe,' She turns seeing his worried expression, 'What is it, what's wrong, darling?'

Grasping her by the shoulders, in a quiet but serious tone he tells her, 'Darling listen to me, please,' a little sterner than he intends, 'I don't want you to panic, but we have a major problem.'

Disconcerted, Katie's smile disappears, 'Problem, what sort of problem?'

'It's Soames. Somehow, he's found out you're both here, living with me, he's on his way here and he's armed too.'

Her hands fly to her mouth and her eyes widen with fear, 'Oh dear God no. Oh Joseph...!'

Wrapping his arms protectively around her, he lifts her face, looks into her eyes, saying, 'Darling, listen to me, please, it's very important. Everyone's here, Stan, Mick, Freddie Tom and Jed, we're gonna sort it,

I promise, darling. Now I'm going to bring Freddie in, and I want you to go upstairs with him to Lily's room, if you can, try not to wake her, please! Do you understand?' he can feel her body quivering in his arms. 'It'll be all right, darling, I swear.'

Trembling she says nothing, just nods.

'Katie, please, I'm begging you, no matter what happens, stay in the bedroom with Lily and Freddie! No candlelight, and most importantly, keep away from the window,' he says firmly, his fear for Kate and Lily resonating in his voice. He holds her close, and they kiss, so passionately it could be the last kiss they would ever share. 'Remember, I love you, with all my heart, my precious darling,' he tells her.

'I love you too,' she croaks, 'oh Joseph, please, please be careful, I'm so frightened,' she confesses, as huge tears well in her eyes.

'Ahem, er... sorry ter interrupt, erm, look, Joe, I don't fink we got long Mate, let me take Katie upstairs,' Freddie offers, and coaxes her from Joe's arms, 'Come, Katie love, I'll look after yer.'

Tugging at Freddie's sleeve, she attempts to pull free from his grip to make for Joe, but Freddie holds her back, 'Go on, Joe, get goin' man, she'll be fine wiv me!'

With fear in her eyes, she reaches out to Joe, 'Oh, darling, don't go, please, don't leave us!'

Joe steps towards her and Freddie yells again, 'Fer Christ's bleedin' sake, if yer wants ter do anyfin' fer Katie and Lilibuff, git yerself outside. Now!'

With his heart pounding thunderously, Joe nods, 'You're right Freddie, take very good care of them both, please!'

Freddie nods, 'Yer know I will, now git goin' Mate!'

Taking a quick glance at Katie, he whispers, 'Never forget how much I love you, darling,' he says, then he's gone, his loaded gun grasped firmly in his hand.

The light was fading fast, there's heavy cloud cover, Joe adjusts his eyes to the darkness.

'Fer gawd's sake, Joe, what the hell have yer been doin', yer been ruddy ages?' asks Stan, clearly agitated.

'No matter Stan,' says Jed, 'Is the gels safe, Joe?'

'Aye, as safe as they can be. Freddie's got them upstairs,' he answers, glancing nervously back at the cottage to check there are no lights showing. 'Are all your guns checked fully loaded?'

They all nod.

'Aye, we're ready and waitin' Mate,' says Tom.

'And you all know where you've gotta stand?' Joe asks.

'Course we does!' replies Stan irritably, 'We ain't bloody daft.'

'Sorry Mate, but I don't want any accidents. So please, everyone, just remember where we are all stationed,' Joe reminds them. 'Oh, and I don't want any of us shooting first, is that understood?' he adds firmly.

Jed puts his hand on Joe's arm, 'Whisht! Listen up!'

As they fall silent, in the distance, they hear the clip clopping of hooves and the grating of cartwheels, as it draws closer.

Albert's drink-fuelled, slurred voice can be heard bellowing out in the quiet night air, cursing and swearing foul obscenities.

Springing into action, Joe barks his orders, 'To your places, quick lads! Stan, no one gets in the back door, and remember, no matter what, we don't shoot first!'

By the time Albert's cart pulls to a standstill in the darkened yard it's eerily still and silent, save the occasional snort from his weary horse.

Stan is now stationed at the rear of the cottage, stood like a sentry, guarding the back door, his gun cocked and at the ready.

From four strategic positions, the tips of four-gun barrels emerge, steadily and silently.

Highly inebriated, Soames lolls unsteadily on his cart, 'Katie Soames!' he bellows, 'I know yer bloody in there wiv yer bleedin' fancy man! Git out here, yer filfy bleedin' whore!' Albert falls silent, straining his ears for a moment or two. 'Git out of his soddin' bed, yer filfy slut! Now! And bring that wife stealin' Markson wiv yer, coz I's gonna blow his bleedin' head orf!' He hollers menacingly as he picks up his gun, waving it in the air.

From the shadows, four long gun barrels emerged further, taking steady aim, for they are all left in no doubt that Albert Sebastian Soames' intentions are obvious, he means deadly business.

Soames stands up shakily on his cart and roars, 'I's comin' ter git yer Katie Soames, and as fer that evil little brat of yourn, yer can bleedin' leave her here. As fer that bastard Markson, I's gonna kill yer, yer dirty bastard!' he threatens, 'Yer ain't having me wife, coz she's mine. She belongs ter me!'

Uncontrollably drunk, he struggles to climb down from his cart, catching his foot in the reins he stumbles heavily to the ground with an almighty thud, floundering like a beached whale. 'Yer dirty filfy whore, yer ain't shackin' up wiv that bloody Markson bastard! I ain't bleedin' havin' it!' he bellows, as somehow, with the help of his cart, he hauls himself up onto his unsteady, fat bandy legs.

Tottering unsteadily toward the cottage with his gun waving in the air, Soames swaggers and sways.

From the shadows, four fingers hover over their triggers.

'Yer mine, and no other dirty bastard's gonna have yer! Out now, or yer gonna git what's comin' ter yer misses!' He continues to threaten menacingly as he makes for the door.

Incandescent with rage, Joe has heard enough of his foul obscene mouth, he can't stand by and let it continue, because despite his faltering unsteady footsteps, Soames is getting nearer to the house. Joe's fury is fuelling his anger to a point where he is prepared to shoot him if he comes any closer, 'That's close enough Soames, I'm warning you.' Growls Joes voice from the darkness. 'My gun's loaded and aimed right at you, one more step and I'll fire, If you've got an ounce of sense in your thick head you will turn your fat arse around and go back to where you came from Soames, you are no better than vermin. There's nothing here for you, so do yourself a favour and fuck off, you drunken bastard!'

'Here, is that you Markson? Where the bloody hell is yer hidin'? Show me yer ugly mug yer bastard wife stealer.' Snarls Soames, squinting his eyes, searching into the darkness. 'So, yer thinks yer can pinch me wife, do yer Markson? Kate Soames! Git yer arse out 'ere now, yer bitch, or I'll blow Markson's bleedin' head off!

'You're a filthy, sadistic, sick pervert Soames, Katie is going nowhere, she's staying hear with me, do you hear me!' snaps Joe,

'Yer reckons does yer Markson?' he sneers, 'Well she's my property, she belongs ter me! Katie Soames, git out here now or yer gonna pay fer it wiv me belt gel!' he threatens.'

'Right, this your last warning, Soames, I know how you badly you abused Katie, and Brodie too, you are a sick bastard and can be strung up from a tree for the way you've used them. Well, I'm telling you now, it is never gonna happen again, so if you know what's good for you, you'll fuck off!'

For some inexplicable reason Soames throws his head back laughing, 'Hah, she's me wife Markson, she's my property, and I'll do whatever I wants ter do wiv her, so stick that one in yer gob!' Slurs Soames.

His patience exhausted, Joe steps out from the shadows, his gun to his shoulder, his finger hovering over the trigger, aimed squarely at Soames' heart, 'You looking for me Soames?'

Hidden in the shadows the men gasp, 'What the fuckin' hell's Joe doin'? rasps Mick.

'Fuck, he'll get himself killed.' Gasps Jed.

'There yer bloody is Markson, yer dirty wife stealer, well I got news fer yer,' Snorts Soames. struggling to lift his gun to aim at Joe, 'I's gonna blast yer brains out!' Heavily intoxicated he's unable to focus his eyes as he stumbles forward, staggering unsteadily towards Joe. He struggles to stand upright as he shuffles one foot in front of the other, tripping over his own feet, he topples, losing his balance completely. He lurches forward. As he hits the ground, there's a loud crack and a brilliant flash of light as his gun goes off, echoing around the yard.

Before anyone can move a muscle, Albert's horse takes fright at the sudden, loud crack of the gun, rearing up, he neighs and bolts, trampling Albert beneath his hooves and the heavy wheels of the trailing cart.

There follows a deathly silence.

Three figures slowly emerge cautiously from the dark, their rifles butted to their shoulders, all three still aimed fairly and squarely at the still heap of Soames, their fingers poised ready to fire as they close in.

Running to the front of the house as fast as he can, Stan is the first to arrive on the scene, he peers down at Soames, 'Aw good gawd, what a bleedin' mess,' he mutters.

Tom bends, taking a closer look and shakes his head, 'Aye he's a goner, that's fer sure.'

Jed smirks, 'Aye, the best dead meat I ever saw.'

Joe stares down at Albert, with a look that is full of loathing in his eyes, 'I think someone should catch his horse and cart,' he says quietly.

They all gawp at Joe, 'What d'yer mean, catch his ruddy horse and cart?' says Jed. 'He ain't gonna need it no more.'

'Aye well, all the same, I reckon it's best to catch his horse and cart and bring them back here!' repeats Joe calmly.

Mystified, Jed shrugs his shoulders and strides off in search of the terrified horse.

'Could you cover 'it' with something, please Tom?' says Joe, looking impassively down at the lifeless, bloodied form of Albert Soames, 'There should be something in the barn.'

Raising his cap, Stan scratches his head, 'Huh, couldn't have happened ter a nicer cretin,' he snarls, 'I hope he burns in hell.'

Tom covers the mangled, bloodied body, 'Now what, Joe?'

'Hum, doctor, I reckon we should fetch the doc,' he answers impassively.

Stan's eyebrows shoot up, 'What the bleedin' hell fer, he's dead ain't he?'

'Aye, definitely dead,' says Jed, who has since returned with Albert's horse and cart.

Joe is still staring dispassionately at the covered crumpled mound on the ground, the mutilated, partially decapitated body that for seven long tortuous years had daily raped, sadistically abused and beat his beloved Katie, there's a wry smile on his face. 'That death was too quick and too good for him,' he comments. Inhaling a lung full of air, he looks up, 'The sky looks pretty clear now, plenty of moonlight. Could someone take my cart, go to Fennydown and fetch the doc, he'll have to sort out the necessary business?' he says then turns and walks towards the cottage.

Entering the scullery, he puts a taper to the oil lamp. At the foot of the stairs, he catches sight of Freddie stood on the top of the landing , the barrel of his rifle aimed directly at him, ready to fire.

'Don't shoot! It's me Freddie. It's all right, it's all over Mate!'

Katie barges past Freddie and flies down the stairs and flings her arms around Joe's neck, tears are streaming down her face, 'Oh Joseph, are you all right, darling?' she asks planting kisses all over his face.

Embracing her he smiles reassuringly, 'It's all over my love, Soames will never bother you again, you're free of him at last, my precious love.'

Freddie gingerly passes by them, 'Er, I fink I'll leave the pair of yer alone fer a bit. I'd better go out and see me old man.'

As he edges by, Joe rests his hand on Freddie's shoulder, 'I'm so very grateful Mate, I'm indebted to you.'

'Fink nuffink of it, Mate.' he mutters. He glances at Katie, safely held in Joe's arms and smiles, 'It's my pleasure,' he says as he goes down the stairs and closes the door behind him.

Sobbing tears of relief, Katie gasps, 'Thank God you're safe. Oh, my darling. I panicked when heard the gunshot. I thought for one terrible minute that you…'

'Hey, hush now, it's all right, darling.' He says, his hand rubbing her back to soothe her. 'Actually no one got shot at all, sweetheart. It was Soames's gun that you heard, he was blind drunk and staggering all over the place, he simply tripped, and as he fell his gun went off,' he explains quietly, 'Startled by the gunshot his horse reared and bolted and Soames was erm… trampled to death. He's gone, my love.' He takes a sharp intake of breath, 'Lily! Is she all right?'

'She's fine, believe it or not, she slept, through it all Joe.'

'So why the bleedin' hell can't we all go in and have a drink, son?' demands Stan, 'We been stuck out here fer ruddy ages.'

Freddie is not prepared to divulge anything he'd witnessed, he figures they need some time and privacy. He chastises his father, 'Fer gawd sake pops, stop yer belly achin', Joe's gotta tell Katie about what's happened, ain't he? Don't ferget, the poor gel was married to the rotten bastard!' Then a big grin spreads over Freddie's face, 'Good riddance ter the fucker. Katie, my Verity and every woman in the land can feel safe now.'

Looking glum, Stan shrugs his shoulders, 'I s'pose so. Is Katie and Lilibuff alwight then boy?'

'Lilibuff's fine, she slept frew it all so she's none the wiser what happened, bless her. As fer Katie? Course, it's been a shock fer her, poor love,' he answers his father, 'but given time, I's sure she's gonna be just fine.'

Stan tuts, 'Tch, I hope yer right boy, she's a right smasher, is our Katie, lovely gel. Bleedin' hell, did yer hear them filfy fings what he called Katie, our Joe and Lilibuff?'

A wide grin spreads over Freddie's face, 'Aye pops, he was a foul-mouthed perverted bastard, but now he's a dead perverted bastard, so we all win.'

'Well at least we seen the last of him,' says Tom, looking down at the crumpled heap, 'If it were up ter me, I would string him up in the bleedin' market so everyone can celebrate. I can't fink of a solitary soul what's gonna miss him.'

'Aye yer ain't wrong there, Tom lad,' agrees Mick. He shivers, it's getting chilly, 'I thought it were right good of my Jed ter go all the way back ter Fennydown ter fetch the doc at this time of the night.'

'Aye it was, your Jed's a good'n. Hum, how long, d'yer fink afore he gets back?' asks Stan, 'I could do with a drop of cider or somefink stronger ter wet me whistle and warm me bits?' he adds, rubbing his hands together. 'It's gettin' parky out here.'

Freddie, Mick and Tom all shrug their shoulders.

'Hang on Pops, I'll go and see what's happenin' indoors,' Freddie offers obligingly.

Freddie knocks politely on the door, there's no answer, so he lifts the latch and pokes his head round the door, to find them both sat on the floor in front of the fire, Joe was sat on the rug with Katie gently sobbing in his arms, they were gazing into the fire. 'Ahem. Only me.' he says softly, there's no answer so he steps inside. 'Ahem! Only me, Joe,' he says a little louder, 'it's alwight, I's on me own, Mate.'

'Oh Freddie, come in, come in,' says Joe, helping Katie her to her feet, 'Sorry Freddie, where are the others?'

'Tom's out in the yard wiv Mick and me old man. Jed's gawn on the horse and cart to fetch the erm... yer know who yer was on about,' he answers diplomatically, glancing at Katie.

Sitting Katie in the chair by the fire, Joe wraps a shawl around her shoulders, 'Bring them all in Freddie, it's cold out there. I'll pour us all a stiff drink. I reckon we all need one.'

Freddie nods and yells out the door, 'Is yer comin' in or what?' He returns and kneels beside Katie; she's nervously wringing her hands and sobbing silently. 'Is yer alwight ducky?'

'Yes... I'm fine, thanks to you Freddie,' she smiles a wane smile.

'Well Soames ain't gonna hurt yer no more, yer safe, and so's the rest of the women around these here parts,' he tells her. 'He's dead and gawn and yer ain't gotta worry yer pretty head about him ever again, so don't be upset lovey.'

'Oh, I'm not upset about Albert. It might sound callous, but... I was only worried for my Joseph.'

'I know ducky,' he said softly, 'and don't worry Katie, I'll say nowt, yer can tell everyone your news when yer good and ready and not afore.'

Blinking through her tears, she says, 'You've got an old head on young shoulders Freddie, thank you very much for everything you've done for us, we're both very grateful,' she leans up, kisses his cheek and squeezes his hand.

Blushing, Freddie stands and grins, 'Maybe I just found out what it is ter love someone, proper like. My Verity's the love of me life, and at last it's sorted between us, well almost. She's a good'n. She lets me know what I's missin' wiv out me takin' too many liberties wiv her, if yer knows what I mean,' he confesses smirking.

Katie smiles, 'I'm really pleased for you Freddie, Verity's a very lucky girl.'

Freddie grins from ear to ear. 'Aye, I know she is,' he agrees cockily.

As the sound of hobnail boots approach the door, he whispers, 'but if yer lookin' fer someone ter give yer away one day, I's yer man, I'd be deeply honoured.'

Her beautiful smile spreads wider, 'Why thank you Freddie, we'll bear that in mind.'

Mick, Tom, and Stan head straight for the fire, 'Gawd it's gettin' ruddy parky out there, the damp gits right inter me bones. Er, is yer alwight Katie love?' enquires Stan, holding his palms to the fire then rubbing his hands together.

Joe walks in carrying a tray of glasses, generously filled with the finest French brandy.

Katie looks at Stan and smiles, 'Thank you, Stan, I'm fine now, in fact, I couldn't be better. Thank you, all of you.'

The men gratefully gulp down their drinks and polish off a whole plate of buttered scones that are sat on the dresser, then Stan politely asks if there's any chance of another top-up going, 'And we wouldn't say no to a slice of yer meat pie Katie love, if it happens ter be goin' beggin', ta ever so ducky.'

She stands, 'Of course Stan, I'll get it for you.'

Freddie, Tom and Mick, crowd the fire, and Stan helps himself to Katie's newly vacated chair.

'Get yourselves warm. I'll make some tea and bring out the meat pie, I'll see if we've got some cream to go on the jam tarts,' offers Katie.

As she follows Joe through to the scullery, Katie glances back, Freddie grins and gives her a saucy wink. He nearly falls over when, so uncharacteristically, Katie chuckles and saucily winks back.

Whilst she slices the pie, Joe disappears into the larder, 'I can't find the cream, Katie,' he calls, 'Can you come and have a look!'

She peeps inside the larder, Joe is standing with his shirt wide open, leaning against the wall, he has a wickedly saucy look in his eyes. Grabbing her hand, he pulls her to him, cradling her head to his bare chest, she can hear his heart pounding loud and strong. 'Oooo, I love you so, my precious Katie,' he whispers. 'You are both safe now, my darling.'

His hands around her tiny waist, he picks her up and sits her on the marble shelf, hugging and her kissing her passionately, encouraging her tongue to tangle with his own, Katie's hands wander over Joe's chest,

Giggling she pinches his nipple making him gasp, but the voices of the men chattering in the parlour, keeps their love play in check.

Just as Katie finishes pouring the cream on the tarts, Mick bursts in the door, 'Sorry lads, but our Jed's back wiv the doc, he says we gotta go outside, he wants ter talk ter all of us, now!'

At Joe's insistence, Jed, looking exhausted and cold from his impromptu dash to Holdean and back, is sat at the table, to be waited on by Katie with a well-deserved supper and a very welcome large brandy.

'I really 'preciates this Katie,' says Jed tucking in, 'I guess they'll be loadin' Soames' body on the cart soon. Yer as free as a bird now gel,' he tells her with a mouthful of pie.

'We're so very grateful to you for your help Jed, but it's very late, won't Joanie be worrying where you are?' she asks as she pours him a generous, second brandy.

'Nah, she ain't got long ter go, bless her. She's as big as a house and strugglin' ter get around at the moment, so she's at Margo's. Hey, they'll be frilled ter bits when they find out that evil bastard's dead and gawn! Thank gawd and all. Cheers Katie love,' he raises his glass to her then gulps down the rest of his brandy.

'Joanie still hasn't had the baby yet then?' enquires Katie, 'Hum, she's taking her time.'

'Nah, Margo reckons it's a boy because he's lazy and late, says Jed chuckling.

Meanwhile outside, by the light of four oil lamps, the doctor examines the body thoroughly, he confirms he definitely hasn't been shot, but his head has been almost decapitated by the weight of the cartwheel and his legs crushed by the hooves of his horse. He listens to each of their separate accounts as to what had happened and declares it to be an accident. Between them, they load Albert's mangled body on his own cart for the doctor, so that he could take him to the undertaker in Holdean.

The four men return to the scullery.

Joe looks sombre, 'I'll top up the boiler Katie, I'm afraid we all need a scrub down, we need some clean clothes.'

They begin to remove their blood-stained clothes.

'We'll need something to wear Katie,' Joe points out.

'There are four shirts, three pairs of trousers, some socks and two jumpers on the clothes horse for a start, and clean towels too. Freddie's roughly your size Joseph, and maybe Tom too, but as for the others, I'll go up and have a look in your bedroom, Joe, we've still got some of Will's clothes there. Um... the water should be hot enough so you can all get cleaned up now, I'll put the clean clothes at the bottom of the stairs Joseph,' she offers, then hurriedly disappears upstairs.

One after the other, they strip and wash, then huddle by the blazing fire to keep warm.

Joe is the last to scrub himself clean.

'Hey up, some lucky beggar's been gettin' some lovin'.' grins Stan. 'Look at that.' he says pointing in the direction of Joe's back.

'Shut it, Pops!' says Freddie stepping in, 'it ain't no one's ruddy business.'

Joe says nothing, he is neither about to confirm or deny anything, but the look on his face said it all. He also knows that Margo would be the first to be enlightened the minute Stan gets home, and by morning, word would have spread throughout the entire village, and it would be common knowledge for everyone, he smiles to himself, it doesn't matter anyway, he has a plan in his head

'Is it all right to come in now?' calls Katie

'Yep, okay,' says Joe, 'we're all washed and dressed.'

'I'll put the kettle on again,' she says, breezing into the scullery.

Casting a stern, lightening glance around to the men, Joe frowns, warning them to say nothing, but as she stands making the tea, they all grin and wink knowingly to each other behind her back.

It's well gone midnight, Joe wants a quiet word in the yard with the lads, 'I'll just see them off, won't be long Katie!'

Outside Joe gathers them all together, 'I'm deeply indebted to you all, it might have been a different story if you hadn't been here, thanks for everything lads.' Glancing back at the house he lowers his voice. 'I know I'm asking a lot, but there's something I'd like you do for me, if you think it's possible.'

They all huddled together for half an hour or more, 'What do you think? Can you sort all that for me?'

They all nod, collectively agreeing, 'No problem, Aye, Joe, yep, of course, Mate.'

'I'll come over to yours the day after tomorrow Stan, we can finalise everything then. Freddie, here's the money for another couple of bottles of brandy if you can get it.'

Freddie chuckles, 'Aye, ain't no problem, Joe, I can git yer some mother's ruin too, if yer want it.'

'Sounds good to me, thanks Mate.'

Mick pipes up, 'By the way, the doc says it's an open and shut case. He could see the cartwheel almost cut his bloody head orf and his legs was mangled ter bits wiv his horses hooves. The doc said he were happy he had been trampled to death coz there weren't no bullet holes ter be found on him, so he's declared it were an accident. Mind you, we'll have ter sort out the burial arrangement fer him while we're at it and all.'

'Well, I s'pose the bastard will have ter be buried somewhere. Hum, I reckon an unmarked pauper's grave in the middle of nowhere,' suggests Tom.

'Aye well he's gotta go somewhere, I s'pose,' agrees Mick.

'I'm gonna have to tell Katie I'm bringing you some more wood Stan, I don't want her to find out, so no one breathe a word. That goes for your Margo, Stan, keep it under your hat.' He says as he waves them off.

'Phew, what a day,' says Joe, standing behind Katie, sliding his arms around her waist. 'All your troubles are gone, my precious darling,' he tells her, kissing the back of her neck. Frowning he sighs, 'I'm wondering about Lily, I suppose she ought to be told something?'

She turns to face him, 'I'm dreading the prospect, I'm not looking forward to it at all, I suppose I'll have to tell her in the morning. If you don't mind, Joe, I'd really like you to be with me when I do.'

'Of course, darling.' he pauses for a moment or two, 'Hum, how do you think she'll react?'

Katie shrugs her shoulders, 'The truth is Joseph, she's lived in absolute terror of him all of her short life, but she's only six, so who knows what goes on in her head?'

The fire is burning brightly, they sit on the floor together, gazing into the flames, reflecting on the evening's events. Thoughts of celebrating their union together now put it on hold until tomorrow night, deeming it to be bad judgement, considering all the drama and consequences of the evening.

Cuddles, loving words and tender kisses, pass the hours away until the first glimpse of morning light comes through the window.

'Dawn's breaking, the cows need milking.' He sighs. 'Darling, why don't you go up and get in bed with Lily for a few hours, I'll grab forty winks in the chair, then I'll see to the cows and the goat, we can collect the eggs with Lily later, sweetheart.'

'But you must be exhausted, Joe.'

He beams, 'sweetheart I'm fine, promise. In fact, I've never felt better in my whole life! So off you go, darling, I'll see you later, I love you.'

Pushing the door open with his shoulder, Joe's arms are filled with logs. Katie and Lilibeth are sat at the table about to eat breakfast.

'Morning Katie, morning Lily,' he said breezily, 'I'm starving.'

Looking tired, or maybe anxious, Katie greets him, 'Good morning, Joe, your breakfast's ready. If you wash your hands, I'll serve it up.' Adding with a wry smile, 'Oh, and Lilibeth wants to know why I slept in her bedroom last night.'

Sat eating her porridge, Lily fidgets, 'Joe, is I a big girl?'

Lily is always full of surprises, she amuses him, he's never sure what she will come out with, he smiles, 'Why of course you are, darling.'

'Ooo, Mammy, Joe called me darling, isn't that nice?'

Katie looked lovingly at her young daughter, 'I think Joe loves you as much as you love him.'

Scrambling down from her chair, Lily offers her arms up to Joe.

Only too happy to oblige, he sits her on his lap.

Clasping her arms around his neck, she pouts her lips and gives him a wet kiss. 'I love you, Joe.'

He cuddles her closer, 'And I, my little Lily, love you too, darling, very much.'

'So, why's my mammy sleepin' in my bed, if I'm a big girl now?' she asks, diverting the conversation back to her previous question. 'You said it was my room now, my mammy's got her own bedroom.'

'Hum, I reckon she wanted a big cuddle from you,' he replies, 'besides, your mamma's room isn't quite finished yet.'

Lilibeth looks at Joe's porridge, and picks up her spoon, 'Joe has got more jam than me, I'll swop, deal?' she says, swopping the dishes and promptly tucking in.

He raises his eyebrows and looks quizzically at Katie.

Shrugging her shoulders, she looks equally puzzled.

'Best get it over with,' he prompts quietly.

Katie breathes deeply, 'sweetheart, can you stop eating for a minute, I've um, I've got to tell you something, it is very important.' Lilibeth, still spooning her porridge, looks up.

'There's no easy way to say this, sweetheart,' her brow creases, 'It's your Papa, he had a very bad accident last night. I'm very sorry, but your... your papa has died.'

Lilibeth takes yet another mouthful of porridge, 'Is he in heaven with Grandma, Grandpa and Joe's mammy, then?'

Katie has to curb her shock at her daughter's indifferent response, she gulps, 'Well erm... perhaps.'

Apparently unperturbed by the dramatic news, Lily carries on eating her breakfast.

Katie looks at Joe, her eyebrows raised in surprise.

Joe shrugs and does likewise.

With her bowl now empty, Lilibeth turns to Joe, 'If my papa's deaded, can you be my new daddy now, Joe?'

Taken aback he stares at Lily, 'Wow, is that what you really want, darling? Oh, I'd dearly love to be your daddy, I'd be deeply honoured, but that's entirely up to your mammy to decide, sweetheart.'

Delighted Katie nods, 'Yes of course he can, sweetheart, what a wonderful idea.'

Delighted at acquiring a nice new daddy, Lily runs upstairs to play with Daisy and tell her she has a lovely new daddy.

Joe grins at Katie, 'How about that, me a real dad in just three minutes flat!'

'Hum, I think that all went reasonably well, don't you?' he says to Katie, as they share the washing up together.

'Yes, I'm amazed, but I suppose when you consider the way we were treated by him, and she is so very young, well I'm thankful for small mercies.'

He pecks Katie on the cheek then playfully pats her bottom, 'Darling I've just got to pop upstairs and get Lily, I want a quick word with her, in the garden.'

'And I'd better get these clothes in the boiler,' she says with distaste, surveying the bloodstained pile of clothes still in a heap in the corner.

Steam fills the kitchen as she plunges and turns the washing with the boiling tongs. Looking out of the window she sees Joe and Lilibeth sat relaxed, heads together, apparently laughing and chatting about something or other. Every so often they'd both look in her direction giggling, waving, then their heads would lock together again.

About to call Joe to ask for help to carry the washing outside, they enter the scullery together. Both sit at the table, grinning like Cheshire cats.

'Mammy, Daddy wants to tell you something, very special,' sniggers Lilibeth.

'Oh?'

'Go on Daddy,' prompts Lilibeth, obviously excited about something, 'you tell Mammy.'

Joe is still grinning, he nods, 'Lily's right,' he pats the seat beside him. 'Here, come and sit down with us.'

Bemused, Katie does as she is asked.

Joe winks at Lily then takes Katie's hand, he licks his lips.

'Go on, Joe, hurry up!' urges Lily, full of excitement.

'Katie,' he begins, looking to Lilibeth for support.

'Aw, just tell, Mammy.'

He takes a long sustaining breath, 'My dear Katie, I have been blessed to have two of the most beautiful girls in the whole world living under my roof, but it's not good enough, is it Lily?'

She shakes her head, 'No Daddy,' barely able to contain her excitement. 'Aw come on, give it to Mammy!' she squeals, sitting on her hands, her legs swinging wildly under the table.

Teasing, he laughs, 'Hum, now where did we put it Lily?'

She slides from the chair and delves into his pocket, then puts something into his hand.

Sinking to his knees he takes Katie's left hand.

Lily is jumping up and down, beside herself in anticipation, her plump little hands cover her mouth she smothers her shrieks of delight.

Spurred on by Lilibeth's enthusiasm he gazes tenderly into Katie's eyes, 'Katie, darling, would you make me the happiest man on God's earth and agree to become my wife?'

'And Joe says he can be my real daddy, if you do!' jumps in Lilibeth, clapping her hands. Before anyone can utter a word, Lilibeth throws her arms around Joe's neck and kisses him. 'Oooo, you're my real daddy now. Go on daddy, you kiss Mammy!'

Looking a tad doubtful, Joe frowns, 'Er, shall we see what your mammy has to say to my proposal first, darling?' he says softly.

A tear runs down Katie's cheek, she brushes it away, smiles sweetly at Lilibeth, then beams at Joe, yelping with joy, 'Oh yes, yes. Oooh, Joseph, I will.'

He slips his mother's ring on her finger, takes her in his arms, kissing her so passionately she thinks she might pass out.

Two plump little arms encircled both their necks. 'Oooo, my daddy and my mammy got loving together!'

If anyone had looked through the scullery window, they would have been forgiven for thinking that the occupants were all bonkers. All three were laughing together, cuddling and sharing kisses.

'Loving!' squeals Lilibeth clapping her hands, 'Mummy and daddy loving!''

'Ooo er, hush, darling, you mustn't say things like that,' Katie's face reddens.

'Hey, calm down, sweetheart, this is really good, it means Lily is accepting and embracing love as a normal thing to do, this a big step forward for all of us, and don't forget the sheep,' he reminds her, smiling wryly.

Delighted, Lily raises her eyebrows, 'Ooo, kiss Mammy again Daddy, my mammy likes it!'

'Mmm, so do I,' he says softly in Katie's ear. 'Well Lily, your daddy is going out tomorrow and guess what I'm going to buy?'

Lily shrugs her shoulders, 'I dunno.'

'I'm gonna buy some sheep,' he winks at Katie. 'Darling, if you can have everyone's clothes ready, I can drop them off whilst I'm in Holdean tomorrow.'

'Of course, I'll do some baking too, they love my cooking, especially Stan.'

The drama of the previous night is put behind them. Joe, plans his trip to Holdean tomorrow, and amongst many other things, he will purchase a dozen sheep, arrange a delivery date with Henry, pay him, accordingly, including the cash for the prize ram that is to be delivered three days after the sheep, he has also made other plans too.

Now every other sentence of Lilibeth's includes, 'my daddy.'

For the rest of the day, the quiet little cottage seems to be bursting at the seams with love and shared affection.

After securing the chickens for the night, Joe strides home with renewed vigour, he can't wait to take Katie to bed.

Picking her up in his arms, he carries her to their bedroom, closing the door quietly.

Eagerly he starts to undress but notices her picking up her nightdress, he shakes his head, 'Oh no, my sexy darling, you certainly won't be needing that in here,' he says, carelessly throwing it aside.

Katie stands looking nervous, gnawing her lip.

Gazing into her eyes he can see she looks unsure of herself, so he decides to invite her to undress him first. 'That's it, darling, keep going, shoes, socks, good girl, that just leaves my pants.'

Gulping, Katie stares at him, 'You um… you want me to take them off for you?' she stutters.

Chuckling, he tells her it won't be easy to make love to her if he's still wearing them. 'Come, darling, don't be shy, undress me.'

Kneeling down, with trembling fingers she unbuttons his fly, and his trousers fall to the floor.

Apparently at ease with his nudity, he stands comfortably naked and relaxed before her.

Gaping she stares, eyes wide at his erection. She's all of a tremble, looking highly flushed.

Joe loves her bashfulness, he finds it extremely arousing, 'Are you gonna get undressed for me now?' he asks softly.

Bashfully she unties the top ribbon on her bodice, looking uncertain, while he stands before her completely naked, patiently waiting. 'But the light is on,' she croaks, eyeing the burning oil lamp.

Mindful of her shyness, he obligingly turns the lamp down low.

His soft, silky voice encouraging her to relax. 'I guess it's my turn, darling.' One by one, he slowly removes every item of her clothing until she stands nervously, in the centre of the room, completely naked.

As his eyes greedily roam around her body, he sighs a long appreciative moan, she is more beautiful than he could ever have imagined. 'Darling you are exquisite, Jesus, you're making me hard, look!'

Katie swallows, his willy was now standing rigid and proud, shocked her eyes fall to the floor. Feeling vulnerable and embarrassed, she drops her hands to cover her modesty.

'Oh sweetheart, don't be shy, look at me Katie. Don't hide yourself from me, move your hands, darling,' he says, grasping his erection in an effort to control himself.

Katie takes a deep breath and gingerly drops her hands to her side.

His heart starts pounding. 'Dear God, you're perfect, so very beautiful.'

Gently picking her up he carries her to their bed. 'I have waited for this moment for so long,' he whispers, stretching his limbs, his leg between hers, he kisses her lips so softly. Moving down he pays special attention to her breasts. 'At last,' he purrs, 'now we are as we should be, your flesh against mine. Shall we make sweet love, my darling,' he purrs huskily.

With his body covering hers she feels less exposed, she wraps her legs around his hips, clasping her hands tightly around his neck, breathless with anticipation she whispers, 'Oh please, I want to feel you inside me.'

Their love making carries on for hours, patiently and gently he encourages her to try different ways to make love. Katie objects to nothing they do; indeed, her only response is to keep asking for more, she's greedy.

As daybreak comes, they lay exhausted, their limbs entangled together. 'Mmm, Katie, my sweet sexy darling, you're insatiable. My own little nymphomaniac,' his lips curl at the corners. 'I love it. In fact, I think that's what I'll should call you, from now on.' He pauses for a moment, 'Hum… perhaps woodnymph would be less obvious, especially in front of Margo,' he teases. 'Are you happy, darling?'

Stretching her body, she rolls over, her leg straddling his belly, her hand resting on his chest, 'Mmm, deliriously so,' her fingers trace over his contoured muscles. I love your body, Joseph. You remind me of one of the statues at Sheybourne,' she purrs, looking dewy eyed. Feeling sated and tired she gives a long, contented sigh, smiling sweetly, saying, 'I know I could never feel happier than I am right now.'

But it's time to get up, the cow have to be milked before Lilibeth wakes.

Katie has made several pies and loaves, washed and pressed all the men's clothes so that he can return them on his trip to Fennydown and Holdean. He'd set off bright and early and gone most of the day, not returning until almost dusk, bearing gifts from Margo and Edna, consisting of a small turkey, recently deceased and already minus its feathers, a leg of pork, plus more tea that Freddie had somehow mysteriously acquired, yet again. 'Have you missed me, darling?' he asks softly, as he swings her around in his arms, 'because if you did, I'll have to make it up to you tonight, my little woodnymph,' he promises with lascivious burning, glowing in his eyes.

Hearing he is home; Lily comes running in to greet him.

Picking her up he gives her a big hug, 'Oh I've missed you so much, sweet little daughter of mine,' he tells her, planting a kiss on her cheek.

Clinging to his neck Lily pouts. 'I missed you too, Daddy dearest, coz you been gone a long, long, long time.'

'Things to do Lily, things to do,' he grins. 'Oh, by the way Katie, the sheep will be delivered in five weeks,' he says giving her a wink, 'and the ram will follow three days later,' he adds with a wry smile.

The next three weeks speed by. Relaxed, happy domesticity is now the norm at Sweet Briars.

Retiring for the night, Joe sits on the bed and tells her about the plans that he's made for the following morning. 'Guess what Katie? We're off out tomorrow, all of us.'

Surprised, Katie looks at him mystified, 'Out? But Margo and Stan are coming tomorrow, aren't they?'

He chuckles, 'They were, but with Soames gone, you're now free as a bird, you can go anywhere my darling, no more looking over your shoulder, so we're all going erm... visiting.'

Katie face lights up, 'Are we going to visit Margo and Stan?'

He nods, 'Yep, I reckon we can call by, we're going to visit a lot of um... places tomorrow,' he says cagily. 'So, I suggest you get some beauty sleep, my precious woodnymph, we're gonna have a long day ahead of us.'

Katie can't help but notice the saucy look in his eyes, a look she now knows so well. She grins, whispering, 'Well that's entirely up to you, darling, I'm sure you could do with a good night's sleep yourself.'

'Mmm, maybe or maybe not, sweetheart,' he said putting his leg between hers, pushing her legs apart.

'Katie, my love,' he said softly, 'have I ever told you, darling, you have the most beautifully firm titties, I just can't leave them alone,' he says as he gently nips, tugging on each nipple in turn.

Grasping his hair, she whimpers, her eyes ablaze burning with desire, she gasps, glorying in the feel of him as he pushes deep inside her.

'Oh, sweet Jesus, yes Katie, yessss,' he moans, closing his eyes and savouring the feel of her clenching around him, drawing him in deeper.

She writhes beneath him, matching his thrusts, encouraging him to give her his love, 'More, Joe!' she pants breathlessly, as her fingers grasp his hair. 'Faster. Faster, Joe, oh please.'

'Come for me Katie,' he groans softly, 'come for me, darling.'

Frantically and noisily, they climax together.

As they lay, sated, he smirks salaciously, 'Again my little woodnymph?'

There was no need for a reply, she sits across his thighs, holding his cock she lowers herself onto him, throwing her head back, zealously riding him, crying out over and over, as he grasps her bouncing breasts, driving him wild.

Replete they lay back, their heated, exhausted bodies tangled as one.

'Mmm, oh my beautiful girl, I love you so much,' he whispers huskily, running his fingertips up and down her back. You never know, perhaps after a good day out tomorrow, Lily will be so tired that she'll go to bed early. Because from tomorrow I intend to come inside you like never before, we're gonna make beautiful babies, my darling,' he announces, kissing her so very tenderly as once again he penetrates her. Lost in passion he pumps her over and over again, savouring the feel of her as she tightens around his zealous throbbing cock, welcoming him. 'God, you drive me crazy. I can't get enough of you,' he murmurs, kissing her, invading her mouth with his tongue, carried away he makes love to her with such fervent ardour that she cries out, calling his name as noisily they climax together.

They lay back on the bed breathless, euphoric.

Mindful of Soames, he asks warily, 'I wasn't too rough with you this time, was I, darling?'

'No of course not. I want you to do it like that again!' she tells him, her face radiant, her eyes blazing.

Their energy drained, they lay with their limbs entangled.

'What's so special about tomorrow, Joe?' she asks, barely able to keep her eyes open.

Holding her close he kisses the tip of her nose, 'Just because it is, my precious, just because it is,' he answers sleepily. 'Cuddle into me, darling, we have a very early start tomorrow, we must leave before six thirty.'

Her eyes widened and her eyebrows shoot up, 'Did you say leave here before six thirty?'

'I did indeed, the sooner we go, the sooner we get home and the sooner you become mine again,' he tells her, his eyes full of lustful promise.

Rolling over to face him Katie lays spent and contented in his arms, she reaches down to hold his willy in her hand. whilst Joe cradles her breasts, he kisses her and holds her so close, they share the same breaths until they drift to sleep, 'Good night my sweet darling, sleep tight. I'll wake you both up as soon as the chores are done,' he says softly. But already she is fast asleep.

Bathed, freshly shaved, and dressed in clean clothes, he peers around the door, Katie is still sleeping, he wakes her with a gentle kiss 'Hey, time to get up, my darling little woodnymph.'

He runs up the stairs and opens Lily's door, 'G'morning, Princess, up you get, we're all off out today!'

She peers bleary-eyed over the blanket.

'It's time for Daddy's girl to get up!' he says all smiles, swishing the curtains open to let in the early morning sun. 'I love you Lily. Up you get.'

'I love you too, Daddy dearest.' says Lilibeth slowly coming to life.

'What time is it, Joe?' Katie calls up the stairs.

Joe's heart is brimming fit to bust, hearing Lily call him daddy dearest, 'Sixish, I reckon.' he shouts back, I'll be right down. Up you get Lily. We're going out!'

'Hey! Your breakfast is ready, sweetheart!' He calls up to Lily, then he disappears into the scullery to join Katie, whistling as he goes.

Unbelievably, half an hour later, they are on their way to Wickers Yard. Despite Katie's protests, they leave empty-handed, Joe had insisted that Margo, for a change, was perfectly capable of providing sufficient food for the day.

Not used to getting up so early, Lilibeth, still tired, has fallen asleep, curled up in a blanket in the back of the cart with Daisy in her arms.

Unable to stop himself smiling he leans over and kisses Katie on her cheek. 'What a perfect day!' he proclaims, 'Snuggle up to me, my sexy little woodnymph.'

Throughout the journey his spirits remain high. 'Still love me, darling?'

'Of course, Joe, I love you more than ever after last night,' she says coyly.

'Tell me again, my little woodnymph,' he says grinning broadly.

'I love you Joseph, very much. Last night was… so… what did you call it, erotic? I loved it. I want more!'

'Mmmm, me too, sweetheart, me too. Hah, it's a funny old world, I couldn't wait for us to go out today and yet, I can't wait to get you home, darling,' he tells her, his husky voice full of promise.

Wrapping her arms around him she coos, 'Ooo, neither can I.'

He kisses the tip of her nose, 'You er, you won't change your mind about tonight my sexy woodnymph, will you?'

'Er… change my mind, Joe?'

'About making our baby tonight, darling. No time like the present, my precious.'

Briefly she wonders what exactly had changed his mind about starting a family so suddenly, but she has no real objections, her hand falls purposely to his groin, he emits a long throaty groan, she smiles, delighting in his response, 'I know, darling, I can't wait.'

As they pull into Wickers Yard, Stan, Margo, Freddie, Jed, Tom, Edna, Verity, and a very heavily pregnant Joanie, all come out to greet them.

'Good heavens above, look at this lot Katie, you'd have thought they were expecting us,' comments Joe, chuckling slyly.

Margo, who is under the threat of no loving for a whole month if she gives the game away, does her level best to appear her usual self.

'Mornin' Katie love. Mornin', Joe. Hey, where's our Lilibuff?'

Lilibeth peers over the top of the cart, her little face full of smiles, 'Here I is!'

Freddie lifts her to the ground.

'Everything sorted Stan?' enquires Joe, lifting Katie gently to the ground.

Stan winks, 'Aye lad, all done, everyfin's sorted, like what yer said.'

'Come on in Katie. Be a love and put the kettle on Verity,' orders Margo, 'Edna, be a love and top them two tubs up wiv more hot water. Stan, yer best git orf wiv Joe now.'

Katie spins round, 'Joseph, where are you going?'

Stan clambers up onto his cart, 'Freddie, see ter Joe's horse and cart like what I told yer, Jed's gonna give yer a hand. Sorry gels, no time fer natterin', come on, Joe lad, Mick will be waitin' fer us.' Joe boards the cart and looks back at Katie, waving his hand and looking the picture of innocence, he winks, grinning at Katie. 'I'll see you later woodnymph,' is all he manages to say, before the cart rattles out of the yard.

CHAPTER 13

'Here's yer cuppa.' says Verity, handing Katie a cup of tea.

'Oh, thank you, I could do with that. I must say everyone is looking extremely smart today, I feel a bit out of place Verity, what's the occasion?'

Margo sweeps into the room interrupting their conversation, 'No time fer idle chit chat gel, fings ter do,' she says, then flies out of the door, dragging Verity with her.

Bewildered, Katie is left alone with the empty cup in her lap. Dazed she watches bemused as everyone dashes around her like scalded cats, it's complete and utter bedlam.

Margo breezes in like a whirlwind. 'Verity, take our Katie's cup. Hurry up Edna, or the water will be cold, take Lilibuff and Katie in the parlour fer a bath. Joanie, put yer feet up, we can't possibly have yer startin' wiv the baby now gel. Freddie! Where the heck's our Freddie? Freddie!' she yells at the top of her voice

Freddie rushes in frowning at his mother, 'Is yer hollerin' fer me Mam?'

'I is, where was yer!' she scolds.

At the age of twenty, Freddie objects strongly to being treated like a six-year-old. He scowls at her, he would have liked to answer back, given half a chance, but Margo is off again.

Giving Freddie a shove in the direction of the front door, she chides him, 'Yer got jobs ter do son, go and find Jed. After yer both done yer can git yerselves changed a bit sharpish. Just look at the state of yer, times gettin' on boy! Hang on Freddie, did yer have a shave?'

Rubbing his chin, he nods, 'Aye, I did Mam, smooth as a baby's bum.'

Sighing, he gives in, bowing to his mother's instructions, without so much as a protest he disappears out the door again.

Exasperated, Katie has seen enough, she stands, flings her arms in the air and stamps her foot, 'Margo! Everyone! Stop, stop!'

Suddenly the room falls deathly quiet, everyone stops what they are doing, and gawps open mouthed at her.

She blushes and lowers her voice, 'Oh, I'm sorry to shout, but, Margo, for heaven's sake, what on earth's happening? Have you all taken leave of your senses?'

Margo cuts a look to Edna, 'I fought I told yer ter take them in the scullery, the ruddy water'll be stone cold if we don't git movin', hurry up gel!'

Shaking her head, frustrated, Katie's about to sit down when Edna grabs hold of her arm, 'Sorry gel, yer knows what Margo says goes when she's delegatin',' she says, ushering them both through to the scullery.

Katie stands stock still. Two tin baths sit side by side in front of the glowing fire.

'These are fer the pair of yer, now yer ain't got long coz we gotta git yer both dressed,' says Edna sternly, and marches out, dragging poor Verity with her. Edna looks back, 'Don't worry yer pretty head Katie, we've got somefink really special fer yer ter wear, so hurry up gel.'

Totally flummoxed, Katie shakes her head, if they had told her Freddie was getting wed, they would have come better prepared, but with all the chaos around her she seems to have lost the will to argue.

As promised, Edna returns, rinses the suds from Lilibeth's hair and wraps her up in a large towel, telling Katie, 'I'm seein' ter Lilibuff. Margo and Verity will see ter you ducky,' she explains, then smiling broadly she departs with Lilibeth in her arms.

Almost immediately Margo enters with Verity trailing behind her, 'Alwight gel?' she grins, holding up a towel, indicating that Katie should get out of the bath. Throwing the towel around her she fetches a chair.

Totally confused, Katie throws her arms in the air, 'I swear this is a madhouse. You're all completely bonkers!' she declares, disconcerted she plonks herself down on a chair, pouting.

Hearing a racket, she turns to see Edna dragging a trunk behind her, taking it through to the downstairs bedroom.

Completely mystified Katie stands abruptly, 'Hey Edna, that looks just like my old trunk. It can't be, can it?' Again, she is ignored.

Margo returns, with something wrapped in tissue paper, 'Now be a good gel Katie, look what yer got, some sexy frilly French knickers and a pretty matching cami fingy. Beaut'ful ain't they? Slip them on gel and Verity will do yer hair.'

Verity says nothing and steps forward with the brush in hand, no one argues with Margo when she is in charge.

Before Katie can open her mouth, Margo has disappeared again.

Completely befuddled and utterly confused, right now Katie is wishing with all her heart that they had stayed in the peace and tranquillity of Sweet Briars. All this mayhem and talk of French knickers and what-nots sets her head spinning. 'Oh, please Verity, I can't possibly wear these, look,' she says, holding them up to show her, 'they're all fancy and frilly. Oh no, I'm sorry, I won't wear them, they're positively indecent!' she protests wildly.

Smirking, Verity chuckles, 'I fink yer should, it'd be indecent ter go out wivout them on gel,' she points out.

Against her better judgement Katie puts them on, grateful at least that no-one would be able to see them beneath her clothes.

'Shut yer eyes Katie love!' calls Margo from the scullery, 'I got a right lovely surprise fer yer.'

Beyond caring any more, Katie huffs and does as she's told.

Verity carries on doing what she had been instructed to do, continuing to brush Katie's glorious hair.

The door opens and in comes Margo with Lilibeth, 'Yer can open yer eyes now Katie love, what do yer fink ter this little angel?'

Hands flying to her mouth, Katie gasps in shock. Lilibeth is stood beside Margo in the most exquisite, three-quarter length, pale pink silk gown, she even has little pink satin slippers to match, and sat on her glossy auburn, almost controlled curls, is a dainty head-dress of tiny pale pink rose buds, in her hands a posy of cream and pink rose buds to match.

Katie is so overwhelmed she staggers and literally falls back into a chair, shaking her head. She holds out her arms to her daughter. 'Oh, my dear sweet Lilibeth... just look at you!'

'Aunty Margo says I'm going to be a flower-girl, does I look lovely, Mammy?'

Katie cries tears of joy, 'Oooh my precious darling, you're... why you look beautiful,' she looks to Margo and stutters, 'I...I'm sorry Margo, but I really don't understand all this. What on earth is going on? Is it Freddie, is he getting m-married today or something?' she asks, completely bewildered. 'I haven't got anything decent to wear. Why didn't you tell me?'

A wide grin spreads over Margo's face, 'Just hold on a minute Katie, that ain't nuffin'. Edna! Joanie!' she yells at the top of her shrill voice, 'Time ter bring it in gels!'

Edna waltzes in with Joanie, their arms filled with a cream silk gown between them.

Clutching her chest Katie comes over all lightheaded and staggers back into the chair again, so astounded she practically faints, 'Oh, my dear God!' she gasped, 'It's my Mamma's gown!'

Margo turns to Verity and Edna looking triumphant, 'Now ain't that the finest frock what yer ever saw in yer whole bleedin' life?'

They have to agree, for they had never seen anything so intricate and exquisite, ever.

It was all too much for Katie, the room spins, she faints.

'Bloody hell Edna! Git me ruddy smellin' salts! Quick gel, quick!'

A whiff of the salts wafted under Katie's nose soon brings her round, she can hear Margo talking, 'I know, our Katie's mammy did make it, beaut'ful, so beaut'ful,' says Margo proudly. She looks at Katie and sighs, 'Oh gawd, come on, pull yerself tergether Katie, it's time fer us ter get yer ready lovey, we can't keep our Joe waitin', can we?'

Her complexion ashen, Katie's eyes are glazed and vacant, 'Joseph? What's Joe got to do with this?'

Margo grins broadly, 'Well, ain't yer gettin' wed ter the most, handsomest eligible sexpot alive?'

Staggering back, Katie's jaw drops open and her eyes widen, she holds her breath, her heart pounding in her chest, 'Joseph...? Us...? We're g-getting m-married? Are you serious Margo?'

Beaming, Margo nods, 'Aye me darlin', in less than an hour,' she declares, wrestling with the billowing full skirt and petticoats.

Disbelieving, Katie trembles, she begins to sway.

'Now come on, pull yourself tergether Katie, we ain't got long, there's no time fer yer to start shilly shallying. Mark my words gel, there's plenty of pretty young gels that'd jump inter your shoes terday.' Beginning to lose her patience, time is getting on, Margo starts to panic, 'Aw stand still Katie, stop yer quiverin', I can't do up all these here buttons. Edna…!' Margo hollers at the top of her voice, 'Bring her head-dress in! Verity! come on, put her satin shoes on her!' instructs Margo as she buttons the seemingly endless row of tiny pearl buttons down the back of her gown. Irritated, Margo tuts, 'Aw fer gawd's sake, where's our Freddie. Freddie! where the hell are yah!' she shrills impatiently.

Flabbergasted, reeling from shock, Katie struggles to catch her breath, 'Oh Margo, is this all for real?' she asks, her voice barely a whisper, 'I can't believe it. Tell me I'm not dreaming, please!'

Margo, a long hat pin clenched firmly in her teeth, turns and mutters something inaudible, and secures her new navy straw hat, adorned with long peacock feathers, onto her head.

Freddie enters in a dark navy suit, looking extremely dashing but a bit grumpy, 'Gawd help us, I's tellin' yer mam, I'd never do this fer anyone, 'cept our Joseph and Katie…' he stops dead in his tracks when he claps eyes on Katie stood in her gown, 'Wow! Aw my, what a beaut'ful picture! Cor! I say Katie, yer looks ravishin'. Wow, ain't she the sexiest, prettiest woman what yer ever saw in yer life, Mam?'

Verity scowls, looking somewhat peeved at the attention and the enthusiastic compliments Freddie is showering on Katie.

Margo tuts and straightens his tie. 'Katie love, it's our Freddie what's gonna give yer away,' she announces, as she re-adjusts the head dress of flowers in her glossy hair, 'And naturally, my Stan is bein' the bestest man fer our Joseph.'

Katie's breathing shallows, her head shaking slowly from side to side, 'I can't believe… all this… you mean it's true… I really am going to marry Joseph?' her frail voice trails away. In shock, she goes completely limp, her legs fail her.

'Good gawd, grab her!' yells Margo in a panic.

Between them, Freddie and Edna manage to catch Katie as she falls, they sit her back into a chair.

Edna dashes off, returning with the smelling salts, again, wafting them under Katie's nose, Verity continues flapping the towel fanning her, giving her some much-needed air.

'Look gel, come on, pull yerself tergever, yer knows full well what I fink of Joe, and if yer don't want him then p'raps I'll take him orf yer hands fer yer.' She grins with a wicked look shining in her eyes.

'Huh, well I fink Joe's the lucky one,' chips in Freddie, unable to drag his eyes from Katie, 'Just look at her, she's the most beaut'ful girl in the world. Cor, and so very sexy,' he murmurs.'

Shocked, hands on her hips, Verity pouts, 'Here Freddie, what about me?'

'Apologies my lovely, no offence intended, Dearest,' says Freddie looking suitably humble.

Verity sniffs, 'Well I suppose she do look beaut'ful.' She begrudgingly agrees.

Feeling strangely numb, Katie is still struggling to catch her breath and take it all in.

Looking Katie up and down approvingly, Margo declares, 'Well that's it, Katie love, it's time ter go.'

Freddie steps forward and offering Katie his arm. 'If yer feelin' alwight, yer carriage awaits me darlin' and so do yer prospective husband, Mr Joseph Markson. Shall we?'

Katie is helped to her feet, she's trembling from head to toe, she has to cling to Freddie's arm for support.

Holding her firmly round her waist, he proudly walks her out into the glorious sunshine where a sleek, shiny black and gold carriage with two fine, gleaming chestnut horses stand in the yard. The carriage is bedecked in pink and cream roses and ribbons.

'Oooh… my,' she stutters, 'Oooo Freddie, hold me up, I think somebody's stolen my legs from under me,' says Katie then promptly swoons in his arms.

'Oh gawd!' exclaims Freddie, 'Edna, get them ruddy salts! Mam, help me hold her up!'

Edna rushes indoors and back out with the smelling salts. It takes a good whiff of salts and several steadying deep breaths before Katie comes too, calms down and composes herself a little.

Tom is sat at the reigns looking very dignified in a dark suit and a shiny top hat. 'Aye, yer looks stunnin' Katie love, yer a real beauty, Joe's a lucky bugger, and that's a fact,' he tells her.

First Freddie lifts Lilibeth into the carriage, 'Sit there, me little darlin' and I'll help yer mammy up.'

Katie is extremely pale and still looks quite faint, so he picks her up in his arms, walking a few paces, out of earshot of the others. In a hushed whisper he says, 'Look. If yer don't want ter marry him, Ducky.'

Tears are trickling down her rosy cheeks, 'Oooh but I do, of course I do Freddie, it's just… all this, it has all been such a dreadful shock, I… I genuinely had no idea at all!'

Freddie beams, 'Good, then we won't keep Joe waitin' no longer. So, what is we waitin' fer?' he says and lifts her into the carriage opposite Lilibeth. 'Mam, yer got a clean hanky fer Katie, she's gotta wipe her pretty eyes?'

Sitting upright next to Katie, Freddie looks so proud to be escorting Katie to the church. 'Right, is we all set ter go?' he asks, relieved to be ready for the off.

Margo swings her arm in the air, 'Stop! Aw gawd, no. Hang on Freddie lad. Edna!! Get her bouquet!' she yells.

Poor Edna, obviously run ragged and wilting, comes puffing out the door, her hat slightly askew, 'There we go gel,' she says, handing Katie a long trailing bouquet of assorted cream and pink flowers. 'Good luck me darlin'. Not that you'll need it.'

Katie smiles weakly, her complexion pallid, 'Oh Edna, they're so beautiful, thank you very much.'

Margo hoists herself up on the carriage, to the greatest pleasure for Freddie and Tom, lifts Katie's skirts and slides a garter up her slim leg, midway up her thigh.

Freddie grins, winking a saucy wink in Tom's direction.

Tom grins and winks back.

Freddie, now exasperated, glares at his mother, 'Aw bleedin' hell, good gawd mam, we're ruddy late as it is, poor Joe will fink Katie ain't ruddy comin'!'

'Alwight, alwight Freddie, keep your hair on, Son! She pats Katie's hand declaring, 'Yer look stunnin' gel, Joe's a lucky man, make no mistake.'

'Thank you, all of you,' says Katie, filled to the brim with emotion.

'Mam!' said Freddie, his patience exhausted, 'That's it! Tom, fer gawd's sake, let's get goin' Mate, we can't keep Joe waitin' a minute longer!'

The elegant carriage moves off, followed by Joe's cart, which in the space of a couple of hours, is now miraculously bedecked in streaming cream satin ribbons and flowers, fully loaded with all of Katie's closest and dearest friends.

Freddie takes Katie's trembling hand, 'Is yer feelin' alwight now lovey?'

'I... I don't know Freddie, I... I think so, but I'm very nervous,' she admits, 'Freddie, this wonderful carriage, the smart suits and lovely clothes, all these beautiful flowers,' she bites her lip, 'My Lilibeth's beautiful dress, my Mamma's dress, everything, oh Lordy, who on earth arranged it all? Oh dear, d...does Joe know about this?'

Freddie throws his head back and roars with laughter, 'Ruddy hell Katie, course he knows, it was him what arranged it all! We just helped him out wiv a few fings.'

'But it must have cost a fortune!' she points out.

'Huh, our Joe ain't short of a few shillin's, I can tell yer. Anyway, he said money weren't no object fer his lady love on the bestest day of his life, he loves yer, wiv all his heart Katie.'

'Yes, yes, I know, I love him dearly too Freddie.'

'So, do I,' Lilibeth chips in, 'and you know Freddie? Aunty Margo says Joe's going to be my real daddy now,' she says grinning, 'and he's the bestest daddy in whole world!'

A raucous gaggle of laughter and whoops of delight from the following carriage gets Lilibeth's attention, she giggles, looks back and waves.

They all cheer and wave back.

Taking a deep breath to steady herself, Katie looks Freddie up and down, 'I must say you look extremely dignified and handsome in your suit. You'll make a good husband for Verity. Today's the first time I've met her, I think she's really lovely.'

'Aye, I can't disagree Katie love, but ter be honest wiv yer, I'm gettin' a bit desperate. I reckons it won't be long afore I has ter make an honest woman of her, if yer know what I mean, she's shy and still holding out on me.'

Hearing the church bells ringing out, Katie turns to Freddie. 'Oh, help Freddie, I'm scared.' She's shaking like a leaf and finding it hard to breathe.

'I dunno why, me darlin', Joe's waitin' fer yer,' says Freddie, 'Yer know, Joe's the bestest bloke I ever knowed, a good, kind, honest man, and more than that, he'll be faithful ter yer till the day he dies. Yer means the world to him, yer both does,' he says, adding, 'it's funny, yer know, his mam and my mam had been tryin' ter fix him up wiv a wife fer years, but he always said he never found the right gel, so yer gonna break a few hearts around these parts terday when yer says "I do". But I'll tell yer somefin', you'll make him the happiest man alive. he worships yer both,' says Freddie patting her hand.

As the carriage pulls up at the latch gate, Katie grabs Freddie's hand, 'Oooo help Freddie, I don't even know what I have to do?'

'Don't worry Katie, Joe said ter tell yer, when the vicar asks if yer will, then yer says 'I will,' then when he says, 'Do yer,' yer says 'I do.' Simple. Anyway, I'm wiv yer so yer gonna be fine Ducky,' he promises, patting her arm reassuringly.

Freddie gently lifts her to the ground, followed by Lilibeth, 'There we go my little angel, now just you remember what yer Aunty Margo told yer Lilibuff, I's gonna walk yer mammy up the aisle and yer have ter follow close be'ind us, alwight Princess?'

Lilibeth nods, 'Yes Freddie.'

He turns to find his mam fussing around Katie, tidying her gown and straightening her head dress. 'Aw come on Mam, fer gawd's sake, in yer go, let the bleedin' vicar know we're, here at last.'

Margo straightens her hat and Edna's too, she grins at Katie, 'Good luck Darlin', yer look so beaut'ful.' She gives Katie a swift hug, sniffs, dabs her nose with her hanky, links arms with Edna and they enter the church.

As they hear the organ play, Freddie looks back at Lilibeth, 'Close behind us Lilibuff, close behind,' he reminds her, he winks, then offers Katie his arm. 'Are yer ready now, Katie? Take a deep breath me darlin', Joe's waitin' fer yer inside.'

Katie gulps, her stomach seems to drop into her shoes, 'Oooo I don't know Freddie. Oh dear, yes, of course I am.'

The congregation all stand to watch Freddie proudly escort her slowly up the aisle on his arm.

There are gasps of admiration from friends, they all give little waves and nods of approval as he walks her towards the altar.

Almost overcome by the moment, she faltered briefly, and Freddie slips his hand around her waist, 'Look Katie love,' he whispers, 'there's Joe, see? He's waitin' fer yer, best foot forward.'

Looking up she sees Joe, standing head and shoulders above everyone, she gulps, he looks so stunningly handsome, stood in his dark suit.

As she reaches the top of the aisle, her heart races when Joe looks adoringly at her, he moves sideways to join her in front of the vicar.

Margo steps forward and takes Katie's bouquet, and hands it to Lilibeth, saying, 'Take hold of these fer yer mammy, and don't drop them Sweetheart.'

Leaning towards her Joe whispers in the lowest voice he can manage, 'Oh Katie, you look so beautiful, darling.'

The portly, red-nosed vicar clears his throat, 'Ahem, are we ready?'

Katie glances sideways at Joe stood beside her, she suddenly feels calm and serene.

'Ahem. Dearly beloved, we are gathered here today, to witness the solemn marriage between Joseph Markson and Katerina Soames.' The vicars monotone voice echoes around the packed church.

'Who giveth this woman?' asks the vicar.

'I does,' said Freddie, proudly offering Katie's delicate hand, he takes a couple of steps back, looks down and smiles at Lilibeth and holds her little hand tightly.

The ceremony continues.

'Joseph, will you love, honour, and obey Katerina, keeping her only unto yourself as long as you both shall live?' asks the vicar solemnly.

Joe smiles lovingly at Katie, 'Oh I will, most definitely, always,' Joe replies enthusiastically.

A titter ripples around the congregation.

Unimpressed the vicar scowls and clears his throat, 'Ahem. Katerina, will you love, honour and obey Joseph and keep him only unto yourself as long as you both shall live?'

'I will,' says Katie in a whisper as soft as a gentle summer breeze.

The vicar, looking sombre, scans the sea of faces, 'If anyone knows of any lawful impediment why these two persons cannot be joined in holy matrimony, let them speak now or forever hold their peace.' There follows a short, hushed silence.

Prompting Freddie, the vicar holds out the open bible, 'The ring if you please?'

Placing it on the bible Freddie stands back, re-joining Lilibeth.

Joseph takes Katie's left hand, and the vicar clears his throat again, 'Repeat after me. I Joseph, do take thee Katerina as my lawful wedded wife, to have and to hold from this day forward. To love and to cherish, till death do us part. With my body, I thee worship, all my worldly goods I thee endow. I give you this ring as a symbol of our marriage.' He slides it on her third finger, as instructed by the vicar.

He turns to Katie, 'Repeat after me Katerina.'

In a quiet but clear voice Katie repeats, 'I Katerina, do take thee Joseph, as my lawful wedded husband, to have and to hold, from this day forward, to love and to cherish, till death do us part. With my body I thee worship and all my worldly goods I thee endow.'

'I now pronounce you husband and wife. For those whom God hath joined together, let no man put asunder. You may kiss your bride,' concludes the vicar.

Lilibeth is so overjoyed she begins clapping, and like ripples on a pond, gradually the entire congregation follows suit.

As Joe holds Katie close to kiss her, he whispers, 'I love you, my wife, my own.'

After the register is signed and witnessed by Stan, Margo and Freddie, Katie is handed the wedding certificate, the organ plays as Joe takes Katie's arm in his and proudly walks his wife down the aisle and out into the glorious sunshine.

Stood in the doorway he turns to Katie and to the roar of the crowd, wraps his arms around her and kisses her passionately taking her breath away. 'My darling Katie, my wife, my own, I love you so much. Thank you for becoming my wife, darling,' he whispers softly in her ear, 'you've made me the happiest man alive.'

Katie smiles sweetly, 'I love you too, my beloved, very handsome husband, but you really should have told me, it was such a shock,' she playfully scolds him.

Joe beams, 'Would you have come if I'd asked?'

Squeezing his hand, she smiles back, 'You know I would, darling, wild horses wouldn't have kept me away. I've told you before, wherever you go, I will always be by you side.'

The church bells peal out in celebration and as they kiss, petals are thrown from all directions, the crowd cheer, surge forward, milling around them, wishing them well, shaking their hands and patting them on the back.

If Katie wasn't so ecstatically happy, she might have noticed in the crowd, the faces of several very pretty young girls all turning green with envy. One young girl in particular, is stood at the back glowering, tears are streaming down her face. She is clothed from head to toe in black, matching her long straight, jet-black hair. Scowling, she's thinking to herself. How could you marry someone like her Joseph Markson? She's already had herself a husband and she got a bloody kid, the bitch. Well, yer better watch yer back Katerina Soames, coz I'll never let you go Joseph. Never! She vows and slips quietly away.

'Mind yer backs, move away now folks!' orders Freddie, taking his duties very seriously, 'Come on now, make way fer the bride and groom!' Katie shrieks and clings to Joe as he scoops her up in his arms and proudly carries her to the carriage, beckoning as he does, to Freddie to bring Lilibeth too.

Joe stands proudly in the carriage, put his hand in the air to silence the crowd. Instantly they fall silent.

Proudly he lifts Lilibeth on one arm, his other arm wrapped firmly around Katie's waist. 'Our dearest friends!' he addresses the crowd, 'Today, I want to introduce you to my beautiful wife, Katerina Markson, and also, my very precious daughter, Lilibeth Markson. I want you all to know that today they have made me the happiest man to ever walk God's earth!'

Applause and cheers run through the crowd.

Raising his hands for silence he adds, 'My wife and I would like to thank each and every one of you, for the hard work and help you have all freely given in making today the best day of our lives! Now if you'd all like to follow the wedding carriage to the market square, we can all enjoy our wedding feast,' he announces, adding, 'We truly thank you all, from the bottom of our hearts.'

Good will messages are called from the cheering crowd, 'Good luck!' and 'All the best,' and, 'Ain't she just the finest woman yer ever clapped yer eyes on?' and, 'Cor, yer a lucky bleeder, Joe!' quickly followed by, 'Not arf, I'd swap me misses fer yourn any day, Joe!'

A voice from the back calls out in reply, 'Bet yer misses would be only too happy ter swop yer wiv anyone and all Mate!'

The crowd roars with laughter and Joe stands again grinning widely, 'I can tell you all, right here and now, this fine, exquisite woman is now a very treasured, deeply loved Mrs Joseph Markson, my wife, and that's the way it stays till the day I die. So hard luck you lot, believe me, the pleasures gonna be all mine!'

The whole crowd roars with laughter and cheers.

He sits in the middle of the carriage seat, Katie to one side and Lilibeth to the other, his arms firmly around them both, and as Tom flicks the reins, the carriage moves forward, with a highly jovial wedding party following noisily behind.

Arriving in the square in Holdean where the market is normally held, they find dozens of various assortments of tables, each groaning with the biggest selection of food ever seen.

Freddie escorts Joe, Katie and Lilibeth, to the top table.

Dumbfounded, Katie is still struggling to take everything in, 'Who on earth did all this Freddie?'

'Everyone,' says Freddie, 'All yer good friends from the markit Katie. They were all so pleased fer yer both, they all chipped in wiv their tables, food and stuff, all tergever.'

A cake sits in the centre of the top table, on the top are two large sugar hearts joined together with a white ribbon, one has 'Joseph' piped on it, and the other, with 'Katerina', propped between them is a little one, on which is piped in pale pink icing, 'Lily'.

On a cue from Jed, a band strikes up the music.

Mick, Stan, Tom, Abe, Jed and Freddie all chip in helping to pour and hand out cups, mugs, and in some cases jam jars of either cider or ale and gin for the ladies.

Stan takes a slurp of the ale and smacks his lips, 'Finest drop of brew yer'll ever taste, try that,' he says, handing one to Joe.

After a quick sample, Joe nods in agreement, 'Mmm, you're right there Stan, delicious.'

'Aye,' agrees Stan grinning, 'Good, ain't it?' he leans closer to Joe and whispers, 'There be four more barrels stashed away under the table, and I got another couple at home ter wet yer first borns head wiv Mate.'

Grinning broadly Joe winks, 'Ta Stan, I'll look forward to that.'

Leaning nearer Stan whispers in Joe's ear, 'A pleasure ter drink, but watch it, Joe, don't drink too much or it will blow yer bleedin' head orf, we don't wanna spoil yer nuptials ternight does we?' he chortles, then adds, 'though I might give Margo a couple, it can be right rewardin' lovin' when our Margo gets squiffy, if yer knows what I mean lad.'

Freddie overhears the conversation and tuts, his eyes roll skyward, 'Oh gawd, here we go agin Pops, yer know I often wonders why I'm the on'y ruddy child.'

Margo and Stan throw their heads back, laughing raucously, 'Well it weren't fer lack of ruddy tryin' boy. I guess the good Lord thought one of yer was quite enough fer this devoted couple,' says Stan.

Freddie sighs and shakes his head.

Almost two large barrels of cider later, the air is filled with hilarious jollification. Men that normally find it difficult to get off their backsides and do a decent day's work, now filled with alcohol, have found a new lease of life, they are dancing and jigging to the music with their wives and getting romantic ideas of their own, as are the young and unattached.

Freddie, now clearly inebriated is standing with Margo, beside Joe and Katie. Picking up a metal jug and spoon, Freddie bangs furiously, hollering, 'Let's be havin' some hush folks!'

After two more attempts, the raucous laughter dies down.

'Ahem, friends, let's have some hush, purleeease!' All eyes focus on Freddie, 'Ahem. My fanks ter yer all. Now Joe, his very beaut'ful wife Katie and his daugh'er Lilibuff, is orf shortly, so I'm askin' yer all ter raise yer glasses and drink to their good health and happiness!'

Mugs cups, glasses and other vessels, are raised high.

'Ter Joe and Katie, long life and happiness, may all yer troubles be little uns,' says Freddie, he grins at Katie, 'Eight, I fink Joe said, weren't it, Joe?'

Katie's eyebrows raise and she blushes, she looks inquiringly at Joe, who was sporting a wry smile, 'Um... excuse me Joseph, eight?' she whispers.

'To Joe and Katie. Good healf and happiness,' they chorus.

Joe beams, leaning nearer he whispers quietly in her ear, 'I thought we could make a start tonight, my darling little woodnymph.'

Katie blushes even deeper, she lowers her eyes, 'But eight Joseph?'

He looks at her with his wickedly sexy deep blue eyes, 'Whatever, I've no doubt we'll have lots of fun trying Mrs Markson.'

After being prompted by Freddie and the gathering, Joe stands to make his final speech. 'My dearest friends. On behalf of my delectable, most treasured, beautiful young wife...' everyone laughs, 'I want to say a heartfelt thank you, to each and every one of you!'

They all clap and shout their approval.

He turns to Katie, picks up her hand and kisses her wedding ring, 'Katerina, my love, my wife, my life, thank you for marrying me. Believe me, I am deeply honoured to be your husband, I will cherish and treasure you till my dying day. Mrs Joseph Markson, I love you more than life itself,' then ignoring all the oooos and aaaahs, he bends down and gives her a long, lingering kiss.

Stood behind them, tears are welling up in Margo's already pink, puffy eyes. 'Awe mam, yer s'posed ter be happy fer them,' says Freddie, putting a comforting arm around his mother.

'I is Freddie, I'm so happy,' she says, noisily blowing her nose.

'Aye Freddie,' sobs Edna, 'so am I.' patting her eyes dry.

Smiling, Joe gives them both a hug, handing them both a gift box, 'Edna, Margo, I have a small gift for you both.'

Opening them, they both shriek, each box contains a heart shaped, gold broach, he is promptly rewarded with a kiss and a hug from them both.

Grinning broadly, Joe holds up his hands in surrender, 'Hey up, leave it out girls, I'll have you both know that I'm a very happily married man!'

The entire crowd roars with laughter.

The band strikes up and merriment fills the air. Edna puts her head on Margo's shoulder and they both bawl their eyes out.

'By the way Freddie, I'll be very honoured to do the same for you, someday,' Joe tells him, shaking his hand

Freddie leans closer and whispers in his ear, 'Might be sooner than yer fink, Joe, coz my Verity's a virtuous gel, and she's holdin' out on me till she gets a ring on her finger.' He frowns, 'I can't wait much longer.'

Joe sniggers, remembering how he hard he'd struggled to conceal his own carnal longings for Katie. 'Hah, I know exactly what you mean, believe me.'

He takes Freddie aside, 'Look Freddie, can I ask one more favour?'

'Anyfin' Mate, yer on'y gotta ask Joe.'

'We're stopping off at your mam's for a bit, so would you take Stan's cart, follow Tom. He's dropping off the horses and wedding carriage, then give Tom a lift home? On your way back, could you call into Briars, I've some jobs need sorting?' he says, handing him a list of jobs.

'Course I will,' says Freddie grinning, 'Call it me wedding present.'

It is time to leave Wickers Yard. Lilibeth is staying at Margo's for the week, giving them time alone together.

Joe wraps his arms around Lily. 'Be a good girl for Mammy and Daddy, and remember, if you change your mind, Uncle Stan or Freddie will bring you straight home, darling.'

Lifting Katie aboard his cart, Joe wraps a blanket around her shoulders.

Margo, looking as anxious as an old mother hen, climbs up to join Katie. 'We should've had a chat about ternight,' she says in a hushed voice.

Joe looks lovingly at Katie and winks, 'Come on Margo, old thing, don't you trust me? Why not let Katie have the pleasure of finding out for herself,' he says grinning broadly?

Margo's eyebrows raise, 'Oh, are yer sure, Joe, on'y it really ain't that simple?'

Katie leans forward, her cheeks reddening. 'Very sure Margo, I trust Joseph with my life.'

Looking somewhat put out, Margo scowls, 'Ahem, it wasn't yer life I were finkin' of gel. Now, Joseph, just remember what I told yer about.'

'Aye I will Margo, don't worry, Katie's mine to worry about now,' he tells her.

Katie does her best to keep a straight face, 'I'll be just fine, thank you.'

Seemingly placated, Margo nods, 'Aye, there's a good gel,' As she climbs down from the cart she whispers in Joe's ear, 'Mind yer take it nice and gentle when yer takes her, Joe.'

Joe nods reassuringly, barely able to hide his amusement. 'I hear you. Don't worry Margo, I'll look after her, don't worry.'

He chuckles to himself, if Margo knew the truth about sweet innocent Katie and the way she has turned into an insatiable nymphomaniac in such a short space of time, she'd have never believed him.

'Time to go, darling,' says Joe, and with a flick of the reins they are off.

Lilibeth waves and blows kisses as they pull away, joined by their friends, all waving furiously until the cart disappears from sight.

'Are you happy Mrs Markson, my precious wife?' he asks, tightening his arm around her.

'Deliriously so, my beloved husband,' she says, snuggling closer. 'Believe me, it was a shock, but a wonderful shock, so unexpected, but today has been glorious, oh I'm so happy, thank you, my darling husband.'

'I told you, I'm a man of my word, darling, didn't I promise you I would take you to church the minute it was possible, my darling wife?'

Expelling a long sigh of contentment Katie smiles, 'You did indeed.'

'Mmm, Mrs Joseph Markson. At last, we are legally married, you are all mine,' he whispers huskily, making her go weak at the knees. 'Oh Katie, my beloved wife, I love you so much.'

'Thank you for today,' she whispers, snuggling up to him. 'I'm happier now than I've ever been in my entire life, my dear impetuous, handsome husband.' Her voice is filled with emotion.

His eyes darken, 'Hum, I like the sound of 'my handsome husband' bit, I think I heard somewhere that all new wives should call their husband handsome, at least twice a day, first thing in the morning and last thing at night.'

'Well, if that's the rule then who am I to break it,' she says giggling.

Eventually they pull into the yard, Joe jumps down and holds up his arms. As he lifts her down, he kisses her tenderly, then, with Katie's shrill squeals, he proudly carries her over the threshold. 'Welcome home, my beloved wife.

Thanks to Freddie and without Katie's knowledge, the parlour is already lit with a small oil lamp and the fire ablaze in the hearth.

'Sit there, darling, and don't you dare move a muscle,' he tells her, 'I'll just see to the horse and cart,' he kisses the tip of her nose. 'I'll be right back!'

Katie smiles coyly, 'I'll be waiting.'

By the time he returns to the cottage, Katie has made two mugs of steaming milk and is sat gazing into the fire.

Hanging his jacket on the back of a chair he holds out his arms. 'Would my precious wife like a cuddle from her husband?'

She flies into his arms, burying her head against his chest, weeping.

Concerned, he lifts her face and kisses away her tears, 'Hey, Mrs Joseph Markson, you're not having second thoughts are you, darling?'

Katie shakes her head, 'No, no of course not, I'm just so happy. Everything was absolutely perfect, though I can't imagine how you managed to do it all, it must have cost you a small fortune!'

Shrugging his shoulders casually he kisses her nose, 'So what, darling, it's only money,' he says. 'But you, my precious wife, look simply stunning, your mother's gown, it is as beautiful as you, my love.' Gazing down at her with an all-consuming, salacious, look burning in his eyes, he adds huskily, 'Trouble is, my delicious wife, I can't wait to get you out of it.'

She gulps nervously, she's under his spell again. 'Oh help, perhaps we should drink our milk first,' she suggests shyly, remembering Margo's prophetic words about him stripping her naked.

Joe swallows a quick mouthful and grins mischievously. Sweeping her into his arms she shrieks, 'Oh help, put me down Joseph!'

Ignoring her protests, he carries her through to their bedroom, kissing her lightly on the lips, 'Will here do, Mrs Markson?'

Looking around the room she bites her lip, 'Yes, er… fine. Oooh Joseph, it's very bright in here.' To her surprise the curtains are closed and there are three large oil lamps burning so brightly it could be daylight, instead of the single small lamp that she has been used to.

Tonight, she is his wife, and he wants to see every glorious inch of her.

Quickly he takes off his cravat, removes his waistcoat and undoes the buttons on his shirt, sitting on the side of the bed he removes his shoes and socks. Sliding his shirt off his shoulders, he puts his hand on his trouser flies then waits, his seductive eyes focused on her painfully slow undressing, looking nervous. 'Hey, don't be shy my beautiful wife.'

She blinks as he drops his trousers revealing his pulsating erection.

'I want to watch you take your clothes off, darling,' he purrs seductively.

'I um… I can't, it's all the buttons at the back of my gown.' She points out, hoping to prolong the moment.

Shaking his head, his lips curl, stepping forward he is only too happy to help. One by one he undoes the tiny buttons on the back of her gown, when he reaches the last button, he plants several light kisses across her bare shoulders.

Now she is left with no alternative but to let it slide down her body to the floor, pooling at her feet. Timidly she fingers the ribbons on the bodice of her silky lace camisole, her heart begins to pound.

'Oh sweetheart, you're my wife now. Shall I do it for you?'

Katie's smile is feeble, 'All right, it's just…'

He moves closer, pushing the straps off her shoulders, 'Oh my beautiful wife.' He groans as her camisole falls to the floor. 'Oh yes, so beautiful, you're making me so hard. Look, do you like what you see sweetheart?' he asks, as he stands before her, desperate to hold her.

To Katie, everything is so different in the brightly lit room. Again, she recalls the statue that she had seen at Sheybourne. It was so like Joseph, very lean, with contoured muscles from head to toe, though one feature is so different to the statue. Gaping at Joe's willy it's standing erect and rigid, eager for her. Katie opens her mouth to speak, but nothing comes out, she nods shyly, trembling as she stands in her fancy, frilly French knickers, and the garter, halfway up her smooth thigh.

'Oh Katie, my beautiful wife,' he moans softly. 'Sweet Jesus, just look at you, you're stunning!' Making towards her he takes her in his arms, kissing her hungrily, sucking her tongue into his mouth, encouraging her to explore his mouth. 'Mmm, my sexy wife, at last, you are all mine,' he mutters softly. 'Can I take the rest of your clothes off, darling?'

Despite dreading this moment, she lowers her eyes and nods shyly.

Gently he cups her breasts, his thumbs teasing her nipples, then with laboured breath he kneels, sliding down her knickers revealing her brown curly mound. Splaying his hands on her buttocks, he pulls her forward, his nose parting her pubic hair, kissing her, moaning throatily as her body jerks to his touch as he circles his tongue around and around her sensitive clitoris.

'Oh, please, Joe. Oooo!' she cries out, her hands tugging his hair.'

'You like?' he smirks. Rising to his feet, his throat emits a long lustful moan as he savours in her perfect pert breasts with oh so tempting darkened prominent nipples, her very slim waist, slender hips, flat belly and the little mound of curly brown pubic hair at the top of her slim shapely legs, the sight of her heightening his desperate need for her.

In the brightly lit room, there is nowhere to hide and nowhere to look, except his beautifully contoured body. She shivers with edgy anticipation and gasps, his hardened cock standing up boldly from the bed of his dark curly hair.

Picking her up in his arms he carries her to their bed and carefully lays her down, not taking his lust-filled blue eyes off her for a second.

Breathing heavily, he takes her hand, leading it to his groin, 'Oh, my precious wife, hold me, darling.' His breathing increases rapidly as she

338

grasps him, he reacts by throbbing in her small hand. 'Oh darling, my beautiful, gorgeous wife.' He's breathless with an insatiable hunger, murmuring huskily in her ear, 'Oooh, my precious wife, play with me.'

His hand covers hers around his erection encouraging her to pleasure him, all the while whispering in his velvety, sensual voice, coaxing her, rousing her, urging her to absorb the pleasure of sharing and giving, driving her need higher.

Unable to control herself any longer, her emotions are heightened beyond belief, lost in the moment she surrenders to her innermost desire to please him. With one hand she tightens her hold on his willy, stimulating him, with her other hand she lightly runs up his inner thigh, cupping his balls, instigating a long soft throaty moan of pleasure as his breathing increases. Spurred on by his reaction, she relishes her newly found power of eliciting the intensity for him. The faster she rouses him, the more his muscles tighten, until, closing his eyes, he grasps her head, moaning in ecstasy. 'Stop Katie, stop! Please, darling, I'm gonna come!' His muscles ripple taut, but she doesn't stop, he shudders violently, letting out a long loud, drawn-out groan, calling out her name as he ejaculates.

Gazing at him in awe, she smiles triumphantly, 'Oooo, did I do it right? Did I please you, my darling husband?'

Groaning deep in his throat he holds her, 'Oooo, my sexy little woodnymph. Oh, sweet Jesus, yes, yes, yes! But you're a naughty girl, you're wasting my babies,.' he purrs, gasping to calm his breathing.

'I'm quite sure there's plenty more here,' she laughs softly as she strokes his manhood.

Raising himself up, he smirks, 'Is that so. Mrs Markson?' he says, playfully threatening her with his wagging finger, his eyes darken.

Still laughing, she springs to her feet and makes a dash into the parlour, her squeals of laughter filling every room.

He's in hot pursuit.

Katie squeals, runs through to the scullery, round the table until he finally catches her.

Stretching her arms out wide, he's filled with adoration, 'Oh dear God! Mmm, just look at my saucy, brazen wife, running around here completely naked. Oooh, bloody hell, I'm loving this,' he looks down, 'I'm so hard already, I want you, now!'

Tittering, her hands cover her mouth, 'And what about you, Mr Markson, running around with nothing on,' her eyes fall to his rigid cock. 'Oooo, especially with such a great big fat...' she giggles, she couldn't say it, could she? 'A great big fat willy. Oh help!'

As he stands stark-naked before her, she brazenly stares at his beautiful, tanned physique, and his willy. Oh, my dear lord, she could never have envisaged his manhood could grow so large. Katie points and gulps, 'oh help, look, it's grown again already!'

Gently he places his hands on her shoulders and looks at her with his sexy, bewitching eyes, 'Have you not heard of the story of Little Red Riding Hood, Mrs Markson? Let me see, how does it go? Oooh, what big eyes you've got. Hum, all the better to see every inch of your beautiful naked body with, my beloved wife. Oooh, what big hands you've got, all the better to caress with every inch of your divine body with, my precious wife.' he grins salaciously, looks down at his hard erection then looks at Katie. 'Oh, look, what a big cock you've got. All the better to take my beautiful wife and make love to her until she's pregnant, my sexy wife.'

Her eyes sparkle, and she cries out, 'Oh no, oh help!' she makes a dash through to the parlour, into the bedroom, where he manages to corner her, pinning her against the wall. 'Do you give in now, my deliciously sexy, precious wife?' he pants, his eyes gleaming with obvious lascivious intent.

Suddenly acquiring a daring gleam in her eyes, she giggles, yelps, and dips under his arm towards the open door. Joe catches her, pulling her into his arms, kissing her passionately, his tongue exploring her mouth, his eager cock pressed against her belly.

'I think it's time I make sweet love to my precious wife,' he declares in a deep husky tone, 'but this time is different, this time it's baby making time.'

Giggling playfully, she nods, 'Feel free my sexy husband,' her bright blue eyes challenging him. 'Take me now,' she purrs brazenly.

The giggling and laughter stops, as they cling together, naked, their hunger growing into primitive lust for each other.

Pleasurable whimpers turn to soft longing moans and groans of desire, 'Oh, my dearest sweet wife, I can't wait a minute longer.' He lays her carefully on the bed and kneels between her thighs, his erection is pulsating, waiting impatiently. 'Katie, my beautiful, sexy wife, I promise,' he pants breathlessly, 'to make love to you, tonight, tomorrow night, and every night that follows, my darling wife.' His velvety voice lowering as his breathing becomes heavier and laboured.

As she gazes into his darkening blue eyes, her hands grip fistfuls of his hair, pulling him down, her eyes are alive with need, 'Make love to me Joseph,' She whispers.

'Now, Mrs Markson?' he murmurs softly in her ear as he nuzzles into her hair.

Katie replies with desperate need in her voice, 'Oh please Joseph, now, my beautiful husband.'

Expelling a long primeval groan, he whispers, 'At last you are my precious wife, I love and adore you, darling.' He closes his eyes moaning softly as slowly he penetrates her, appreciating the exquisite tightness of her as her body welcomes him enthusiastically.

To Katie's joy, Joe proves to be gentle and loving, as they share the pleasure of their bodies joining as one, arousing, giving, and taking. All the while he talks softly, telling her he loves her, wants her and needs her, encouraging her to absorb and enjoy every pleasure radiating throughout her body. 'You're so beautiful, my darling wife, Oooo... sweet Jesus, I want you to come for me,' he gasps as he thrusts deep inside her again and again.

Her nails dig into his flesh as she cries out, 'Please Joseph, oh please!'

His eyes darken, glistening as he relishes the tightness as she clenches him in the throes of her orgasm, they come together, crying out noisily, joyously.

Replete they sleep, contentedly, their bodies and limbs interwoven together.

CHAPTER 14

What the time is, he can't be sure, he doesn't care anyway. He has awoken from his sleep to find his beloved wife curled naked, on top of the bed clothes, her gorgeous breasts pressed against his chest, her leg draped over his thigh and her hand still firmly clutching his cock, she's sleeping soundly.

It isn't easy to prise himself away from her, but doing his best not to disturb her, he carefully eases himself from under her and out of bed. Standing quietly, he drinks in her delectable, flawless naked body as she lays sprawled, peacefully sleeping, her unruly, auburn hair spread out on his pillow, her clear pale complexion, now tinted a delicate pink, he admires her small, tight rounded bottom, sighing a long, contented sigh he carefully pulls the throw over her body.

In the scullery the fire beneath the boiler is out, it feels chilly. Wrapping a towel around his waist, he tops up the boiler with water, stokes and adds logs beneath. It's time to cook his darling wife's breakfast.

Carrying the tray, he picks his way back from the scullery to the bedroom, he smiles to himself, her wedding shoes lay discarded on the floor in the parlour, their clothes, mixed with her underwear is scattered around the bedroom.

A tender kiss on her lips wakes her from her slumber.

Standing above her with the tray in his hands he smiles lovingly, 'Good morning Mrs Markson, did you sleep well, my sexy wife?'

As Katie stretches her body, her breasts pop out from under the cover, she looks serene and beautiful, she smiles dreamily, 'Mmm, I would have done Joseph, but a very handsome man with a great big fat willy made mad passionate love to me five times during the night, so no, I didn't get much sleep at all,' she teases with a wry smile on her lips. 'But I really didn't mind at all, in fact I loved every single minute of it!'

His flirtatious eyes shine, he sets the breakfast tray down on the table, shakes his head and tuts, 'Only five times my sexy little woodnymph, now that really won't do. We can't have my wife feeling neglected, can we?'

With a saucy glint in her eyes, she suddenly throws back the cover. Springing from the bed she snatches the towel from his waist, fleeing through to the parlour, shrieking wildly as he chases her into the scullery, around the table and back into the parlour.

Both stand laughing and panting, waiting for the other to make a move.

A sound by the front door startles her, 'Joseph! Who's that?' she asks, covering her modesty with her hands.

Covering his groin with his cupped hands, he tiptoes to the window and peers out.

As soon as his back is turned, Katie giggles, seizing the opportunity, she pinches his backside then makes a dash back to the bedroom with Joe in hot pursuit. 'Ooo, look at you, it's a good job you've got big hands,' she sniggers

Grabbing her wrists, he holds her hands high, backing her against the wall, 'So my teasing little wife wants to play games, does she?' he murmurs, kissing her hungrily. Laying her carefully on the bed he plants kisses from her head to her toes, his hands gently caressing her body, 'I think it's time to make our baby, darling.'

Katie responds eagerly, and once more they make tender love.

By mid-afternoon, they both wake feeling ravenous, the fire under the boiler has long gone out. Still naked, Joe opens the scullery door to collect some logs.

Katie yelps, 'Oooo, help, Joseph, don't go out like that, put some clothes on!' she calls after him as he rushes out of the door.

Joe returns, grinning, 'And pray who's gonna see me? The birds?' he asks, as he carries in several logs.

Katie appears to have had a miraculous loss of all her inhibitions, after twenty hours of very erotic lovemaking. Despite the fact it now broad daylight and she is still completely naked; she'd seemingly found herself a wickedly saucy and daring sense of humour too. Giggling, Katie puts her hands to her mouth and quips, 'I was thinking of the thieving magpies, in the garden. They have big strong beaks you know,' her eyes twinkle, 'they might fly down and peck off your big fat willy!'

Taking hold of his cock he waggles it temptingly. 'Would you miss this if I lost it, my darling wife?' he asks with the look of devilment and lust burning like fire in his eyes.

Breathing rapidly, Katie giggles, 'Oh my dear Lordy, of course I would, my sexy beloved,' she squeals and sprints into the parlour.

As Joe chases her out of the scullery, he spots something that's been slipped under the door. 'Hold up, darling, what's this?' he asks, handing her a piece of paper.

As she stands reading the note, his hands wander over her body, playing special attention to the sensitive, responsive areas that he'd found the during the night.

Katie wriggles and squirms as she reads the note, 'Mam says ter tell yer that Joanie's gotta baby boy, a real whoppa. Lily's happy and sends her love. We'll see yer on Friday. I've milked the cows and the goat and taken the eggs as promised, coz yer both probably too busy. Freddie.'

Katie gasps, her eyebrows shoot up, 'Oooo help, oh, Joe, that noise we heard earlier, it must have been Freddie!'

'Whoops, sorry sweetheart, I forgot to tell you, Freddie's gonna see to the animals this week,' he admits. Grinning he shrugs his shoulders, 'Huh, as you're both very busy indeed. Typical of the Hoopers, they're all sex mad. Hey up, better watch out young Verity, you're going to have your hands full with Freddie, or is it, he'll have his hands full with Verity. Hum, it seems our Freddie's as saucy as his mam and dad,' he says, laughing raucously, then he flees to the bedroom.

Flushed, Katie chases after him, 'Oh Joseph, you can be very rude sometimes, fancy saying things like that about Freddie.' She stops dead in her tracks, 'Do you... do you think he saw us both with erm... no clothes on?'

Pulling her down on the bed, he chuckles, 'Nah, he's not a peeping Tom sweetheart. So, I suggest, in future, you simply close the curtains before chasing after me around the house with nothing on!' he quips light-heartedly, then falls back on the bed laughing.

'Joseph, stop it, you're teasing me, it's not funny,' she pouts.

'I think it is, darling, I also think we should work on broadening your sense of humour, my wonderful sexy wife.'

Giggling she climbs on the bed, straddling his sleek body, deliberately arching her back tantalising him with her breasts, 'Is that right husband, so, what can we do about that?'

His hands go up to cup her breasts, 'Oh sweetheart, I've got lots of ideas,' he says as he pulls and rolls her nipples. Inwardly he's loving her newly found brazen enthusiasm. At last, her horrendous past is behind her, and best of all, she is happily embracing intimacy with her beloved husband. He feels that at last, she had been liberated and blossomed into a free spirit. 'Humm, let's make babies darling.'

Exhausted and replete they lay, their bodies entwined together and drift into another blissful sleep.

Hours later, Joe lights the fire and the fills the tin bath so they can bathe together, whilst Katie prepares their first proper meal since they were wed.

Until Lily returns, as a special request by her sexy new husband, Katie happily wears nothing. Saying her dress is completely unnecessary, as it blocks his view of her pert breasts. He tells her they are his, and he is entitled to easy access to them at any time, as he is her loving husband.

Katie fully agrees and unashamedly complies to her husband's wishes.

They've not eaten for at least twenty-four hours, and both are ravenous. 'Happy, darling?' he asks, as they sit eating.

Smiling, Katie stretches across the table and kissed him, 'More than you can ever know, my darling husband,' she answers, 'and you?'

He smiles tenderly, eyeing her oh so tempting breasts, 'So much so that I think I've died and gone to heaven, my beloved wife.'

Between cuddles and kisses and so many playful long, drawn-out intimate moments, including four more different, exciting ways of making love, they manage to share the menial but necessary chores of washing up, cooking meals and stoking the fires.

As they relax on the bed, he shuts his eyes, picturing the vision of Katie in her wedding gown, he sighs, 'You know, sweetheart, I will never forget our wedding day. When you walked down the aisle on Freddie's arm, you actually took my breath away, you looked... simply stunning in your beautiful gown. You're so right, it is the most exquisite gown, darling.'

'You know it's funny how things turn out, Joe, it was as if the dress was made to be my wedding gown,' she says wistfully, remembering the moment when her precious mother had given it to her.

'You could well be right my love; I reckon life's all down to fate. If it hadn't rained, if you hadn't sheltered in my barn, if you hadn't milked my cow... hum, definitely fate,' he says philosophically, 'Oh yes, because when fate deals its hand, it's up to us to pick up the cards.'

Katie can't pretend she knows what he's on about, she exhales, 'I'm sure you're right, Joe. You know I still can't believe you organised so much in such a short space of time. You quite literally thought of absolutely everything, it was all so perfect. Thank you, darling.'

He laughs. 'Good friends, a lot of delegating and money, that's all it took, my precious wife.'

'I know, but I mean everything, right down to my Mamma's dress and shoes!'

Joe hugs her close, 'You told me about it, remember. You told me you had to leave the trunk behind when you left Penfold Grove.'

'I know, but how, when?'

'Darling I knew how much the gown meant to you, it seemed obvious that you should be married wearing your mother's splendid gown, so I took a ride over there myself. Not a problem, is it, darling?'

'Joseph, it was simply perfect, I actually fainted when Margo brought it out. You are so considerate, darling, it was unbelievably thoughtful of you to even think of it,' she says. 'You know, when I put on the gown, I really felt that Mammy was there, with me.'

'I'm quite sure she was, my precious,' he tells her as his hand caresses her naked back.

'Joseph,' she frowns, 'I swore that I'd never go near that place, ever again!'

'Well, you didn't have to, I did. Anyway, what are you going to do with it?' he asked nonchalantly.

'What, my gown?'

'No, darling, Penfold Grove.'

Her expression changes instantly, her body goes rigid, she stares at him with pain in her eyes, 'What do you mean, do with it?'

He rolls on his side to face her, 'Soames is dead, and at the time of his death you were still legally married, so everything is now yours, the smallholding and everything in and around it, all the land, the lot.'

Agitated, she sits up, scowling, 'But I don't want it, I hate the place!' she insists fiercely.

Annoyed with himself for raising the subject and upsetting her, he takes her in his arms. 'Darling I'm so sorry, I shouldn't have mentioned it, I wouldn't upset you for the world. I guess we can discuss it when you feel you're ready, there's no rush,' he hugs her close in his arms and murmurs in her ear. 'I hate upsetting you, forgive me sweetheart?' he apologises profusely. 'Come, Mrs Markson, give your very handsome husband a cuddle, I love you, my beloved wife.'

Wrapped safely in his arms, the nightmare memories of her time at Penfold Grove fade to the back of her mind, 'And I love you too, my darling husband,' she purrs.

At Joe's insistence, late in the afternoon, still naked, they stroll hand in hand to collect the chickens' eggs, 'No regrets my sweet love?'

'Maybe just one,' she answers.

He stops dead in his tracks. 'You have?'

Struggling to hide her mirth, Katie nods, 'Yes, that I didn't meet you seven years ago,' she says, flashing her pale blue eyes at him.

He frowns, pulls her down in the grass and sits beside her, 'We've discussed all this, darling, we can't alter the past,' he sighs. 'I swear I will do my level best to wipe those memories away, I promise.' He changes the subject quickly, 'Our Lily was a perfect little angel on our wedding day, she looked so sweet bless her, she's so like you Katie. And now she's my daughter, I love her dearly. Lily's a very precious gift to both of us, but I'm missing her dreadfully.'

'I know Joseph, me too, but she'll be home with us tomorrow, then we can be a proper family.'

Gazing at her, his eyes darken and carnal longing burns in his eyes, 'So my most precious, sexy wife, shall we make our baby now?'

There was a suppressed giggle from Katie, 'Ooo, I thought we'd already made a pretty good start, my insatiable husband.'

347

He looks smugly proud, 'Well you've not done too badly yourself, my brazen little woodnymph. The mischievous look in his eyes suddenly turns to one of intense desire, 'Now back to that regret I mentioned earlier.'

'Regret, oh Joseph, you have a regret?'

'Uh huh, didn't I say? I regret that until now, we've never made love, naked in the grass, under the warmth of sun.'

'Oh eek! I don't know if I could do that Joseph, it's broad daylight!' she protests.

Taking her comment as a challenge, he chuckles as he takes her in his arms, gently laying her back in the long grass, he's already hard and desperate to take her. His lips curl, 'What shall we have first, my darling wife, a boy or a girl?'

Flushed with a highly arousing ache for him, Katie groans with need, 'Oooh, Joseph, take me. A boy or a girl, whatever? Though I don't think we have a choice, darling. I just need you to love me!'

Beneath the warmth of the sun, they savour the joy of sharing their love for each other. Katie writhes uncontrollably beneath him as gently he rouses and encourages her with his finger teasing her clitoris, then oh so lovingly fills her with his love.

As he helps her to her feet he smiles broadly, 'Hum, not a single regret left.'

By the end of their honeymoon, they have become inseparable.

Beyond Joe's expectations, Katie's proves to be insatiable, they even made love as they bathed together, in the tin bath in the scullery, all new experiences eagerly and enthusiastically embraced by Katie.

After six uninhibited, erotic days of marriage, they are due to collect Lilibeth from Margo's.

Rising before dawn, Katie cooks him a special breakfast. 'Good morning, beloved husband of mine, wakey, wakey. I've brought your breakfast.'

He opened one eye then the other then sits bolt upright, Katie is stood completely naked, holding a tray. 'Good morning, my sexy husband, your breakfast is served,' she repeats.

Stretching his body, he gazes at her with pure unadulterated lust in his eyes, 'Mmm, forget the food, my love. The only appetite I have, is for my sexy wife.'

No coaxing needed, she sets the tray down, and without any hint of embarrassment, she mounts his thighs, ensuring that it turns into highly charged, voracious lovemaking that culminates in both crying out in ecstasy as they climax together.

As she comes, Joe's muscles tighten, he groans deep in his throat as he holds her hips, pressing her down so that he can come deep inside her again. 'Sweet Jesus. Katie!' he cries out as he fills her with his love.

'Oooo, Joseph,' she coos, sighing contentedly, 'I love you so much,' she mutters, as she lay replete on his heaving chest.

Opening her eyes, she sighs. 'What's the time, darling?' she asks sleepily.

His fingers run down her spine, holding her firm buttocks, pressing her to him. 'Oh hell, you have such a peachy bum, my darling, you have a perfect fanny too, in fact you have a perfect everything.'

Blushing, Katie smiles, 'Why thank you kind sir, you're pretty perfect yourself. So, what time do you think it is, Joe?' she asks again.

This time it is Joe, that sighs, 'I've no idea my love, but I think we should get up. We've got to fetch Lily.'

They set off to collect Lilibeth, blissfully happy, 'I can't wait to see her,' says Katie.

He nods, 'Me too, I've missed our little princess.'

Almost to Fennydown, they can't resist stopping, to take advantage of their last few moments alone together. In the back of the cart, they made love, she cries out, whimpering in ecstasy as he grunts and moans pumping her until joyfully elated, they both climax as one.

Joseph smiles to himself, her response to their lovemaking, always passionate, highly satisfying and very noisy, 'Mmm, I think, my darling wife, we should stay in the downstairs bedroom, because with Lily back home, you'd wake the hibernating squirrels right down in the spinney, when we make love, let alone Lily, if we are in the room next door.'

Katie, who just weeks ago, would have died of sheer embarrassment at his comment, giggles, putting the blame fairly and squarely on his shoulders, for being such an expert teacher, driving her to distraction with pleasure. Besides, Katie points out, he was far from a silent lover himself!

Joe liked the sound of being termed her lover and is instantly stimulated, his sensual flirtatious eyes flash with desire, it's only their anxiousness to be reunited with Lilibeth, that curbs their ravenous sexual appetites.

With a flick of the reins, he urges the horse to break into a trot, his arm firmly around her waist.

'Do you think she's been all right?' Katie asks anxiously.

'Believe me, if she wasn't happy, Freddie or Stan would have brought her home. Lily has Daisy, and there's the new baby to occupy her too.' he gives Katie a kiss. 'Hopefully, it will be our turn next darling.'

Their cart pulls into Wickers yard. Lilibeth, her little face beaming, is carried out on Freddie's arm to greet them, closely followed by Margo and Edna.

'Mammy, Daddy!' she squeals, holding up her arms.

Joe lifts her onto the cart, giving her a big hug, 'We've missed you so much, my little princess.'

'I missed you too, Daddy.' she says wrapping her arms around both of their necks.

'Have you been a good girl for Aunty Margo?' asks Katie, on the receiving end of a big wet kiss.

Lilibeth nods, 'Course I have, Mammy.'

'She bin a little angel bless her, a real joy ter have her here.' Margo says beaming. 'Come on in, we've cooked yer both a dinner. They are all here ter see yer.'

Greeted with a resounding cheer as they enter the scullery, hugs and kisses are exchanged all round.

'Congratulations on the birth of your son Jed!' says Joe, vigorously shaking Jed's hand.

'What's he called?' Katie asks.

Proudly Jed puffs his chest out, 'Noah, on account of the day he was born, the heavens opened, and it rained so hard we thought we'd have a ruddy flood!'

Katie laughs, she didn't recall any rain that day, but then she'd been pretty occupied with her handsome, extremely virile husband to notice the weather. 'Are they both all right?' she inquires.

Jed beams with pride, 'Couldn't be better, ta ever so. Joanie reckons all the jiggin' about on the cart comin' back from yer weddin' did the trick. I'll take yer both up when we've eaten, yer can meet me first born son, Noah,' he says grinning.

'Oooo, we'll look forward to that,' says Katie.

'I saw Noah when he was just been borned!' says Lily excitedly, 'I want a baby brother for me too,' she declares. 'Can I have one, daddy?'

Everyone laughs, all looking at Katie, who blushes profusely and lowers her eyes.

'I fink it'll take a little while Lilibuff,' says Margo, 'Yer see, little babies takes a long time ter grow from a tiny seed, sweetheart.'

Lilibeth's face is serious, 'From a seed? What seed? So how long has I got to wait then, two weeks?' she asks innocently.

Everyone chuckles then falls silent, all ears waiting for Margo's answer, which was likely to be amusing, if not blunt and to the point.

Joe's arm tightens around Katie's waist, her eyes widening, and her mouth dropping open, he gives her a squeeze chuckling. 'Hang on Katie love, this should be interesting,' he whispers. 'Come on Margo, let's hear your explanation,' he prompts.

Margo shrugs, 'Yer needs plenty of lovin' Lilibuff,' she explains, looking straight at Katie and Joe.

Taking it all in, Lilibeth's expression is serious, 'Well that's all right then, coz my daddy is always tellin' my mammy he loves her and keeps kissing her all day,' she informs them, then carries on eating as if it was a satisfactory the end to the matter.

Katie is more than thankful that Margo doesn't go into more explicit details, because until Stan's enlightenment she had never understood the meaning of the expression loving, Ooo er, she certainly does now.

'Leaning across to Katie, Joe whispers, 'Sheep, darling, don't forget the sheep.'

Everyone agrees that the wedding was the finest, happiest wedding the village has ever attended.

'Well, ain't this a right nice family gatherin' now,' says Margo, sitting next to Katie, she leans closer and whispers, 'Katie love, was everyfin' alwight wiv you and Joe, in his bed like?'

Turning bright red, Katie bites her lip and swallows, 'All right?'

Margo smiles kindly, 'Yer know what I mean gel'

She stares at Margo, shared intimacy between herself and Joseph was one thing, but she wasn't about to share any details with Margo, best friend or not, 'Mmm.' Is all she volunteers and gets on with eating.

As the meal progresses, the happy mayhem of mixed conversations and laughter grows louder, reminding Katie of the confusing, yet glorious day of her wedding, when her life had changed forever. Was it really only six short days ago?

Sat curled up on Joe's lap, Lily asks, 'Does you want to see baby Noah now, daddy?'

'We'd love to princess,' says Joe, 'wouldn't we Katie?' Margo leads the way upstairs.

'You have to be very quiet, coz he is only little,' explains Lilibeth putting her finger to her lips.

'I dunno about that,' laughs Margo, 'I reckon he must be a good ten pounds, not bad fer a ruddy first.'

Katie frowns, for a fleeting second, she remembers all her miscarriages.

Joe reassuringly slides his arm around Katie, 'It'll be our turn next, darling, if we're lucky,' he whispers in her ear, giving her a squeeze.

Katie smiles at Joe. Somehow, he always makes her feel better.

Sitting on the bed, Katie holds the crying infant in her arms, Lilibeth is one side of her, Joe the other.

'He's tiny,' comments Joe, studying the crying bundle.

'But isn't he adorable?' coos Katie, stroking his fair downy hair.

Soothed by Katie's soft voice, the infant stops crying.

Watching Katie cradling the tiny infant, Joe glows inside, it brings out paternal feelings that, until recently, he didn't even know he had. He couldn't wait for the day when he could hold their own baby in his arms and make their lives complete.

Lilibeth saunters round beside Joe and puts her arm around his neck, 'Can I have a baby brother like Noah Daddy, pleeease?'

Winking at Katie he sits Lily on his knee, 'I know princess, your mammy and me, we'd like one too, but we have to be patient and wait a while,' he explains. 'Besides, we're a pretty new family and your mammy and me, want to make the most of having our little princess all to ourselves for a while.'

'But we will get one Daddy, promise?'

Looking at Katie he smiles, 'I certainly hope so, my little princess. Will you help mammy look after it sweetheart?'

'Course I will Daddy.'

After much badgering on Lilibeth's part, before they leave for home, arrangements have been made for her to stay with Margo and Stan every weekend, weather permitting.

'We'd love her ter stay, she's a little angel, and besides, it'll give the pair of yer a bit of time on yer own,' says Margo smirking. 'Our Freddie says he'll ride over ter pick her up every Friday afternoon, he can pick up our wood order at the same time, it'll save yer both a journey.'

'Would you like to stay, Lily?' they ask.

A very enthusiastic grin and nod from Lily is their answer.

'Right, well that's agreed. Thanks Freddie, you're a real pal. Hum, best we make tracks then,' says Joe rising from the chair.

Wrapped in a blanket, Lilibeth, clutching a parcel containing her clothes, and bed covers for Daisy's cradle, sits in the back of the cart with Daisy.

Joe settles into married life so easily he amazes himself, he feels like a new man, with a strong sense of purpose in life. By the time autumn turns to winter, he'd built an extension to provide a more spacious parlour. They purchased several thick rag rugs from Margo to cosy the rooms. There were ongoing discussions regarding extending and improving the scullery when spring came, along with the added luxury of building a separate washroom that would include a chimney and fireplace, providing warm accommodation for a large tin bath.

Katie, still as euphoric as the day she married Joseph, is counting her blessings daily, thriving on the ever growing, deep love she shares with her beloved husband.

Lilibeth is, for the first time in her life, enthralled with the rewards of their marriage, having gained something that she had never known in her short life, the most wonderful, devoted and loving father. She had also slipped happily into the routine of spending the weekends staying with Margo and Stan. Every Friday afternoon, weather permitting, either Stan or Freddie would collect a supply of wood and take Lilibeth home with them. Come Sunday afternoon, Joe and Katie would travel to Fennydown for afternoon tea and collect Lilibeth.

The most enlightening occasion for Lily came when the sheep were delivered. Joe explains that they are all lady sheep called ewes.

The day the ram is delivered to be let loose on the sheep; Joe insisted they were all there together to witness the event.

Looking curious Lily looks up to Joe. 'Daddy, why's he painting that new sheep red under his tummy?'

Joe kneels beside her; he glances at Katie who is biting her lip nervously. 'Ahem, he's a man sheep, called a ram, he's got a willy under there,' he explains, he looks at Katie, but she just shrugs her shoulders. 'All the rest are lady sheep, called ewes. Henry paints the ram so that we'd know if he'd coupled with the ewes, if he does then we will have little lambs born in the spring.'

Lilibeth nods, listening pensively. 'We'd like some baby lambs in the spring, wouldn't we, Mammy.'

Katie chews her lip, nods, but remains silent.

'Ahh look daddy!' says Lilibeth, pointing to the ram, 'He's cuddlin' that lady sheep, isn't that nice?'

'So, he is, darling. When he climbs on the ewe's back, he puts his seed in her tummy and it will grow into a baby lamb, it will be born early next spring.' He clears his throat. 'Ahem, do I need to explain it again, darling?'

Lily shakes her head, 'No Daddy. The man sheep puts his willy in the lady sheep and makes baby lambs, just like Uncle Jed did to Auntie Joanie.'

Both Joe and Katie stared wide eyed at each other and gasp, raising their eyebrows.

'That's right, darling, aren't you clever!' says Joe.

'Yes, I am, coz Aunty Margo told me about boys and girls. She told me when I saw Noah's willy. Have you got a willy, Daddy?' she asked, looking straight faced at Joe.

Taken aback, he nods. 'Yes, my darling child, I have.'

Then she looked up at Katie, 'You haven't got one, have you, Mammy, coz you're a girl like me?'

Katie shakes her head and croaks, 'Er... you're quite right sweetheart.'

'If Daddy puts his willy in you, Mammy, we can have a baby brother like baby Noah,' she says smiling sweetly, 'Coz aunty Margo told me.'

Poor Katie could have fainted with shock. Dear Lordy, that blasted Margo Hooper had a lot to answer for!

Joe smiles down at Lilibeth, she had obviously taken it all in, 'You're right, my clever daughter, but we'd better leave the ram to it, we can see how many sheep have got red paint on their backs tomorrow, but right now we'd better go home, I'm starving.'

That evening, Joe's looking pleased with himself. Before her bedtime, he tells Lily the magpie story whilst she sits on Katie's lap. As usual, she falls asleep mid-story, together, they she settle her in bed in no time.

'Oh, dear Joseph, today was so awkward, what with Margo and her brazen loose tongue.'

Giving her a squeeze, he kissed the nape of her neck, 'Honest and simple my darling, Lily is very bright for her age. I think we can safely say that our daughter has learned a great deal about Mother Nature in the past week or more.'

Katie sighs, 'I know you're right my love, you did so well, I know I couldn't have done it, but thank goodness it's all over with.'

With the early onslaught of winter and shortening daylight hours, Joe is more than happy to spend less time working in the spinney and more time at home with his family. He also notes the marked difference in Katie since they'd married. Katie is blooming, and thankfully no longer suffering from the debilitating fainting spells that had worried him in the past, though he's becoming a little concerned that she still isn't pregnant, after all, they had had more than enough practice. He worries that her time with Soames had damaged and affected her in some way and that it might never happen.

Never-the-less, she had certainly put her terrible past behind her, she was no longer innocent as far as their sexual activities were concerned, unbelievably adventurous she now embraced all forms of their lovemaking with an arduous passion.

Life, he decided, was as good as he ever thought it could be. With Christmas almost upon them, he had carved a handsome wooden rocking horse with leather reins, now safely hidden in the barn, away from Lily's inquisitive eyes.

He had bought Katie, a long, dark blue coat trimmed with a fur collar, with a hat and gloves to match from Margo, along with a sensual promise to make this Christmas, one they would never forget.

From the money that the cheeses and her baking brought in, Katie had bought Joe two thick jumpers, knitted by Edna, a pair of sturdy boots, a thick, pure wool jacket and a hand knitted scarf with matching gloves, plus a discreet whispered promise of sharing a sexy, sudsy bath with her handsome husband before they went to bed on Christmas Eve.

Three days before Christmas, Stan and Margo visit, bringing Freddie and his newly announced fiancé, Verity, over to celebrate the event, a couple of brandies and a flagon or two of Joe's strong cider, ensured a very jolly night, and it was way after breakfast the following morning when the visitors finally went, tired, a bit too merry and exhausted, home to their beds.

At the end of January, they spend their winter evenings eagerly planning their future together. Katie is talking of overhauling his mother's flower garden, so that they can sell their produce at market in the summer.

Irritatingly, Stan is asking for more and more wood, no easy task when Joe is working on his own. Besides, he wants more time to spend with his family. However, the problem appears to be solved when the old blacksmith in Holdean dies suddenly. Mick's son Jed, had worked there as a Smithy for more than seven years, living in the Smithy's tied cottage.

On his death, the Smithy's widow had sold the business, including the cottage that Jed and Joanie occupied, now they were in dire straits.

With their predicament in his thoughts, inspiration strikes him, he broaches his idea to Katie, suggesting they might consider converting the outhouses between the barn and the dairy, for Jed, Joanie and baby Noah to live in, and offering Jed a job, working mainly in the spinney and the vegetable garden, pointing out that Joanie can help Katie in the dairy and scullery, whenever possible. Telling Katie, he wants to spend more quality time together.

'Why that's a wonderful idea, Joe. But can we afford it?'

Joe is straight to the point, 'Well money is a bit tight, though I do keep some by for a rainy day, what with winter and all. Of course, I can't afford to pay him as much as he earned at the Smithy, then there's all the furniture they'll need, but the walls of the outhouses are stone, and I've got all the wood we need to convert the buildings. Business can be quiet during the winter so if maybe Mick, Jed, Tom, Freddie and Stan can muck in, then I'm sure we can do it.'

Katie feels guilty, he had not only spent a fortune on their wedding day, but he had spent a great deal more on refurbishing their cottage to date. Then it comes to her, 'I... I um, I'd like to sell Penfold Grove, Joe.'

His eyebrows raised, shocked, 'You'd sell Penfold Grove, darling? No, I can't let you to do that!'

'It's just sitting there going to ruin, and there's all the furniture too, Jed and Joanie are welcome to it, it makes perfect sense to me.'

'But it's your inheritance, Lily's inheritance. No, darling, I can't let you do it. It's up to me to provide for my family! Look, I do have money, we'll be fine, with a good spring and summer working with Jed I'll soon build the coffers back up in no time,' he tells her stubbornly.

But Katie looks wounded, she's not about to be palmed off, 'Joseph Markson, I thought we were a partnership, we share everything!'

He wraps his arm around her, 'Aye, of course we are, of course we do.'

'Then, I want to sell Penfold Grove, I need to be rid of it!' she insists stubbornly, 'So if that place is our inheritance, like you say, then it makes good business sense to sell it and expand Briars, for us and for both our children's future.' She clams up and bites her lip, she had let the cat out of the bag way too soon.

It takes a moment or two for her last sentence to sink in, he sits with a quizzical look on his face, 'Katie?' he lifts her chin, looking her directly into her eyes, 'Katie, you said both our children, darling, are you saying what I think you're saying?'

It's no good, the prospects of producing their first born is something she simply has to share with him. Katie smiles shyly, but before she can open her mouth to answer, he stands, takes her in his arms and whoops for joy, 'Way hey! I'm gonna be a dad again!' he whoops again, 'Oh my clever darling, are you quite sure?'

She sighs, 'No Joseph, if I'm honest I'm not completely sure. I just think I might be.'

He promptly sits her down on the bed and joins her, 'Perhaps you should see a doctor sweetheart?' he suggests, trying to mask his concern. He's thinking of all the babies she had lost in the past.

'But I'm not ill, darling, I just might be pregnant.'

Joe can't contain his excitement, 'Just pregnant, just pregnant!' and he whoops again, darling how far gone are you, a week, a month, two months even?'

She shrugs, 'Calm down, Joe, I'm not absolutely sure, it's just… I've not felt too clever in the mornings recently, and I do feel different… sort of… well, pregnant,' she admits, splaying her hands over her belly.

Now he'd mentioned it, her tummy is no longer flat, in fact it feels quite firm and rounded.

There are tears of joy in his eyes, 'I'm taking you to Holdean to see a doctor. I'm sorry sweetheart, I can't risk anything happening to you, I don't know what I'd do if…'

'Hush now,' her finger on his lips to silence him. 'It's too soon, I've only missed one period by a week or two. So please Joseph, let's wait a while, just to make sure.'

Unconvinced, he shakes his head, 'Hum, I don't know, I don't think we should wait sweetheart.' Although she's always very slim, he can definitely feel a very firm bump. 'Our first born, oh, darling, you're so clever. Oh Lordy, I love you so much,' he says, cradling her in his arms, gazing at her lovingly, he whispers, 'I want to tell the whole world.' his deep blue eyes fired up with excitement, 'A little brother or sister for our Lily. Oh Katie, she'll be as thrilled as I am!'

'Oh, please Joseph, I don't want Lilibeth to be disappointed, or you for that matter, let's keep it between ourselves, just a little longer.'

His hand slides over her belly. 'You've definitely put on weight, darling,' he says smirking.

Katie giggles, 'I've probably eaten too much over Christmas,' though come to think of it, her clothes did feel uncomfortably tight around her waist.

But Joe, who after four months of wedded bliss, knows every inch of his wife's body, is adamant, he takes Katie's hand and places it over her belly. To her surprise her belly feels solid, bewildered, she sits bolt upright, 'Oooh! But I can't be that far gone. I don't understand.'

His eyebrows shoot up, he grins, 'Oh my sexy little woodnymph, do I have to spell it out for you.'

Blushing she digs him in the ribs, 'No, what I mean is… I could be as much three months gone!'

'Christ, this gets better and better!'

All too aware of Katie's previous problems, Joe insists that they will travel to Holdean in the morning, to pay a visit the doctor.

Running her fingers through his hair she coos, 'Make love to me, Joe.'

Caressing her breasts his eyes shoot to Katie, 'Sweetheart, your belly's not the only thing that's changing. Mmm, your lovely titties are rounder, sort of bigger, your nipples are darker too. Oh, my sweet love…' Moaning with pleasure he tugs on each nipple in turn. His erection is throbbing painfully, he wants her badly, but should they? Unsure he frowns, 'Do you think it's it safe to make love, darling?'

Her need for him is equally as strong, but she knows he's concerned about her many early miscarriages, 'If I'm three months and we're careful, I'm sure it'll be fine, I need you, Joe. Make love to me, please.' Her hand slides down to his groin. 'I need you.'

Slowly and gently, they made love.

The following morning, unable to contain his joy, against Katie wishes, he announces to Lily that she's going to have a brother or sister.

As expected, Lily is over the moon, demanding to know when she was getting her baby brother.

'That, sweetheart, we don't know, so were visiting the doctor today to find out Lily. Um, we don't know if it's a boy or a girl,' he points out, 'we'll just have to wait and see.'

CHAPTER 15

Rapping at the door, Joe, paces impatiently up and down until it is eventually opened by a wizened little woman, and they are cordially invited inside.

'Name?' she asks curtly.

Mr and Mrs Joseph Markson and our daughter, Lilibeth,' obliges Joe.

They are invited to sit and wait in a sparse little room, furnished with four wooden chairs, a small table and two framed certificates on the wall, and nothing else. 'Good day to you. I'm Mrs Entwistle,' she says stiffly, 'Doctor Jerimiah Entwistle will see you after his present patient leaves. Do take a seat,' she tells them and bustles out of the room.

Fifteen minutes later, a door marked 'Doctor' opens, a young man with a heavily bandaged hand is escorted out. Joe stands but the door is closed on him.

Not used to being kept waiting, especially when he's paying, Joe scowls, irritated he sits back down again.

Lily clambers up on his lap which helps break the tension, relaxing him enough to calm his frustration.

A hand bell ringing breaks the silence. Mrs Entwistle scurries back into the waiting room, 'Doctor Entwistle will see you now, which one of you is to see the doctor, may I ask?'

Joe stands, towering above her, 'All of three of us ma'am, thank you,' he says politely, ushering Katie and Lilibeth forward.

Eyeing them suspiciously, Mrs Entwistle frowns, as she reluctantly directs them all into the doctor's office, following closely behind them, she closes the door, standing with her arms folded.

Much to their surprise, the doctor turns out to be quite young and good looking.

The woman clears her throat, 'Ahem, Doctor Entwistle, this is Mr and Mrs Joseph Markson, and their daughter, um...'

'Lilibeth Markson,' Joe reminds her.

'Hum, yes, well, do take a seat,' says Mrs Entwistle, beckoning them to sit.

The Doctor looks up, smiling pleasantly, 'Thank you, mother, I'll call you if I need you,' he tells her, waving his hand, directing her to leave the room.

'Good morning, what can I do for you all,' he asks as he studies his three prospective paying patients.

'It's my wife, Katerina, she's pregnant, in actual fact we think she might be three months gone,' explains Joe.

'Hum, I see,' replies the doctor nodding, he reaches for the hand bell and rings it.

His mother enters the room so fast that one could have been forgiven for thinking she'd been listening at the door, 'Yes Doctor?'

'I wish to examine Mrs Markson, would you escort Mr Markson and the child outside to the waiting room, then come back in?'

His mother nods, looking triumphantly at Joe, 'Certainly Doctor, this way Mr Markson.'

Joe stubbornly stands his ground, 'I'm sorry, but I... we, all three of us would like to stay.' Leaning forward he lowers his voice, 'You see I've got my worries about all this.'

Mrs Entwistle cuts Joe an old-fashioned look and tuts, her pinched face full of disapproval, 'Sir, it is always customary for the husband to wait outside. I shall accompany your wife, so, if you don't mind...'

The doctor raises his hand smiling kindly, 'It's fine mother, take Mrs Markson behind the curtain and help her undress, I'll be with you in just a moment.' He waits until Katie and his mother disappears behind the curtain and then leans towards Joe, lowering his voice 'You said you have worries?'

Joe glances nervously at Lilibeth and leans even closer, saying in a hushed voice, 'Er... my wife was married before sir, she was very badly treated and severely abused by her first husband. Because of that she has had several early miscarriages in the past, if you understand what I mean,' adding, 'I need to know that Katie and our baby, are all right.'

'Right Mr Markson, well then, let me see if we can put your mind to rest,' he says, rising he scrubs and dries his hands then disappears behind the curtain.

When he emerges, some fifteen minutes later the doctor is smiling and offering his hand, 'Congratulations Mr Markson, I have given your wife a thorough examination and I'm pleased to say that your wife and baby are coming along just fine. The baby has a very strong heartbeat, and I can't foresee any major problems,' he said confidently.

Lilibeth's look is one of amazement, 'You can hear the baby Doctor, is he talking then?'

Chuckling at the young child's forthright curiosity he nods, 'Indeed I can hear it, though it's not talking, but if you put your ear to your mammy's tummy with this,' he says holding up a small trumpet shaped metal object, 'you will hear the baby's heart beating. Here,' he says offering it to Lilibeth, 'you can take it home with you, your mammy will show you what to do.'

Lilibeth looks as pleased as punch, proudly holding it up, 'Oh thank you very much doctor. Look, Daddy.'

Katie joins them from behind the curtain, looking highly flushed, to find Joe and Lilibeth beaming.

'When's I getting my brother then, please?' asks Lilibeth impatiently.

'Hang on Lily, let us hear what the doctor has to say first,' says Joe.

'Let me see, it's the end of January, hum,' the doctor studies something on his desk then looks up, 'I would say... hum... I would say, probably around the 20th to the 28th of April.'

Wide-eyed, Joe and Katie gape open mouthed at him.

'Yes, about eleven weeks till your confinement. Now the baby is on the small side, so I'd like to see you again in four weeks, just to keep an eye...'

Shocked they are still staring at the doctor in amazement.

Clearly Katie is stunned, 'But that makes me just over six months pregnant! Good grief, I had no idea I could be that far gone!'

The doctor relaxes back in his chair and clasps his hands over his waistcoat, he glances at Joe and back to Katie, 'Yes well it's not at all unusual Mrs Markson, with your past history. You see it upsets your monthly workings, so to speak. Now I want you to take reasonably light exercise daily, at least eight hours sleep, a good diet, including plenty of milk. Both you and the baby need to put on weight, most importantly, make sure you put your feet up and rest more often.' The doctor stands, 'Would you see them out, please Mother. Make a note of all their particulars and make an appointment for Mrs Markson in a month,' he smiles pleasantly, 'Good day and congratulations, once again.'

'I'll join you in the waiting room, darling, I need to pay the bill,' says Joe, closing the door behind the girls.

'Is there be anything else I can help you with sir?' inquires the doctor.

Joe shifts from foot to foot, 'You said the baby is small., sir, we have a friend that until recently, was pregnant, she was huge, are you quite sure about the dates doctor?'

Doctor Entwistle nods, 'Yes, yes, I'm quite sure. Allow me to put it simply. All pregnancies are varied and different. Your wife is very trim, the length and size of the baby, how much water there is, etc, etc, tells me so,' adding, 'Mr Markson, babies come in all sizes, and grow quickly in the last two months or so. Now, you need to look after her, feed her up and make sure that she rests.'

'Um, yes thank you doctor, I certainly will,' Joe dithers.

'Well? Is there anything else I can help you with?' asks the doctor.

Joe looks around to make sure that his mother is out of the room, 'Yes sir, erm... man to man Doctor, my wife and I... we only married a few months ago and I'd really appreciate your advice,' Joe's frowns, he might be a doctor but he's very young, 'In view of my wife's past history of miscarriages, erm... making love... it won't harm my wife or our baby, will it?'

The doctor smiles compassionately and pats his shoulder. 'Yes well, I'll be perfectly frank with you, as you might have noticed, I'm not of the old school. Young doctors now-a-days have new ideas.' If truth be known, he was highly impressed with the novelty that a man would have the slightest interest in his wife and her pregnancy. Most men that he came across would wait until the child is born, before picking up where they'd left off. 'Mr Markson, your wife is in remarkably good health. However, the baby is a tad on the small side, so your wife needs to put on more weight. Apart from that. Shall we say a contented mother-to-be, ahem, in bed, makes for a happy baby, and indeed, that includes the father too, for that matter.' Pausing he looks Joe straight in the eye, 'Though as she gets nearer to her confinement, you will probably, shall we say, improvise positions somewhat. I um, I can offer you further advice if you so wish,' he offers genially.

Joe grins, 'I'm sure we can manage sir, thanks all the same.' and shakes his hand vigorously.

Joe walks out into the sunshine, his head held high, his shoulders back, he inhales a lung full of air, yelling at the top of his voice, 'Were having a baby!'

'Oh, my clever darling, we'll take a nice easy ride and call in at Fennydown on the way home, I can't wait to see Stan and Margo's faces when we give them our wonderful news,' he beams.

With Lily on his lap and Katie snuggled up close, he throws a blanket over them all. 'It looks like the idea of employing Jed and renovating the outhouses for them is a necessity now, darling. What do you think?'

Katie pulls a face, 'To tell you the truth, I feel a bit torn. I know you need help with the business, and yes, they do need somewhere to live… but I love it, being just the three of us, well three and a half of us,' she tells him.

'Sweetheart, they can live with Mick and Edna till the cottage is finished. Then they'll have their own front door across the yard and so, my darling will we. But I like the idea of having someone around, now that you're expecting our precious baby.' He pecks her lovingly on the cheek.

'Oh, don't take any notice of me, Joe, I'm being selfish. Of course, it's a good idea.'

'Nay Never!' I don't ruddy believe it, Katie Markson, yer not on'y pregnant but yer say yer over six monfs gone!' Margo does some quick calculations in her head and smirks, 'Good gawd, well I never did!' she exclaims, all agog, 'My, yer a fast worker Joseph Markson, make no mistake!'

Stan coughs, 'Well he must have done gel,' he quips grinning, he's equally delighted for them both.

Overjoyed but not really surprised at Katie's bemusement, finding out she was so far-gone Margo pats Katie's belly, 'Humm, I fink yer needs building up a bit gel. I'm so happy fer the pair of yer,' She declares sincerely, sending Stan outside to fetch a jug of cider.

'Ter wet the baby's head,' Stan explains to Katie who is tutting.

'See what I got,' says Lilibeth, producing the little trumpet with the earpiece the doctor had given her, 'it's to listen to my little brother with.'

Margo chuckles, 'Ooo really? Well, yer never know Lilibuff, the good Lord might send yer a little sister, we has ter have what the good Lord sends us, darlin'.'

'I don't mind,' replies Lilibeth, 'Coz I'm gonna help look after him, with my mammy and daddy.'

Deciding that with Katie pregnant it is even more important than ever that he should get some extra labour sorted out, so that he can spend more time with his family, he decides to run past Stan the possibility of offering Jed and Joanie a job and a home. 'Stan, what's happening with Jed and Joanie, have they found somewhere to live yet? What about his job?'

Looking glum, Stan shakes his head, 'Nah, it's worryin' it is. I mean, me and Margo can put them up fer a little while, but what wiv a growin' baby.'

'Well, I've got a proposition for them, if they're interested,' states Joe, then outlines the possibility of converting the outhouses into a home and giving Jed a job.

'Well blow me down, what a bloomin' God send, that's right good of yer Mate. There ain't no call fer anover Smiffy round these parts fer Jed, in fact there ain't that many full-time jobs at all round these parts. The bloke what bought the Smiffy has got two strappin' sons workin' fer him, so...'

'Tell you what.' says Joe, heartened by the possibility of much needed help. 'Perhaps we should go and...'

As he speaks the door opens. 'Well blow me down, talk of the devil and he opens the ruddy door,' says Stan laughing raucously, as if on cue, Jed and Joanie walk in carrying baby Noah.

'Hey Jed, Joanie. You'll never guess, my Katie's expecting!' says Joe grinning, 'Stan, give Jed a drink.' Adding, 'Not only that Jed, but I've also got a proposal for you both!'

Shaking Joe's hand Jed chuckles, 'Hold up, yer proposed ter Katie and she said yes, remember.'

Everyone laughs, then listens closely as Joe outlines his plans.

'If you give me a hand converting the outhouses Jed, then the cottage will come rent free with your job, hopefully it'll go some way to make up the short fall in your wages. There's all the wood you need for the fire, the heating and the water and there's plenty of fruit and veg in my vegetable garden and if Joanie wants to give my Katie a hand, when she can, I'd be grateful,' he offers, to which a very relieved Jed and Joanie look at each other and enthusiastically accept immediately.

Stan and Freddie chip in, agreeing that business was often quiet through the winter months, and they are more than willing to give a hand with the building, adding that Mick and his two other sons would probably muck in too.

Katie stuns the room into silence when out of the blue, she announces she will be selling Penfold Grove and all the acres of land that go with it. Telling them that if they hear of anyone interested in purchasing the property, they are to contact Joseph, through Stanley.

Feeling pleased with himself, Joe takes his pregnant wife and daughter home, he has so many plans and ideas running through his head, he can't wait, their future is looking rosy.

Joe and Katie jointly agreed it will be a golden opportunity to include Lily in the progress of the pregnancy, so each evening they would take it in turns listening to the heartbeat with the trumpet the doctor had given them. Both Joe and Lilibeth are amazed at how quickly Katie's bump is growing and even more so when they actually feel and see the movements. Every night they both cuddle the bump and kiss it goodnight before Lily goes happily up to bed.

Dropping his pyjama bottoms, Joe slips into bed and cuddles Katie close, 'You're so beautiful, let's make love, darling,' he whispers, enthusiastically pulling Katie's nightdress off, caressing her breasts and teasing her nipples.

'Help me sit on your thighs Joseph,' Katie purrs, 'I want to pleasure my sexy husband, I love making you come.'

Sat above him is a sight to behold for Joseph, two gorgeous full, rounded breasts and protruding hard nipples to play with, and a swelling baby bump to caress.

He moans softly as she sweetly kisses the tip, beginning to arouse him, she grips him firmly, pleasuring him, up and down, up and down, faster and faster enthusiastically. The more she tightens her hand and fastens her pace the louder he moans, hastening her action she whispers softly, 'Is this nice, my darling husband? Come Joseph, come for me!'

As the muscles in his body tighten, he grasps the sheets, 'Oooo Katie,' he groans, 'Mmm I'm coming! Ooo… yessss… Katie!' he cries out with a long, satisfied, deep throated moan as he ejaculates, absorbing the feeling of ecstasy coursing through him. 'Sweet Jesus, oh Katie,' he cries.

'Oh, my precious wife.' Joe's eyes darken, he rolls Katie onto her back and slides his hand between her legs, 'Now it's time for me to give you a thrilling orgasm, my sexy, clever wife.'

As time passes by, they adapt their lovemaking, he would lay behind her, slip one arm beneath her and hold her breast, the other arm holding her belly as she curled up her legs so that he could penetrate her from behind. Sometimes she would kneel on all fours, and he'd bend over her, supporting her belly and take her that way, his favourite was for Katie to lay on the edge of the bed with her legs around his hips, he could play with her breasts and tease her nipples and see the reactions on her beautiful face as they make love. He delights in Katie's body, as it changes so quickly. Mortified at her expanding belly, she feels fat and awkward when he sees her naked, but Joe is constantly reassuring her that she had never looked more beautiful, telling her he loves her and he wants her even more, he's so sincere, he makes her feel beautiful, special.

A week later, after a light fall of snow, Joe ushers the flock inside the barn, for the imminent expectation of lambing, it is cold, hard work.

Lambing takes three whole days, working virtually twenty-four hours a day. Joe's exhausted.

During the daylight hours Katie stands watching with Lilibeth, totally fascinated, in awe when the first sheep gives birth to twins. 'Oooo, look what came out, Mammy, two little baby lambs!' Lilibeth coo's when each lamb is born, she watches in awe as the mother's cleans each new-born, squealing with delight as each lamb in turn, takes its first wobbly steps then begins suckling its mother.

With the last of the lambs safely delivered, Joe sinks fatigued, but happy into bed, 'I think that was a job well done, don't you, darling?' he says as they cuddle down. 'We only had one stillborn, and we've got five sets of twins amongst them. Hum, good job we're gonna have Jed with us, or I don't think I'd be able to cope. I think Lily enjoyed watching them all being born, don't you, darling?'

Sleepily she nods, 'You're always so right, my very clever, handsome husband.'

The peace and tranquillity that Katie has come to love at Sweet Briars is broken, when for three weeks, sawing, banging, hammering and mayhem reigns, as the necessary construction takes place in the yard. Fortunately, there's welcome respite when for a whole blissful four days, work ceases as the freezing weather takes hold. Then work resumes at a pace. Luckily, Margo, Edna and Verity come most days to help Katie provide the food for the ravenous workers.

Mid-way through the fourth week, Stan announces that he'd found someone very interested in buying Penfold. The news comes as a welcome relief to Katie.

Joe takes care of all the necessary, agreeing a price and dealing with the sale and paperwork etc. She'd made it perfectly clear to him that she wanted absolutely nothing to do with it!

'Five thousand, eight hundred pounds, he's offering, darling,' he tells Katie, two days later.

Her eyes widen in disbelief, 'But that's a small fortune!'

'Aye it is, but remember, Penfold has so many acres of prime land, there are four wells on the property, not forgetting the three cottages, two barns, six outhouses and the farmhouse to renovate,' he points out. 'But I'm pretty sure we can hold out for more if you want. The buyer is obviously worth a few bob. He's pretty keen. It's up to you, darling.'

'No Joseph. I want it gone, and as soon as possible!' she says curtly.

Joe shrugs his shoulders, 'Don't you even want to know who's buying it, sweetheart?'

Uninterested, Katie shakes her head. 'No!'

'Perhaps you should think about it, darling,' he suggests, 'there's no rush.'

But Katie is adamant, 'Just sell it, as soon as possible. Please Joseph, I want rid of it, for good!'

'Hum, well if it's what you really want. Of course, you have to sign these papers, darling,' he says, sliding them over to her to read, 'but I really wish you'd...'

Too late, the deed is done, she doesn't want to spend a second more on the subject of Penfold Grove. 'There, I've signed it. Would you take Jed and Joanie to Penfold Grove tomorrow, let them pick anything they need, furniture wise, for the new cottage?'

Shaking his head slowly, he sighs, 'If that's what you really want, darling.'

Folding the papers, he slides them into an envelope and sighs once more, 'I'm sorry, darling, are you very upset about all this business?'

Slipping her hands around his waist she whispers, 'Actually Joseph, I feel relieved, that place reminds me of nothing but pure evil. Let someone else take it over and turn it into a happy house. Huh! if that's at all possible,' she retorts caustically.

He gives her a squeeze. 'Fine, darling, consider it the end of the subject. I'll collect the money when I hand over the signed papers on Thursday.' Taking her in his arms, he kisses her so passionately that Penfold Grove is, at last, banished from her mind forever.

'Come, my precious, let's go to bed, I want to listen to junior and spoil his gorgeous sexy mammy.'

Appreciatively, Jed and Joanie chose the furniture from Penfold Grove and discreetly store it in the barn, out of Katie's sight, with the exception of a brand-new double bed that Katie has personally bought for them, the mattress stored in Joe's old bedroom to prevent it getting damp.

Katie treasures their bedtimes even more now, what with the constant noise and people in and out of her home all day long.

Alone in the privacy of their own room, despite her ever-swelling belly, Joe still makes her feel as if she's the most desirable woman on earth. Each night, before they slip into bed, Joe helps her undress then admires her ever changing naked form. His face is a picture when he feels the baby move, completely fascinated he would hold his splayed hand over her belly, to feel it, 'Oooo, Katie, look, there he is, again!'

Katie smiles, 'Who says it's going to be a boy?'

'I honestly don't care what we have, just as long as you're both all right, my precious,' he tells her, and she knows he means it too.

Despite Katie's strong objections they are visiting the doctor again, sitting side by side in the surgery waiting room.

Perhaps it's familiarity, but old Mrs Entwistle greets them with a thin smile this time, 'Good morning Mr and Mrs Markson, do take a seat.'

Almost immediately, the hand bell rings, 'Ah, that will be for you,' she tells them, beckoning for them to follow her into the doctor's office. 'Mr and Mrs Markson,' she announces formally.

Sat at his desk, the doctor is studying Katie's notes, he looks up and smiles. 'Please, do take a seat. That will be all, Mother, I will ring, if I need you,' he says, waving his hand dismissively. She nods, though her attitude has not changed, she cuts Joe a very old-fashioned, disapproving look, 'Very well Doctor, as you wish. Ring when you need me,' she says haughtily and sweeps out of the room, closing the door behind her.

'Good day to you both, not brought the little girl with you today?' asks the doctor, instantly putting them at their ease.

'No sir, we are having work done at home, so she is staying with friends,' explains Katie.

'You have a very bright little girl if you don't mind my saying so.'

'Oh, she is, believe me,' agrees Joe, 'bright as a button and as sharp as a knife. Normally we like to involve her in everything, including the pregnancy, you can't beat Mother Nature,' he brags openly and proudly.

Katie smiles and nods in agreement.

'Quite so Mr Markson, most commendable. Well now, how have you been Mrs Markson, any problems at all?' he asks, as he washes his hands.

'I feel fine doctor, thank you,' answers Katie shyly.

Joe nods, confirming his wife's words.

The doctor rings the bell and waits.

'Ah, good, there you are mother, would you take Mrs Markson behind the curtains and help her undress please?' he looks at Joe. 'If you wait here Mr Markson, we won't be long.'

Frustrated at being omitted from the examination he sits waiting. Despite straining his ears, all Joe can hear is softly spoken mutterings, both male and female.

Eventually the doctor, his mother and a highly flushed Katie re-emerge. 'Thank you, Mother, I think we can manage now,' he opens the door and ushers her out.

'Hum, let me see, seven and a half months, uh huh. As baby hasn't turned yet and it's still high, hum, I think another six weeks is about right.' The doctor explains. 'Baby has put on some weight, keep it up, Mrs Markson. Now I'd like to see you again in two weeks. Do you think you can make the journey?'

'Er, I'm sure we'll manage thank you,' says Joe.

They sit hand in hand, watching the doctor make notes, waiting to hear his verdict.

'So, the good news is the baby is putting on some weight, it's coming along nicely. I can't see foresee any major problems,' he tells them as he rinses and dries his hands.

Relaxing back in his leather-bound chair, he gives his opinion, 'The baby is still a little on the small side and you don't seem to be carrying much water, which gives me slight cause for concern. However...'

Katie stiffens, Joe leans forward frowning, 'What is it, what's wrong?' he asks, searching the doctor's face for answers.

'Right now? Absolutely nothing, but going by what you've told me about your previous confinements Mrs Markson, in view of your numerous miscarriages, you've had a very difficult time in the past,' he looks serious, 'I can't promise with any certainty that we won't encounter...'

'But that was when I was with my first husband,' Katie points out, interrupting him mid-sentence again, she's overcome with emotion. 'My life is very different now doctor.'

Joe eases her back in her chair and puts a comforting arm around her, 'Hey, don't upset yourself, darling, please. Doctor Entwistle, my dear wife and I are very much in love, I adore her, we are devoted...'

The doctor smiles and holds up a silencing hand, 'Of that fact I have no doubt.'

'So, what are you suggesting?' Joe asks anxiously.

'One of three choices. Either you move closer to me for the last few weeks, so that I can attend your wife's confinement, maybe you could stay with a friend, here in Holdean...? Alternately, I can assign a nurse to you, ideally staying at your home, for at the very least, the last three weeks of your pregnancy. After all, your abode is very remote. Baby is still on the small side and in the unlikely event that a problem arises, and you need urgent medical care...'

'I won't leave my husband, not for a minute!' Katie retorts vehemently, immediately dismissing his three alternatives out of hand, 'Never!' and she grips Joe's hand even tighter.

'Fine, well after your visit, then I'll find a nurse to call on you weekly, it's a long trip, and definitely not one I would recommend for you, when you get down to the last few weeks.'

'But I don't want a midwife, my friend Margo will deliver me,' Katie insists.

Concerned, Joe intervenes, 'I'm sure the doctor knows best, darling,' his wife and child's safety being his priority.

But Katie's ambivalent, 'Margo has delivered lots of babies, she delivered my Lilibeth safely, and she was born really early, and she delivered Joanie's baby too.'

'Ah, do I understand we're talking of Margo Hooper, Stanley Hooper's good wife of Wickers Yard?' the doctor inquires.

Katie nods.

'Mrs Hooper, ah yes, a fine woman, and I agree, more than competent. Fine, well then it's agreed, Margo Hooper will be your nurse,' he relents.

Katie sighs, relieved.

'Though I would like to see you again.' He turns to Joe, 'Mr Markson, if you don't think your wife can make the journey, please send word to me and I will make a home visit.'

As he pays the bill, Joe voices his concern, 'You say the baby is still small, should we be concerned?'

Patting Joe on the back he says patiently, 'Mr Markson, I can assure you that babies come in many sizes, and babies come when they are good and ready. So, try not to worry, I'm sure everything will be fine.'

He thanks the doctor and pays the bill.

Joe helps Katie climb up on the cart, it's the beginning of March and the days are bitterly cold, so he settles her comfortably, surrounding her with cushions and wrapping her in a couple of rugs. 'I thought the doctor was reassuring, but are you quite sure about Margo? I think it might be safer if the doctor delivers the baby.' He is having doubts.

Katie snuggles up close, 'I'm sure he's a very good young doctor, but Joe, that's my problem, don't you see?' her face is still highly flushed, 'He is very young, it's so embarrassing for me! Do you know I have to take everything off from my waist down then lay down on the bed so he can examine me, I hate doing that! Even worse Joseph, the first time we visited him I had to open my bodice so he could examine my breasts. Oh Joseph, I'm so embarrassed about all this. No, I'm sorry, I've decided, Margo can look after me from now on. And as for delivering our baby? Good heavens no, I would die of shame!'

Joe smiles to himself, he has to agree, Doctor Entwistle is very young by doctors' standards. But on the other hand, he liked him, he was very open and put you at ease, he felt he could talk to him frankly about anything, but never-the-less, he could understand Katie's objections. He shudders, loathed at the very thought of this young man carrying out such personal, intimate examinations on his beloved wife, Katie's delightful body is for his eyes only. 'Oh Katie, I do understand. I confess I didn't realise what the examination entailed, I'm so sorry, darling. I can tell you, I feel exactly the same as you, my love.'

Looking relieved Katie says, 'So Margo will deliver me then?'

'Of course, my darling, as you wish. Um, do you have any objections if your handsome husband wants to be with you and hold your hand whilst our baby comes into the world?'

Katie is glowing inside, what a difference this pregnancy had been. Joe is proving to be the most considerate, attentive husband, and she loves him dearly for it, she kisses him on the cheek, 'Thank you, Joseph, I love you, so much, darling.'

'I'd really like to be with you when our baby is born,' he repeats.

Katie's genuinely surprised, surely it wasn't the done thing, for men to be in attendance when their wives give birth. However, she doesn't want to upset him, 'I'll speak to Margo and see what she thinks,' she answers diplomatically.

Meanwhile, in an effort to complete the new cottage, the band of workers had grown, Jed had enlisted the extra help of his two brothers Abe and Tom. Most days, when the weather is good enough to travel, Margo brings Edna and Verity with her, to help with the cooking for the men and to clean and polish all the furniture that's being stored discreetly, in the barn, out of Katie's sight.

They are on the go all day until they all leave, two hours before dusk.

Nearing completion, Stan, Freddie, Mick, Jed and his two brothers, Abe and Tom are bedding down in the barn at night now, so they don't have to waste their time travelling back and forth.

Regretfully, everything is getting on top of Katie, she feels as if the tranquillity of her sanctuary at Sweet Briars has been invaded and she's beginning to wish that she had never agreed to the build. Lilibeth, on the other hand, is thriving with all the attention she receives from everyone, but Katie…? She longs to be alone with Joseph, but there's always someone around. Even bedtimes have changed, she's so tired, and Joe is always so exhausted they are often both asleep within seconds of putting their heads on the pillow.

'I really don't want to go to the doctors today, please don't make me, Joseph!' begs Katie, she's visibly upset.

He hates to see her so distraught, 'Hey, don't cry, darling.' He pulls her into his arms. 'If you don't want to go, that's fine. Just promise me you will rest and eat the meals Margo cooks for you. Do you promise?' he asks, hoping he's doing the right thing.

'Yes, I promise, thank you, darling.'

True to her word, Katie does as she's told.

The following week, Joe has to admit that with regular meals, putting her feet up and a lot of gentle loving, Katie is thriving. The gaunt, tired look has gone, now she is positively blooming.

Regardless of what work needs to be done, Joe joins his family indoors at teatime. Quality time is spent with Lily, and when she goes to bed, the doors are locked and the curtains drawn, to ensure complete seclusion.

Every night, a bath is filled with water, and they savour the enormous pleasure of an intimate bath together in the scullery, enjoying their privacy. Playfully caressing each other with sensuous sudsy hands, then making love together.

Joe would gently pat her dry and then wrap his strong protective arms around her swollen belly. 'Oh Katie, my beautiful darling, I love you, I adore your belly, darling,' He'd whisper, 'Just a few weeks to go now my precious sexy wife.'

'I love you so much, Joe, take me to bed and make love to me, darling,' is always her predictable response.

Their lovemaking continues, though not as vigorously as it had been before. 'Dear God, you're so beautiful,' he would tell her when he saw her stood naked.

'It's a strange feeling,' says Katie, 'I don't feel at all embarrassed with you seeing me like this.'

Joe looks at her, quizzically, 'Why on earth should you feel embarrassed, darling?'

Katie shrugs, sliding her hands over her bare, pregnant profile, 'Sharing my pregnancy with you like this, my fat body. I thought it would put you off me.'

He's shocked, 'Good grief, darling, no. I told you, you are beautiful, and what man would want to miss seeing his precious sexy wife, growing his baby in her perfect body, why on earth would you think that?'

Kneeling down he wraps his arms around her, kissing her belly. 'Oh Katie, my love' he groans, looking up at her, 'if I died this very minute, I would take these moments with me to my grave, as the happiest moments of my life! I worship you, darling, I love you so much it hurts.' Full of emotion he kisses her passionately, his hands caressing her breasts, rolling and tugging her nipples, stirring her desire. In desperate need of relief, he slides her hand around his eager erection, moaning with pleasure, 'Here, play with me sweetheart. I crave your touch.'

Her eyes darken as she licks her lips, her hand tightening around him, she whispers, 'I love it when you talk low and sexy, I love you so much.'

With just a day to completion, Joe walks into the scullery looking shattered, 'Well that's it, sweetheart, just the last of the furniture to go in tomorrow and Jed and Joanie can move in with Noah,' he declares, too exhausted to have a bath he strips out of his clothes to wash.

'I can't say I'll be sorry; it's been mayhem. I had no idea it would create such upheaval,' she says, washing his back, 'Still, I suppose it will be nice to have Margo on hand.' With less than five weeks to go before she is due to give birth, she seems to feel permanently tired lately. 'Joanie told me Margo can stay with them, when they move in tomorrow, just till the baby's born,' she says, drying his taut rear.

Joe turns, taking her in his arms, 'After this weekend it will be good to get back to work. I've neglected the business long enough. I'll give them the weekend to settle in and then Jed can start work with me on Monday, and Joanie can help you out with some cleaning and stuff.'

Katie pouts, she'd become accustomed to having Joe around twenty-four hours a day, she would miss his constant loving care and attention.

Completing his strip wash, Joe stretches his arms out for Katie to dry the front of his body, giving Katie the golden opportunity to let him know exactly how much she loves him. She sinks to her knees to pleasure him. Cupping her head in his hands, his eyes close, moaning softly, loving the pleasure she is giving him as her fingers grasp him firmly. Her soft lips kiss the tip, licking the bead of moisture as she gazes up at him, her love shining in her beautiful bright eyes. Shielding her teeth with her lips, devotedly she begins her slow, sensuous assault with her mouth and tongue. Pushing his hips forward, he runs his hands through her hair, thrusting further into her mouth, as she gradually increases her rhythm. His legs tremble, emitting a long, drawn-out moan, as she goes on and on, 'Katie! Oh, sweet Jesus,' he moans, calling out, 'Katie!' as he comes in her mouth.

Struggling to stand, he gives her a helping hand, noticing her grimace with pain as she stands.

'So why the glum face, darling?' he asks, assuming it's because with Margo living on the doorstep, she might invade their private time. 'Sweetheart, at least if Margo's sleeping at Joanie's, we'll still have our privacy, and I'll feel happier going off to work knowing she's here for you.'

Katie smiles, 'I know, I'm being silly,' she tells him, stretching her aching back.

'Are you all right, sweetheart?' he asked, 'You look very pale.'

'I'll be fine when we get to bed,' she assures him.

Joe puts a pan of milk on the hob, 'There's still plenty of hot water in the boiler, I'll fill you a warm bath. A nice soak will relax you sweetheart, I can rub your back,' he suggests, 'Here, put your feet up and drink your warm milk first,' he pats the cushions in the fireside chair to make her comfortable.

Feeling grateful, she isn't about to argue, she's so tired, and her back is aching so much. Anyway, it would be pointless to argue with him, he can be quite stubborn when his mind is made up.

'There we go, darling, nice and easy does it,' he says carefully helping her into the soothing bath water.

Laying back she closes her eyes, sighing with relief, 'Mmm, Oooo that feels better. Mmm.'

'Relax, darling,' he says as he builds up a lather in his hands. Gently he massages her aching feet and legs, 'Is this nice sweetheart?'

'Mmm, Oooh, that's lovely Joseph. Oooh, I feel better already.'

He smiles fondly, 'What was it the doctor said? Happy mother, happy baby.'

'Then we should have the happiest baby ever born,' she coos.

He grins. 'Sit forward, darling, let me give your back a rub,' he says, soaping his hands, 'Have you thought of any baby names yet?'

Eyes closed, Katie is purring with pleasure, enjoying his firm soothing touch on her back, 'Um, no, not really. Mmm, lower, Joe. Oh, that's lovely. Um… names. I thought we should wait until it's born, then we can choose a name between us. Ahh, that's so nice,' she sighs with contentment.

His eyes darken with longing, he moans softly in his throat, 'Ooo, Katie, you're so sexy. I'm so tempted to get in with you.' His hands slide round to cup her breasts.

Katie winces, 'Ouch, Joseph!'

'Katie?'

'She smiled reassuringly, 'It's all right, they're just a bit tender, that's all, believe me. I'm not telling you to stop.'

'Wow! I love your fabulous tits baby. Have I ever told you what gorgeous breasts you've got, my darling wife?' he asks as he gently caresses them with his sudsy hands, paying special attention to her oh so tempting, hardening nipples with his fingertips.

'Mmm, oh yes, every single day, darling,' she giggles, 'But I'm not complaining. Ooo... Ouch!' she yelps, grabbing the sides of the bath, giving Joe the fright of his life, 'Ouch, Joseph... Ouch... oh help!'

Horrified, he sees her serene expression turning to an agonising grimace, her knuckles turn white as she clings to the edge of the bath rim.

'Katie! What's wrong, darling?'

Her contorted expression fades and she relaxes her grip, 'Joe the baby, oh no, I think it might have started!'

'But you've still got four weeks to go!' he points out. He bites his lip when he remembers the doctor's prophetic words. Baby will come when baby is good and ready. 'Christ, are you sure sweetheart? Oh, Katie love, why didn't we get Margo to stay tonight?'

'Perhaps it'll go off if I lay here and relax,' says Katie, hoping against hope that it will.

As he's about to lift her out of the bath, she grips the bath again, crying out, 'Oh no Joseph, wait!' As the pain passes, she sinks lower into the water, 'Ooo, that's better, it's fine, it's going off now.'

Unconvinced, he grabs a towel, 'I need to get you out, darling. Here, I'll help you.' his arms plunge into the bath water lifting her out. 'Stand still, I'll wrap you in a towel,' As he does, he spots a smudge of blood on the towel and an ever-expanding puddle on the floor. 'Katie... darling you're bleeding and there's water running down your legs, are you peeing?'

Doubling over with pain, she clings to his arms for support. Terrified, she groans, 'Please Joseph, it's my waters, they've broken. Please, I need Margo. Please!'

Taking a deep breath, he does his best to sound calm, 'It's gonna be all right Katie, we mustn't panic.'

Hearing a noise, he spins round, Lilibeth is stood in the doorway, rubbing the sleep from her eyes. 'What's wrong with Mammy?'

'Mammy's fine, darling, I think the baby might be coming.' Though far from calm, he explains in a tone that sounds almost matter of fact. 'Can you do something for me, sweetheart?'

Lilibeth nods.

'Would you put on your shoes and coat, run across the yard and fetch Freddie for me, sweetheart?'

Lilibeth nods again, immediately she turns tail and runs.

Alarmed, Katie panics, screaming, 'No Joseph! No! I don't want Freddie in here!'

'Hey, don't worry, darling I'm just gonna send him to Fennydown to fetch Margo. Now, can you make it to the bedroom if I help you?' he asks gently.

Gripped by another bout of pain, Katie screws her face and shakes her head, 'No!' she cries, 'Not yet...!' as she doubles up in agony again.

'No problem, darling, we'll wait until it goes off.'

Between the contractions, he carries her in is arms to the bedroom, plumping up the pillows and making her as comfortable as he can, 'I won't be a minute, I need to get a clean towel and another sheet.'

'Don't go, please!' she reaches out to him, 'Don't leave me Joseph!'

'I'll only be a minute, darling, we need a clean sheet,' he explains. 'I can hear someone coming, darling, it must be Freddie.' He doesn't want to leave her, he can see the fear in her eyes, but the sooner he sends Freddie to fetch Margo, the sooner they'll get back, 'I'll be one minute, I promise.'

Stan is standing in the parlour, with Lilibeth in his arms wrapped in a blanket, Freddie is stood by his side, 'What's up, Joe. Lilibuff said the baby's comin', it ain't is it?'

'She's started all right. Christ, we need Margo, like now!' Joe explains.

'No problem, I'll take your horse and ride bareback,' offers Freddie, 'It'll be quicker, I'll bring me Mam back on the old man's cart.' And with that he's gone.

Stan chuckles, 'Don't worry Mate, it'll be hours afore the baby gits here. There's plenty of time. Now why don't I take Lilibuff back over ter Jed's fer a while,' he suggests. The sound of Katie groaning in dire agony, halts the conversation. 'Get back ter Katie, she needs yer. Lilibuff will be fine wiv me, won't yer, me little darlin'?' Stan smirks, 'By the by, Joe, it won't hurt fer yer ter but some trousers on Mate, and yer better put some pans on ter boil the water, and all.'

Bemused, Joe frowns at Stan, 'What's the water for?'

Stan scratches his head, 'I dunno Mate, but that's what our Margo always does, and I fink yer need some brown paper and clean sheets too.'

There was another shrill cry from the bedroom, this one bordering on a scream.

Joe nods to Stan, pecks Lily on the cheek then dashes back to Katie, 'It's all right, darling, I'm back.'

'Arrrrrgh. Oh Joseph,' she gasps, 'I want Margo!'

'It's all right, Freddie's gone already. She'll be here in no time, try to rest in between the pains, my love,' he says, taking her hand and patting it to pacify her.

Joe is trying to think straight, but it isn't easy when he's watching his beloved wife writhe in agony. 'Erm yes, my trousers,' he mutters something inaudible as he tries to drag them on, 'Sheets, bloody hell, I forgot the damn sheets, brown paper, oh hell, and boiling water. I forgot to put on the ruddy water,' he mutters getting flustered.

As the pain subsides, Katie lets go of his hand. Seizing the opportunity, Joe says calmly, 'I'll just be a minute,' and dashes back to the scullery.

A few logs are thrown under the boiler, two large jam making pans, filled with water are sat next to the kettle, before he can do any more, he hears Katie cry out again, 'Joe...! Arrrrrgh... Joseph! Help me!'

Returning, with his arms full of towels and sheets, he finds Katie red face, clinging to the bedstead, she's perspiring so much that her hair is clinging to her face.

Cursing Margo under his breath for going home, he uses the corner of a towel, dips it in the cool water of the washing bowl. 'There, my precious, that's better, you're doing really well, take it easy, try to rest, my love,' he whispers soothingly, mopping her brow.

Between contractions, Joe cools her down with the damp towel, and when each contraction returns, he holds her hands feeling helpless. 'Hold on, darling, Margo will be here soon, you're doing so well, sweetheart,' he encourages her.

'Everyfin' alwight in there, Joe?' yells Stan from the parlour.

Prising his fingers from Katie's grasp, he pops his head around the door, 'She's doing all right, I think. How much longer before Margo gets here, for pity's sake?' he demands.

Stood in the scullery with his hands on his hips, Stans brow creases, 'Erm, I dunno Mate, anytime soon, I hope. Is yer sure everyfin's alwight?'

'Christ, I dunno, she's in so much pain, I don't know what to do to help her,' says Joe, no longer able to hide his anxiety.

'Tell her ter breave deep and then pant fast when the pains come, and rub her back and all, I fink it's s'posed ter help, Joe.'

'What good will that do?' he retorts, She's in agony.'

Stan lifts his cap and scratches his head, 'I don't rightly know, but that's what I heard Margo sayin' when she delivered Joanie's baby, and a few others and all.'

An ear-piercing scream has Joe rushing back to her bedside.

Almost half an hour later and to Joe's frustration, Margo still hadn't arrived, the pains were coming every minute or so now. Fraught with fear, at that moment Joe is feeling nothing short of useless. 'You're doing really well, darling,' he encourages her, trying and failing to sound calm. 'Keep breathing, nice and deep. There we go, nice and deep, darling, pant when the pains come. There we go, good girl. Squeeze my hands, darling.'

Katie grabs his hand and screams out as another contraction engulfs her.

He is shocked at her immense strength when, as with the onslaught of yet another painful contraction she grips him like a vice.

'Arrrrgh, oh no, it's coming, oh dear God. Joe, help me, I think the baby's coming, I want to push!'

From nowhere, he suddenly feels calm and in control. 'I'll have a look, darling. Stooping down he opens her legs wider, 'Bloody hell, I think I can see its head, Katie. Breathe deep, darling, hold my hand sweetheart!'

As her fingernails dug into his skin, she squeezes so hard that he grimaces at her unbelievable strength.

When the contraction eases, he encourages her to pant. 'That's it, darling, good girl, try to relax now. Margo will be here any minute!'

'Bugger Margo, bloody help me Joseph!' She yells gripping his hands so hard that her fingernails draws blood. 'Oh no, help me Joseph, I've got to push…! Arrrrgh! I've got to push…! Oooo please, Joe, help me!' she screams. Grasping the iron bedstead, writhing in agony she grits her teeth. 'Never again, Joseph bloody Markson! Do hear me?' she screeches, as memories of her agonising three days of labour with Lilibeth comes surging back to haunt her.

Joe's hopelessness turned to despair, 'Don't talk, darling, please,' he whispers softly, 'save your strength.'

As another contraction overwhelms her, she doubles up in agony, crying out again, 'Arrrrrgh, don't you ever come near me again, Joseph! Oh God! Arrrrrgh. Oh no. Arrrrrgh!' She screws up her face, summoning up every ounce of the strength she can muster giving an almighty push, gripping his hand so fiercely she brings tears to his eyes.

At the bottom of the bed, he opens her legs wider, 'Can you pull your knees up sweetheart.'

In no position to argue, Katie does as she's told.

Opening his mouth in awe he can see the head is right there.

'Another push, Katie. That's it, darling… oh yes, it's coming, it's coming! Good girl. Another push… Oh, sweet Jesus… the heads nearly out! That's it, darling, another push! Push again, Katie, push again!'

'I can't. I can't!' She screams out, sinking back on the pillow.

Supporting the baby's head Joe calmly urges her again, 'The head's actually out, Katie! That's it, one more push, my love. Come on, you can do it, try again!' he urges.

Gritting her teeth, Katie pushes as hard as she can muster, but there's something wrong, very wrong. She falls back on the pillow gasping for breath, 'I can't, Joe, please… I'm sorry… I just can't.'

Joe's complexion pales, the head has emerged, but he can see the cord wrapped round the baby's neck, 'Stop, darling, don't push yet!' Holding his breath, he carefully slides his finger beneath the cord and gingerly eases it over its head, 'That's it, you can push now, darling. Come on, Katie. Push! Push! And again! Push!'

'Arrrrrgh, Dear God, Joseph…! Arrrrgh…!' Katie screams, her face now purple as she grits her teeth, giving one last almighty push, the baby slides out into Joe's hands, 'It's a baby!' yells Joe, 'You clever darling, it's a bloody miracle!' His delighted face is dripping with sweat.

'Here, Joe, let me,' said Margo calmly, ready to take over.

Joe looks up at Margo, his eyes wracked with fear, 'Margo, it's not breathing! For Christ's sake, do something…! Please!'

Calmly stooping to pick up the lifeless infant, Margo blows sharply into the baby's face, grabs a towel and rubs the baby's back vigorously.

For a few agonising moments, there's nothing.

In anguish, Joe puts his head in his hands and cries out, 'No, God no!'

Suddenly the infant cries out in protest, Margo beams at Joe, 'There we go little one, tell yer daddy what yer fink of the outside world then.'

Joe breathes a huge sigh of relief and tears fill his eyes. Margo lays the infant down, cuts and ties the cord. Calmly she cleans the infant, then wraps the baby in a little blanket and places the infant on Katie's chest.

Overcome with emotion, Joe slumps beside the bed and grasps Katie's hand, tears of joy running unashamedly down his relieved face, 'Oh, my clever, sweet darling, you've done it! He exclaims, his voice choked with emotion, 'We've got our baby!' Insanely euphoric, Joe is barely able to contain his joy. 'My brave, clever darling!'

Margo clears her throat, 'Ahem, will yer fetch us the hot water, Joe, some towels and more sheets, it ain't over yet, we got ter deliver the afterbirf. Come on, move yerself, sharpish lad!'

Grinning proudly through his tears, Joe rises to his feet and kisses Katie, then the baby, 'I won't be a minute, darling, I love you,' he tells her, and with the encouragement of Margo, who is anxiously beckoning him towards the door, turns, grinning broadly, he blows Katie a kiss and rushes out, with the baby's first cry wringing joyfully in his ears.

By the time he returns, Katie is laying back on the pillow looking exhausted, but happy, he gazes at his infant, amazed, the baby is blinking and opening its eyes.

'It's alwight, Joe, I've got the afterbirf, no problem, it's all here,' says Margo, dropping it into a bowl. Then she grins a smile to match Joe's, 'Yer got a beaut'ful baby boy, and he's perfect, absolutely perfect!

Gazing in wonder at his new-born son, Joe's tears fall like rain, 'A boy? We have a son! Darling, did you hear that? We've got a son!'

Katie smiles back and nods wearily, 'Yes, darling, isn't he just perfect. just look at all that hair, he looks just like his lovely daddy?'

Filled with elation he grabs Margo and twirls her round the room, planting a smacker on her cheek, 'You're an angel Margo, a real live bloody angel!' he declares, 'We've got a boy, me and Katie, we've got a son!'

Margo is easily caught up in his joy, 'Yes Joseph. He's a bit small, but there's nowt wrong wiv his lungs. He's fine. But it was nuffin' to do with me, yer did it all by yerself, Joe, and yer done a right grand job and all.' She adds soberly, 'Yer know if yer hadn't released the cord from around his little neck so quick, he would've died, bless him, and maybe our Katie and all. So, all's well what ends well, fanks ter you, daddy Joseph.'

'Did I, really?' he pants.

'Aye yer certainly did, Joe. Well done lad. Most men would've run a bleedin' mile.'

Joe's so elated his face positively shines with pride, 'Lily! I've got to tell Lily!' he gives Katie a soft kiss on the lips, 'I've got to fetch our daughter, introduce her to her new little brother!'

Margo and Katie laugh together as they hear him bounding downstairs and out of the door, the sound of his rapid footsteps, clattering over the cobbles towards the new cottage, echoing around the bedroom. Joe is yelling at the top of his voice, 'Lily! Lily! Come with Daddy, we've got a baby!'

In no time at all, Margo has cleaned Katie, ripped a towel up to make her a pad, dressed the baby and wrapped him in a blanket, then gathering all the soiled sheets together she rolls everything in a ball, an efficient job of clearing up both the room and Katie. By the time Joe returns, holding Lily in his arms, peace and tranquillity has returned to the bedroom

Margo props Katie up in the bed, Joe, with his arm held lovingly around Katie's shoulders, sits beside her, his eyes fixed firmly on his new-born son, Lily is sat on his lap, gazing adoringly at her baby brother.

'Has I got a little brother all for me, Aunty Margo?' asks Lilibeth.

Margo opens the blanket, 'There you go darlin' look, he's got a little willy and ball bag, see, he's a beautiful baby boy.'

'Oooh, he's so lovely. What's his name?' whispers Lilibeth.

Joe looks to Katie, 'Erm... Katie?'

Thinking for a moment Katie looks at Joe, 'Perhaps... Jack, in memory of your dad and Joshua, after my dad,' she announces. 'Jack Joshua Markson, how does that sound, darling?'

Joe beams with pride, 'Ruddy grand, Jack Joshua. What do you think, Lily?'

'Jack Joshua, smashing, I like it. So, where's he gonna sleep then?' she asks.

A blank look comes over Joe's face, 'The cot, it's still at yours Margo!'

'I know. Jack Joshua can have my Daisy's cradle!' suggests Lily.

Everyone laughs, 'Well I suppose he is really very little,' says Margo 'and it'll only be fer a few days.'

'Baby Jack Joshua is settled in his temporary cradle and Katie, who had just enjoyed a very welcome cup of tea, yawns. She looks completely exhausted.

'Time fer Katie ter get some sleep,' declares Margo, 'Come on Lilibuff, let's get yer orf ter bed.'

'It really is a miracle Margo, I'm so proud of my wife,' Joe whispers, his eyes gazing adoringly at his tiny offspring, 'Isn't he just perfect Margo?'

Margo nods and smiles in agreeance, 'Aye he certainly is, he's a bit on the small side, but yer know, Joe, yer really did save his little life, and Katie's and all, gawd bless yer. Any other man would've been out the ruddy door,' she tells him, 'Here, I've made yer a nice cuppa, you've earned it, Joe.'

'I wouldn't have missed this for the world. I'm so proud of my Katie, she did brilliantly, isn't she a clever darling?'

Margo nods, 'Aye, she certainly is. But it's been a long night fer the pair of yer, now get yerselves some sleep. I'll go in wiv Lilibuff. Just call if yer needs me.'

Joe gives Margo a hug, 'You're truly the best friend we could ever wish for, thank you Margo, for everything.'

Margo's face reddens, 'Aye, well, come on Lilibuff, bedtime. It was my pleasure, Joe, good night Daddy, good night, Mammy.'

Joe grinned broadly, and gives Lily a kiss, 'Good night Margo, goodnight my darling daughter, we'll see you in the morning.'

Feeling highly emotional, Joe gazes lovingly at his first-born son. 'I love you so much, my little Jack Joshua, my son, and you Katie, if it's possible I love you even more, for giving him to me, my clever precious wife.'

Then he strips naked and slips into bed beside Katie, careful not to disturb her, tenderly he kissed her on her lips, whispering, 'I love you so much, my clever wife, our precious son is just perfect, thank you.'

Desperate for sleep, Katie smiles through bleary eyes, 'Thank you, my darling husband, for giving him to me.'

'Oh, my sweet, darling Katie, I'm so sorry I put you through all that terrible pain. After all that, I think two children are quite enough,' he tells her.

Katie smiles wearily, 'Oh Joseph, take no notice of me, darling. Women say all sorts of stupid things whilst they're in labour. Believe me, I really didn't mean a word of it.'

'Oh no sweetheart, I could never expect you to go through that awful pain again, ever!'

Katie's still smiling, 'Joe, I swear the minute he was born it was all forgotten, darling.' Sliding her hand across his chest she looks at him, her lips curling up at the corners, her blue eyes filled with love, so now we have our first baby there are just two more to go. Now snuggle up to me, my handsome husband, the proud father of our son. I so need to feel you close to me,' she tells him as her eyelids droop.

'Goodnight, my clever, beautiful wife. I love you so much.'

'Goodnight daddy Joseph, the father of to two of the most precious children in the world. I love you more.'

At last, the house falls into blissful silence.

Joe cradles Katie gently in his arms and they both drift to sleep.

CHAPTER 16

Barely two hours have passed, and Joe is rudely awoken by Margo shaking him, putting her finger to his lips, she whispers urgently, 'Shush… Joe… yer gotta get up!'

He screws up his face, 'What's up Margo?' panicking he sits bolt upright, 'Oh my God! Jack Joshua?'

Margo shakes her head, putting her finger to his lips again to silence him, lowering her voice to a barely a whisper says, 'Quiet, you'll wake Katie. No lad, it's the new cottage. Get up, Joe, we got a ruddy fire!' she tells him.

He can hear the sound of agitated voices outside in the yard and the nauseating smell of burning.

Margo quietly closes the window to keep out the smoke, 'Hurry, Joe, get dressed, quick lad!' she urges, then rushes out of the room.

Standing gaping in the open doorway, Joe is in total shock, one end of the new cottage is well ablaze. All hell has broken loose.

Everyone's running around with buckets and yelling at each other.

He cries out in anguish, 'Lily!' As he bolts towards the flaming cottage Stan staggers towards him, his face blackened, he is coughing and gasping for air, he bends over, retching from his congested, smoke-filled lungs and vomits.

'Stan, where's Lily?' in a blind panic he yells frantically.

'We're here, Joe, don't worry, I got Lilibuff, she's safe wiv me. Yer better help them wiv the bleedin' fire!' shouts Margo, then flees back indoors with Lilibeth in her arms.

Utter chaos reigns, they all take it in turns pumping water from the well outside the dairy and passing buckets, milk churns and anything else they can find to fill with water, passing them along the chain of men.

'Fuck! We'll lose everyfin' we got!' bellows Jed above the roar of the fire, 'I gotta get the furniture out!' he covers his head with his jacket and runs blindly into the burning building.

'Jed!' His brother Abe is about to follow him when he's forcibly restrained by Freddie, 'Don't Abe, fer gawd's sake, the buildin's gonna collapse any second!'

Stan holds Abe back, and Freddie, shielding the heat from his face with his arm, makes a dash through the open doorway, but within a couple of seconds he comes stumbling out, alone. Coughing and spluttering he collapses on the ground, burying his heat seared face and body into the cool, wet grass.

Tom drops his bucket and runs to Freddie, falling to his knees, he grabs Freddie by the shirt, 'Where's our Jed...! Tell me... where's me bruver!'

Forlornly, Freddie shakes his head, 'I tried Tom, I really tried Mate...'

As the roof caves in, Joe, Freddie, Mick, Tom, Abe and Stan stand shoulder to shoulder, numb with disbelief, watching helplessly as the cottage crumbles inwards, all six weeping openly, Jed has perished.

Filled with shock and grief, Joe turns and looks up to the bedroom window, Margo is stood with Lilibeth held on one arm and the other round Katie's shoulder. Despairingly he shakes his head.

'Someone's gotta tell me mam and Joanie,' Abe croaks, he buries his head in his hands, sobbing.'

Stan shakes his head, 'Fuckin' hell, Joanie and little Noah, gawd bless them.'

The yard is completely silent, save the crackling and spitting of the burning fire and the deep throated sobs and woeful cries. .

Margo, a stalwart in any crises, leaves Lilibeth with Katie and slips down the scullery, puts the kettle on the hob and re-lights the fire beneath the boiler. She surveys the grieving, wretched faces of the men and sighs. She rests her hand on Joe's' bowed head, 'I fink yer should go and see Katie and Lilibuff, they need yer,' she says quietly, 'I'll make us all a cup of tea.'

He finds Katie sat in a chair staring out of the window, her arms tightly wrapped around Lilibeth, 'Katie, darling, you should be in bed, and so should you, Lily.'

Katie turns to him, 'W...what happened, Joe?'

Solemnly he shakes his head, 'I honestly don't know, darling, I really don't.'

Margo enters carrying a tray, her face sombre. 'I've brought yer a cup of tea, Katie love, and a drop of brandy fer you, Joe. I hope yer don't mind lad, I helped meself ter yer brandy ter give the boys a drop, and all.'

Shrugging his shoulders indifferently, Joe gulps a grateful swig.

'Yer know Katie should be in bed Joseph, she needs her rest, we don't want her ter bleed out. Here, let me take little Lily back up ter bed fer yer.'

Lilibeth's face is ashen, 'Bad lady burn!' she whispers and puts her arms up to Margo.

Frowning, Margo looked quizzically at Joe, 'Shock I 'spect. Come on Lilibuff, kiss yer mammy and daddy and yer little bruver good night, yer can see them all in the mornin' lovey.'

Joe slumps down on the bed shaking his head, 'Gone,' he whispers, 'gone.'

'It's only a building, we can build it again, darling,' says Katie softly, wrapping her arms around him.

Joe shakes his head, grimacing, 'No, darling, It's Jed.'

Her eyes widen, her face pales, 'Jed, what do you mean?'

'He went back in the building, the roof collapsed. Oh, Katie love, he's... he's dead!' he buries his head in his hands as his tears flow.

Shocked, Katie tightens her hold on him, as the news sinks in, her tears flow freely, for Jed, Joanie, and baby Noah.

Half an hour later, Margo taps the door and peeps inside, her red blotchy face and puffy eyes cannot be hidden. 'Just ter let yer know, I had a bit of a job ter settle young Lilibuff, I think the fire's really upset her, but she's asleep now, bless her.'

Unable to speak, Joe nods gratefully.

After checking that the infant is sleeping, Margo retires to join Lilibeth upstairs.

Totally distraught and exhausted, Katie has cried herself to sleep in his arms. Gently he kisses her forehead, lifts her, and tucks her into bed. With tears in his eyes, he gazes at his precious son, trying to make sense of the bittersweet day. Dog tired he slips into bed and pulls Katie close.

Margo pops her head around the door an hour later, 'Sorry to disturb yer, but I thought I'd check on Jack Joshua,' she says quietly apologising, 'are yer sure you're alwight, Joe?'

The face that stares back at her is devoid of expression, he simply shrugs his shoulders.

'We've gotta talk, Joe,' she whispers, pulling a chair beside him, 'What happened ternight, it's tragic...' she gnaws on her bottom lip, 'I know this is gonna sound hard, but yer gotta fink about yer family, yer new son.'

Joe sighs and stares vacantly towards the window.

'Yer know Katie could easily loose her milk, even afore it comes in, wiv all this upset,' Margo points out, 'Jay J's really small, so we gotta make sure Katie stays calm, coz I doubt he'll survive wiv out her milk.'

He sighs. 'I hear you, Margo.'

She pats his hand, 'I'm serious,' she warns, and she leaves Joe with even more to think about.

From the cradle, a lusty cry from Jack Joshua disturbs everyone, Margo comes rushing in, 'Here,' she says, gently placing the infant in Joe's arms. 'Put him ter Katie's breast. I'll get a couple of nappies.'

Looking down at his son, he smiles, he is burying his head to his bare chest, his mouth desperately searching for a nipple. He smiles lovingly, 'Hah, you won't get anything from me Son. Come, let's latch you on to Mammy,' he whispers soothingly as he lays him carefully in Katie's arms, helping the tiny infant to latch onto her nipple. 'Are you comfortable, my clever darling?'

Katie gives a half-hearted smile as the infant instantly stopped wailing and sucks furiously. Three pairs of eyes watch in awe at the little soul, takes to his mother's breast. 'There yer goes, right as ninepence. When yer proper milk comes in, yer can soon build him up. Yer doing fine Katie love,' says Margo, managing a thin smile.

'I've got to go out and talk to the lads,' says Joe grimly, 'Try to sort things out.'

'Nay, no need, there's nowt yer can do, lad. Our Freddie's taken Mick and his boys back to Edna's on our Stan's cart, they gotta break the terrible news ter Edna and Joanie,' Margo explains, 'Best yer stay wiv Katie, she needs yer.'

'But what about Stan?'

'Don't go worryin' about him, Stan's gawn ter sleep in the parlour, there ain't nowt none of us can do right now.'

'You look all in yourself Margo, you should rest,' He says.

Margo smiles wearily, takes the sleeping infant from Katie's arms, winds him, changes his nappy then hands him to Joe. 'Aw don't worry about me, I ain't just had a little baby. Come on Katie love, let me tuck yer in gel, little Jay J's gonna want feedin' again, in a couple of hours.'

Hum, Jay J? Joe likes the sound of that, 'Don't worry about us Margo, we'll be fine, you get off to bed with Lily, I can manage,' he assures her.

'Call me if yer needs me,' she says, 'and puts little Jay J down in his cradle, yer gonna need all the sleep yer can git.'

Just as dawn breaks, Joe brings in a cup of tea for Katie, she had just finished trying to feed Jack Joshua for the third time, 'I'm just going to check on Margo and Stan. Here, let me put Jay J in the cradle, darling.' As he settles his son in the cradle, he hears coughing out in the yard.

Outside he finds Stan, stood with his head bowed and his hands sunk deep in his pockets, he's staring blankly at what is left of the new cottage.

A pungent smell fills the early morning air, whilst defiant wisps of smoke spiral from what is left of the charcoaled shell.

'Fuck, what the hell happened?' asks Joe, putting his arm around Stans shoulder.

'I just dunno,' rasps Stan, shaking his head, 'There weren't no lamps nor candles in the bedroom. It were a full moon and warm last night, so we never even lit the ruddy fire in the parlour!' He lifts his cap and scratches his head.

'Dear God, Jed gone, I can't believe it,' says Joe grimly 'This is all a bloody nightmare.'

Stan staggers uneasily on his feet, 'What a bloody fool, fancy going back in like that, and all fer a few sticks of bleedin' furniture!' he coughs violently, grasping Joe's arm for support, 'Gawd. I'm so sorry, Joe.'

'Take it easy Stan. Come, let's get you inside.'

As he sinks into the chair, Stan breaks down and weeps, 'Why… why the bloody hell did he go in there, Joe?' he sniffs, 'Fuck, I can't believe it… Jed gawn, he weren't no age at all!'

Handing Stan a brandy, Joe's face contorts with pain, 'I've got no answers Stan,' he says, bewildered he looks helplessly at Margo, 'Why?'

She tuts, 'Come on now boys, pull yerselves tergether, remember, Katie's in the bedroom wiv yer brand-new little son Joseph.'

Topping up Stan's drink Joe pours what's left in the bottle for himself, downing it in one go, 'I just can't take it all in,' he says, staring into the bottom of his empty glass.

'Huh, just look at yer Stanley, yer as black as a chimney sweep, 'Margo grumbles, 'Be a love, fetch the bath in Joe, there's plenty of hot water in the boiler.' She tuts and occupies herself cooking them all breakfast.

The atmosphere is decidedly strained at the table and although they are ravenous, most of the food goes to waste. No one utters a word until the table is cleared and the dishes washed.

'Where's our Lily?' asks Joe anxiously, his face creased with worry, he looks as if he'd aged ten years over night.

Margo is about to take a breakfast tray into Katie, 'She's alwight, she's in wiv Katie, dotin' on her new bruver Jay J, bless her little heart.'

Joe stands, 'I'll take it Margo, sit yourself down with Stan and have a cup of tea and something to eat,' he insists, 'Then perhaps yer can help Stan get in the bath, he's a bit shaky.'

Lilibeth is sat bedside Katie, with Jack Joshua cradled in her arms.

Before opening the door, Joe takes a deep breath and fixes a smile. He looks lovingly at Katie, 'Absolutely perfect, isn't he, darling?' says Joe proudly, 'Hah, Margo keeps calling him Jay J, suits him, don't you think?'

Katie nods her approval, 'I suppose Jack Joshua is a bit of a mouthful, Jack or Jay J is fine by me. What do you think Lilibeth?'

Sat on the bed, cradling the baby, Lilibeth's eyes are firmly fixed on her baby brother, she just nods and continues gently rocking him back and forth.

'Humm, Margo says you've gotta eat Katie, she says you've got to build your strength up or you'll lose your proper milk before it comes in,' he tells her, giving her a kiss.

After helping Katie to sit up, he puts the tray on her lap, he turns to Lily, 'And you, young Lily, had better go and have your breakfast, Aunty Margo says it'll go cold if you don't hurry up.'

Lilibeth looks up, saying nothing and carries on rocking the baby.

Puzzled by Lilibeth's reaction, Katie looks at Joe, 'You don't think she's jealous, do you?' she mumbles.

'Maybe. Hey, come on Lily, breakfast. Shall I give my favourite daughter, a piggyback?'

'Dunno,' she mutters sullenly.

Joining her on the bed, he puts his arm around Lily's shoulder, 'Isn't he lovely, you know he's a very lucky little boy to have a very special big sister like you, do you think you can manage to look after him with Mammy when Daddy goes back to work?'

Lilibeth nods, but keeps her eyes fixed firmly on her brother.

'Well how about giving your Daddy a hug and a kiss then?' he persists.

Lilibeth looks up at Joe and offers her pouting lips.

'Humm, you're not sorry you've got a little brother are you sweetheart?' he asks concerned.

'No daddy, he's mine, I love him, very much.' she proclaims, and promptly clams up again.

'I'm not sure what's wrong with Lily,' Joe says returning the tray to the scullery, 'I can barely get a word out of Lily.'

'Could be she's jealous,' suggests Margo.

'Katie thought that, but somehow I don't think so, she's holding the baby and can't take her eyes off him. I asked her straight out and she said she loves him very much.'

'Kids is funny sometimes,' says Stan, breaking his silence.

'Aye, yer probably right,' agrees Margo, 'I'm gonna take in some clean sheets and nappies, can yer give us a hand carryin' in the washin' bowl, Joe, I got ter check Katie, make sure everyfin's alright. I'll give her a nice wash and change the sheets. Then per'aps I can talk Lilibuff inter helpin' me barf Jay J, she'll like that.'

'What sorta name's Jay J?' asks Stan, at last beginning to show a modicum of interest.

'It's short fer Jack Joshua,' she explains, picking up a pile of nappies.

'Huh, I fink I prefer Jack Joshua, a good strong name, so when does I get ter see him then?' he asks.

'After I've seen ter Katie and Jay J, and after yer both have had a shave.

The sound of Jack Joshua hollering sends her scurrying to the bedroom.

Stan removes his sooty cap, 'Hum, well that's us well and truly told, Joe.'

'Heart of gold, your Margo, what would we ever do without her?' Joe replies.

Joe, stripped, washed, and shaved, helps Stan take off his grimy clothes and into the bath, then leaving Stan to have a well-deserved soak, he follows in Margo's footsteps, carrying in the bowl of fresh warm water to Katie.

'Ain't nuffink wrong wiv Lilibuff.' declares Margo, making a pot of tea. 'She really loves her little bruver, she even helped me give him a barf.' She smiles approvingly at Stan and Joe, both are now clean and freshly shaven, 'Good as gold, Lilibuff were, she enjoyed every minute of it. But now I come ter fink of it, she were sort of quiet when I put him back in his cradle ter sleep.' Margo looks at Stan and scowls, 'Gawd look at yer Stanley, yer ruddy clothes is miles too big, yer ruddy trousers are all rolled up at the bottom. Huh, I s'pose they fits round yer belly,' she retorts sarcastically.

'It's the best we could do,' Joe tells her, 'They were Wills, and they're not that big, Margo.'

Margo snatches Stan's cap and throws it into the flames of the boiler.

'Hey, what the hell did yer go and do that fer? I'm lost wiv out me ruddy hat!' says Stan looking sorely aggrieved.

'It's filfy black Stanley, we'll just have ter get a new one.' Margo retorts, sniffing and wiping a tear from her eye with her pinny.

Stan put his arm around Margo, 'Hey sweetheart, don't get upset gel.'

'Aw sorry Stan, take no notice of me,' she sniffs again, fighting to stave off the tears that are bubbling up inside, 'I'm all sixes and sevens.

I dunno what I got ter moan about, yer looks grand, me old love,' she says, giving Stan a peck on the cheek.

'Thanks saucepot, I suppose we've just gotta make the best of fings.' His smile vanishes, 'Anyway, me and Joe been talkin'. We gotta go and attend ter Jed, bless him. But first I'll pop in ter see Katie, and the little ones. But like I said… we can't leave him out there… we're gotta get Jed out…' he pauses, wiping his eyes on his sleeve, 'We can't put it orf… then me and Joe ought ter go to Edna and Mick's and see Joanie.'

Nodding slowly, Joe sighs deeply, 'We've gotta give our condolences and help to make arrangements for poor Jed.'

'Yer'll have a job Joe, our Freddie took yer horse ter fetch me last night, and we came back on yer cart Stan. Don't forget, our Freddie took Mick and the boys back ter Edna's last night, and he ain't back yet. So short of walkin' yer gonna have ter wait,' she informs them.

'Oh right.' He doesn't want to bring up the subject again, but it has to be done, 'Margo, can you keep Lily with Katie and Jay J. Pull the curtains, coz me and Stan's gotta get Jed out of the ruins, clean him up and wrap him up decent, until we can arrange things properly?' asks Joe.

Biting her lip, Margo fights the tears that are threatening to crupt again, 'Course I will lovey, I'll get yer some sheets.'

With Jed respectfully taken care of and laid out in the barn they return to the cottage.

Stan puts his arm around Joe's shoulder, 'I fink I'd like ter put me head round the door and say hello ter Katie and the nipper, if that's alwight wiv you.'

He nods, 'Come on Stan, I'll introduce you to my beautiful son.'

For the first time since the fire, Stan manages a smile as he bends over and gives Katie a kiss on her forehead, 'So how is yer ducky?'

Katie smiles. 'I'm fine, thanks to Joseph and Margo.'

'Aw get away wiv yer, it weren't me, it was your Joe what did it, and all by himself, bless him. I take my hat orf ter him, he did a grand job, he saved little Jay J's little life he did.' declares Margo, lifting the baby from the cot and placing him in Stan's arms, 'Here Stanley, say hello to Jay J.'

Stan looks down at the infant and beams, 'Well I be blowed, he's the spittin' image of his daddy. Gawd love us, what a mop of hair. Hello baby boy, I'm yer Uncle Stanley.'

'He's smiling at you Stan.' Joe points out proudly. 'Look.'

'Wind,' says Margo smirking, 'Jay J's got wind.'

Stan delves into his pocket and pulls out some half crowns and florins, 'Er, hope yer don't mind Margo, it were yer purse love, is it alwight?'

Margo nods, 'Of course Stan love.'

'These are fer you little man, give yer a start in life. Yer can be very proud of him, Joe, he might be little, but he's a mighty handsome lad, just like his daddy.' Suddenly Stan's face screws up, as if in pain, 'Oh gawd, the Lord giveth, and the Lord taketh. Shit! What a bittersweet day,' he cries out in anguish, and a morbid silence, envelops the occupants of the room.

'Nasty black lady, burned her arms,' whispers Lilibeth sombrely.

They all frown and stare at Lilibeth, baffled.

Kneeling down beside her, Joe softly asks, 'What do you mean, darling, who was burnt? What lady?'

Lilibeth flings her arms around his neck and weeps and despite all the gentle coaxing, she says nothing more.

'Time ter put some washin' on, what wiv all these here nappies and sheets, then we'd best make a start on dinner,' announces Margo. 'Come on Lilibuff, yer can help me lovey,' and without giving her a chance to protest, she takes hold of Lilibeth's hand and leads her through to the scullery.

'So, what was that all about wiv Lilibuff? Stan asks.

'I really don't know,' says Katie, 'but something's upset her, and it's definitely not Jack Joshua.'

'I reckon it's the fire what's upset her,' suggests Stan.

'You could well be right,' Katie agrees, 'She got really upset watching the fire raging.'

Joe shakes his head, 'Take a seat by the bed Stan, you look all in. I want to talk to Katie, and I want you to hear what I've got to say,' says Joe drawing him up a chair.

'What's on yer mind Mate?' asks Stan, who was still clearly shaken and only too glad to be able to take the weight off his feet for a while.

'Joanie,' says Joe grimly, 'she's not only lost her home, but she's lost her loving husband, and left with baby Noah to bring up, alone. I thought, um... me and Katie, could help them out. We owe them.' He says, looking to Katie for her approval.

Katie slips her hand in his and nods. 'I know where you're going with this, Joe, and yes, of course.'

'I was thinking,' Joe continues, 'we could easily buy a little place for Joanie and Noah, we could afford to give her some money to keep them going too.' Admiring, Joe's generous sense of justice and thoughtfulness she agrees, 'It's the very least we can do.'

Stan raises his hand to lift his cap to scratch his head, then realises Margo thrown his sooty cap in the fire. 'It's mighty good of yer, but I reckons wiv Jed gawn, Joanie will want ter go back ter Edna and Mick's now.'

Joe sighs, 'Maybe you're right Stan, but if that's the case, we can buy Edna and Mick's place for them. It's big enough after all, they've got two bedrooms,' he points out. 'Granted they don't have a lot of land so I reckon we could pick it up fairly cheap. At least they won't have to worry about paying rent and stuff.'

'Yer don't have ter do this, Joe,' says Stan, 'I mean yer spent a lot of time and money doin' the old outhouses up, and you were givin' them work and all. Now it's all gawn up in smoke, yer back where yer started, and out of pocket, ain't yer?'

'Humm, Hardly, that's as maybe Stan, but the point is, I'm sitting here with my beautiful wife, sweet daughter and my precious new son,' he squeezes Katie's hand, 'I couldn't live with myself if I didn't... we didn't look after them,' he says, burying his head in his hands and weeping shamelessly.

'Yer gotta do what yer finks is right,' says Stan, getting up and stretching his aching back, 'I'll go and give our Margo and Lilibuff a hand wiv dinner.' He walks to the door and turns, 'Jay J's beaut'ful, congratulations ter yer both.' He gives them a cheery wave, closing the door quietly behind him.

Wrapping her arms around him to comfort him, Katie strokes his cheek fondly, 'I think it's the most generous, caring thing we can do for them, darling, well done.'

'It's only money, sadly it won't bring Jed back' says Joe miserably. 'Anyway, we still have plenty left, so if we buy Edna's cottage, we could give Joanie a small lump sum to keep them going.' He sighs, 'But... of course it's entirely up to you, darling, it's your money after all.'

Katie stares at him indignantly, 'My money! What do you mean Joseph, my money?'

'But don't you see? It is your money by rights,' he points out.

Holding her up left hand out she retorts, 'Do you see that?' Wagging her finger with her wedding ring on it, 'Mr and Mrs Joseph Markson, husband and wife, everything we do is shared between us. Your money, my money, Joseph, whatever we have we share! Never normally raising her voice she blushes and softens her tone, smiling wryly she adds, that includes making and delivering our beautiful first-born son.'

Their conversation is rudely interrupted by Jay J crying gustily for his feed again. 'Hey up, Daddy's little man, are you hungry?' he whispers soothingly, picking him up, kissing his forehead. 'Here we go son, Mammy will feed you.'

Tears of joy run down his face as he watches his son suckling at her breast. 'I love you so much, my darling wife, you're so very clever, thank you for giving me our precious son.'

'I love you too Joseph, isn't he just perfect, he looks just like his handsome daddy?'

'I'll help,' said a little voice at the door. Lilibeth creeps in, 'Me see my little brother have his dinner,' she whispers, clambering onto the bed.

For a short while they sit together as a proud, contented family unit, their sorrows left outside the room, until Margo taps the door, 'Sorry ter disturb yer, can yer come inter the parlour, Joe? We got visitors.'

Mick, Abe, Tom and Freddie are gathered in the parlour with Stan. Margo starts noisily manhandling the dishes in readiness for yet another brew of tea.

Their conversations are hushed and full of grief for Jed's untimely death.

First comes the sadness and sorrow.

'It's a stupid question I know, but how are you Mick, how's Edna and Joanie?' Joe asks, his face filled with torment.

'Understandably shocked, but bearing up, ta Mate,' answers Mick quietly.

Joe wraps his arms around Mick to comfort him.

'It don't bear thinkin' about,' says Freddie shaking his head.

'Aye, you're right there, I still can't take it all in,' says Joe, 'One minute everything's fine, then...' his voice fades away.

Though Margo has prepared a tray of tea and cake, her good intentions are wasted when Freddie produces three large bottles of brandy and a bottle of gin. Not that she minds one bit, in fact she takes a glass of gin herself, for medicinal purposes she explains.

There follows the inevitable string of questions, so Margo pours them all another stiff drink.

Three more top ups and the alcohol relaxes the morbid atmosphere, just a little, it loosens a few tongues, then anger takes over.

Freddie shakes his head, 'Why the fuckin' hell did he go in there? The place was nearly empty, there were hardly any furniture in there anyway, 'cept what were in the bedroom.'

'I only wish I knew. I've been over it with Stan, time and time again, but we just can't work it out,' says Joe shaking his head and gulping down another large slug of his brandy.

'What I'd like ter know is how the fuckin' hell the fire started? There weren't a naked flame nowhere, and definitely not in the bedroom? We was all tergether in the parlour,' Abe points out.

'A fire don't start up on its own, so what the fuck happened, I wanna know?' growls Tom, 'Well some fucker was walkin' around wiv a lamp burnin'.'

'I think we should take a good look around, see if we can come up with some answers,' declares Joe grimly.

The conversation moves on to practicalities, and Margo topped up their glasses once again.

'We've brought the um... the coffin fer our Jed...' whispers Mick. 'We wants ter take my boy back home, yer know, ter make arrangements.'

400

'Which of course I will pay for,' says Joe, grimacing at the thought of Jed laid out in the barn. He sees Mick shaking his head. 'Me and Stan... we found Jed face down, so his front wasn't burned at all, we've cleaned him up...' he croaks, 'and like I said, Katie and me will pay for the funeral.'

Mick stands and sighs, 'That's really good of yer, Joe, but me and Edna... we can manage, ta ever so.' he says resting his hand on Joe's shoulder.

Shaking his head, Joe sighs heavily, 'I'm sorry, but I can't let you do that Mick, and there's no need for anyone to manage. I er, that is Katie and me...'

Mick opens his mouth to protest but Stan jumps in, 'Here, don't be hasty Mick, come on, let Joe have his say.'

Weary from grief, Mick shrugs his shoulders indifferently and sits back down and empties his glass.

'I er... I feel responsible Mick,' Joe tells him.

'Yer wasn't even there, Joe lad, so don't go takin' the blame,' Mick gallantly points out.

Distraught, Joe intervenes, 'That's as maybe Mick, but it was me that offered him the cottage and job!' he says, uncharacteristically raising his voice, 'and it was me that had you all working on the bloody building!'

'Hey, hey, come on lads,' chivvies Margo softly. 'Ain't there been enough upset?' and she empties the second bottle between them all, with the exception of Stan who is looking decidedly grey around the gills and quite peaky.

One large gulp and Joe's glass is empty again, his voice returning to normal, 'Please Mick, I... that is me and Katie want to do something, we've been talking,' he says seriously, 'we want to buy Joanie a little cottage, somewhere that Joanie and Noah can call their own. We know we can't bring Jed back, but me and Katie...'

Mick frowns, shaking his head, 'There ain't no point, coz our Joanie and little Noah will be livin' wiv Edna and me...' He glances at Joe, who is beginning to lose his self-composure. In an act of courage, Mick's deep-rooted sorrow turns to sympathy for Joe, 'Look I knows yer means well, Joe... I does, really, but...'

Joe gnaws on his lip, 'Then hear me out Mick, please!'

Mick huffs, 'Go on, Joe, I'm listenin' ter yer.'

'Me and Katie regard everyone in this room as our dearest friends, as near as you can get to family,' says Joe, rising from his chair. 'Over the years we've always been here for each other, through thick and thin, surely?' he looks to Margo for support. Margo nods.

'Mick, if Joanie's gonna be living at yours then, me and Katie, want to buy your Honeysuckle Cottage, for you all.'

Mick's eyebrows lift in surprise.

'And we want to give Joanie a sum of money to help her keep going.'

Astounded, Mick shakes his head, 'I dunno what ter say, Joe.'

Joe offers Mick his hand, 'Come on Mick, shake on it, please. It's only money Mate, and me and Katie value our friendship above everything. Now please, what do you say Mick?'

Rising to his feet, Mick flings his arms around Joe and cries on his shoulder, 'I s'pose it'll m...make things easier fer our J...Joanie. Alwight Mate, t...thank you.'

Opening a new bottle of brandy Margo charges their glasses, once more, 'I want yer all ter stand and give a toast,' she tells them raising her own glass and unashamedly allowing her tears to flow, saying, 'Ter our Jed, may God rest his sweet soul.'

'Ter our Jed!' they chorus.

'And while yer all on yer feet, ter little Jack Joshua and all...' she adds.

'Jack Joshua!' they chorused again.

'And finally, ter the most special fing of all. True friendship!'

Everyone empties their glasses, 'True friendship!'

The mention of Jay J and a bellyful of brandy lightens the atmosphere a touch. 'So, Joe, what's he like, your little Jack Joshua?' asks Mick.

'Oh, he's just perfect,' Joe brags, trying hard not to sound too joyous, 'Would you er, would you like to see him Mick?'

'Aye, course I would, er, and how's Katie?' he enquires.

'Jay J is on the small side, but they're both perfect, and all fanks ter Joe playing doctor,' states Margo looking smug.

'Aw it was nothing,' says Joe.

Margo laughs heartily, 'Well you might ruddy well fink it were nuffin', but I bet poor Katie wouldn't agree wiv yer. Joe saved his little life and Katie's and all. Anyways, I'll go and see if our Katie's decent, then yer can take it in turn ter go in and see them. Only a couple of minutes at a time mind.'

By midday, the coffin has been soberly loaded on the back of the cart and covered with a clean sheet in readiness for Jed's solemn, final journey home.

'I reckon it won't hurt ter give the old ruins the once over afore we go,' suggests Freddie, 'see if we can't fathom out what the bloody hell happened.'

A morbid dark cloud surrounds them as Stan, Mick, Abe and Tom along with Freddie, cautiously follow Joe inside the fire blackened shell. Surveying the scene of devastation, each are filled with stomach churning wretchedness.

Apart from the newly built chimney breast that is still stood stubbornly, like an epitaph to Jed, they find the stone sink and marble larder slab is also intact, sat caked in a shroud of heavy soot, everything else, save the blackened stone walls, are reduced to huge pieces of charcoal, beneath which lay two mangled and warped iron bedsteads, even the thick horsehair mattresses is gone.

Despairingly, Joe runs his fingers through his hair and sighs, examining the bedroom where the fire had started, he shakes his head. 'How the fuck can we tell what started the fire from all this? Just look at it!'

Stan put a sympathetic hand on his shoulder, 'Don't torture yerself, Joe, come on lads, there ain't naught we can do in here.'

Freddie trips over a charcoal covered beam, 'Sorry Mate, looks like even yer dairy's gawn, Joe, there ain't nuffink anyone can do, 'cept knock the ruddy lot down and build it agin.'

'It'll be gone by next week, even if I have to work, day and night,' vows Joe, 'but I won't be building it here again, it wouldn't be right.'

Heads bowed, one by one, they start to troupe out, resigned, feeling next to useless.

'I'll stay on wiv yer, Joe, give yer a hand,' offers Stan.

Freddie stumbles on something, turning his ankle, 'Shit!! What the devil... glass?'

Stan looks back, 'What's up son?'

Freddie bends down to pick something up 'What the fuck is this?'

They all turn to take a look.

'Look here, Joe, I reckon this is a ruddy oil lamp, a bit busted and sooty maybe, what do yer fink?'

They all stand looking whilst Joe slowly turns the broken blackened object in his hands, 'You're right Freddie, but where did it come from?' he asks, 'I thought you said there weren't any naked flames in here, Stan.'

'Aye I did, so where the bleedin' hell did it come from?'

Freddie pipes up, 'If I didn't know better, I'd say someone must have chucked it frew the open winder and it landed here.'

'But who?' asks Joe. 'Who would do that, it's insane?'

A puzzling thought comes to Joe, 'Our Lily, she said something about a naughty black lady, didn't she? Hum, she's really upset, and there's definitely something she won't talk about.'

Margo, who had brought out a tray of tea nods, 'Aye, yer right, Joe, perhaps yer should have a talk wiv her,' she suggests. 'But gently mind, we don't wanna frighten her.'

Deep in thought he frowns, 'Freddie, d'yer think you could take Jed home to his family with Mick and the boys?'

'No problem, Joe, I'll come straight back Mate, we gotta get to the bottom of this,'

'I hate to keep putting all this on you Freddie, but before you go, can you put some stuff on the cart, for Edna? There's a churn of fresh milk up by the door, some eggs and plenty of vegetables and Katie's got a larder full of food. Edna might be glad of it.'

'Aye of course Mate. It won't take long,' says Freddie, only too pleased to do something constructive to help. 'Come on Abe, yer can give us a hand.'

Taking Mick aside, Joe hands him a package, 'It's the money I promised, to buy your house with, it should be enough. If not, we can sort it out later. Tell them... tell them I'm so very sorry.' His voice breaks so they hug, sharing their grief.

Soberly Joe and Stan stand shoulder to shoulder, their tears falling freely as they watch them leave the yard with Jed on his final journey home.

As they return to the cottage, Stan spots Katie at the bedroom window looking highly distressed, he points her out to Joe, 'Your Katie's in tears, yer better go and see her, all this upset ain't gonna do her no good,' advises Stan.

Joe strides straight through to the bedroom.

CHAPTER 17

Subdued conversation on the practicalities and arrangements are shared between Stan and Margo, over a cup of tea in the scullery, until Joe returns and joins them.

'Me and Stan's decided we're gonna stay on here, ter help yer wiv and Katie and the kiddies,' Margo informs him. 'Is Katie alwight?'

Joe gives a thin smile and sighs, 'I think she's in shock, she's keeps staring out the window at the ruins.'

'I was afeared this'd happen,' says Margo wiping her hands dry on her pinny. 'Your Katie's milk won't come in properly, at this rate, gawd knows where we's gonna find a wet nurse. Course, in different circumstances, Joanie could have done it, but after losing her Jed that's impossible now.'

Joe stares at her mortified at the very idea. 'No Margo, no bloody wet nurse!'

Looking somewhat apologetic, Margo gently explains, 'Katie's hardly got enough milk as it is. She's gotta look after herself, eat more and drink a lot of milk. I s'pose she might be able to manage, just about... but any more upset Joe, and I'm tellin' yer, we'll have no choice, Jay J's only little he needs building up, bless him. If Katie can't feed him, we'll have no choice, we'll just have ter find a wet-nurse fer Jay J, and pretty damn quick and all!'

Putting his head in his hands, Joe groans in despair.

'Look, it might not come ter that, Joe, but Katie's only got little tits as it is, and Jay J needs feeding up. Let's see how it goes, Joe,' she pats his shoulder, 'but at the end of the day, yer gotta fink about Jay J. In the meantime, it's best yer ask yer doc if he knows of a wet nurse in the area?' Margo suggests kindly.

Joe's horrified, 'No. I said no Margo! I'll talk to Katie, leave it with me!' Fuming he storms off to the bedroom.

Katie is sitting in the chair trying to feed Jay J again, 'How's it going, darling, is he feeding any better?'

Katie shakes her head, taking Jay J from her breast, 'I'm getting sore nipples. They're so painful,' she tells him, 'Look.'

He winces. They looked very red and cracked. He tries make light of the situation to calm her down, 'Oh my poor darling, he's not an expert like his daddy, is he?' he quips, he puts his arm around her shoulders. 'Listen Katie, I've been talking to Margo. She reckons you're not eating and drinking enough, so you can't make enough milk. Now I know you're upset, darling, but for Jay J's sake, you must start to eat and drink as much as you can. You see he's hungry, he's not getting enough milk to fill his tummy. That's why he needs to keep latching on to you all the time, he's still hungry.'

'Really, Joe, do you think so?'

'Yes, my love, if he gets more milk each feed then he won't need your breasts so much. He'll have a full tummy and won't need to suckle so often.'

A polite tap on the door and Margo enters, interrupting their conversation. 'Here Katie love, I've brought some warm milk, and I'm making some broth fer yer dinner, be a good girl and drink it all up.'

Joe cradles his son, watching Katie sat by the window, making sure she's drinking it all.

'That's a good girl, Joe will bring you some dinner in a bit, a couple of days and you'll soon be sorted and so will little Jay J,' says Margo kindly.

'Please, come away from the window, darling, sit with me and our beautiful son,' he says patting the bed.

Katie snuggles up to him, 'You're so clever, my husband. I promise to eat and drink a lot more.'

'I know you will, darling. But I'm not really clever, Margo explained it to me,' he confesses with a wry smile, omitting to mention Margo's advice to find a wet nurse.

Under Joe's watchful gaze, Katie does as she's told, eating the chicken stew, plus the egg custard that Margo has made especially. He's so proud of her.

Early next morning the baby is crying. Joe hops out of bed to pick him up, he opens Katie's bodice 'Oooo Katie, look, you're actually leaking proper milk, you clever girl.' Gently he places the baby to the nipple that looks the least sore, helping him to latch on, Jay J sucks hungrily, 'Hey, that's my boy!' he grins. 'Just like his Daddy.'

Jay J doesn't cry when he takes him away from her breast, he changes his nappy, winds him and settles the satisfied infant in his cradle. 'Perhaps you can both come through and sit in the scullery with us sweetheart,' suggests Joe, hoping to distract her from the view through the window.

'I'd like that, Joseph. Can you give me a hand?'

Settling Katie beside the fire with a blanket over her knees, Joe puts Jay J on her lap, 'Are you sure you are comfortable sweetheart?' he asks, plumping the cushion behind her.

'Yes, thank you, I'm fine.'

'Right, I'll warm some milk for you. Do you fancy scrambled eggs, darling?'

After milking the cows and goat, Stan and Margo collect the eggs and return to the cottage. They find Katie sitting in the scullery with Jay J sleeping in his cradle.

'What are you doing in here lovey, where's Lily?' enquires Margo.

Katie frowns, 'I'm worried about her, she doesn't seem to have any interest in anything, well apart from Jay J that is.'

'So where is she now lovey?' she asks, topping up the teapot for the umpteenth time, 'Lilibuff didn't eat her breakfast.'

'Upstairs, on her bed with Daisy.'

'Just leave her ter me, I won't be long,' she says, disappearing upstairs to Lily's room. 'Make sure Katie drinks her milk!' she yells back to Joe.

'Now yer horse is back, we can make a start on clearin' the rubble terday,' offers Stan sitting gratefully back in the chair opposite Katie.

'Sooner the better,' agrees Joe handing him a freshly made cup of tea.

'Yer ain't got a drop of brandy ter put in me tea, ter cheer me up have yer?' Stan asks, keeping his voice low, watching the door in case Margo reappears.

Joe gives Stan a wink and a smile, 'Of course Mate, here we go.'

'What's this about clearing the rubble, darling?' asks Katie.

Joe hands her a cup of hot milk and picks up Jay J, 'I'm afraid the dairy's gone along with the rest. We're gonna have to rebuild it, but I want to put it on the other side of the barn, nearer the cows and sheep, what do you think, sweetheart?'

Relieved that the ruins will be gone from view, Katie smiles, 'You know I'm more than happy for you to make all the decisions Joe, and for what it's worth, I think it's a good idea.'

Tickled pink at the way his son is gripping his finger, Joe gazes lovingly at his son. 'Hum, I'm glad you agree, darling, because I've got other plans too.'

Jay J, is sleeping soundly, so Katie takes him from Joe and places him in the cradle, 'Oh, what plans are these, Joe?'

'Yep, I've got plans, I'm gonna build us a new cottage for us darling, something bigger, more room for us all.'

'What's this?' asks Margo coming back with a subdued Lily in tow, sitting her down an giving her some buttered toast, she's just in time to hear the end of the conversation.

'Joe says he's gonna build a bigger place,' says Stan, with a lopsided grin on his face.

Hands on her hips, Margo eyes Stan suspiciously, 'Stanley 'ooper, have yer been drinkin' agin?'

He grins at her with a twinkle in his eyes, 'Course I has, me old darlin', I got me tea ain't I?'

Due to the current circumstances, Margo decides to give him the benefit of the doubt, just this once, 'Humm, well perhaps I'd better pour yer next cup. Now what's all this about a new cottage?'

'Well,' says Joe gazing adoringly down at his sleeping son, 'I have decided me, and Katie and the children need more room, and...' he says looking at Stan and Margo in turn, 'I was wondering what you'd both think if we offered you Sweet Briars, compliments of your good friends, me and Katie?'

'Good gawd, have yer taken leave of yer senses lad?' asks Stan.

Katie smiles at Joe and she gives him a nod of approval.

'Not at all Mate. From what I gather, your Freddie's planning on getting wed soon,' he says, knowing full well that on the quiet, Freddie had been searching high and low for a place for weeks. 'They deserve a house of their own, and he's perfectly able to run your business for you. Now don't take this the wrong way Mate, but you're not getting any younger, you deserve to take things a bit easier, you know, a bit of quality time spent with Margo. So, what I'm proposing is, you let Freddie run your yard and live in your place, and you Stan, take a slice of the profits every month, like a sleeping partner, so to speak. You and Margo can come to live at Sweet Briars then you and me can work together in the spinney. So, what do you think?'

'Humm,' Stan scratches his head, 'I dunno as I'll be much use ter yer Mate, like yer said, I ain't gettin' no younger.'

'Hah, I'm not looking for you to start felling trees or anything heavy, but if you don't think you'll be able to milk the cows each morning, see to the sheep, collect the eggs and take a cart load of wood to Freddie, once a fortnight...?' says Joe smirking.

'Eh... course I can, Joe, I ain't that far past it!' exclaims Stan. Clearly bowled over by Joe's offer, he looks to Margo for guidance.

Shaking her head, Margo frowns, 'I don't rightly know what ter say, Joe, I mean it's a lovely idea but, our Freddie could never run the yard on his own, it just ain't practical,' she points out.

Settling himself at the table, Joe pours three small measures of brandy. He hands one to Margo and slides another over to Stan. 'But he wouldn't have to. Tom's nearly nineteen, he's a strapping lad who's willing to graft, don't forget, he's worked with you off and on for years, and young Abe can work with Freddie too.'

'What about me basket making?' asks Margo.

Joe takes her work worn hands and gives them a gentle rub, 'It's about time you looked after your poor hands Margo, get them all nice and soft. Perhaps you could use the second bedroom upstairs as a sewing room to make your lovely quilts and clothes. Maybe you can teach young Abe how to make your baskets,' he suggests, adding, 'both of Mick's lads could do with full-time work, so we all win.'

Katie intervenes, 'We really would like you both to consider it. You would have two incomes coming in, a share of the yard's profits and the wages we'd pay you,' she points out. 'Freddie and Verity could have your house and yard, and we will give you Sweet Briars,' she explains. 'Think about it. Joe and I, we're asking you to consider our offer, very seriously. Please?'

'Well, we's more than tempted Katie love, ain't we Margo? But we'd have ter speak ter young Freddie, and Micks lads too.'

The pain that they've all had etched on their faces fades a little, Katie stands to give Margo a hug, 'Oh Margo, say you'll think about it, you won't be sorry.'

'Aye a new start all round,' says Stan grinning. 'So how about we have a little drink ter celebrate?

Margo tuts, raising an eyebrow but picks up the bottle anyway, 'If Freddie agrees then, yes please Joe. Bein' as we got somefin' ter smile about, maybe we could have just a little one.'

Light-hearted chatter lifts the gloom that has been hanging over the cottage.

It suddenly dawns on Joe that Lilibeth has sat completely silent throughout the entire conversation, shredding her toast into little pieces, weirdly she has not shown an iota of interest at all, not even making a single comment. He's extremely concerned, this is not Lily at all. Hoping to cheer her up he stands and grabs her from behind, lifting her up and twirling around enthusiastically, 'Hey Lily, daddy's gonna build a big new house for us sweetheart!' 'Stop it daddy, if you make a big noise, you'll wake my little brother up,' she chastises him pouting.

'Lilibeth, please, darling? Did you not hear? Daddy's going to build a big new house for us, and Aunty Margo and Uncle Stan are going to come and live in this one, then we can see them every day, isn't it wonderful?' says Katie.

For the first time, since the fire, her little face breaks into a beautiful smile. Picking Lilibeth up Joe sits her on his knee and kisses her cheek. 'Can you tell Daddy something, darling?' he asks softly. 'Do you like having a baby brother sweetheart?'

Her little face lights up, she smiles sweetly, 'Oh yes Daddy, I love him lots and lots, coz he my baby brother, and I helped Aunty Margo wash his dirty bum and we gave him a bath.'

'Then can you tell me why you are so sad, sweetheart?'

Lilibeth frowns, looking at everyone to see if they are cross with her.

It's worrying Joe, he needs to get to the bottom of this. He picks her up he carries her through to the bedroom, sitting her on his knee again, 'You do know how much Daddy loves you, darling. You are very special to me, and I will never be cross with you, and I will always keep you safe, because you are my very special daughter?' he says softly.

Lily had no idea what he's talking about but nods anyway.

'So, I'm wondering sweetheart, do you remember the naughty black lady because silly Daddy's forgotten.'

Lily screws up her face to think, 'Umm… yes Daddy, very bad lady,' she replies scowling.

'Indeed, she was very naughty. Erm… what did you see her do, darling? Because Daddy can't remember, no matter how hard I try,' he prompts.

'Naughty lady threw flames in Uncle Jed's bedroom,' she replies.

Joe takes a deep breath to stay calm, 'And you actually saw her do it?' he asks quietly. 'How?'

'Yes, I did Daddy, through the window, the nasty lady hurt her arms with the fire.'

'What did the lady look like Lily, can you tell me?'

'Lady got a black dress, with very long black hair, she's not a pretty lady coz she was very bad.'

'Do you know, my darling daughter, you are the cleverest girl in the whole world,' he tells her. 'Don't worry, darling, Daddy will sort this out.' He picks her up and takes her back to the scullery to sit with Katie, deciding to talk to Stan privately, later.

Jay J is making it known that it's time for his feed, so Margo suggests Lily goes up to bed for a nap. Joe walks Katie and the baby into the bedroom, lifting Katie into bed, he opens her bodice and helps Jay J latch onto her breast. 'Is it getting any easier, darling?' he asks caringly, as he watches his little son suckling. 'Your breasts are definitely more swollen.'

'Much better, now my milk has come in. My nipples aren't so painful, and he sleeps so much longer in between feeds, thank goodness.'

She spots saucy look in his eyes. 'What?'

'Mmm, I hope they stay that size. I've missed them so much. I know it's early days, my sexy little woodnymph and I probably shouldn't say it, but I really miss making love to you.'

Giving Joe a sweet smile she agrees, 'I know, I'm really missing you too, but we're going to have to wait till I stop bleeding. Why don't you get into bed with me, Jay J's nearly finished his feed?'

No need to be asked twice, he strips off and gets in beside her. He waits until his tiny infant is fed and winded, then after a decent attempt at changing his son's nappy he gently settles him into his cradle.

Patting the bed, Katie smiles, gazing at him with her come-to-bed eyes. 'Come, cuddle me, my darling husband,' she purrs.

Snuggling into her he gasps as her hand slides beneath the cover, closing his eyes he emits a long throaty moan as she grasps his cock firmly, her index finger toying with the bead of moisture on the tip. 'We don't have to wait, my sexy husband. I want to make you come, darling.'

Moaning lowly, enthralled with her tender ministration, as she skilfully increases the intense sensation, driving him wild, pushing him higher, building him even higher. 'Come on Joseph, I want you to come,' her soft, sensual voice encouraging him to absorb his increasing pleasure, and submit to his impending orgasm. 'Katie! Oh, sweet Jesus!' he cries out as he savours his release, ejaculating at her bidding.

Still content, with a full tummy, Jay J thankfully carries on sleeping soundly, affording them the luxury of sleeping undisturbed for two heavenly, peaceful hours.

Waking, Joes' mind is working overtime, he needs to talk to Stan, to discuss the conversation he'd had with Lily. Carefully, not to disturb Katie, he slides out of bed, checks that Jay J is still asleep then gets dressed and goes in search of Stan.

'Alwight, Joe?' Stan greets him. 'Look Mate, we like yer idea of movin' in here. Me and Margo says if it's alwight wiv Freddie, of course we would love ter take yer up on yer generous offer.'

Slapping his thighs, Joe chuckles, 'That's great news. Freddie will be well pleased. Welcome aboard to you both.'

The room falls quiet. Joe is thinking of his talk with Lily earlier.

'So, what's up, Joe, yer bein' ruddy quiet?' asks Stan, noticing the pensive look on Joe's face.

'Er, fancy a stroll in the yard Stan?' Joe asks, nodding towards the door. 'I'm gonna check on the chickens.'

Once outside, Joe repeats to Stan, his talk with Lily. 'Now I don't want to influence you, but I'm asking if Lily's description rings a bell with you Mate.'

Without even pausing to think Stan declares, 'Izzy Perkins! Wiv out a shadow of doubt. Long black hair, dressed all in black, of course, it's Izzy bloody Perkins! The mad cow never got over yer rejectin' her advances, did her? Followed yer round fer a year or more, wouldn't take no fer a bleedin' answer, she was obsessed wiv yer, Joe.'

'My thoughts exactly,' says Joe frowning.

'Shit! Yer knows what that means, don't yer?'

'Sadly, I do Stan. She's a cold-hearted murderer,' says Joe, trying to fathom out what to do about it. 'Look, Freddie and Mick are coming tomorrow afternoon. I think we ought to tell them, then decide between us what to do?' he suggests.

Stan is all for going to Izzy's and dragging her out of her house there and then, after all, she had callously murdered poor Jed and left Joanie a young widow with a small baby!

But Joe feels differently. 'I dunno, think about it, we've only got our Lily's word for it, I know she'd never lie but she's only six, the problem is we need proof.'

Suddenly a thought pops into Stan's head, 'If what Lilibuff says is right, she'll have burns won't she,' he reasons.

'Good point Mate. She will, but I still think we should wait for Freddie and Mick. After all, this business affects us all, especially poor Mick and his family.'

'Alwight, if yer fink it's fer the best,' Stan agrees.

'Good, in the meantime we can make a start on demolishing what's left of the outbuildings, it'll be best for everyone when it's gone,' suggests Joe.

Stan agrees, 'Aye, sooner it's gawn the better lad.'

With the necessary chores behind them, they make a start on the ruins. Joe swings the heavy hammer and Stan picks up the rubble, loading it onto the cart. They work with determination and with the chimney finally raised to the ground, there's little left other than a pile of rubble, but the stench of smoke still lingers in the air, getting up their nostrils and into their clothes.

'Stan stops and stoops down, 'Here, hold up, Joe, what's this?'

Joe glowers, 'Looks like a black beaded purse with a broken handle. Where did you find that?'

'Down here, under winder,' Stan is about to hand it over when there's a sound of breaking glass beneath his boot, 'What the…?' he picks up the blackened, broken bottle and sniffs, 'Ugh, it smells horrible, like um…'

'What is it?' asks Joe.

Stan's face contorts at the pungent smell, 'It smells of…'

Grabbing the bottle Joe sniffs, 'Lamp oil!' he declares, 'What the fucking hell…? It's lamp oil.'

Stan face pales, his eyes narrow, 'Is yer finkin' what I'm finkin' Mate?'

'Aye, too bloody right Stan. This is the proof that the fire was started deliberately!' he shakes his head in disbelief.

'Well, I'm blowed! Here, what's we gonna do about it?' demands Stan.

There was a pause whilst Joe thinks for a moment or two, 'This is the proof we need Stan; it all fits together now. We'll take the purse and the bottle with us, and collect Mick and the lads on the way, this is a job for the law.'

'Christ! Can yer believe it, that bleeding Izzy's a cold-blooded murderer!' Stan holds up the purse frowning, 'I s'pose it might belong ter one of our gels, I could ask our Margo…'

'Don't bother!' jumps in Joe, 'What would the girls be doing with a fancy thing like that? No, you say nowt to them, keep it under your hat till we get to Fennydown,' Joe tells him. 'This is a matter for the law to deal with. Hide them under the bench of your cart, out of sight for now. We'll leave soon as we've eaten.'

With the knowledge that they'd be informing Mick and the lads that the fateful fire was actually arson and that they know who is responsible for it, Stan and Joe work with fury, searching for further evidence, but they find nothing more.

'I'll tell yer, I ain't lookin' forward ter tellin' the lads what we found,' says Stan heaving and puffing as he works.

Stripped to the waist, Joe stops and stretches his lean frame, wiping the sweat from his brow with the back of his hand. 'I know Mate, we'll just have to cross that bridge when we come to it.'

'Dinner's ready!' Margo yells from the door.

'Remember, not a word to the girls,' Joe reminds Stan.

'If there's enough hot water in the boiler, me and Stan needs to get cleaned up, we're gonna take a ride to Fennydown,' says Joe casually.

Stan nods, 'Aye, we're gonna have a word wiv Freddie about the house and business,' he says, mopping the last of the gravy from his plate with a crust of bread then licking his fingers.

Suspecting nothing, Margo and Katie nod.

'Let us know about Jed's funeral arrangements,' says Margo.

'We'll know more when we see them love,' says Joe, feeling guilty holding back secrets. Suddenly it dawns on him that if the fire was deliberate, there was always a possibility that she might come back.

'I'd like to go with you,' says Katie.

Margo frowns, 'That ain't a good idea lovey, a cart ride won't do yer no good.'

Tears well up in Katie's eyes, 'But it's only right I go. Oh, poor Joanie and Edna.'

Margo turns to Joe and shakes her head, 'Look Katie, you're still strugglin' wiv yer milk, and yer can hardly take little Jay J, the last fing yer want is ter be travellin' on a bumpy old cart, and yer don't need no more upsets, do yer.'

Joe kneels and puts his arm around Katie, saying, 'Katie, Mick knows you want to be there, and they'll understand, believe me, but you've got to think of Jay J. Margo says if your milk dries up, we'll have to find a wet nurse, you don't want that for our son, do you, darling?'

'No of course not! You know I don't.'

'Then be a good girl and stay here, let Margo look after you all,' he says softly. 'I won't be too long, darling, I promise.'

Katie sighs, 'All right, Joe.'

Taking Stan aside, Joe lowers his voice, 'I don't want to worry you Stan, but I've got concerns about leaving the girls here, alone.'

'What do yer mean, concerns?' asks Stan.

'If someone can set a fire once Stan...'

'Oh, my gawd, I git yer,' whispers Stan, cottoning on to what Joe's implying, he turns back to Margo and Katie, 'Yer know what gels, I'm fair jiggered, if Joe don't mind, I wouldn't mind stoppin' here and puttin' me feet up, I ain't gettin' no younger.'

'Aye, you look all in Mate,' says Joe backing him up, 'Course I don't mind.'

Freshly shaved and scrubbed, Joe says his farewells. 'Katie, darling, I'm taking some money with me, to pay for Jed's funeral,' he says patting his pocket.

'Good idea, Joe. Please tell them I'm thinking of them.'

Joe nods, 'Of course I will sweetheart.'

'Can yer bring some of our clothes back wiv yer, Joe? We can't keep walkin' around in the same old fings,' asks Margo. 'Freddie knows where ter find them.'

'Yer can always go wivout them gel.,' says Stan, trying hard to make light of the situation, he gives her an affectionate pat on her rump.

'Get away wiv yer Stanley, I thought yer was so tired yer couldn't travel.'

'Well, I s'pose some lovin' wiv me missus will soon perk me up,' he suggests with a twinkle in his eyes.

Margo glances at Lilibeth who seems to be taking in their every word, 'Yer can wait till ternight Stanley 'ooper, then per'aps I'll give yer old back a rub and all that,' she suggests smirking.'

Stan winks at her, 'Ooo here, I'll look forward ter that gel.'

Cottoning on, Katie forgets her old attitude to brazen talk, 'I um, I could take Lilibeth and Jay J in the bedroom for a while, we could do with a rest,' she offered subtly.

Margo grins, 'Yer can stay put gel, it doesn't hurt ter make a man wait, yer know.'

'I take it you'll all be fine till I get back then?' says Joe, relieved that the girls would have someone keeping an eye out for them.

He picks Lilibeth up giving her a kiss, 'Will you look after Mammy and Jay J for me, darling?'

Lilibeth smiles, 'Course I will Daddy.'

He kisses Katie, perhaps a little too passionately for Katie's liking in front of Stan and Margo, but she isn't exactly complaining, 'I won't be long, darling, I love you.' He plants kisses on Lilibeth and then Jay J, who is sleeping soundly in Katie's arms, I love you Lily, I love you, my son.'

As Joe hoists himself up on the cart, his boot gets caught in a sack and it falls to the ground.

Lilibeth rushes to pick it up then drops it, as if it's burning her fingers, she makes a dash to hide behind her mother's skirt.

'Lily, what is it, what's wrong, darling?' asks Joe.

Lily scowls, whispering, 'Lady's bag.'

Jumping down from the cart, Joe scoops her up in his arms, 'Lady's bag? What do you mean Lily?'

Unsure if she had said something wrong, Lilibeth's bottom lip quivers, she hides her face under his chin.

Picking up the purse, Stan holds it up, 'Does yer know who this belongs ter, Lilibuff?'

Lilibeth buries her face under Joe's chin again, expecting repercussions.

'Here, what's goin' on?' demands Margo, 'Where did yer get that fancy purse from, and what the bloody hell's it doin' on our cart Stanley 'ooper?' she demands in an accusatory manner.

'I think we'd better go back indoors,' says Joe quietly, his expression serious, 'I'll go on ahead with Lily, give you a chance to explain things to the girls Stan,' adding, 'give me ten minutes.' And he strides away with Lilibeth in his arms. About to follow him, Stan catches Katie's arm, 'Don't worry love, sit yerselves down here a minute, I'll tell yer both what's happened.'

Alone in the bedroom, Joe sits with Lilibeth on his knee, he lifts ed her face, 'Don't look so worried, darling,' he said softly, 'Daddy isn't cross with you.'

Lilibeth pouts, her eyes fall to the floor.

'Do you know who the purse belongs to Lily?' he asked gently.

Pursing her lips, she nods.

'Well why don't you tell me; you know Daddy won't be cross.'

On the verge of tears, Lily sniffs, 'It broke on the window Daddy, the lady dropped it.'

Joe lowers his voice to a pleasant lighter tone, 'What exactly did you see?' he gently coaxes her.

Lilibeth shrugs.

'Well, I think you'd be a very brave girl if you can tell Daddy what you saw, sweetheart,' he urges.

'The black lady put the fire in the window and broke her bag.' she volunteers quietly.

Inside, Joe's brain is working overtime, somehow, he manages to maintain an air of calmness for Lily's sake, 'You actually saw her drop it?'

'Yes Daddy,' she whispers, 'me and Daisy saw her.'

'Humm, thank you for telling me, darling, I think you are a very clever girl. I'm so proud of you.'

The door opens, Stan, Margo and Katie troop in, looking to Joe for answers, especially Katie. Taking her in his arms, he whispers, 'I'll explain about Izzy when I get back, darling, don't worry.' He kisses her then turns to Stan, 'Um, can I have a quick word before I leave Stan?' nodding to the door indicating he wants a private word outside.

Jay J starts to cry, 'Lily, darling, why don't you go with Mammy into the bedroom and help Mammy feed Jay J,' he suggests.

'Stan, after what Lily's just told me about the lamp and this purse, it's all the proof we need,' says Joe, 'Lily saw everything.'

'Oh gawd, ain't no doubt about it then!' says Stan, eyes blazing with fury.

Bowing his head in despair Joe sighs, 'Definitely, and before you ask, 'I have a bloody good idea why she did it.'

'Aye, Joe, so have I, mad bloody wench.'

'I hate to admit it, but this is all my fault. Izzy thinks she's a woman scorned, by me. She once told me, a long time ago, I would eventually realise I was meant to be with her,' he says shaking his head.

'Aye, well yer better git yerself gone, Joe, I'll see that the gels will be alwight here.'

'Don't leave them for a second Mate, keep the doors and windows shut tight, I'll be back just as soon as I can,' orders Joe soberly.

CHAPTER 18

So much runs through Joe's mind on the journey to Fennydown. He recalls Izzy Perkins and the totally unfounded infatuation that she once had for him. It was all in her mind, it seemed to him at the time, somehow, she'd been obstinately fixated and followed him around for a year or more. He thought long and hard, wondering what had become of her. He frowns as a lump comes to his throat, never in a million years did he think she would take revenge on him by trying to destroy his beloved family and friends, successfully killing poor Jed in the process!

At Wickers Yard, Freddie gathers Stan and Margo's clothes together, along with Jay J's cot, and with Verity, they travel on to Mick's. On the way, Joe explains the whole sorry saga of Izzy and her misguided obsession with him. He then explains how Lily had witnessed everything that took place and the evidence they'd found after the fire.

Needless to say, the news shocks Freddie, he's beyond furious.

To shorten their journey, they call in to find the bobby, but after a fruitless search and many inquiries, they are forced with no alternative but to leave a message with his wife and carry on without him.

To lighten the atmosphere Joe goes on to explain the proposal he'd made to Stan and Margo, pointing out that Freddie would take over the business and Stan and Margo would give Freddie their house and Wickers Yard, with a monthly slice of the profits going to Stan' 'Your dad would be a sleeping partner.' He looks at Freddie, 'So what do you think, it all depends on whether you agree with the arrangements.'

Sat gawping with his mouth open wide in amazement, Freddie stutters, 'B…but what about you and Katie, where are you gonna live?'

For the first time since the fire, a broad smile spreads over Joe's face, 'I'm building a bigger place for us, but I haven't told Katie where I plan to build it yet. So, what about my offer? You and Verity would have your own love nest and your own business for a living.'

Freddie grasps his hand shaking it vigorously, 'If yer serious about this Joe, then yes, yes please!'

All too soon they arrive at Mick's cottage. Joe had been dreading this moment. He sends Verity indoors as Mick comes out with Tom and Abe. There are no verbal greetings only heart-rending hugs all round. 'I need to talk to you Mick,' Joe tells him. 'But first I have some business to discuss with you, Edna, and Joanie, regarding the funeral, so if you can hang on out here for a bit, lads, I won't be long.'

Joe puts his arm around Mick's shoulders, and they go inside. After many tears and hugs, sharing their deep sorrow, the funeral is paid for, Joe emerges outside with Mick.

Business complete, the men huddle round and listen intently whilst Joe relates the story of the fire, giving Lily's full account of what happened and the subsequent evidence, the items found in the fire ravaged building, adding, 'Izzy will have burns to her arms too, according to Lily.'

Their response is as predictable as expected.

'Fucking hell. Izzy Perkins, the sick murderous bitch!' snarls Tom through clenched teeth, 'You wait till I get my hands on her, I'll fuckin' kill her!'

Pale faced, Mick, stands in a daze, shaking his head in disbelief. 'Izzy Perkins killed our Jed?'

'Let me git me hands on the bitch. So, what's we waitin' fer?' snaps Tom clenching his fists.

If he's honest, inside, Joe feels exactly the same sentiments as Tom, but he isn't a violent man. He decides the right way to deal with the matter is to leave it to the law to handle it, Izzy has to answer for her heinous actions.

He shakes his head, 'Well in the absence of the law's availability, I think we should go to Izzy's cottage,' suggests Joe, 'Get her to give herself up and hand herself in to the law to face the consequences.'

They all pile onto the cart and head over to Izzy's home.

CHAPTER 19

'Git yerself out here now, Izzy Perkins!' hollers Tom, his face dark as a thunder cloud.

'Aye,' shouts Mick, hammering on the door, 'yer murdered my boy and now yer gonna pay fer it. Mark my words gel!'

'Come out and face yer punishment, Izzy Perkins, or else!' threatens Freddie.

'Aye, come on out, yer evil murdering bitch! Git out here now! What are yer fuckin' waiting fer!' screams a ferocious, red-faced Tom.

The door slowly opens, just a little. Izzy peers out. There's sea of vicious angry faces glaring at her. 'Sod off, the bleedin' lot of yer!' she shouts.

She spots Joe stood amongst them, his hands on his hips. 'I ain't talking ter none of yer, so bugger off!' she calls out, then adds, 'I'll only speak ter Joseph,' she says, slamming to door shut and bolting it.

'What the fuckin' hell can we do? She ain't comin' out, the mad bloody murderer.'

'Well, I reckon we ought ter rush the place,' says Abe, 'smash the bloody door down.'

Several suggestions are proffered. 'We can always smash the winders,' suggests Tom.

Freddie is so enraged he's all for setting fire to the place with Izzy inside it!

Violence is not in Joe's nature, there has to be another way, he shakes his head. 'It's all right, I'll talk to her, I think I can persuade her to come out,' states Joe calmly. 'I'm sure I can talk her round.'

There was a chorus of strongly voiced objections from all of them, but Joe chooses to ignore them, saying, 'Don't worry, I'll be fine.' He walks steadily to the door.

Gingerly Izzy opens the door to let him enter, then quickly bolts the door behind him.

The place in utter disarray. 'Izzy,' he says quietly, 'I want you to come outside with me.'

Izzy smiles triumphantly, 'Oh I knew you'd come ter me in the end, Joe.' Despite her heavily bandaged arms she begins tearing at her clothes. Her eyes are blazing with excitement. 'I knows yer really loves me. Oh yes, I knew yer really wanted me all along Darlin', here, take me now,' she says, with a sickly smirk, sidling up to him and waggling her bare breasts in front of him. I'm all yours now Joseph.'

Repulsed, Joe steps back out of her reach, 'Stop it Izzy, stop this nonsense right now!' he snaps.

Undeterred or unhearing, she suddenly launches herself at him. 'You're mine, all mine now Joseph,' she pants, flinging her arms around his neck, standing on tip toes, trying desperately to kiss him.

Grappling to free himself, Joe holds her firmly by her wrists at arms-length. 'You've gotta stop this Izzy, now! You're acting crazy.' He alters his tone, 'put your clothes on, now Izzy, you're making a fool of yourself!' he says, releasing her from his grip.

Though his words don't register, she appears momentarily to calm down. 'Don't shout at me like that,' she says pouting, 'I know yer wants me, I can see it in yer eyes, hold me, take me, make love to me, Joe,' she whispers as seductively, she saunters towards him, batting her eyelashes. 'I'm all yours now, Joe, take me.'

Utterly repulsed, he steps back, his anger building 'Listen to me! I don't want you and never have done! This is all in your head Izzy!' Frustrated they are going around in circles and getting nowhere he lowers his voice, loosening his grip on her, trying to reason with her. 'Look, I'm a very happily married man Izzy, I love my wife Katie dearly, we've got two beautiful kiddies too!'

'No! Yer wrong, Joe,' she spits vehemently, 'That's why yer here, I know yer wants me, Joe.

Unfortunately, he underestimates her strength, she breaks free from his grasp, flying round the room screeching excitedly, 'Hah, I knew you'd come ter me, now she's gawn, Joseph!'

'Stop this nonsense! Now Izzy! My Katie's fine. I know it was you that started the fire, I've got a witness and evidence too!' Joe's angered voice begins rising in frustration. 'Stop Izzy, I've heard enough! Get yourself dressed girl. Now!'

Eyes widening, Izzy's deep brown eyes are wild, she shakes her head zealously, unwilling to hear or believe him.

'Yes, you are right, you killed someone Izzy, because you started the fire,' he tells her, struggling to keep his voice low and composed.

Throwing back her head she laughs hysterically, her eyes register her fury, 'So what if I did, bloody Katie Soames deserved ter die, good riddance ter the bitch! She's already had herself a husband, and she's got a bleedin' kid and all. It weren't right fer her ter have another man! I hate her fer takin' yer away from me. Anyway, now she's gawn yer mine, all mine Joseph!' she screams, waving her arms in a frenzy.

Joe shakes his head, frowning, he keeps his voice low, 'No Izzy, I'm sorry you're delusional. My Katie is at home with our children. She's fine. Sadly, you killed a lovely young man, a married man with a new baby.'

Spinning round she grabs a knife from the table, 'No! No! Well, I'm tellin' yer now, Joe, if I can't have yer no one else will!' she threatens, waving the knife around crazily.

Horrified, watching helplessly though the window, Mick yells to the others. 'Fuck me! Quick lads, she's gawn bonkers, she's gotta bleedin' knife! Git Joe out of there afore she kills him!' He bangs frantically at the window. 'No Izzy, stop! Open the bloody door!'

But Izzy is irrational, she hears nothing. 'It's yer last chance Joseph, I mean it!' she points the knife menacingly towards him, 'Take me now or we die tergever!'

Joe shakes his head, trying to placate her, 'I'm sorry Izzy, that's never gonna happen. Put the knife down and get dressed. You're coming with me, you're gonna hand yourself in to the law.'

'Never!' she screams wildly. 'Never!' In a frenzy she springs forward so fast that Joe has no time to avoid her, viciously she stabs him in the chest with the knife, Joe falls to the floor striking his head on the hearth. Panting she stands over him with the blood-stained knife in her hand, she starts wailing, then screams an ear-piercing scream, 'You're not alone, my darling! We'll be together forever, my love!' she says as she thrusts the blade in her belly.

What Mick witnesses makes his blood run cold. Horrified, Mick screams to the others, 'Fuck! Batter the bloody door down, I fink she's killed Joe!'

Freddie smashes the door in with his shoulder and together they run inside. It's a stomach-churning sight that greets them, there's blood everywhere. Joe is laid on the floor with Izzy's naked body strewn partially across his prostrate body.

Tom frantically drags Izzy to one side, then he and Freddie stoop down, Freddie put his head on Joe's chest.

'Whisht. Quiet everyone!' Tom yells.

Everyone holds their breath, fearing what is to come.

'He's alive, I can just hear about his heart beating!' gasps Freddie, 'It's very faint but it's still beating. Help me git him on the cart, we gotta get him home, fast!'

Pale as a sheet and shaking, Stan yells, 'Someone fetch the doc, hurry!'

'I'll git him,' volunteers Abe, 'he ain't that far away.'

'Git him to come ter Sweet Briars, fast as yer can lad!' Stan yells.

'Christ, there's no time ter waste, time's precious,' says Tom. 'Nice and easy does it, help us git Joe outside and onto the cart, gentle like.'

All the way back to the cottage Freddie cradles Joe's head in his arms. 'Come on, Joe, hang on in there, Mate, we're nearly home.'

Margo has been to collect the eggs and is on her way back up the yard when the cart pulls in. 'Here, what's the rush lads?' she sees the serious look on their faces. 'Freddie, what is it love, where's Joe?'

Tom helps Stan from the cart, he looked grief-stricken, 'I'm so sorry Margo. It's Joe, he's... he's been stabbed. Come on lads, let's get him inside!'

Dropping the basket, Margo stands ridged, disbelieving.

Tom turns to Margo, 'Don't just stand there, gel, git Katie, we gotta put him on his bed! Abe's gawn fer the doc, he should be here pretty soon.'

Margo runs indoors, 'Katie! Come quick! It's Joe! They've brought him home; they says he's been stabbed! Hurry ducky!'

Rushing to the door, Katie's face is white as a sheet. 'Joseph, my Joseph he's been... stabbed? No!'

'Aye lass, we gotta put him on yer bed, the doc's already on his way here lovey.'

Margo slides her arm around Katie to support her as their friends very carefully carry Joe indoors and through to the bedroom.

Katie is shaking violently, 'Oh my dear God! No! Joseph, oh my precious darling,' she spins round. 'What... what happened?' she searches the sea of faces for answers and gets none.

Freddie,' says Margo, 'Lilibuff is playin' in the barn, can yer see if she's alwight? Er... best you don't let her come in ter see her daddy like this.'

Margo fills a bowl with freshly boiled water, 'Come on Katie, help me tear up some sheets fer bandages, we'll clean Joe up best we can, Doc Entwistle's on his way.'

Stood dumbstruck, Katie is shaking violently, staring unbelieving, down at Joe, she's mortified.

'Katie!' Margo shouts, shaking her vigorously, 'Git a grip of yerself! Come on, yer gotta help me!'

There was so much blood on Joe's sodden shirt that they don't know where to start.

The minute the doctor arrives, Tom runs out to him, doing his best to enlighten him as to what had transpired as they run inside.

There was a polite tap on the bedroom door, 'Good afternoon, Mrs Markson,' it's Doctor Entwistle. He looks at Joseph, laying covered in blood and unconscious on the bed. 'Right, I'll need to cut his shirt off then I can see what we're dealing with,' the doctor says calmly, he looks at Katie kindly, 'Please Mrs Markson, do take a seat, you're in shock my dear, try not to worry. Mrs Hooper, could you get something to drink for Mrs Markson please?'

Under Katie's tearful gaze, Joe's blood-soaked shirt is cut away.

Using a torn-up sheet, the doctor bathes the blood from his chest, 'Hum, there appears to be only one wound on the front of his chest, though it could be deep, there's so much blood. 'Right Mrs Hooper, can you give me a hand to turn him on his side? Carefully, I need to look for wounds on his back.'

Between them they roll him on his side, Margo cleans the blood from his back but there are no further wounds to be found.

'Hum, just the one wound, ah, that's good news.' he mutters as he takes a stethoscope from his bag, he listens to Joe's chest, 'Uh huh, very good, his lungs sound clear, so no damage there.' Next, he listens to his heart, 'Uh huh, yes, it's very slow but a good heartbeat. Now, apart from this wound, he seems to have lost an enormous amount of blood, though from what I've been told it probably isn't all his blood, which is heartening.'

'Please doctor, can you save my Joseph?' Grabbing his arm, Katie beseeches him. 'Can you help my Joseph? Oh please, I'm begging you?' she cries, desperately wringing her hands as the tears stream down her face.

Doctor Entwistle stands, looking at Katie with an understanding compassion, he clears his throat, 'Ahem, Mrs Markson, he's no longer bleeding from the wound, I'm sure the knife hasn't penetrated any vital organs, so I will stitch and close the wound and put on a bandage. My main concern then is that he might get an infection.'

Carefully the doctor cleans the wound and stitches it up.

Katie's face is scrunched with fear. 'Why won't he wake up Doctor?' she croaks, silently praying that the doctor had good news.

The doctor closes his bag, rinses his hands in the fresh water that Margo has supplied. 'Mrs Markson,' he addresses Katie with his appraisal. 'Apart from the single wound, he also sustained a nasty knock to his head. Hopefully, he should come round soon. I can also tell you that your husband is incredibly fit, he also has youth on his side, both factors will work in his favour, I'm sure.' He gently places his hand on Katie's arm, 'However, Mrs Markson you are newly confined, and it is imperative that you take good care of yourself,' he advises sternly. 'You will be no good to your family or your husband if you let things slide. When he wakes up, he's going need you to be there for him.'

Margo nods in agreement, 'Leave it ter me doctor, me and my husband will be stayin' here now, ter help them out.'

'Grand Mrs Hooper, thank you. Now mind you take heed of what I've said, Mrs Markson,' he smiles reassuringly wagging his finger at Katie. 'I will be back tomorrow to check on my patient. Now if you will excuse me, I need to speak to the gentlemen outside. I'll bid you good day Mrs Markson. I'll see you again tomorrow morning.'

In the scullery, a grey faced Stan relates all the happenings from the past forty-eight hours or so, from the devastating fire, in which Jed was tragically killed, the evidence they found in the ashes that pointed to Izzy, along with Lilibeth's brave account of what she'd actually witnessed. Finally including a brief description of Izzy's past, one sided, irrational obsession towards Joseph, and finally how Mick watched in horror through the window as she savagely plunged the knife first into Joe's chest and then herself, describing how Freddie had to knock the door down to save Joseph.

Doctor Entwistle shakes his head. 'Dearie me, and where is this Izzy person now?'

'At her cottage on the way to Holdean, Pipkins, it's called. She's still on the floor where she fell on top of Joe,' Freddie informs him, 'but yer can't help her Doc, I did check, but she's dead. Ruddy killed herself after stabbing our Joe,' he explains. 'There weren't nothin' we could do fer her, so we got our Joe straight home, and Abe called fer yer ter come as soon as.'

Apparently satisfied, the doctor nods, 'Fair enough. Thank you. Of course, I will have to call in to this Pipkins place to verify everything, sir.'

He says turning to Mick, 'As you witnessed everything, I'd like to speak with you, then I will inform the authorities.'

'Huh, you'll have a job, we looked high and bloody low fer the rozzer, afore we went ter Pipkins. He wasn't nowhere ter be found, so we left a message wiv his wife. We had ter go wivout him,' sneers Freddie, sounding contemptuous of the law.

'Hum, I see, well the way you found them also accounts to the large amount of blood found on Mr Markson's body, a lot of it must have been from this Izzy person.'

Picking up his bag he nods. 'Thank you, I must be off, leave everything to me.' He tips his hat, 'I'll bid you all good day, gentlemen.'

Freddie flies through to the bedroom, 'Mam, how's Joe? Katie love are you alwight Darlin'? What did the doc say about Joe? Is it bad, Katie love?'

Scowling, Margo tuts, 'Whisht Freddie, stop yer ruddy questions boy. Yer can see how it is. Anyway, I thought yer was looking after Lilibeth.'

'Aye, I was but while the doc was talkin'…'

Before he can utter another word, a little voice from the doorway pipes up, 'Here I is.' Spying her father laying on the bed with bandages swathed around his chest she runs to Katie, crying out, 'Mammy, Mammy, what's wrong with my daddy!'

'I'm afraid yer daddy had a nasty accident sweetheart,' Margo jumps in.

Scrambling onto the bed Lily grabs his arm, shaking him, 'Daddy, Daddy, wake up!' she cries. 'It's me, your darling little Lily.'

'Hush little one,' says Stan trying to prise Lilibeth away from Joe, 'Yer poor daddy bumped his head and he's very tired, we must let him sleep fer a while me darlin'. Best we go in the parlour wiv Freddie.'

Lilibeth was having none of it, refusing point blank, 'No! No! I'm staying with my mammy; we can make Daddy better!' she insists stubbornly.

Margo sighs, 'Best leave her Stan, I can hear Jay J crying fer his feed. He's in the scullery, can yer bring him in fer Katie lovey?'

Stan does as he's told and goes to fetch the crying infant.

'Right out, the lot of yer! Katie's gotta feed Jay J, go on, shoo!' says Margo flapping her hands, taking charge.

Katie, who's eyes haven't left Joe for a second, shakes her head, 'I'm sorry Margo, I don't think I can.' She croaks.

Margo stands above her with her hands on her hips, 'Stuff and bloody nonsense gel! Yer heard what the doc said, yer gotta be strong fer Joe. Poor little mite is starving and yer upsetting Lilibuff and all. Now pull yerself tergever gel and get and feed him!' she orders forcefully.

Knowing she sounds harsh, Margo stands her ground, it has to be said. 'Here,' she says firmly, placing the crying infant in Katie's arms, undoing Katie's bodice and putting Jay J to her breast. 'Feed him!'

Instantly the baby stops crying. Lily and Margo watch as the infant suckles furiously. 'There we go, that's better, yer know Joe would be very proud of yer gel. Yer gotta be strong fer the whole family now Katie love.' Happy that Katie is feeding Jay J to her satisfaction, Margo grabs Lily's hand, 'Come on Lilibuff, it's time fer yer tea.'

After preparing tea for everyone, including Katie, Margo finally sits down to put her feet up for a few minutes.

'So, what did the doc say?' enquires Stan.

All eyes fall on Margo.

Sighing heavily, she scans the concerned faces, all staring at her, all worried and anxious for news. 'He reckons a lot of the blood on his shirt was from Izzy. Thankfully, there was just the one wound. After we cleaned him up, the bleedin' stopped so he stitched him up and bandaged him. The doc says Joe is very lucky, it went frew his ribs and somehow missed his heart and lungs. He reckons it's the bump on his head what made him unconscious. He also said he was worried Joe might git an infection. The doc told Katie he'd be back termorrer mornin'. Anyway, enough of that,' says Margo, pouring herself another cup of tea. She glares at each of the men in turn, 'Well? I fink it's about time someone told me what the hell happened, and why Joe ended up half bleedin' dead!'

Unsurprisingly there was a shortfall of offers to enlighten her.

Freddie suggests that he takes Mick, Tom and Abe back home. He points out that Jed's funeral was to be held in two days, and the family will be worried about them getting home so late.

Margo can't argue that statement and nods, 'Alwight son, I'm sorry. Yer all been so helpful gettin' him home so quick and callin' the doc, we're very grateful. God willin' yer probably saved our Joe's life, thanks ter each and every one of yer.'

'No worries Margo, we know he would do the same fer us.' says Tom.

'Aye' says Mick, chiming in, 'we hope he'll git better real soon. Give Katie our love. And if yer needs anyfin', anyfin' at all, yer only gotta ask.'

There are tears in Margo's eyes, 'Thanks lads, we're all one big family. Anyway, I'd best go and change Jay J's bum and get Lilibuff orf ter bed, if I can. Bless her, she's sat on the bed beside her daddy, sobbing her little heart out along wiv Katie.'

Everyone stands to leave, in turn they each give Margo a hug. 'We'll be back,' they all promise, one after the other.

Stan stands up to see them all off.

'Er, not you Stanley 'ooper, I dunno where yer fink yer goin'!' snaps Margo, 'Yer got some explainin' ter do.'

'I'm on'y gonna see them orf, I won't be a minute,' he says, dreading having to face his angry wife and explain the chain of events thus far.

'Joe should never have gone in there alone! What the bloody hell was yer all finkin' of?' demands Margo, thumping her fist on the table. 'Yer know the damn gel's mad, and yer all just as bleedin' daft fer lettin' him go in there on his own!'

'We hollered, hammered and banged on the doors and winders, but she wouldn't come out, so given their past history tergether, Joe said if he went in alone, he'd be able ter get her ter give herself up.'

Shaking her head, Margo stares at Stan through squinting eyes, 'Is that right Stanley? And how do yer know what happened if none of yer was wiv him then?'

Stan exhales a long breath, 'Coz our Mick saw her do it wiv his own eyes. He was lookin' frew the winder when she stabbed him. He reckons Joe didn't stand a chance coz she was so quick.' Looking thoroughly miserable, Stan frowns, 'Mick yelled at us she'd knifed Joe, so our Freddie did his best and battered the ruddy door in. Accordin' ter Mick, he saw it all, she started shriekin' like a rabid dog as she stood over Joe wivout a stitch of clothes on, kinda laughin' and screechin', waving the bleedin' knife around like she was possessed. Izzy yelled somefin' like they would always be tergever. She stabbed Joe, then she stabbed herself in her belly, and that's how we found them, she were layin' across Joe's body, dead.' Stan closes his eyes, grimacing as if in pain.

Handing Stan a small brandy, Margo shudders, 'Yer say she were naked? Why the fuck were she naked? Good gawd, best we don't tell Katie about that bit, it won't help matters if we do, she's upset enough.'

'Aye, yer right there Darlin'. Then ter cap it all, poor Mick had ter tell the doc all over agin what he saw in detail,' explains Stan. 'Poor bugger, as if he ain't been frew enough, what wiv losin' his Jed.'

'Aye,' Margo agrees, 'Poor Mick, bless him.' She sighs, 'The trouble is Stan, all this upset could dry Katie's milk up, and Jay J is only little le.' Margo sighs, 'I feel ruddy rotten now, me and Katie ain't never fallen out afore, ever. I just couldn't help meself, I lost my patience wiv her. I know I was shoutin', but I had ter be really tough wiv her, coz of little Jay J. I told her, she gotta pull herself tergether fer the sake of the poor little mite. Huh, she weren't really listenin', so I told her in no uncertain terms, she had ter snap out of it. I told her she had ter eat and ter drink and all. I told her Joseph would never fergive her, if anyfin' happens ter his new-born son. Oh gawd, she got really upset.'

'Aye I know, it's hard love, but yer did what yer had ter do, fer all their sakes lovey,' agrees Stan putting a comforting arm around Margo. 'Yer look all in lovey, you toddle orf ter bed wiv Lilibuff, I reckons little Jay J will be hollering for his grub in the night. I'll put the chickens away and lock up, me darlin'.' He pats Margo's bum. 'Nighty night lovey.'

'Twice Jay J woke fer his feed in the night,' says Margo yawning. 'Yer know Katie lay next ter Joseph, holdin' his hand all night agin, she kept talkin' and strokin' him all the time, she never stops. I mean it's bin three ruddy days now. Then Lilibuff went down and joined her mammy at daybreak,' says Margo, eating her porridge. 'Be a love Stan, warm some milk fer us, I'm gonna take some breakfast in ter Katie. I'll change Jay J's bum then I'd better clean up the place and do some washin'. The doc will be here soon.'

'I've already milked the cows and goat, so I'll give yer a hand ducky. I've lit the fire under the boiler, and I'll fetch more water from the well, then perhaps we can take Lilibuff wiv us ter feed the chickens and collect the eggs when the doc gits here, keep her out of the way of the doc' like.'

'Come on, eat up Katie, then me and Lily can give Jay J his bath. You'd better have a good strip wash Katie, afore the doc gets here,' she orders firmly.

Katie says nothing, just shrugs, staring back at Margo vacantly.

There were no voiced objections from Katie as Margo strips her and gives her a good wash, whilst all the while she sits by his bedside clasping Joe's hand, whispering to him constantly. But when Margo brings in clean water to wash Joseph, Katie stands, 'Please Margo, I'll do that, if you take Lilibeth outside I will wash Joseph myself.' His body is hers and she wasn't about to share it with anyone, not even Margo, it was for her and her alone to bathe her beloved husband.

Pulling back the covers he lay completely naked, save the bandages swathing his chest, Katie sighs a long mournful sigh, 'Oh my poor sweet Joseph. Please wake up, darling.' she murmurs, 'I need you so much. I long for you to make love to me again.'

Starting with his beautiful face, she does a top to bottom, she tenderly washes his strong muscled arms, carefully patting him dry. Next, she washes his long legs and feet. Last, his genitals, with tears in her eyes, she soaps her hands into a lather and tenderly holds his soft willy in her hands, with great care she gently kissed the tip, licking away the bead of moisture, then begins washing him.

To her astonishment, a long soft moan rises from deep in Joe's throat. Holding her breath, she gazes up at him she could swear his eyelids moved. Still talking softly to him she grasps his willy, almost instantly it begins to visibly grow and stiffen in her hands. Gasping she stares at him. Although his eyes are still closed, he has the most beautiful smile on his lips. Moaning softly from his throat, he rasps 'Ooo, oh my darling little woodnymph, don't stop...' he mutters in a hoarse whisper.

'Joseph? Oh my God, you're wake! Oh, my precious darling, you're awake!'

Holding his head in her hands she kisses him all over his face, running her fingers through his hair, holding his head, rubbing her nose through his prickly stubble and kissing him on his lips.

About to shout for Margo, it occurs to her that he doesn't have a stitch on except his bandaged chest, so hastily she dries and covers him with a fresh clean sheet. Feeling giddy with relief Katie kisses him tenderly on his lips, 'Oh Joseph, oh my sweet precious husband, you're awake, thank God,' she murmurs, with her heart pounding. She's breathless with joy.

Slowly he opens his eyes and focuses on Katie. 'Oh, my sweet love. Water, darling,' he croaks then closes his eyes again.

Fleeing to the scullery she finds Margo doing the dishes, 'He's awake! Quick Margo, Joe's awake! He wants a drink!'

Drying her hands on her pinny, Margo pours a glass of water and follows Katie to the bedroom. 'Joseph?'

Supporting his head, she puts the cup to his lips, so he can sip the water, he coughs, 'Easy does it, Joe,' says Margo, 'not so fast.'

'Oh, thank God. How do you feel, darling?' asks Katie clutching his hand to her breast, deliriously overwhelmed with happiness.

As he tries to raise his head from the pillow, he screws up his face in pain and falls back groaning.

A discreet tap on the bedroom door and Doctor Entwistle enters. 'Mrs Markson, Mrs Hooper, good day.' he greets them, he looks at Joe. 'Ahh good, I see you're awake at last Mr Markson, wonderful,' he declares. 'I would like to examine my patient if I may. If you will excuse us, Mrs Hooper.'

Margo nods and leaves the room, closing the door quietly behind her. Katie stands, about to follow.

'Not you Mrs Markson, I'd like you to stay,' he says, opening his bag. Carefully unwrapping the bandages, he inspects the wound closely. Nodding he looks at Katie, 'Hum, good, no infection at all, it'll need regular bathing, freshly boiled water and salt should do the trick, my dear.' Out comes his stethoscope, he listens to his heart, 'Hum, not so slow today, good, good. His heart sounds much stronger now, Mrs Markson. Right, let me check your lungs, Mr Markson. Take a deep breath, and out, again. Uh huh, yes, lovely, all clear.'

'There's a light tap on the door, 'I've brought a bowl of freshly boiled water and a clean towel doctor,' calls Margo.

'Do come in, Mrs Hooper,' he acknowledges her with a smile. 'Ah yes, set it on the table if you will. Thank you, Mrs Hooper,' then dismisses her with a wave of his hand. 'I'll re-dress the wound.'

Margo leaves the doctor to it.

'I could do with a cup of tea, darling,' Joe whispers hoarsely. 'I'm parched.'

Katie kissed him gently on his lips, 'I won't be long, my precious husband.'

The doctor watches Katie leave the room, 'You're a very lucky man, you have a lovely wife Mr Markson, and a fine son too, I see.' He says, peering into the cradle, nodding his approval. 'Yes indeed. Mrs Hooper tells me how you not only delivered him on your own, you actually saved his life by removing the cord quickly from around his neck. Most commendable if I do say myself. Well done, I'm highly impressed.'

'Um, thanks, look, before my wife returns, I'd like to ask you something Doctor, man to man, I feel we have an understanding?' he whispers.

'Of course, Mr Markson. Go ahead.'

'How long before I can make love to my wife?'

Keeping his voice level, he says, 'Now let me see. You have a wound that needs to heal, which fortunately is not too deep, luckily it missed your heart and lungs Mr Markson. Also,' he points out, 'your wife is recently confined. Yes, well if you can wait… a further, um, shall we say two weeks, your wife would have stopped bleeding by then. So, if you take it easy you should both be fine.'

Dejection is written all over Joe's face. 'Two weeks?'

The doctor tries and fails to supress a chuckle, 'Of course there are many ways you can both satisfy each other in the meantime, without having full intercourse. Would you like some advice in that direction Mr Markson?'

Joe grins, 'No thanks Doc, I've got some pretty good ideas myself, thanks all the same.'

'Grand,' he said, picking up his bag, 'I'd like to visit you again in a couple of days, to check and redress your wound.'

'Yes Doc', fine, I'll look forward to seeing you.' says Joe.

'Good day Mr Markson, I'll see you in a couple of days then.'

'Peek-a-boo Daddy dearest, it's me,' says Lily, excitedly dashing round his bed closely followed by Katie carrying their son, Jay J.

'Well bless my soul, ain't that a pretty picture,' says Margo to Stan. They are both standing in the doorway watching the four of them cuddled up on the bed together.

'Yep, a real happy picture,' Stan agrees, 'But I reckon young Lilibuff is tired, she should go up fer her afternoon nap now,' he points out to Margo. He shuffles his feet, 'Er… excuse me folks, I was wonderin' Katie, our Margo's a bit tired, what wiv all the comin's and goin's, and I ain't getting' no younger. Do yer mind if we go up ter bed fer a couple of hours, fer a sleep like? We'll put Lilibuff down fer her nap first.'

Both Joe and Katie knows the look in their eyes, they glanced at each other and smirked knowingly, 'Not at all, off you go. Aunty Margo is going to take you up for your nap now Lily, so give Daddy and Mammy a kiss, darling. Oh, and don't forget Jay J.'

Alone once more Joe leans a little closer, whispering in her ear. 'Hey, my beautiful sexy woodnymph. I have a big surprise for you. How long between feeds for Jay J, sweetheart?'

She sees his eyes have that wickedly saucy look in them. 'Three hours at least, I think,' she replies smirking. 'But your wound, darling?'

He slides his hand into her bodice, very gently cupping her breast he tweaks her nipple, moaning with pleasure he purrs in his oh so sensual velvety voice, 'Mmm, I think I should show our son what your lovely titties are for. Mmm, so full,' he murmurs, lightly stroking his thumb over her ripe hard nipple.

'Hush, darling, they will hear you!' She exclaims, blushing profusely.

'Hey Mrs Markson, don't be shy. We are married, my precious wife,' he reminds her, as his eyes darken with lascivious intent.

'Squirming at his touch, she giggles. 'Oh, my naughty husband, I've missed you so much.'

'I've missed you too, darling, but luckily I've got a few ideas, my sexy woodnymph, though you might have to help me out a little bit. It's a good job you're so good with your hands and mouth, darling, and I'm pretty good with my mouth and hands too, don't you think, my deliciously sexy woodnymph?'

'Mmm, kiss me, my darling husband.'